MURDER IN NEW ENGLAND

MURDER IN NEW ENGLAND

Edited by
Eleanor Sullivan & Chris Dorbandt

CASTLE

Printed in the United States of America.
ISBN 1-55521-528-9

Grateful acknowledgement is hereby made for permission to reprint the following stories, all of which appeared in *Ellery Queen's Mystery Magazine*: *New England Equinox* by Isaac Asimov, copyright © 1986 by Davis Publications, Inc., reprinted by permission of the author; *The Sisterhood* by Gwendoline Butler, copyright © 1968 by Davis Publications, Inc., reprinted by permission of the author; *That Day at Connally* by Stanley Cohen, copyright © 1974 by Davis Publications, Inc., reprinted by permission of the author; *Off the Interstate* by Brendan DuBois, copyright © 1987 by Davis Publications, Inc., reprinted by permission of the author; *A Quick Learner* by Brendan BuBois, copyright © 1987 by Davis Publications, Inc., reprinted by permission of the author; *A Ticket Out* by Brendan DuBois, copyright © 1986 by Davis Publications, Inc., reprinted by permission of the author; *Unacceptable Procedures* by Stanley Ellin, copyright © 1985 Davis Publications, Inc., reprinted by permission of Curtis Brown, Ltd.; *Death of a Harvard Man* by Richard M. Gordon, copyright © 1958 by Davis Publications, Inc., reprinted by permission; *Lizzie Bordon in the P.M.* by Robert Henson, copyright © 1980 by Robert Henson, reprinted by permission of the author; *The Problem of Santa's Lighthouse* by Edward Hoch, copyright © 1983 by Davis Publications, Inc., reprinted by permission of the author; *The Problem of the Boston Common* by Edward Hoch, copyright © 1979 by Davis Publications, Inc., reprinted by permission of the author; *The Chalk Line* by Ryerson Johnson copyright © 1985 by Davis Publications, Inc., reprinted by permission of the author; *Mifflin Must Go* by Shannon O'Cork, copyright © 1986 by Davis Publications, Inc., reprinted by permission of Ann Elmo Agency, Inc.; *The Day the Children Vanished* by Hugh Pentecost, copyright © 1958 by Judson Phillips; copyright renewed © 1986 by Judson Phillips. Reprinted by permission of Brandt & Brandt Literary Agents, Inc.; *The Rhode Island Lights* by S. S. Rafferty, copyright © 1975 by Jack J. Hurley, reprinted by permission of the author; *The Stone Wall* by Steve Sherman, copyright © 1985 by Davis Publications, Inc., reprinted by permission of the author. *A Tasty Tidbit* by Janwillem van de Wettering, copyright © 1984 by Davis Publications, Inc., reprinted by permission of the author; *Something Like Growing Pains* by Lika Van Ness, copyright © 1972 by Eleanor Sullivan, reprinted by permission of the author; *Nice, Well Meaning Folk* by N. Scott Warner, copyright © 1986 by Davis Publications, Inc., reprinted by permission of the author.

CONTENTS

INTRODUCTION

New England, a region that is synonymous with some of America's proudest and most enduring cultural traditions, is the setting for the stories in this collection from *Ellery Oueen's Mystery Maaazine.*

The tales in this volume are as varied as the New England landscape and allude to many facets of New England legend and folklore. Cape Cod beaches, Vermont villages, steaming lobsters and ivied campuses are emblems that are part of the collective American heritage. These pleasant aspects of New England culture are painted in many of the stories included in this collection.

However, the reader also will encounter images and characters that reflect darker aspects of the region's geography and folklore: the craggy Maine Coast, taciturn natives who endure isolation and loneliness winter after winter, long after summer tourists have flocked back to their urban havens. Such references and characters contribute to the turbulence that the reader will encounter in many of the stories.

Whether or not one believes that New England is the ideal locale to stage a mystery readers will enjoy the shrewd detection, startling plots and sardonic wit that have been the hallmarks of *Ellery Queen's Mystery Magazine* since its founding nearly fifty years ago.

In any case, we don't want to spoil anyone's vacation plans!

Chris Dorbandt

NEW ENGLAND EQUINOX

Isaac Azimov

"That was typical of Hazlett," Ingoldsby said. "He had a passion for getting detail correct. I've read a great deal about him, including his autobiography, and he would indulge in serious research in order to settle some small detail in his paintings..."

Jennings walked into the library of the Union Club with a clearly discontented expression on his face.

"My wife," he announced with a tremor of outrage (which we were sure he would have repressed if he were in his wife's actual presence), "is up to her old tricks again."

The statement did not elicit an immediate response. There are old tricks and old tricks, and Baranov and I knew Mrs. Jennings well enough to doubt that some of the more spectacular old tricks were part of her makeup.

"What old tricks might those be?" I finally said, with a studied air of frank innocence.

"She's been buying paintings," said Jennings with an aggrieved air.

"For how much?" asked Baranov, getting down to the nitty-gritty.

"For more than I want to pay," said Jennings flatly. "And they're modernistic stuff that I can't bear to look at. Just junk, as nearly as I can tell."

I said, "Don't be a Philistine. Your wife may be making careful investments. Good paintings, however nauseating they may appear to the naked eye, have a habit of appreciating. You, or your heirs, may someday outpace inflation with those paintings and, at need, sell them for ten or twenty or fifty times the purchase price."

"Not every painting," said Jennings intransigently. "Some go up in value and some remain worthless, now and forever. I can't tell the two kinds apart, and you can't, and frankly I don't think art experts can. It's all bluff and circumstance. If enough people say some artist is great, everyone else is afraid to disagree and proclaim that the Emperor has no clothes. Only how do you get people to start saying it about the paintings *you* buy—and if they're already saying it, how do you keep them from no longer saying it as soon as you make the purchase?"

"You *are* a Philistine," I said.

It was at that point that Griswold stirred in his armchair. He had obviously been listening to the conversation under his usual pretense of being fast asleep—though I've never been able to figure out how he maintains that soft, regular, and utterly authentic snore.

Griswold said, "It is sometimes very easy to make a judgment concerning a painting, even if one is not an art expert, which I'm not."

"There is something you're not?" I asked, turning up my irony faucet to the full.

"There are innumerable things I'm not," said Griswold with dignity, "but unlike you, I never pretend I am what I am not, which leaves me with my integrity."

I had no chance to answer him as he deserved, for he was already well and truly launched into his story.

It happened (said Griswold) precisely here in the library of the Union Club. It did not take place on *our* night of the week, however, so you three were not present. That pleasant fact was counteracted by the presence of two other individuals who were not members of the club as far as I know. I had never seen them before and, for that matter, I have never seen them since.

I presume they were waiting for a member whose guests they were, and while they were doing so they engaged themselves in an intense conversation, paying no regard to me, since they supposed me to be asleep, I presume. If so, however, they showed scant concern for my comfort, for they didn't bother to lower their voices very much.

This was three for four years ago, soon after the death of Louis Hazlett. Since none of you three is what might be considered knowledgeable in contemporary art, or in much of

anything else for that matter, I will go to the trouble of explaining who Hazlett was—and please don't interrupt to tell me
you know all about him. Such a statement would be utterly
unconvincing on the face of it.

Hazlett was an old-fashioned painter, you might say, intent
on producng representational art. His barns looked precisely
like barns, his trees strongly resembled trees, and sunlight il-
luminated his landscapes precisely as sunlight does in the case
of what we refer to as "reality."

You (he pointed to Jennings) would undoubtedly find Hazlett entirely satisfactory, for you could look at a painting of his
and know exactly what you were looking at. If you were looking at what you thought was junk, it would only be because
Hazlett was deliberately portraying junk—old bottles, scraps of
paper—and not because the painting consisted of colors and
forms you could not understand, leaving you to suspect nervously that the fault might be yours rather than the painting's.

And you (he pointed to me), with your easy blathering
about "Philistines," might dismiss the paintings as merely a
photography in oils, but that would be nothing more than pre-
tentious ignorance on your part. A photograph is a literal presentation and is helpless, or relatively helpless, to alter that—
though photography in the hands of an expert can be art, too

A painter—however representational and accurate his paintings—is more than a camera, for he can be selective. He can add,
subtract, arrange, and rearrange, correcting deficiencies and
supplying omissions. The painting my look real but still have a
beauty and symbolism that a particular reality cannot—that is, if
the artist has genius. Hazlett had genius.

Naturally, then, Hazlett's paintings grew more valuable with
time and, as he produced them prolifically through a long life,
he grew wealthy indeed, and, moreover, added to the wealth of
those who bought his paintings, for one and all proved good
investment.

After his death, it was not surprising that his paintings in-
creased sharply in value, that being the ghoulish state of affairs
when death puts a final limit on the number of an artist's
paintings and the fight grows sharper for those that exist.

Imagine, then, the delight of someone who discovers a Hazlett painting in an out-of-the-way place, one which he can

buy for a fraction of its value.

This apparently was what had happened to one of the two conversationalists on that evening—one who was referred to by the other as Ingoldsby.

Ingoldsby was describing how he had come across a painting in a New Hampshire farmhouse a few weeks before, one which seemed to him to be an authentic Hazlett. The farmer said his wife had bought it at a garage sale because it looked pretty, but he wouldn't say how much they had paid for it. Apparently Ingoldsby looked too interested for the farmer to fix a value too quickly.

Ingoldsby said, "It had Hazlett's signature, and it *looked* like Hazlett's signature to my untutored eye. What's more, it's a picture dealing with precisely the sort of thing Hazlett loved to deal with. It's a painting of a small town at dawn.—Or it might be sunset, but if it were there would be some people in the one street he shows and that street is deserted. So it must be dawn. There's additional evidence for that which I'll come to later.

"There is nothing so crass as half a sun at the horizon, but there is a ruddy bit peeping through a gap in a stretch of clouds just at the line where the water of a lake meets the sky. It is a subtle but absolutely unmistakable suggestion of sunrise.

"The buildings," Ingoldsby went on, are lined up at the lower right of the painting, which is about three feet wide and one and a half feet high—it's no miniature—and those buildings seemed authentic New England in every detail. The town hall, in particular, was exactly what it should be, and there was just an indication, somehow, that it was on the point of needing a paint-job.

"To the left and above are fields and a grove of trees, and the lake, of course, and a sky with a scattering of beautifully handled clouds from pink-lined at the bottom to a gathering grey above. It is clear that Hazlett is showing how the works of man are dwarfed by nature, and even though the buildings are beautiful and possess a charmingly imposed unity they cannot compete with the sheer majesty of world-without-man. Hazlett strengthens the point by leaving human beings out of the painting. It's as though people shrink to such unimportance in Hazlett's universe that they disappear altogether.

"And yet there is one intrusion, Lomax. The scene might be bucolic Nineteenth Century, but in the one street before the line of structures, right in front of the town church with its graceful steeple, as though to emphasize the contrast, is an automobile. The machine age is invading paradise, you see, and it's enough to make your heart break.

"Another thing that made me think it was really Hazlett was the absolute accuracy of detail. I studied that automobile and I could swear it was a 1955 De Soto. I had one of those when I was younger—second-hand, of course. What's more, the clock on the town hall, which registered six o'clock, didn't have the hands shown as a single vertical hairline of black paint. I studied it with a hand-lens and there were two strokes, one for each hand.

"What's more, there was a weathervane on top of the town-hall tower and the hand-lens showed a plain E for East, done with jeweler's precision. Hazlett had the E pointing in the direction of the sun-glow, a clear indication he was portraying dawn and wanted to make the face unmistakable.

"That was typical of Hazlett. He had a passion for getting detail correct. I've read a great deal about him, including his autobiography, and he would indulge in serious research in order to settle some small detail in his paintings. You should have seen the foliage on the trees—just a suggestion of beginning to turn. A touch of orange-brown here and there."

Ingoldsby's friend, Lomax, who had listened patiently, said, "Did you buy it?"

"Yes, I did. I certainly didn't go about it shrewdly, though. My scrutiny with the hand-lens was a dead giveaway, and when I asked the price the farmer said quite calmly, 'Five hundred dollars.' He had probably bought it for five.

"I didn't begrudge it, however. In fact, just to ease my conscience, I told him it was worth closer to a thousand, which I certainly felt was true, and he settled at once for that sum. I didn't feel cheated. If the painting is authentic, it's easily worth fifteen thousand and in a few years that value should double."

Lomax said, "*If* it is authentic? Is there doubt?"

"Well, I don't have its provenance. I have no record of previous owners and bills of sale and all that. In the world of art, a potentially valuable painting is considered a fake until it is proved authentic and it's hard to prove that without documents. You can take it to an art expert, but unless the expert is trying to sell you the painting himself he's extraordinarily cautious and won't commit himself. He has his reputation to think of. Mind you, the thousand dollars isn't wasted. I'll easily get a thousand dollars' worth of pleasure looking at it."

"Aren't there lists and descriptions of all the paintings Hazlett produced?"

"All those we know about," said Ingoldsby. "My painting isn't in any catalogue of his works and there are no descriptions of it anywhere in the listings. Of course, that's not conclusive. In his earlier days, Hazlett gave away many paintings he wasn't satisfied with. He was an easily dissatisfied man. In later years, he would buy back a number of the paintings he had given away just so he could destroy them. It wouldn't be surprising if he never referred to a painting he was dissatisfied with, and if he never put it up for sale or placed it on exhibit it wouldn't be in the catalogues."

"It's a pity you don't know the name of the painting," Lomax said. "That might give you a valuable lead."

"Oh, but I do know the name," said Ingoldsby, "and unfortunately it doesn't help at all. Burned into the wooden frame along its lower border is "New England Equinox'–that, I presume, is the title."

It was at this point that I stirred. I had heard enough.

I opened my eyes and said, "Mr. Ingoldsby, I could not help but overhear your conversation, and I feel I must tell you that the painting is in all likelihood a forgery. That would be so even in the unlikely case that the experts agreed it was authentic."

Ingoldsby and Lomax looked at me with startled surprise as though they thought I had materialized from nowhere.

"What do you mean?" said Ingoldsby, frowning. "What do you know about this?"

"Enough," I said, and explained. Naturally, I was convincing. Since, as I said, I never saw the two men again, I don't know what happened with the painting, but I strongly suspect Ingoldsby must satisfy himself with getting a thousand dollars' worth of pleasure out of looking at it and nothing more. It is *not* a Hazlett. It may be just as good, but it is not a Hazlett.

With that, he sipped the last of his drink and lapsed into silence. I said, "You took a big chance, Griswold, in making artistic decisions on a picture you didn't even see. You're probably wrong."

"Not at all," said Griswold stiffly. "I should have thought that even you halfwits would have seen the mistake the artist had made."

"What mistake?" said Jennings, looking all at sea.

Griswold sighed. "Then I'll explain.—Look, the painter was showing a New England town at equinox. The title tells you that. But there are two equinoxes, the vernal equinox on March twentieth and the autumnal equinox on September twenty-third. The one that was shown in the painting was unmistakably the autumnal. On September twenty-third, the trees in New England, particularly in northern New England, are beginning to show signs of autumn coloring, as they were doing in the painting. On March twentieth, the trees of New England are bare. So the day being shown in the painting is September twenty-third.

"The scene is not Nineteenth Century. There's an automobile shown that is possibly a 1955 De Soto, so such a thing as daylight saving exists—and the two equinoxes are not identical in that respect, either. Daylight saving runs from the last Sunday in April to the last Sunday in October, so the vernal equinox, March twentieth, is in standard time and the autumnal equinox, September twenty-third, is in daylight

"In standard time, sunrise would be at six A.M., give or take a few minutes since the earth's orbit about the sun is elliptical, not circular. In daylight saving time, with the hands of the clock moved ahead one hour, sunrise at equinox would be at seven A.M. Consequently, sunrise on September twenty-third should be at seven A.M. and not at six A.M. as shown in the painting. The ever-meticulous Hazlett would not have made that error."

THE SISTERHOOD
Gwendoline Butler

I was serving the first coffee of the day when the two women came in. It's a hot day, so I'm slow, but I'm a hard worker and I'm getting on with it. That's the picture I see looking back. I could do with help but conditions are bad just now and I don't get help. Frankly, I'm glad to have a job, and I need one. When my husband died (his Feed and Grain business failed the year President Grover Cleveland came into office) he left me penniless.

So I do what I can. I can make coffee and tea and serve it neatly, polish china and cutlery, and give the right change. Also I'm honest; I don't steal from my employers. My employer is the Railroad, an impersonal one but we get along well enough. It don't overpay me and I don't fill my basket with its coffee and sugar, and that's about it. We don't owe each other a thing. At first, I wondered if there'd be any talk about me serving tea and coffee, but no, no one said anything.

The two women came in so early I knew that there'd been another delay on the line. I don't think our Railroad will ever pay for itself while we have these little incidents so often. This time it was only the engine caught fire and no one hurt. These two women were the forerunners; I could hear other angry voices behind.

"It's only a little delay," one of them was saying. "We shall get there in the end. Only Father is cross; we need not be." She was a nice-looking young woman, plainly dressed in poplin, but not poor. I know the sort—no show but plenty of money tucked away in the family moneybags. Who controls the purse strings, though?

"And he's the one that counts," said the other one. So this answered my question: in this family it was the father who held the money. This woman was younger than the other one— not a girl, but a woman approaching her prime. She looked as though she feared this prime would come and go unnoticed. I recognized that keen searching look.

They had got on to the subject of marriage by the time I served their coffee, which showed how their minds were running.

"Marriages are made in heaven," the older one was saying. I suppose I've served thousands of cups of coffee and overheard thousands of conversations; but I've never heard anyone say that.

"Marriages are made with money, Emma," snapped the younger one. *Snap.* Her jaws went like little traps. Well, she was right enough there. "Father has the money and Abby will make the marriage."

"Do you think she will, Elizabeth?"

"Yes."

Father and Abby put in their appearance then. He had been help up by a quarrel with the engineer. Abby asked for iced tea and Father for water. He'd have an extra glass with it, please. I kept my eyes on him to see what he did with the two glasses. Father and Abby didn't sit at the same table as the two girls but a little way off. There wouldn't have been room for them, with Abby the size she was. She was wearing a fine silk dress, though.

"My, I'm hot." That was her size, of course. The dress was red silk too, which didn't cool her off any. "Do you have any cologne, girls?"

Elizabeth silently handed over a small flask of cologne for Abby to dab her face, and Father took some too and held the bottle while she fanned herself. This seemed to be his manner of doing his courting and Abby nodded and chuckled, and this was her way of doing hers. I never did get to see what he did with his two glasses. Perhaps he had some medicine to take, but he looked a fine healthy man that would live forever. He drank his water, though, then gave the cologne back to Elizabeth and put his hand down on the table near to Abby's.

So Abby sat there cooling off, insofar as she was able, and Father sat there warming up. Every so often he looked at the door as if he might get up and leave soon. It's true there were a few train noises every once in a while, but I knew better. There are only three trains a day through here. The 9:10 in the morning running west, which was not broken down. Then the midday train running east. Then the 5:00 p.m. train running west again. I knew they wouldn't be moving for a spell.

Then the girls started talking again in low voices.

"I don't think she looks at all nice," the older one said and I knew what they were talking about. They were talking about the only other customer.

She'd been there all the time. She hadn't come off the train. No, she'd been there waiting. She was wearing a watered silk dress and a satin-edged bonnet. She made Abby look cheap. I'd served her the first coffee of the day and she was still sitting there sipping it. She was going some place, no doubt, but I didn't know where and she was giving me no sign–I'm good at reading even very little signs. I'd say she'd come a long way. Was going a long way too.

"Not nice? What does that mean?" asked the younger one.

"Don't flash at me. I know what I mean. She looks worldly. Experienced."

"She looks interesting." Elizabeth was dabbing at her own face with cologne. "Clever. If that's what worldly means." The cologne was putting a shine on her nose. She had a plump face with full cheeks which might lengthen into a long hatchet face later. Now she was a bouncing young woman with the nearest to good looks she'd ever have.

The smell of cologne has done nothing for me since my husband died. Funny, I can smell coffee and feel fine. Cologne, and I'm sick straight away. I used cologne for him a lot in his last days. It was an easy death. I was there and I can tell you: it was an easy death, but he didn't want to go.

To take my mind off my nausea I moved closer to the girls.

"I'd like to get to know the world better," said Elizabeth.

"Perhaps we could go to Europe."

"With Father? With Abby? Does Abby look like a traveler?"

No, Abby did not.

I'll tell you how I could get their conversation although they were talking low. I'm something of a lip reader. I taught myself; it's one of my tricks. They were talking soft but I could read them. Abby was talking away too but I couldn't read her. She had her head down. I guess Abby could lip-read too.

The other lady (unknown I was going to say, but of course they were all unknown to me) looked towards them. Just a glance. No more. But I'll bet her eyes and her observation were good. She was the sort that took everything in and wrapped it away in brown paper for future use. Funny way of looking she had—just glancing up under heavy lids and deep lashes. A pretty face really. Or had been. It was lined now, and she used rouge, too.

I just glanced at my own in the mirror. Ah, there was a *look* there. It seemed to me this look was growing and growing—the only live thing about me.

"She looks interesting, but she doesn't look honest. Not straight," said Elizabeth, as if she'd made a discovery.

"Not straight! The way you talk. Like a man."

Elizabeth seemed flattered as if she'd received a compliment and I can tell she's one of the simple ones who hasn't grasped that she *is* a man. That's why she'll never get a husband. Not because Abby has Father and Father has the money and money makes a marriage, but because she's a man and another man will notice it.

"More coffee, please," sings out the lady. It was a strange little voice, soft yet mighty penetrating and with an accent I couldn't place.

"She's an English lady," whispers Emma.

"Scottish," says the lady, in that gentle lilting voice of hers. She smiled. No one else did.

It was an encounter all right, I could see that, a real moment in life. I haven't traveled much, so I don't know where she came from; but it was a strange place, I'll say that.

"May I join you ladies?" She was carrying her coffee over to their table. "We must pass the time somehow, must we not?" She sat down close to Elizabeth. "It would be coarse and common to make a fuss. Still, it is tedious waiting."

"No," answered Emma.

"Yes," said her sister.

So that was the effect she had on them—not that they'd ever spoken with one voice, I reckon. Take care, I wanted to warn them: she knows something you don't know and if you don't watch out you'll know it too.

There was plenty of noise going on outside. Not the noise of a train which was what they were hoping for, but the noise of something, and I could see Abby and Father looking curious. They'd soon be out there to investigate. I knew what it was. It was a funeral. We have noisy funerals in this little spot. Well, we have had lately. And there have been so many of them. Why, we die off like flies round here.

Abby was heaving herself up and out of the room and Father was hurrying after her, as if his blood was hot, whereas you could tell by the cut of his suit it was cold. It was going to be a marriage all right, the sort I knew about. A kind of exclusive club with only two members.

A suitor of my own came in as they went out, brushing against them with an apology. At least, I supposed he was a suitor. He's always in here talking to me. He sells insurance. I don't imagine he thought he would sell me any. My buying days are over. I bought some for my Willy; that's enough for one family; I won't be buying any for myself.

"I heard the noise," I said, nodding outside. I gave him his coffee.

"Yeah, terrible sad thing. Maisie Gray."

"I heard she was going."

He drank his coffee.

"Bad time?" I said.

"Worse than most."

"I heard."

We stood in silence for a minute. Our tribute, you might say, to the dead.

"So it wasn't an easy end? Funny thing. I'd have sworn Maisie was a woman as'd have an easy end. She seemed made for it somehow."

"Oh, they've all been bad lately. It's something in the season, I think." He sounded depressed. He kept in with the doctors and the undertaker in the way of business, so he always knew about the ends we made.

"Who was making all the noise out there?'

"Oh, Maisie's sister. Crying to beat the band. You heard? It was the *way* Maisie died," he burst out. "Little by little. One day it was a foot, the next day a finger. No telling what next. Then at last it was over her like wildfire."

"What was it supposed to be?"

"Some infection. That's the way they've been lately."

My Will had an easy death, but he didn't want to go, and for that you couldn't blame him. He knew what would be waiting for him. His brother whom he'd cheated, his mother he'd neglected, and his sister he'd help kill. He was leaving me this side, but I doubt that was much comfort to him.

"Was she insured?"

"No. She didn't carry insurance. There wasn't no one who benefited by her death. No one." He shook his head. "Bad business."

He went on drinking his coffee. Watching the three women at their table I saw Emma get up. I guessed the Scotch woman had sent her out. She knew how to say, "Do this," and it was done. She had a pretty elegant way of holding her lips when she spoke. I quite admired her. Elizabeth was just a good plain ordinary speaker. You wouldn't have picked her out from any crowd for the beauty of her diction. I could read both their lips fine.

"So kind of your sister to do that little errand for me. I feel the need for some cologne like you."

"She was glad to go."

"Yes." She sounded doubtful, forming her lips in a little cooing shape. "I think she doesn't like me."

"Emma doesn't consider whether she likes you or not, she doesn't know you." Only a fool would expect flattery from Elizabeth.

"Oh, you Yankee ladies are so smart. You put us poor European creatures to shame." She could live with her lies and even love them. Perhaps this was what she was going to teach the other one.

"Who is that woman?" It was my suitor speaking. I had forgotten him there drinking his coffee.

"I think she's a teacher."

"Where does she teach?"

I shrugged. It was my idea she was teaching right now. But I'd reminded him of something.

"Why do you do this work?" He pointed to my hands, red

and stained. "You taught school once. You could teach it
again."

"No," I said. "No school."

"She doesn't look like a teacher to me. No. I'll tell you what
she does look like–" He frowned.

I could see them both in the mirror behind me, still talking
away.

"Why, she looks like you," he finished, in a surprised voice.

"Yes." I'd noticed it myself. "Perhaps we're related."

"What? Not by blood."

"By blood."

"I don't understand you."

"Hush. Listen."

The two women were deep in conversation. I've never seen
what that meant before. Now I saw it meant that they were
talking at all levels. They were talking with their eyes, with
their bodies, and with their silences. And some of the most important things get said that way.

"As soon as I saw you I knew you were someone I must talk
to," the Scotch woman was saying.

"Do you feel that way often?" I cannot describe the peculiar
note the speaker put into that question. Off-hand, sceptical,
and yet profoundly interested in the answer. The one thing
that perhaps she didn't want to show was what came across
strongest.

"It comes. I can often tell when it will happen. I get a warning."

"So you were getting warnings while Emma and I sat here?"

"Before." She smiled. "Before. I don't say that's why I came
here."

"You can't say that's why you came here. I didn't know I was
coming here myself. We were going straight through but the
engine broke down."

"As if that mattered." She still smiled. "But I don't say so.
Notice, I *don't* say so."

They sat looking at each other.

"I am on my way to help a sister. An American girl married
to an English businessman. In Liverpool. Cotton, I believe. She
is in great trouble and I am going to help her. She has been
rather careless, poor girl."

"She's an American girl and she is your sister? But you are

not American."

"No, I was Glasgow-born. A Miss Smith before my marriage."

"And she's your sister?" Elizabeth was getting lost. I wasn't though. I was beginning to see my way. I've always been quick on the uptake.

Looking out of the window I could see Abby and Father pacing up and down; they were not talking. No sign of Emma. The funeral had become quiet. They were doing the burying, I suppose.

There's no noise louder nor stronger than the thud of earth against the box.

"I call her my sister," answered the Scotch woman.

"And what does she call you?"

"Oh, we've never met. No, I am on my way now to our first meeting. Even this may not be easy to do. No, it will not be easy to meet her, but I shall try. I know my duty."

"Well, I know *my* sister," declared Elizabeth. "I meet her face to face every day. That's what I call being a sister."

"You have many sisters that you don't know. I must teach you about them." See, I said she was a teacher.

"I know all I want to know about my family."

"Have you noticed," said the other, "that although this is a very hot day there is no sun? This is a sunless town."

This I had noticed. We all do. It can get quite trying in high summer. The deaths are always worse then.

"I don't want any more members added to my family," said Elizabeth, in a pointed kind of way.

"You mean the lady who went out with your Father? That makes you bitter?"

"I don't trust her. We should have our rights."

"Rights?"

"Money," said Elizabeth sullenly. Emma pushed open the door.

"I'm sorry I was so long," she panted. "It was impossible to find a shop open in the town for your cologne. On the way back I came across a large crowd in the town square and I had difficulty in getting through. I don't know what they were doing. Every so often a man would say something. But he didn't speak very loud."

We don't speak very loud in our town. You can't call our voices soft, but we don't raise 'em much. Except at funerals.

"Every so often someone would call out a name and then they would all be silent again. I wonder what they were doing?"

They must be starting the election for mayor. And that means Tom Edwards must be going downhill fast. He's younger than most. The average life expectancy in this town is 45, and we age quick. Tom's still a young man but he looks old. It's a shame he should go. He made a good mayor. He has a growth, I've heard. Back of his throat. Certain he didn't speak well these last years.

But a lot of us have trouble this way. We intermarry a good deal. There are only three or four big family groups, kin we call them, and we're all related. Tom's mother married her cousin. Some people said *his* father was also his brother, but I don't know about that. You hear these stories every so often round here, but I don't know that any one of them has even been proven.

No one said anything to Emma standing there and in a minute she muttered something about getting some air and went out again. I doubt if they noticed her go.

"You must learn to defend yourself," the old one was saying. I couldn't hear even the breath of these words, I could only read them on her face. "Money is important. Yes, and you should have yours. A woman may get justice, but she must usually get it for herself."

"How can she?"

"A man won't give it to her, that is certain. Oh, he can be persuaded into it, but is has to be contrived. In the end one relies on oneself."

"I always do."

"Yes, you have made a good beginning, but it is not enough. Are you a woman of education? Anything of a scientist? A doctor perhaps?"

"No."

"A pity." She sounded regretful. "There would be so much scope for a sister who was also a doctor. Well, then you must exercise a good deal. Keep in good health. Develop your muscles."

"Why?"

"It may come in useful." She leaned over and felt the girl's arm. "Yes, I thought you looked strong," she said with approval. "Suitable bouffant sleeves will mask a lady's arm muscles. I should not advise you to make a show of them. Always think of a practical point like that. It may be the saving of you. Some sisters have wasted time on theory that would be better spent in attending to the practical details."

"And my legs too?" said Elizabeth, withdrawing her arm.

"Oh, I can't foretell the future. I can't tell you what your need may be. Perhaps at some future date I might advise a lady to cultivate strong legs, but I can't say. It may be that you will invent some ingenious little plan of your own that needs strong legs. I leave it to you. And in any case a strong mind and good manners are your best protection. Many a lady owes her life to her manners."

Oh, how I had needed someone like her in my life. She gave good advice. She said words I wanted to hear. I moved away unsteadily to sit down. My right leg always troubles me worse in hot weather.

"How lame she is, poor thing," said the young one. Much she cared. "I'm afraid she has been badly used at one time."

"She may have been born like that."

"No. You can see by her face. She has not the expression of someone who has been used to it since birth. She has had to learn how to bear it."

"She's listening."

"Nonsense. She cannot possibly hear." So then I saw that my lady from Glasgow had this limitation: she only believed what she wanted to believe. I suppose this was what made her strong. Because she was strong. I'm strong myself and I could measure hers.

"If I might suggest," she was going on. "You might pay a little more attention to your dress."

"Ladies where I come from don't bother much with their dress."

"Ladies everywhere bother with their dress," the Scotch woman corrected. "A well trimmed bodice or a becoming hat can make a good deal of difference at your time of crisis."

"My time of crisis?"

"You will have one, my dear," she said softly.

"Ah." It was a long, long breath. I felt it more than heard it.

"And when that time comes you must accept your crisis. Be proud. Wear it like a crown."

"We don't have queens in this country. And I don't aim to be a martyr."

"Oh, on no account. They are our least successful members."

"Is this a sort of club?"

"Yes, but it's more important than that. More sacred."

"Do I take an oath or something?'

"You have already taken it."

"What?" Elizabeth recoiled.

"Yes. You took it...Now, let me see." She looked thoughtful. "You must have taken it a few minutes after our conversation began. When you said: 'I know all I want to know about my family.'"

And it's true, she had taken it then. From then on there was no looking back for her.

"Now you are one of us. My sister," and the Scotch woman stretched out a fleshy hand.

"So, it's a sisterhood," said Elizabeth, just beginning to take in what she had joined.

"Yes." There was a radiant smile. "Oh, we are a great band stretching out hands down the centuries. Mary Stuart was one of us, Madame Brinvilliers was certainly another."

And what about the nameless ones, I wanted to shout out, the ones who didn't get their names in history books?

"I remember my own initiation," the old one was going on. "I was walking in the country near Glasgow. The old crone frightened me with what she said. But I never forgot it." She looked amused. "Still, do you know, I believe I must have re-solved then that when my time came it should all be neatly and tidily managed and nothing sordid like that old woman. Pah, I could smell the blood on her."

Elizabeth took a sniff of her cologne, for which I didn't blame her.

My suitor woke up. I'd forgotten him dozing over his coffee.

"It's all in the womb," he said as he came awake. He's the only man I know that would say "womb" right out. I think he drinks.

"What is?"

"Wickedness." That's another word he can say outright.

"You'd better go off home."

"Thanks. I will."

He shuffled out. He'd be back tomorrow.

She was still talking about death when I turned back.

"Of course you must not take me literally when I say I smelled blood. What I smelled was probably something quite different. Dirt, I dare say."

"I don't think blood does smell."

"Not to you. No. You are one of the lucky ones. But it does to some people. Blood will never smell to you, or stick to you, or in any way worry you. You should be glad."

"I am."

"It was because I was tender of the sight of blood that I was obliged to find a different weapon. Come Louis, my love, I said, drink this chocolate, you will be better for it."

"And was he?"

"We must all be the better for casting off this world and its troubles, must we not? In the end."

She was willing to tell more.

"Mine was an affair of the heart, you understand? I truly and tenderly loved my poor Louis. But then he was poor, and showed no signs of trying to better himself." She sighed. "Poor creature, he tried so hard to cling to me. In the end I had to be brave for both of us. But I was too innocent to live then, my dear, and the result was there was a great deal of nasty talk, quite ill informed, and my trail had to be moved to Edinburgh."

"Oh, so there *was* a trial?"

"One cannot hope to escape all unpleasantness," She said placidly.

"And the result was?"

"The verdict was 'Not Proven.' "

"And that means?"

"It means you go free."

"Is that all?"

"My dear, allow me to say that in the circumstances it is very nearly everything."

Elizabeth became quiet. She hadn't quite accepted the reality of all this, but it was coming. I knew her kind–slow to take anything in, but very tenacious. Hadn't I taught girls like her? I knew their ways. Obstinate, yes, and ruthless too. Stupid sometimes; you could talk to them forever and ever and get nowhere. Then *snap*, they took something in and it was theirs for life. She was like that.

"And never forget," the old one way saying. "You are a gentlwoman, and in that is your protection. Who will believe a gentlewoman could be violent? Go naked if you must to commit your deed. No one will believe it."

Elizabeth covered her ears with her hands. The other pulled them away.

"You heard me? You listened? You will never forget. Remember, we are sisters."

She was talking quite loudly now, not caring if I heard, but then she was a gentlewoman see, and I was just a stone in the wall to her.

I wanted to call out, "I'm here. I'm listening. You are talking to the converted. Can't you see we look alike? I have done my deed, I am one of you, I am your sister. I gave my husband arsenic in his coffee. And I did it all on my own."

Perhaps I ought to have been proud of my independence.

The train was going to come in soon, the one running east. Already I could hear a noise in the distance. The woman from Glasgow got up, gathered her possessions together, and slowly moved towards the door. We watched her go.

The train came in and still we stood, silent.

Then Emma put her head in at the door.

"Come on, we are going back home. Papa has canceled the trip. We are going back on this train."

Her sister still stood there. Emma became impatient.

"Come *on*, Elizabeth. Come on, Miss Lizzie Borden."

SOMETHING LIKE GROWING PAINS

Lika Van Ness

Ralph Boalt came in from putting the car away and found his wife weaving back and forth on her toes, looking through the still unfamiliar kitchen cupboard. "What are you dong?" he inquired, locking the door.

"I'm looking for something to wash this sand out of my mouth."

"Water's good," he suggested, shutting both kitchen windows against the raw sea air and turning to face her. "You look like a sand sculpture. Why don't you go take a bath?"

Outside, the surf splashed methodically, one hefty sigh following fast on another. "Come on," Ralph said, going to the bathroom off the kitchen and turning the squeaky faucets in the tub. "Get the sand off and I'll make you a fire and that silly rum and grapefruit drink you like."

"Is there any juice left?" Harriet opened the refrigerator door and peered in, rubbing a lock of sand-encrusted brown hair between her fingers. A large can of unsweetened grapefruit juice stood between the bottle of milk and a pickle jar containing one dill pickle sunk in pale green water. She removed the can of juice and shook it.

"What gets into you at the parties down here?" Ralph called, a deceptive, amused-sounding note in his voice. "You were all over that beach tonight like the sand was stardust. Not that you'll remember it tomorrow."

"I'll remember it." she assured him.

"You'd think you'd remember your first swim in two years, but you don't."

He was referring to the swim she had taken on Sunday with all her clothes on. Harriet ran her finger thoughtfully over a long dark cigarette scar she had already made on the pine-board countertop, then walked to the bathroom, stepping out of her sandals on the way.

Ralph was down on one knee, testing the water with one hand and adjusting faucets with the other. "You thought you were Esther Williams, for God's sake," he was saying.

"Are you preparing me a bath," she asked quietly, "or a lecture?"

"Have you got a fresh change?" He dropped a bar of soap and a drying, balled-up facecloth into the water.

"My nightgown is on the back of the bedroom door."

He wheeled the faucets shut, slapped the water, and wiped his hands on a worn towel on the rack. "There you go," he said, leaving her.

She heard him climb the wooden stairs as she shut the door and got out of her scratchy clothes. Stepping into the shallow tepid water and sitting, she frowned as he started to whistle overhead and she wondered why the things she had loved five years before, like his whistling and his good posture and careful manners, drove her wild now.

Shutting her eyes, she sank back, letting the water soak off the sand. She ran her tongue over her teeth, still gritty with sand, stopping at her broken front tooth. She hadn't really stopped being self-conscious about the tooth since she had broken it in a stupid fall after a high-school football game, but she had never had it capped, she didn't know why.

The door opened and Ralph set the pink gown, neatly folded, on the john lid by her head. She quickly closed her eyes again, but he did not leave. He fished for and found the washcloth and knelt by the tub. She sat up and pulled the cloth out of his hand.

"Go away," she said. He stood and wipes his hand on his corduroy trousers, his face taking on the arrogant expression he used to recoup his dignity, and then left, shutting the door behind him.

"All right," he called in later. "What's keeping you?"

She was sitting with her head forward, her forward resting on her knees. The room was cold. "I'm coming."

"Hurry up. You'll catch cold."

The sand on the bottom of the tub was sharp. "All right."

"Don't forget your hair."

"All *right*."

When she joined him in the living room she was wet under the pink cotton gown and her hair was slicked back and dripping down her collar. He gave it a disapproving glance.

"You told me to soak my head and I did," she explained.

"Have you ever heard of a towel? Your drink's there." He gestured from the flowered sofa where he lay with a glass of whiskey and soda on his chest.

"This?" She lifted a tall glass off the pile of newspapers on the hassock.

"What's wrong with it?"

"It should be pink."

"I can't help that. You told me equal parts applejack and juice. Does it have to be pink grapefruit or something?"

"Grenadine makes it pink, it's got nothing to do with the grapefruit."

"What possible difference can the color make?"

"It's not just to make it pink—it's for flavor. It makes a big difference in the taste." She went to the kitchen, remembering there was no grenadine but pretending to look. In the living room Ralph sang, "'And He walks with me and He talks with me—'"

" 'Oh, the Bowery, the Bowery,' " Harriet finished, " 'I'll never go there anymore.' " She returned to the living room and stretched across the armchair opposite him, swinging her legs over the frayed sailcloth-covered arm so that she too was facing the fire. "No grenadine," she said, lifting her glass. "Here's mud in your eye."

"Here's to the kids," he returned solemnly.

"To the kids. Long may they wave goodbye to us as we leave for vacation."

"You haven't missed them for a second, have you?" Ralph said.

"I've missed them all right, don't you worry. I don't *ache* for them. When I start to ache I remind myself how fond Ronnie's

grown of whining and Barbara can't ever stop and think once
before she does anything. I think of the sleepless mornings and
the squalor and I know I can survive to the end of the week
without too much pain."

"If your life strikes you as squalid don't blame them. You've
got the time to teach them manners without any interference
from me. I'm on the road five days a week. I'm no distraction."

"You're no *help* either."

"What do you want me to do, find a job in the office? At half
the salary?"

"I want you to stop trying to make me feel guilty about enjoying a vacation away from them just because you think you
should feel guilty because you're *always* away from them." An
honest talk can't hurt, she told herself, wanting to run but taking a drink instead.

"You're as truthful with yourself as you've always been," he
said, throwing her a quick sinister smile.

"Truth? What's that?" she said lightly, scared, deciding honest talks did hurt. When her friend Bunny's marriage was at the
breaking point, Harriet had insisted that if Bunny would only
talk it out with Art it would be all right. Communication was
the answer. But Art didn't have a hot-potato smile like Ralph's
to scare the hell out of Bunny, that was a big difference. "This is
nice," she said, changing her tone. "I should build more fires at
home."

"I forbid you to build any fires at home when I'm not there.
Just keep your fires confined to the inner woman, please."
Forty feet away, outside the window, the tide beat the shore. "I
forbid you to build a fire in my absence."

"I was a Girl Scout. First-class."

"You'd leave the damper closed or forget to put back the
screen or some foll thing. No fires."

"You're a fine one to forbid," she said, lighting a cigarette.
"Who left the bottle of gin on the stove last night?"

"*You* did, for God's sake!"

"*I* did! Who was sitting on that very soda—*sofa*—drinking
from that same bottle of gin when I went up to bed?"

"I was. Who got up later in the night after I was in bed and
came down for a nip?"

"I came down once, to the *john*. I didn't see that bottle again
until I got up this morning, *hours* before you did, and there it

was, smack on the open pilot. If I hadn't thought fast and grabbed a pot holder, I might have burned my hand off. We're lucky it didn't explode."

He swung his feet to the floor and went purposefully to the kitchen, returning with an almost empty bottle of gin. "How come when I went up to bed this bottle was more than half full?"

"Have you ever heard of evaporation?"

"I don't buy that."

"Will you buy the possibility that you could be mistaken about how much you left?"

"I'm sold on the fact that you left it on the stove. I put it on the counter here when I went to bed."

"You're a dream," she said softly into the fireplace.

He slammed the bottle down on the table near the porch door and threw himself back down on the sofa.

"I myself—" she began.

"I *myself*," he repeated scornfully.

"I myself *personally* say it was an accident, no harm done, let's forget it."

"Easy for *you*," he told the ceiling.

Why did I marry him? she asked herself, taking more of the drink and regarding him across the woven-straw rug. His mouth was a dry line and the planes of his nose were hard and sharp even in the artificial light. Why did *he* marry *me*? What made us think we could be happy?

They had left home early Saturday morning in the company car, leaving the children with Harriet's mother, who had convinced them they needed a vacation by themselves in a rented cottage on the Connecticut shore, where they had friends. Ralph had insisted on driving the whole way, declaring, "*No*body's got that much insurance" when she asked to take the wheel.

The drive had been the best part of the vacation—the only good part, in fact—the lush green country leading to the shore-line, the blood-red barns and antique shops and the proud little restaurant where they had stopped for lunch.

For a few brief hours she had thought that her mother was right and that the vacation might be the answer to the last few demoralizing years. But they had done nothing but drink and fight since the Longmires' beer party on Saturday night. Their arrival there, and seeing Steve and Judy Longmire and other old friends jubilant and tanned, was the last good moment she could recall. They had stayed until the part went dry and on Sunday had got straight out of bed and gone to another party, a clambake on the beach, very little of which (including her first swim in two years) she could remember...

"Do you think you're a better person for this marriage?" Ralph asked.

"I'm not a compulsive cleaner any more."

"That's only because you'd rather booze with the neighbors than stay home and clean, it has nothing to do with me, or the children."

"I only drink with you."

"That's a feeble lie."

"I'm sorry you think so."

"*Some*thing's occupying your time besides the children. Or some*body*."

"I'm not a kaffee-klatscher."

"I believe you."

She drew herself up straighter to look at him, the applejack doing its work at the pit of her stomach. "Let's not start with the really damaging words now, please."

"No, but what can I believe? Yours is a deceitful nature."

She ignored his meaning.

"You've got a nerve. The gay deceiver himself."

"Are we coming to Grace Ordway?"

"You lead the way every time."

"I might deceive you but Grace Ordway wouldn't."

There's only one thing honest about Grace Ordway and that's her being so honestly ugly. In that department she's very honest."

"She has beautiful teeth."

"So you've said. You've also said she is a quote salty gal un-quote."

"I was entitled to Grace Ordway."

"I used to think I was something of a salty girl myself."

"*I was entitled to Grace Ordway!*"

"Go to heaven."

"When a man finds his wife was committed to a mental institution before she married him and didn't think to mention it, he's got a right to react when he finds out."

"I was an outpatient. Just a little crackers for a short time. Something like growing pains, the doctor said."

"You're on the records for extensive psychotherapy, that's all I know. Plus two shock treatments."

A wide blue flame wrapped itself around the front log. The room was warm and the slipcover wet from her hair. She drained her glass, forbidding herself to cry. "You may recall—" She reached down and returned the empty glass to the floor. "You may recall a conversation before we were married in which you explained to me the wisdom of two people keeping certain aspects of their past a secret."

A mental breakdown wasn't the kind of thing I meant."

"How did I know you were protecting yourself from your raunchy past?"

He went to the fireplace, moved the screen to the side, and stoked the fire.

"Let it die," she said.

He continued to prod the logs, creating sparks. "I wish I could forget it," he said finally, "but I can't."

"You can though," she insisted, "if you don't make a memorandum of it."

He replaced the poker and the screen and brought his empty glass to the kitchen, leaving behind an offensive smell of perspiration, like scalded chicken soup. Harriet sat watching the flame flick shadows on the walls and furniture, hearing the ocean play its steady rhythm against the beach.

"Are you going to bed?" she asked as he started back through the room toward the stairs.

"What does it look like?"

"I didn't hear you brush your teeth."

He started up the stairs.

"Is it such a crime that I was sick, Ralph?"

I couldn't have cared less that you were sick," he answered, out of sight, his climbing a tired scrape on the uncarpeted stairs. "The crime is that you didn't tell me."

"*Why?*"

It was a whisper she decided he hadn't heard when finally he answered from the top of the dark stairwell.

"Because you didn't trust me to understand, you destructive, insensitive foul-up of a broad, how many times do I have to tell you?"

She heard him undress, shut the bedroom window, and climb into the creaking bed. Her empty glass was a disappointment but she resolved not to mix another drink. The ship's-bell clock on the mantel chimed eleven. Crossing to the sofa she plumped up the dry pillows and lay on her side, breathing the fragrant wood-smoke and wondering where the sweet peace of sleeping with Ralph had gone.

The clock sounding midnight roused her and she sat up, her head aching loosely. She walked stiffly to the bathroom for an aspirin and washed her face, noticing as she did that her nightgown was inside out. She took it off, turned it right side out, and slipped it on again. She took a second aspirin and sprayed the mud out of the bottom of the tub down the drain. In the kitchen she rinsed the glasses, filled the ice-cube tray, and put out the light.

Back in the living room she knelt on the sofa, holding the curtain aside to look out. It was too dark to see the surf and she rose and unbolted the door, walking out onto the sandy porch and down the stairs in her bare feet.

Billions of stars swept in brilliant arcs through the black sky. The air was spicy with smoke from the chimneys along the beach. Lowering herself onto the steps she sat facing the sea, the breeze stirring the still-damp ends of her hair.

Her mother hadn't liked or trusted Ralph and had fought the idea of her marrying him. But once convinced the marriage was inevitable, she had made Harriet promise not to tell him about the breakdown, persuading her that he would plague her with it afterward whenever they quarreled and that eventually it would ruin the marriage.

Would he have done that if he had known from the start? Harriet's head ached as she climbed back up the porch stairs and went inside, locking the door behind her. She would never know.

Except for the sigh of the ocean, Ralph's light snoring from upstairs, and the mouse-like sounds in the fireplace the cottage was very quiet. The almost empty bottle of gin on the table caught her eye and she brought it to the darkened kitchen, draining it on the way. Placing it on top of the trash barrel by the sink, she then walked with interest to the stove.

In the small hole in the center of the stove the tiny flame of the pilot light burned steadily. Harriet turned on the gas under each of the four burners, slowly, one at a time, then lit all four, increasing and diminishing the intensity of their flames before extinguishing them again.

She went to the narrow linen closet by the bathroom door and felt around the upper shelves for the two army blankets they had brought with them for the beach. Leaving one on a chair by the table, she placed the other across the floor by the back door, pushing its thickness snugly against the threshold. She checked the windows to make sure they were fully shut and returned to the stove where she blew out the pilot light on the top of the stove and then the second one inside the oven. Finally, turning all the gas jets full twist, she moved to the living room, sensing the whisper of the escaping gas behind her, and tucked the second blanket neatly against the floor by the porch door.

There was an old *Life* on the table she didn't remember having seen and she browsed through it standing, dusting sand from one foot with the sole of the other. Then she flipped the last page and stood a while, absently patting her hair, which was now completely dry, before starting for the stairs.

Halfway across the room she hesitated a few seconds longer to stare at the embers, touching the lukewarm screen with her fingers. She wished she could have built more fires for the children. Well, they would be all right. They could remain with her mother. Her mother was still young. They would be no better and no worse off with her

With a last look at the small sealed-off room she started up to the bedroom and her sleeping husband, who would probably, as was his habit these days, turn his back to her when she climbed in beside him.

THAT DAY ON CONNALLY
Stanley Cohen

Sighting through the heavy snowfall, he lined up the cross-hairs on her chest as the cable brought her into view. He focused on a brightly colored emblem on her parka, perfectly and conveniently located, and after following it for a second or two he squeezed off the shot. The girl heaved against the safety bar, then slumped back into the ornate seat. Another perfect hit.

How many was that? Eleven? An even dozen? Maybe even thirteen. He had lost count. All clean kills. Only one had required two shots. A big man who had shifted in the seat just as he fired. The man began struggling after the first bullet hit and he fired a second with greater concentration, instantly stopping the man's wild thrashing movements. But he'd hated having to fire a second time—it was a blow to his otherwise perfect score.

He leaned the rifle against the wall of the shed and pressed the handle of the chair-lift drive. A little farther. Another twenty feet or so. As the chair glided into the landing area beneath the shed he cut the power, just as the ski-patrol attendant would have done to help a skier out of the seat.

He moved quickly up to the chair, pushed the sagging body backward, raised the safety bar, and pulled the man onto the platform. Then, turning him over, he gripped the man under his armpits and dragged him along the planked floor to the back of the platform and toward the convenient little hollow behind the shed. When he reached the dropoff into the hollow, he gave the body a push and then a kick and watched it slide on its own, downward and into the pile with the others.

He hustled back into the shed and grabbed the ski poles out of the holder on the lift-chair. He wheeled and hurled them toward the array of bodies, skis, and poles. Then he returned to the lift drive control and started it again. Time to bring another nice live target into view.

The girl in the seat still some fifty feet out showed no signs of life. Why should she? Fish in a barrel. A human shooting gallery. A helpless human form moving slowly in a set path at 50 yards or less. And with a scope sight. Almost unsportsman-like.

He thought about snipers who'd made the news in recent years. Kids with 22's, popping at cars on parkways near big cities, never hoping to score a clean kill. Or butchers, hauling an arsenal to the top of some tall building and blasting away at everybody in sight. Suicidal exhibitionists! Morons! With no hope whatever of walking away from it. No imagination. No planning. No class. He'd show the world how it was done by a master. A real master. And in the process he'd return a small favor to the ski community.

His mind riffled back through the countless interviews he'd had with the honchos of all the ski mountains.

"I'm sorry, Mr. Griggs, but we've completed our recruiting for this year's ski patrol."

"But sir, I'm no ordinary skier. Look, I can make these guys you've been hiring look like beginners."

"I'm afraid we're just full up at this time."

"All I ask is a chance. Before Vietnam I was the lead instructor at Stratton. I taught the advanced classes. I even trained most of the ski patrol. All the college hotshots. Don't you understand? I'm a pro. The best."

"I can appreciate that, Mr. Griggs, but we're just not taking on any more men this season."

"Look, somebody's got to give me a break. Skiing's my life...It's because of my war record, isn't it?"

"I'm sorry, Mr. Griggs, we're just not hiring."

"You've been running ads, looking for guys."

"We've finished filling our roster."

"You know, this isn't a fair shake. I couldn't help all that publicity. I had no way of stopping it. I didn't want it. Besides, I was acquitted. Completely. They let me go clean. I was only a noncom. I was acting under orders at all times."

"I'm sorry, Mr. Griggs."

"Look, if you'd been over there as long as I was, you'd have reacted the same. All I wanted was to stay alive and get back. It got to where you couldn't tell the women from the men, or the kids, either, for that matter. There were even instances where our guys *did* get it from kids or women. That was a mess, over there. You've got to have been there to know about it."

"I'm sorry, Mr. Griggs."

"Look, I was given a clean bill and all I ask is to get back into skiing. I couldn't help all that publicity. You can't keep me out forever. I want to make my living on skis."

"I'm sorry, Mr. Griggs, I'm sorry, Mr. Griggs, I'm sorry..."

He set himself and took a breath and followed the next target that moved into view and fired and smiled at the whispered crack of the silenced rifle and at the way the young man lurched in the seat and then collapsed. Another clean hit. And he watched the chairs move closer. Almost time to stop the lift and take off the chick with the plugged emblem.

He was a master at two skills. Skiing wasn't his only area of expertise. He could shoot. And he liked shooting. Back in Nam he had become his company's cleanup man. As the unrelenting tension of the hide-and-seek fighting worked on him, he found he could best keep his head by taking pleasure in doing what he did well. If he was to kill to survive, he might as well be good at it. And to be good at it he had to like doing it.

His C.O. had recognized his instinctual capacity and had given him all the "special assignments." He soon grew to feed on them. He liked good clean kills because they were a challenge. Tough to pull off in the jungle. But he also liked those "special assignments," the closer-range "less competitive" jobs. And he had liked doing them with neatness and finesse.

He stopped the lift and began struggling with the dead girl's body. She'd been good-looking. A dish. He would have liked knowing her a little better before she decided to take the chairlife up Old Imperial that particular morning. But too bad. There would be other chicks.

Since she was light and feminine, he put his shoulder into

her waist and hoisted her up and carried her to the edge of the little pocket where he had been piling the bodies. He dropped her onto the incline and she slid down among the others. Too bad about her. She was nice. Really nice. She'd picked the wrong day to ski Old Imperial.

How many more should he take before skiing down and driving away? He probably had enough already to leave his mark on the ski world for a long time. How many people would start thinking twice and maybe just stay home and watch TV before planning a weekend of skiing? A weekend of being a helpless target, dangling from a lift-cable, moving slowly toward the top of a mountain? The operators were going to pay for keeping him out.

He'd returned from Nam in the summer and could hardly wait for the snow. But that one sticky morning when the story broke about the incident in the town by the river marked the beginning of a nightmare even greater than all those in the stinking jungle. Who the hell ever heard of locking somebody up for defending his country? "Everything I did I did under orders, sir."

"Some of our witnesses feel that you seemed to have more than just a desire to carry out orders on the morning in question."

"Sir, I was doing as I was told. We were at war, regardless what college kids might say. I was mainly interested in survival. It could have been them or me."

"That's for the court to decide."

The punishing uncertainties of the trial and the confinement dragged out for months, during which he was restricted inside the base, and he watched the season come and go, reading the daily ski reports when he could get a paper. He was finally acquitted and released but his name, Wesley Griggs, had become a familiar phrase, almost a synonym for the senseless excesses of the war.

As soon as the next season approached, he began his tour of the Northeastern ski areas, looking for a job, a full-time skiing job, ready at last to begin living again, to buckle on the new boots and the gleaming new Mark II's and hit the slopes and let the ski air with its exhilarating clarity flush the glooms and stenches of jungles and army posts out of his head.

He sensed he was a marked man after the first job interview.

He was apprehensive on the second and the turndown came without surprise. Thereafter he went from mountain to mountain, playing out the complete dialogue, all the way to the final, repeated, "I'm sorry, Mr. Griggs." Anticipating each rejection, he would become so antagonistic the operators found him oppressive, almost frightening.

After he was completely certain no operator would have the likes of him with his record and reputation working their precious mountain, he decided to spend a little time hunting. Get out his rifle, his other love, and get off a round or two at a deer. After watching the animal drop with a single, clean, perfect shot he suddenly made up his mind about what he was going to do. He immediately began planning details.

He had been a ski fanatic even as a child, a scrawny kid, often cutting school, always skulking around one or another of the mountains near his home in Vermont, listening to instructors teach rich kids, sneaking onto the lifts or stealing lift passes off jackets in the main lodge and skiing the slopes from sunup to dusk on a progression of stolen skis. He dropped out of high school in his junior year, bought an old heap, and drove from mountain to mountain, all over New England, satisfying himself that he was master of every slope. Having become a brilliant skier, he managed to get into a ski patrol the following year and within the two more years was the youngest No. 1 ever in the patrol at Stratton, one of his favorite mountains with its profusion of runs. Then he was drafted.

When he began planning his payoff to the operators for their kindness and consideration, he remembered the Old Imperial run at Connally Mountain, a tough isolated slope with an antiquated lift, bucket-like seats strung out some 75 feet apart, slow-moving, the patrol member in the shed at the top stopping the lift and helping each skier out of the bucket. The run was steep in places, and long, a challenging and satisfying run for even the best skiers, which explained its popularity despite the time-consuming ride to the top.

And he also remembered the bend in cable direction as the run approached the summit so that only two chairs at a time were in view from the shed. He had only to get a rifle with a removable stock, ride to the top of Old Imperial with the dismantled weapon strapped under his coat, shoot the attendant in the back, and take over the mountain. After making a good solid kill he'd simply leave the lift stopped, ski down, get into his car, and drive away. He'd be gone before the patrol could get up to the summit on the "cat" to check out the problem...

He watched the next chair turn the corner and move into view with another target, a guy in a fancy sweater and stocking cap. No heavy jacket. Probably a good skier. This would be the last one. Pop him off and call it quits. He'd gotten enough to leave his mark, to make that day on Connally long remembered. No use taking unnecessary chances.

He sighted in on a couple of stripes in the sweater's design, a hair left of center. Perfect. Follow the target for a second or two, maintain concentration, squeeze. But a split second before he fired, the skier reached down to touch his boot. He'd missed completely!

The skier looked up abruptly, stared at the shed and at patches of woods to the right and to the left. Then he flipped up the safety bar on the chair and leaped quickly out of the seat, not even bothering to take his poles, dropping the ten or fifteen feet to the snow and falling over.

How had he missed? He had to get off another shot! Drop him quick before he got to his feet and skied around the bend and out of sight. He lined up on the skier as the skier struggled upright to start downhill. The same two stripes, from the back instead of the front. He squeezed but the gun clicked harmlessly. Damn! Why hadn't he reloaded? Why hadn't he kept count? How could he have been so stupid?

The skier, starting a little slowly without poles, moved downward, gaining speed, and finally swept to the right, around the crook in the slope and out of view.

No need to panic. Just get rid of the gun and ski down. No clues. Nothing. He didn't know from nothing. Tht's all. No, he didn't see or hear anything. No fingerprints, even if they found the gun. He'd handled it with glove-linters and had rubbed it carefully to make sure. No panic, no panic.

He ran a few yards along the path to the summit, a spot just beyond the little hollow. The bodies were becoming speckled with snow. He stuffed the rifle into a drift near the base of a tree and smoothed over the spot where the gun went in. A few minutes of fresh snow and there'd be no trace. Nothing to worry about.

He hurried back to the shed, set down his skis, and stepped

into them. Grabbing his poles and gloves, he moved back along
the path. The lift was motionless, the nearest chair containing a
crumpled body wearing skis, the second chair empty except
for poles. He pushed off, skiing down the slope with style and
grace.

The long ride down gave him time to think, to anticipate
questions and plan his responses. No, he hadn't seen anything
unusual going on. Accidents? No. Anybody with a gun? You
kidding me? No. And no, he didn't know of any reason why
nobody'd come down the slope in the last little while. No, he
didn't know why the lift wasn't moving—it was running fine
when he got up there and he'd taken a bad fall on the way
down and had stopped and rested a few minutes to get himself
back together.

He began to feel strangely chilled and realized that despite
the air temperature and the wind of skiing and the snow in his
face, his body was steamy with sweat.

He glanced up at skiers stranded in the unmoving chairs
and hoped they'd still be hanging there, freezing their noses
off, when he drove away. He looked down and ahead. A good
slope. One of the best. Let the people in the chairs watch a pro
take it down.

As he reached the lower stretches of the run and the main
lodge came into view, he saw the "cat" just starting up the
slope, carrying two members of the patrol, each wearing his
bright blue jacket and blue hat. They had a long ride to the top.
He was moving a lot faster. He had plenty of time. More than
enough. He'd had much closer calls than this in Nam.

He continued down toward the area around the main lodge
where all the lifts took on their loads and headed up the
mountain. Lots of skiers. They'd remember this day at Connally. They might even lose some of their interest in skiing. He
had only to get through the crowd unnoticed, over to the
parking lot, then get the hell out of here.

As he drew nearer he was able to separate the crowd into
individuals. He picked out the skier in the fancy sweater, the
one he'd missed with his last shot. The guy was standing in a
group, right where the slope leveled out, watching him approach. Nothing to worry about. They couldn't possibly know
anything yet.

Several in the group wore the mountain's bright blue jackets. He recognized the honcho who ran the mountain, a big over-age college Joe. He thought about the interview with him several months back and wondered if the creep would remember him. Then he spotted the fat guy who ran the ski school. And one or two more from the patrol. And a cop, the trooper, the big one with the mustache who'd been directing traffic, wearing his shiny, navy-blue jacket with the big badge and the fur collar, and the hat with the fur-lined earmuffs tied up and sticking out like wings. When it became obvious the group was waiting for him, he began plowing and slowed as he reached them.

"Excuse me," the honcho said, "but did you notice what's wrong at the top? The operator has stopped the lift and we don't know why."

No look of recognition. The creep didn't remember him. Still, his heart was pounding. This was it. The last hurdle. The parking lot was less than a hundred yards away. "Uh, everything looked okay to me when I was up top. I noticed the lift stopped, too. Why is that?"

We thought you might be able to tell *us*. You just came down."

"No, as a matter of fact I left the top some time ago. Had a fall about halfway down. Stopped and rested a while. Sprained my ankle a little." He felt dizzy from his churning pulse and wondered if they could tell.

"You seem all right, now."

"Yeah, it's a lot better."

"This man says someone took a shot at him up there. Did you hear anything that sounded like a shot?"

"Shot? You kidding? What kinda shot? Hell, don't say that. I'll be scared to go back up. No, I didn't hear any shot."

Did you see anyone with anything that might have been a gun of any kind?" the cop asked. "Anything at all?"

He hesitated, to appear to be trying to remember. "No. Not a thing."

"Well, we've sent up two members of the patrol," the manager said. "We should know something in a few minutes."

"Probably nothing serious." He started to ski slowly out of the group and toward the parking lot.

"Hey," one of the ski patrol said. "What's that all over the shoulder of your jacket? Blood?"

He stopped and froze. His mouth fell open and he looked at all of them, his eyes going from face to face. The chick! He dropped his poles and clutched at his right shoulder with his left hand, still looking from face to face. As he did, his right arm dropped against his side and he felt the box of shells, still about half full in his jacket pocket. He'd forgotten to bury them with the gun.

"Well? What about it?" The cop studied his face, then reached out and tugged at his shoulder to look at the stain.

He didn't answer.

"I think you'd better wait here with us till the patrol gets to the top," the cop said.

"Uh, I can't. I gotta get going. I really got to go." He thought about trying to run but he was on skis and he'd dropped his poles. And he was surrounded by blue jackets.

"So early?" the cop said. "You've got an eight-dollar lift ticket there and it's not even time to break for lunch yet. You'd just better wait here with us till we hear from the patrol."

The manager squinted at him and said, "You look very familiar. Have we met before?'

But he hadn't even heard the question. He'd just remembered something funny. The blood on his jacket wasn't fresh. He had worn the jacket hunting and had messed it up lifting the doe he'd shot. A silly grin spread across his face and he began to snigger and then laugh uncontrollably.

THE PROBLEM OF THE BOSTON COMMON

Edward D. Hoch

It was a warm summer's afternoon and old Dr. Sam Hawthorne was pouring a bit of sherry at a little table on the back lawn, obviously enjoying the opportunity to be out of doors. "The air is so clear and fresh today," he commented. "When I was young it used to be like this all the time, even in the cities. Sometimes folks ask me if I ever solved an impossible crime in the city, and there were a couple over the years when business of some sort took me away from Northmont. The first one–a terrifying case–happened in Boston, in the late spring of 1928..."

I'd gone to Boston with my nurse April (Dr. Sam continued), to attend a New England medical convention. It was my first opportunity to take a long drive in my new car–a tan Packard Runabout that had replaced my beloved Pierce-Arrow. Though the roads weren't nearly as good as they are today we made the drive in under two hours, and I was quite pleased with the Packard's performance. It was warm enough to ride with the top down, which April especially enjoyed. Some years back I'd taken her with me to an engagement party up at Newburyport and she still talked about the excitement of that auto trip. Now she was equally excited as we drove up to the fancy hotel facing the Boston Common and the uniformed doorman hurried over to help us with our bags.

"Are you here for the medical convention, sir?" he asked.

"That's right. Dr. Sam Hawthorne from Northmont."

"Go right in and register at the desk. The bellman will take your bags and I'll park the car for you."

The first person we encountered in the lobby was gray-haired Dr. Craig Somerset, vice-chairman of the New England Medical Association. "Well, Sam Hawthorne! How've you been? How're things out in the country?"

"Fine, Craig. Good to see you again. This is my nurse, April. I brought her along to see the sights while I'm involved in all those dull meetings."

His look made April blush at once, but Craig Somerset was always the New England gentleman. "Nice to meet you, April. I hope you'll enjoy our city."

"I haven't been to Boston in ten years," she told him. "It's changed so much!"

"It has that," Dr. Somerset agreed. "This hotel wasn't even here ten years ago. There's a great view of the Common from the upper floors. A word of caution, though—don't walk across the Common in the early evening. We've had some trouble here in recent weeks."

"What sort of trouble?" I asked, assuming he spoke for April's benefit. "Someone molesting women?"

"More serious than that, I'm afraid." The lightness had gone out of his voice. "Three people have been murdered there, all in the early evening while it was still daylight. The killer seems to be absolutely invisible."

"I'll bet Dr. Sam could catch him," April said. "He's solved the most impossible-soundin' crimes you ever did hear of, back in Northmont."

"No, no," I protested. "I'm here for the convention, nothing more."

"And I want to talk to you about that," Somerset said. "I'd like you to fill a little gap in our program the day after tomorrow and speak to us on the problems of country medicine."

"I'm no public speaker, Craig."

"But you could do a fine job. It's an area of medicine most of these men know nothing about."

"Let me think about it overnight."

"How were the people killed?" April persisted, her curiosity aroused.

"It seemes they were poisoned by a quick-acting substance injected into the skin," Somerset said. "The police are trying not to alarm the public, but I was called in as a consultant on the poison question."

"Back in Northmont I swear Sheriff Lens calls on Dr. Sam as much to solve crimes as the sick folk call on him to get healed."

"You're embarrassing me, April."

I'd completed the registration forms by that time and I could see the bellman waiting to show us up to our rooms. "We'll see you later, Craig."

In the elevator April remarked, "He thinks you brought me 'cause I'm your girl, Dr. Sam." Even the words made her blush.

"We won't worry about what he thinks." April was in her thirties, a few years older than me, and she'd been my nurse since I came to Northmont in 1922. She'd lost some weight since those earlier days but she was still a plain-looking country woman. I'd never thought about her romantically, though I did enjoy her company.

"Are you going to solve the murders for them?"

"No, I'm here to attend a medical convention."

But events were working against me. That evening, shortly after eight, the invisible killer claimed his fourth victim.

Dr. Somerset came to my door around 8:30, looking quite alarmed. "We'd like your help, Sam. There's been another killing."

"On the Common?"

"Yes, right across the street! Can you come down?"

I sighed. "Give me five minutes."

We crossed the street in silence to a spot just inside the Common where the body of a young woman lay sprawled against a tree. The police were busy photographing the scene, using flash powder in the beginning dusk. A burly detective who seemed to be in charge came over to us. "Is this your great sleuth, Dr. Somerset?"

"This is Sam Hawthorne, a physician from Northmont. He's here for the convention, and I understand he's had great success solving seemingly impossible crimes back home. Sam, this is Inspector Darnell."

I could see right away that this was no Sheriff Lens. Darnell was a big-city cop who obviously resented interference, especially from a country doctor. "Do you use a magnifying glass, Doc? Want to crawl around on the ground like Sherlock Holmes?"

"To tell you the truth I want to go back to my room."

Dr. Somerset was exasperated. "Look, Inspector, will it do any harm to tell Sam what you've got so far? He just might come up with an idea."

"Hell, we've tried everything else. What we've got now are four dead bodies. Two men, two women. This last one seems to be the youngest so far. One of the men was a drifter who panhandled in the park. Another was a young lawyer on his way home after working late at the office. Then there was a middle-aged woman out for a stroll in the early evening. And now this one."

"All poisoned?"

The detective nodded. "That's how Dr. Somerset got in on it. We needed a doctor's advice on the kind of poison. The autopsy showed the first three died of minute injections of curare, the South American arrow poison. That fact hasn't been released to the papers yet."

"Curare? On the Boston Common?" It was hard for me to believe. Even in medical school the subject of curare poisoning had been barely touched on. It wasn't something the average doctor ever encountered.

"Curare acts within a few minutes in humans, paralyzing the motor and respiratory muscles," Dr. Somerset explained. "The speed of death seems to depend somewhat on the size of the victim. A thousand-pound ox took forty-five minutes to die from curare in an experiment described in Charles Waterton's book *Wanderings in South America*."

"You know a lot more about curare than I do," I admitted.

"That's why I was called in by Inspector Darnell." He was staring down at the dead young woman. "It's a particularly insidious poison for the killer to use, because there is no pain and very little warning to the victim. There is some double vision and inability to swallow, then asphyxiation as lung muscles are affected. Admittedly it's a painless death, but it's also one that gives the victim no opportunity to call for help."

"How was the poison administered?" I asked. "With a hypodermic needle?"

Inspector Darnell knelt by the body and turned back the

collar of the dead woman's white blouse. A tiny feathered dart protruded from the skin of her neck. "It's so small she might never have felt it—or if she did she thought it was an insect bite. In two of the earlier killings we never found the darts. The victims must have felt them hit and brushed them to the ground as one would a pesky mosquito. In the first killing the dart was snagged in the victim's clothing."

"A dart gun of some sort?" I suggested. "An air pistol might have a fairly long range."

"In South America the natives use blowguns six feet long," Dr. Somerset said.

"I can't picture a murderer using one of those," I said. "He wouldn't stay invisible for long. Have all the killings been at this time of day?"

"All in the evening, but before dark. We doubled the police patrol after the second killing, and filled the Common with plainclothes men after the third one. Now I guess we should close it to pedestrians altogether."

"I'd advise against that," Somerset argued. "The killer would simply move elsewhere, or wait for the Common to reopen. You want to capture him, not scare him off."

"We're finished with our pictures," one of the detectives told Inspector Darnell. "Can we move her?"

"Sure. Take her away."

"Any identification in her purse?" I asked.

"Rita Kolaski, a nurse at Boston Memorial. Probably on her way to work."

The Inspector moved away from us without a goodbye, following the covered stretcher to the street. I turned to Dr. Somerset and said, "I really don't see how I can help here, Craig. Back home in Northmont I'm dealing with people and places I've known for six years. I know the way they live and how they think. I'm out of my element here. Boston people even talk different."

"I'm only asking you to look for something the rest of us might be missing, Sam."

"The killer is a madman, there's no doubt of that. And it's hard enough to catch anyone who's rational."

"Sleep on it, Sam. If you think you can help us in any way, see me after the first session in the morning."

They walked back to the hotel and Somerset asked the

doorman to get him a taxi. "Aren't you staying here?" I asked, surprised.

The doorman ran down to the corner blowing his whistle for a cab, and Somerset fished a coin from his pocket for a tip. "No, I'm staying at home. My wife insists on it."

Up in my room I sat for a long time by the window overlooking the Common, watching the lights of the policemen as they searched the area of the killing. After a time I pulled down the shade and went to bed.

Another Common Killing, the morning paper screamed in a bold black headline. April read the story over breakfast and I admitted that Somerset had come to my room for help.

"You were over there, Dr. Sam? You saw the body?"

"I've seen a lot of bodies, April."

"But in the city like this—"

"She'd have been just as dead in Northmont."

"You've got time before the first session. Take me over and show me where it happened."

There was no talking her out of it, so we crossed busy Tremont Street and I showed her the spot where Rita Kolaski had died. We strolled farther into the park then, past the burying ground and all the way to the soldiers monument. Then we turned west, walking across Charles Street to the Public Garden that adjoined Boston Common.

"Look at the swan boats!" April exclaimed as we came to an artificial lake. "The people pedal them with their feet!"

She was like a child on Christmas morning, and I took her for a ride around the lake in one of the swan boats, knowing I'd miss the first session of the convention. Afterward we walked along the Arlington Street side, past the Washington monument and on up to Beacon Street. Presently, circling around the north side of the Common, we came to the State House with its golden dome glistening in the morning sun.

"The morning paper says the first body was found over on this side of the Common," April said.

"It doesn't concern me."

"Honestly, sometimes you can be so stubborn!"

"We're here to enjoy the city, not to solve murders. Come on, tonight I'll take you to the movie at the new Metropolitan Theatre. They say it's a regular palace."

We walked back across the Common, which was almost empty for ten o'clock on a weekday morning. The newspaper scare headlines were apparently having their effect. April left me at the hotel to do some shopping and I went upstairs just in time to catch the end of the opening session.

Dr. Somerset caught me on the way out. "I have a noon meeting with the Inspector. Care to sit in?"

"This business really isn't for me, Craig. April and I walked around the Common this morning. It's like a foreign country to me."

"There's one thing about the murders we didn't tell you last night," Somerset said, lowering his voice. "The killer has been in communication with the police."

"Just like Jack the Ripper."

"Exactly. Come along and you can see the letters."

Somerset knew how to pique my curiosity. There was no way I could turn down that invitation. I sat through the second morning session only half attentive, listening to a professor from Harvard Medical School discuss the latest polio research. The subject was much in the news that month, since Al Smith had just asked polio victim Franklin D. Roosevelt to run for governor of New York.

I offered to drive Somerset to police headquarters in my new Packard but he insisted we take a cab. They were easy to get at the stand near the hotel and during the day at least there was no need to tip the doorman. Riding up Tremont, I watched the faces of the people we passed, wondering if one of them might be the killer. In Northmont I would have known their names. Here they were strangers. In Northmont I might have had a half-dozen suspects. Here, the whole city of Boston was suspect.

"This is your city, isn't it, Craig?"

"Always has been. You should set up practice here and you'd learn what medicine is all about."

"Oh, I'm learning that."

"Six years in the country! Are you going to spend your life in Northmont?"

"Maybe."

"We've got three-quarters of a million people in Boston, Sam, and we need more good young doctors like yourself."

Why?" I asked with a smile. "Is Boston the hub of the universe?"

"It could be. How many cities do you know that have daily steamship service to New York?"

"Maybe your killer comes up from New York by boat every week."

"No," Somerset answered seriously, "he's from this area."

We alighted from the taxi and walked up the steps of Police Headquarters. Off in the distance I could see the pointed tower of the custom house, the city's tallest structure. I had to admit that Boston had a certain charm. It was different from the simple country charm of a place like Northmont, but no less appealing.

Crime here was also different. The letters that Inspector Darnell spread out on the desk before me could only have been described as the work of a madman. *Last evening was the first of the Common killings! There will be more! Cerberus!* And another: *Two dead and more to come! Boston will remember me! Cerberus!* And a third: *Another must die because of what you did! Remember me! Cerberus!*

"And last night's killing?" I asked.

"Nothing yet." Darnell sighed and relit the stub of a dead cigar. "It's probably in the mail."

"These haven't been released to the press?"

The Inspector shook his head. "This sort of maniac thrives on publicity. We're trying to give him as little as possible."

"I agree completely," Somerset said. "The public doesn't even know the killings are connected, though it's bound to come out soon."

"The mayor wants to close the Common completely till this Cerberus is caught, but as you heard last night Dr. Somerset has advised against that."

"You need to capture him, not just send him into his hole."

I was studying the notes, but I could make nothing out of them. "I can't help you on this," I said. "I have no idea who he could be."

"That's not what we want you for," Craig Somerset said. "We want to know how he's doing it."

Inspector Darnell nodded agreement. "*How*, Dr. Hawthorne. We already know *who* he is."

I must admit their words took me aback. "You know who the

killer is and you haven't arrested him?"

Craig Somerset smiled. "It's not like Northmont, Sam. In the city a man can hide out for months without ever being found."

"I didn't spend the whole of my life in Northmont, you know. Just the last six years. I know what city life is like."

But did I, really? Had I been away from it too long?

Inspector Darnell cleared his throat. "You must realize, Dr. Hawthorne, that what we tell you must go not further than this room. The lives of innocent people could be endangered if this Cerberus becomes aware that we know his identity."

"It was the curare that led us to him, of course," Craig Somerset explained. "It's not the easiest substance in the world to obtain, and once it was identified as the cuase of death I began checking around at various hospitals and research centers in the Boston vicinity. As you may know, Sam, research is under way to find uses for curare as a muscular relaxant. It's a difficult task, because even in tiny doses it seems to cause nausea and a drop in blood pressure. But I found a research lab in Cambridge that's been running tests with the poison. About six months ago a quantity of curare disappeared from their lab, along with a part-time research assistant named George Totter."

"Why would he take it?" I asked.

It was Darnell who answered. "They laid him off. The research was being done under a grant from a local charity. When the money ran out, the research had to stop. Apparently Totter wrote to the city for more funds, but they ignored him. He made the remark to a co-worker that maybe they'd pay attention if a few people in Boston died of curare poisoning. Shortly after that he disappeared, and the lab discovered a vial of the poison was missing too."

"How much was in the vial?" I asked.

"Enough to kill twenty or thirty people. They didn't report it at the time because nobody believed Totter capable of murder. But when Dr. Somerset started checking for missing curare the story came out quickly enough."

"Is there any other possible source of the poison?"

Somerset shook his head. "It's highly unlikely. As you know, curare comes from the bark of various South American trees. The lengthy and laborious process is a deeply guarded secret among certain native families and tribes. Some attempt has been made to duplicate the process in a laboratory, but thus far researchers must depend on the real thing, brought in from the jungles. Our killer must be using a laboratory supply, and this lab in Cambridge is the only one that has it in this

"All right," I said, "I'll accept this man Totter as your killer. And I'll accept the fact that he could remain hidden in Boston for months. Now tell me why you can't stop him from killing these people."

Darnell ground out the stub of his cigar. "The darts are fired from either an air pistol or a blowgun. If he's using an air pistol of some sort he could probably be fifty feet away and still hit his target."

"Farther than that," I suggested.

"No, not with these hand-made wooden darts. We've tried it. After fifty feet they start wobbling and tumbling in the air. With a blowgun the effective range is only twenty-five feet. And there's our problem. These killings have been in broad daylight, in a park at the very center of a large city. There are no out-of-the-way trails or heavily wooded places in the Common. It's roughly an irregular five-sided park that's only seventeen hundred feet across at its widest point. You can see from one side to the other. There's no place to hide, except behind a tree or statue, and there are people constantly passing through—especially in the early evening hours on spring days like this."

"A blowgun disguised as a cane?" I suggested. "It would take just an instant for the killer to raise it to his mouth."

"Maybe for the first two killings it could have been something like that, but the park was filled with plainclothes police when the third victim got it. Yet nobody saw a thing." He picked up a folder on his desk. "Rita Kolaski, last night's victim, was actually under surveillance at the moment she was killed."

"What?" This was news to Dr. Somerset, and he reacted with surprise.

"I just learned of it this morning. She was suspected of being party to a Volstead Act violation. Two Treasury agents were following her in hopes she'd lead them to her boy friend who's been running boatloads of liquor in from Nova Scotia. She crossed Tremont Street at the corner beyond your hotel and entered the Common at exactly 8:10. There was still plenty of daylight and both agents had a good view of her. They were especially watchful of anyone who came close because they were waiting for a contact with the boy friend.

"But nothing at all unusual happened. No one even glanced at her. Nothing was pointed in her direction. She'd been walking in the park for only about two minutes when her walk became unsteady. She paused to lean against a tree and then collapsed. Our plainclothes men moved in at once, but it was too late. The Treasury agents filed a report with their superior and a copy was sent to me this morning."

"Surely she must have felt the dart hit her," I argued.

Darnell held up one of the feathered wooden shafts, half the length of a matchstick. "Notice there's the point of a common pin embedded in the wood. Don't touch it, there's still poison on it. When the dart hit it would feel like little more than a pinprick. She might have reached up to her hair, but the Treasury men would think nothing of that."

"I can't believe this pin point could carry enough curare to kill a person so quickly," I said. "Besides, what if she'd brushed it off her neck before the poison could act?'

"She didn't, and she died. We don't know how many people this Totter—or Cerberus—might have fired at. Maybe there's a dozen more that brushed the dart off and lived. All we know is that four of them died."

"Just where on the Common were the bodies found?" I asked.

Darnell referred to a large-scale wall map where four red pins dotted the green area of the Common. "The first one, Pete Jadas, was found on the other side of the Common near the State House. He was a former wrestler who'd fallen on hard times and taken to panhandling. Simon Falk, a young lawyer who'd been working late at his Tremont Street office, died right here, about in the middle of the Common. The third victim, a waitress named Minnie Wiser, died there, on the next walkway over from Rita Kolaski."

"Wrestler, lawyer, waitress, nurse," I mused. "I guess there's no pattern there."

"No pattern at all. He kills whoever happens to be handy."

I was staring at the map, but it wasn't telling me a thing. "What about that Cerberus signature?'

"A dog with three heads," Darnell snorted. "Greek mythology!"

"A dog from Hades," Somerset added.

"He must have chosen that name for a reason."

"What is reason to a madman?"

"All right," I said, getting up to leave.

"Where are you going?" Darnell asked.

"For another stroll on the Common."

It was the lunch hour now and the walks were more crowded. On benches people sat and chatted. One man was reading about the latest murder in the newspaper, but nobody seemed terribly concerned. They didn't know about the poisoned darts, or the letters from Cerberus.

I crossed over Charles Street to the Public Garden and went down to watch the swan boats again. That was when I noticed the man with the picnic hamper. He was dark and heavy-set, with unfriendly eyes, but the thing I especially noticed was the way he kept his right hand beneath the lid of the hamper at all times. He might almost have been holding something.

Like the trigger of an air pistol.

Whatever it was, he didn't look the sort who'd come here for a picnic. When he started walking back toward the Common, I followed, wishing that Inspector Darnell had shown me a photograph of George Totter.

The man's right hand was out of the hamper now, but still near its lid. I stayed just a few steps behind, watching that hand. When it moved, when the lid came up again, I ran forward. I needed only the briefest glimpse of the gun within and I slammed my fist down on the lid, pinning his hand inside. He let out a gasp of pain and released his grip on the hamper.

Then, before I knew what was happening, a second man spun me around from the rear. I felt a glancing blow to the side of my head and everything went black.

I must have been unconscious for several mintues.

When I finally came to, with a throbbing headache, I saw a circle of men bending over me. One of them was Inspector Darnell. "What in hell were you trying to do?" he demanded.

"I—"

"That was one of my plainclothes men you jumped on!"

"I'm sorry."

"You should be! If Totter was anywhere around you certainly scared him off!" He helped me to my feet and brushed the dirt from my suitcoat. "In the future you'd better stay off the

Common, Dr. Hawthorne. If we need your help we'll call on you."

I mumbled more apologies and moved away, feeling like a fool. I just wasn't used to the ways of big-city police. Back in Northmont, Sheriff Lens could hardly be expected to fill the town squared with deputies because he had only a couple of part-time men whom everybody knew. Here in Boston it was different, maybe too different for me. Had six years in Northmont changed my perceptions that much?

I found April in front of the hotel, asking the doorman for directions to Paul Revere's House. "I figured I might as well see some historical sights while I'm here," she said. "Want to come along?"

"I don't think so, April."

I turned my head and she noticed the bruise where the second cop had hit me. "What happened to you?"

"Just a little accident."

"Let me get you upstairs and wash that! Did you fall?"

"I'll tell you about it."

She listened to my tale with much clucking as she bathed the bruise with cold water. "You're not even safe from the police in this city!" she decided.

"Don't be too hard on them, April. It really was my fault."

"Well, a gun in a picnic hamper! What were you to think!"

"They called Inspector Darnell right away. They must have thought they had the killer." I told her what I'd learned.

"Don't they have a picture of this fellow Totter?"

I shook my head. "And only a general sort of description."

I opened my medical bag and found a powder to take for my headache. Then I settled down to relax. Almost at once there was a knock at the door. April opened it and Craig Somerset hurried in. "I just heard what happened. Are you all right?"

"I guess I'll live."

"Good God, they didn't have to slug you with a blackjack!"

"I suppose they thought I was the killer."

"Darnell is sorry about it."

"So am I."

"The afternoon mail brought another letter from George Totter."

I came alert at once. "If it really is Totter. What does it say?"

"Darnell let me make a copy to show you. Mailed just before

midnight from the main post office." He held out a page from his notebook and I read: *Four down and more to come! I won't wait so long next time! Cerberus!*

"What is Darnell's plan to do next?" I asked.

Keep watching the Common. Hope they can spot him the next time. What else is there to do, except close up downtown and throw the city into a panic?"

"Sooner or later—"

"Sooner or later! Doesn't Darnell realize he's dealing with an invisible man? Someone like Chesterton's postman who's there but isn't there?"

Craig Somerset pursed his lips. "Could it be one of the plainclothes men assigned to the park?"

"Stranger things have happened. But if Cerberus—"

"What is it?"

"Just an idea. That map on Darnell's wall showing the location of the killings—do you think we could borrow it? Or make another?"

"What for, Sam?"

"You asked me to speak to the convention on the problems of country medicine. Suppose I speak instead on curare poisoning."

"What? But you're no expert—"

"I think I've learned enough these last two days. Let's see, I'm scheduled to speak late tomorrow afternoon. Is that right?"

"Four o'clock."

"Good. I think I'll spend the morning out at that research lab, brushing up on curare." As an afterthought I said, "And be sure to post the topic of my talk on the schedule in the lobby. I want as large an audience as possible."

As the time for my speech drew near, April was beside herself. "What if the killer learns you're givin' this talk, Dr. Sam? He might pick you for the next victim!"

"Now don't you worry your head, April. I'll be all right."

But she stuck by my side all the way down to the second floor, where a big meeting room had been assigned for my talk. I looked out on the rows of chairs, just now receiving the first arrivals, and felt just the least bit apprehensive. But to be honest I think I was more afraid of speaking in public than of the murderer. Directly behind me the large curtained windows looked out on the Common across Tremont Street.

"He could be down there in the park, watchin' us through binoculars right this minute!" April said, obviously worried.

"I think he's a lot closer than that," I said, watching the doctors file in. I was surprised to see Inspector Darnell take up a position near the door. Somerset had obviously alerted him to the subject of my talk, in order to obtain the map I needed.

Exactly at four o'clock, with the room more than three-quarters full, Craig Somerset strode to the podium. "Are you ready, Sam?"

"Ready as I'll ever be."

He turned to the audience and spoke loudly so that his voice would carry through the room. "Gentlemen—and I note a few ladies with us today as well—our speaker this afternoon is Dr. Sam Hawthrone, a relatively young man who has spent his six years as a physician in caring for the ills of the people of Northmont, about two hours' drive from here. Yes, Sam Hawthrone is a country doctor—the backbone of our medical practice. He was planning to speak to us today on the problems of medical practice in a small town, but as most of you know he's chosen to change his topic. In recent weeks four persons have died on the Common across the street from this hotel. Only today the police admitted to the press that all four died of curare poisoning. And it is that poisoning—so rarely encountered in general practice—which is the subject of Sam Hawthrone's talk."

When he'd completed the introduction I stepped to the podium and began to read from my notes, covering a history of curare and the early experiments by Charles Waterton in Dutch Guiana. Then I touched on the Boston-area experiments before getting to my main point.

"You see behind me, on my left, a large-scale map of downtown Boston. The points where the four curare victims died are clearly marked. But as you know from my previous remarks, curare does not kill instantly. You might say, the police have said, that a poison which kills within a few minutes is instant enough. But the truth is that a person can walk all the way across the Common in a few minutes I've done it.

"The idea occurred to me that the invisible killer the police are seeking might not be roaming the park seeking out victims at all. His poisoned darts might all be fired from one location, and it might have been the dying victims who moved rather than the killer. Looking at this map, is such a possibility feasible?"

There was a stir of interest from the audience and I saw Inspector Darnell straighten up in the back row. I glanced over at April and hurried on. "We've already seen that the speed with which curare kills depends very much on the size and weight of the victim. An average person lives only a few minutes. A thousand-pound ox lives forty-five minutes. I checked the weights of the four victims this morning, but even without knowing them I could make certain guesses.

"The first victim, a drifter who'd been a wrestler, was found on the far side of the Common near the State House. My guess was that a former wrestler might be the heaviest of the victims—since the others were a young lawyer and two women. In that I was correct. He weighed the most, and therefore—assuming the curare doses to be about equal—would have taken the longest to die."

I could see I had them now. The doctors were hanging on every word, and all my early nervousness had vanished. "The young lawyer was found in the middle of the Common, and the two women closer to this side. The latest victim, being the smallest of the four, died the quickest. She was actually observed entering the Common from Tremont Street, just down at the corner here. The lawyer, we know, was coming from his office on Tremont Street. The waitress and the ex-wrestler both could have entered the Common from Tremont as well.

"I submit to you, Inspector Darnell, and to my distinguished audience, that the invisible killer is not in the Common at all, but right here on Tremont, hitting his victims *as they enter the park.*"

My wind-up after that was anti-climactic. I couldn't give them the name of the murderer, so I ended with a few generalities about police work in poisoning cases, and then stepped back while Dr. Somerset said a few words of thanks. Doctors from the audience were grouped around me at the end, asking questions, but after a few pleasantries I made my escape.

"You were great, Dr. Sam," April assured me. "I can see Inspector Darnell coming our way."

"Come on, let's get out of here."

"Dr. Hawthrone!" Darnell called. "Let me have a word with you! I'm sorry about yesterday."

"That's all right."

"That was a very interesting theory. You seemed to be saying that the killer might be someone right around here. But how—"

"I have to go now." I broke away and headed for the elevator. If my idea was right, I could be in great danger.

Craig Somerset was hurrying after me too, but I jumped between the closing doors of the elevator and left him standing there with April and the Inspector. I knew it would be only a few moments before they caught the next elevator and came after me.

Downstairs I hurried across the lobby and out into Tremont Street. "Get me a cab, will you?" I asked the doorman.

"Certainly, sir."

He stepped behind me and blew his whistle and I felt the pinprick of a bite on my neck.

That was when I moved, as fast as I could, plucking the tiny dart from my skin and throwing myself on the uniformed doorman. Darnell and April and Somerset came through the revolving door as I wrestled the doorman to the sidewalk.

"Here's you killer!" I shouted. "Mr. George Totter, in person! April, there's a hypodermic needle in my right-hand pocket with an antidote for curare poisoning. I need it—hurry!"

What with all the police business and newspaper interviews after that, it wasn't till the drive back to Northmont the next afternoon that April and I had any time alone. "What a foolish thing to do!" she berated me. "Setting yourself up as a target for that madman!"

"Someone had to do it, April. The police were content to wait for the next victim, but I wasn't. I figured that the curare speech, advertised in the lobby, would attract his attention. But I probably wouldn't have risked it if that research lab hadn't given me a hypodermic full of an antidote they've been testing."

"Who would have thought of the doorman!"

"Once I established the victims had probably entered the Common from the Tremont Street side I started looking for somebody who was stationed there regularly. The doorman, whistling for taxis—sometimes even going up to the corner to get them—was in a perfect position to fire those darts at people crossing the street to enter the park. People saw him put something to his mouth and blow, but it was such an innocent gesture for him that they never noticed it. His whistle—a long slender one similar to the ones London bobbies use—had a tube like a short pea shooter taped to it. The tiny darts would be inaccurate at more than five or ten feet, but the point was he could get quite close to his victims before firing. He chose people heading for the Common so they'd die there. In his confession he said he'd fired more than a dozen darts in all, but some missed and the others were brushed off by the victims before the poison could take effect."

"Dr. Sam, you purposely ran ahead of us all in the hotel yesterday. You knew he was going to try for you and you didn't want us in danger."

"I was sure he would try. All the killings were in the early evening, so I figured it was the doorman who came on duty in the late afternoon. He knew I was the curare speaker and I thought I'd offer him a tempting target."

"You were that sure it was the doorman?"

"People like that want to be caught, April. Totter was telling the police who he was in those notes he sent, only they didn't understand him. Cerberus was a three-headed dog from Hades all right—he guarded the entrance! The word is sometimes used to signify a watchful guard or doorkeeper."

"You did pretty good in the big city, Dr. Sam."

"But it's good to be home."

"And that's how I caught the Boston Common killer," Dr. Sam Hawthorne concluded. "He was invisible only because nobody noticed him. But this sherry is invisible because the bottle is empty! Come inside and I'll give you another small—ah—libation. And if you have time I'll tell you about what I found back in Northmont that summer—an impossible murder right in our general store."

OFF THE INTERSTATE
Brendan DuBois

Brad Poole thought, Business sure is bad. Through the open door of the store, propped open by the last year's rakes he couldn't sell, he could look down the porch steps at the twin gasoline pumps and the empty tarmac of Route 4. He sat behind the wooden counter on a stool, a *Union-Leader* in his hands. The counter held the cash register and some packaged candy and cookies. Coolers flanked both sides of the counter, chilling beer, soda, milk, and fruit juice. Off to the left were racks of chips and pretzels, and to the right was what Brad called his "junk corner"—more rakes, shovels, jumper cables, inflatable water cushions, maps, and the like.

He turned a page of the newspaper, the hot July afternoon wind tugging at it some. Business was worse than he could ever remember it.

He glanced down below the counter, where he kept a few receipts, a lot of bills, and his old Army .45, one of the few things Dad had left him before coughing out his lungs at the Veterans Hospital in Vermont. The pistol was clean. He was sure of that, cleaning it every day as he did. Just in case.

Ever since that damned Interstate extended itself thirty miles last summer, the tourists who had streamed along Route 4, heading to Palmer Lake, now kept on going up the Interstate and hardly came by any more. Brad had timed it once, driving up the Interstate in his rusty Ford pickup, going past the Route

4 exit at Purmort and on to the lake. Going directly up the Interstate saved ten minutes for those tourists coming up from
Massachusetts, ten lousy minutes. Goddamned government,
spending all those millions so sweaty tourists could save ten
minutes and Brad Poole could be ground into the dirt. It wasn't
fair.

But then again, nothing much *was*. Which was why he kept
the pistol handy. After all, he was pretty much alone out here.
Who knew what might happen if a certain car pulled up?

The air-hose bells out front rang and he looked up expec-
tantly from the paper. He rubbed at his thinning black hair,
put on his glasses, and ambled outside.

The sun was hot on his back and he remembered all the
tourists that had come through before the Interstate was finished, buying out his beer and chips, making the cash register
sing. They'd be dressed funny, the guys in shorts, showing off
their hairy legs, a lot of them not bothering with shirts. And the
gals—hell, what they wore made him blush most of the time.

The car at the pumps was a dull-yellow Buick, hubcaps
missing, a Purmort dump sticker on the windshield. A woman
was driving and in the back seat in a jumble of blankets and
toys, three kids were squabbling.

"What'll it be?" Brad asked.

The woman, her long black hair greasy-looking, said, "Two,
Mr. Poole."

As he undid the gas lid, he remembered the woman—Jackie
Dow, one of the Dows from up on Summer Ridge. Married the
no-mind Mark Goodson, who worked when he had to and
drank whenever he could. Now, you want to talk fair, he remembered Jackie being chosen Miss Wentworth County some
summers ago, and now here she was, with scared-rabbit eyes in
a doughy face the three brats screaming in her ear.

Pumping from the no-lead side, he filled her tank with four
dollars' worth of gas, then took her two singles and walked
back to the store. Behind him, he heard it take six tries for the
car to start, then saw it fumble off in a blue cloud of exhaust.
He went back up the steps to the front porch, under the sign
that said ROUTE FOUR GENERAL STORE, and went back to
his stool and his newspaper. He didn't bother ringing up the
sale on the register. He was already a month and a half behind
in paying the fuel company.

The afternoon dragged on. Occasionally a car or truck droned by, but none stopped. It's the empty store. They felt better if they saw a couple of cars outside, other customers around. He wasn't sure why it was like that, but it was. He took off his glasses and rubbed them clean with his handkerchief. He couldn't understand why anyone would be fearful of stopping at his store.

In the paper he saw a couple of stories that made his blood boil. One was about the governnment spending six million dollars on some dam over in Maine. A small dam, barely big enough to do the job, and here in the story some experts said that by the time the goverment finished building that dam it would be worthless, anyway. Six million dollars. If he could have just one-hundredth–hell, one-thousandth–of that, he'd be set. He'd no longer have to worry about the cars not stopping or about the bills or the pink notices piling up in his post-office box. He wouldn't even have to worry about the pistol.

He rubbed at his eyes. The afternoon sun was starting to stream into the store, lighting up the uneven wooden planks on the floor, highlighting the grease spots on the wall. What a place. The only job he ever knew, ever since old man Dumont took him on before he croaked. It had begun to come together for a time, before those yellow machines came in, noisily digging up the dirt, tearing out his life.

A truck pulled into the dirt lot and Brad felt like burrowing his head in the newspaper when the truck came to a stop. The snack man. He was a young pup of about twenty, swaggering up the steps in his brown uniform pants and vest with the cartons of popcorn, chips, and pretzels. Last summer he'd come in and shoot the breeze while pulling off the dated bags and putting up the new stuff, and if he was ahead of schedule he'd pop a bottle of Coke and sit on the porch with Brad and talk women and politics, two of the best talking subjects ever invented.

But that was last summer.

The boy came in, glanced at him once, and then set down the boxes and started replacing the bags of snacks silently. Brad pretended to read the *Union-Leader's* travel section. When the boy was done, he came over and dropped his slip on the counter. As he walked out, carrying the dated snacks, Brad dropped the bill into the open shoebox at the bottom of the counter with the rest, not bothering to look at it. One of these days, probably pretty soon at that, the kid would come in with empty boxes and leave with every snack in the store.

With the afternoon sun setting down toward Vermont, it got hotter instead of cooler, and the wind died down. Sweat trickled down Brad's neck and back and he stepped out onto the porch to try to get a stray breeze. He blinked at the sun's glare. It sure was hot. He folded his arms and looked down the empty road as it curved around the corner, heading out to the old exit by the Interstate. The heat made the air over the road shimmer in queasy waves.

Closer down the road, a group of black crows swooped down and started hopping around, poling at whatever road kill was on the gravel. Not many ways to go, Brad thought. He could put the place up for sale, but even if he could get someone to buy it, what would he do after that? Work like those guys he went to high school with, bagging groceries at Mountain Mart and acting grateful for a fifty-cent tip?

He remembered a movie on television one night last winter, watching it from Dad's old rocking chair upstairs with a down comforter wrapped around him and the woodstove chugging out a little heat. It was about a businessman who was losing money at his garment factory and was thinking about burning the place down for the insurance money. Brad couldn't remember how the movie ended, but right now he didn't care.

Down in the cellar was enough junk and newspapers and the like—well, if it happened, he was sure the Purmort Volunteer Fire Department would poke around and blame it on faulty wiring. The insurance was paid up, eh was pretty sure of that.

Down cellar. It would be easy. He turned and looked at the store, catching a bit of a reflection from the front windows. After Hurricane Dennis had blasted through last summer, he'd had to replace both front windows. Up on the roof was the shingling job he'd done a few years back. How hot those asphalt shingles had been, sticking to his hands and wrists and clothes. Up there he'd been able to see a glimmer of water on the horizon that marked Palmer Lake.

He stamped his feet a couple of times, like a nervous horse waiting to gallop away from something. Damn it, he had sweated too long and even bled a few times for the store, sawing wood and the like—he wasn't going to torch it like some common criminal—no, sir, even if the fire insurance was there. What he needed was debt insurance.

He heard a faint squeak-squeak. A boy on a bicycle was coming this way, and he watched as the boy rolled the bike to a stop and leaned it against the base of the porch—he looked to be about ten or eleven. He wore jeans with knee patches on them, dirty sneakers, and a white T-shirt knotted around his thin waist. His hair was light brown and cut short, and he squinted up at Brad from the gravel lot. "You open, mister?"

"Sure am."

"Then how come you're not in your store, working?"

Brad tried not to smile. "I was workin' hard all day. You just caught me taking a break."

He walked into the store, the boy climbing the stairs and following him. "You from near here?" Brad asked.

"Yeah, I live with my mom up on Orleans Street."

"What's her name?"

"Sullivan. Mine's Bernie."

"Good to meet you, Bernie." The boy's mother must be Alicia Sullivan—she was a couple of years ahead of him in grammar school, but her name back then was Alicia Stoneham. Long blonde hair, always getting in trouble.

The boy came to the counter, a cold can of Mountain Dew beading sweat in his dirty hands. He put the can down, reached into his jeans pocket, and dropped some coins on the counter. Brad counted them as they fell. Forty-three cents.

"That all you got?" he asked softly.

Bernie nodded his head.

"The drink's sixty cents, you know."

Bernie bit his lower lip. "It sure is hot out there," he said.

"It sure is," Brad agreed. "Here." From his shirt pocket, he took out a pen—Bank With Us At BankUs, it said—and tearing off a piece of register tape, he wrote: I.O.U. seventeen cents, B. Sullivan. He slid the piece of paper across to the boy.

"This here's an I.O.U.," Brad said. "You get yourself seventeen cents the next few days, then you come back and pay me. But make sure you do, now, 'cause I know where Orleans Street is, and where to find you if you don't pay me back."

The boy nodded seriously and picked up his can and the piece of paper and ran out of the store. Take care of yourself, boy, Brad thought. Some years from now you'll wish all you had to worry about was a seventeen-cent debt.

It got near six o'clock, his usual closing time, and Brad went back out on the porch again. The Sullivan boy had been the last of the traffic and he folded his arms again, wondering, as he did all the time now, if he'd be here next summer. And if not here, where? This was the only place he knew, and sometimes, like now, when he was hot and his head was throbbing with a headache, he knew he'd do almost anything to keep the store going.

He was going to close up and head in for his usual late-afternoon beer when a bright-blue pickup truck rounded the corner and slowed down. It had Massachusetts plates and Brad almost grinned with pleasure as it rolled up to the gas pumps. A man and a woman were in the cab and the woman had a map in her hands. Some tourists that had slipped off the Interstate. He felt like giving the man a free tank of gas just for doing that.

In the bed of the truck was an inflated yellow life raft, tied down. The young man stepped out, dressed in sandals, khaki shorts, and a T-shirt that said SIMMONS in blue lettering. He had a thick brown moustache that matched the color of his hair. "Afternoon," the man said. "Fill it up, will you?"

Brad went around to the passenger side, where the woman sat. She was about the same age as the young man and she was fiddling with an expensive-looking camera in her lap, the map set aside for the moment. She was blonde and wore big sunglasses, and had on white shorts and a black bikini top. He tried not to stare as he went by, but he noticed a gold chain around her neck. A chain like that would bring some good money over at Earl's Gold and Silver.

The gas cap came off slowly, his hand trembling with the effort, and he spilled some gasoline on his work boots as he put the nozzle in. The fumes made his eyes ache. He tried to watch the rolling numbers through the cracked glass of the pump, but his gaze kept returning to the woman in the front seat. His mouth was dry, and he glanced up the road some. All alone, except for those damn crows.

The pickup took a little over ten gallons and Brad went back into the store. The young man was by the counter, two cases of Michelob beer and three bags of potato chips on the counter before him. The sight was wonderful. Look at me, Brad thought, I'm all excited about this man and his girl coming in here and spending money. Last summer they would've been only two more faces in the crowd. Just like those two that came by three weeks ago. How times change. He started ringing up the register.

"That'll come to twenty-nine fifty," Brad said.

"Right." The man pulled out a wallet. "And no sales tax, right?"

"That's right."

The man's wallet was fat and his nimble fingers skimmed across a thick sheaf of bills before pulling out a ten and twenty. "Here you go," he said, handing over the money. "And keep the change—I hate carrying all that silver around."

Brad carefully put the bills in the register. "Where you headed for?"

The man piled the chips on the two cases. "Palmer Lake. A cousin of mine gave me directions to the lake, said it was right at the Purmort exit. Thing I can't figure out is that the Interstate keeps on going. My cousin said it gave out right after Purmort."

"Your cousin was right, up until last summer. Now the Interstate keeps on right to Palmer Lake."

The young man looked at his watch. "Damn. We were late as it was." As he picked up the beer and chips, Brad placed both hands on the counter and stared down at the wide planks of the flooring.

"I know a shortcut," he said. "It's kinda complicated to describe, but I was starting to head up that way when you came by."

"A shortcut? You sure?"

"Sure as truth," Brad said, wiping his hands on his pants. "Comes in on the other side of Palmer Lake, heads out by an abandoned quarry. You can follow me if you'd like."

The man's moustache curled up with his grin. "That's great. I'd really appreciate it."

Brad said, "No problem at all. Just give me a minute or two to close up."

With the beer and chips in his arms, the man went out to the truck and slid the load into the bed, then clambered up into the cab and waited. Out on the porch, Brad dragged in the sacks of fertilizer and potatoes, and then took down the rakes that propped the door open. He went back to the register, totalled it up, and then locked it. Almost as an afterthought, as he started toward the front door, he reached under the counter, brought out his pistol, and tucked it into his waistband under his shirt.

The air seemed cooler and his headache was gone as he approached the front door, keys jingling in his hands. Lord, he thought, the things we have to do.

Unacceptable Procedures
Stanley Ellin

The meeting, surprisingly summoned on only one day's notice, was held in the Chief Selectman's office at the far end of the upstairs corridor of the town hall. Not much of an office for size and thriftily furnished with essentials acquired cheaply over the past century, it still provided sufficient accommodation for the Board of Selectmen around the well worn oak table there.

Of course, since the room was at the rear of the building, it did offer to anyone with an eye for that sort of thing the view of a vast rolling woodland extending to the faraway horizon. A spectacular view especially this mid-autumn time of year, what with those hills showing as much scarlet and gold as evergreen. And even more so at this hour of day, when the star-spangled darkness already shadowing Maine to the east could almost perceptibly be seen flowing westward toward Vermont to dim the flaming sunset there.

However, the gathering around the table took no notice of this familiar scene: it was the ancient Naval Observatory clock ticking away on the wall between the windows that engaged its interest. Five selectmen, all greyhaired, thin-lipped men of substance. Chief Selectman Samuel Sprague, president of the Merchants Bank. Jacob Sprague, younger brother to Samuel and the bank's treasurer. Abner Perkins, real-estate sales, rentals, and property maintenance. Benjamin Starr, Starr's

Cars–Sales and Service. Fraser Smith, Smith's Market–Quality
Meats and Groceries. All five of them done up neatly in jacket
and necktie as was the tradition at selectmen's meetings, they
sat silently with eyes fixed on the clock. The meeting had been
called for six. The clock now plainly marked three minutes
past the hour.

It was Fraser Smith who broke the silence. He cleared his
throat and addressed Chief Selectman Samuel Sprague. "You
said special meeting, Sam. Special how? Not getting started on
time?"

"Seems so," admitted Samuel Sprague. "But what we're
waiting for is our police chief. Told me last night to get us all
together so we could meet with him in strict private. Make it
for when the building's cleared out, said he, so there wouldn't
be any ears at the door."

Benjamin Starr raised an eyebrow. "Considering that Chief
Ralph Biggs has the biggest and busiest ears in town–"

"And worse than ever these last few months," put in Abner
Perkins. "Matter of fact, he's getting downright peculiar. Could
be that what we just gab about now and then –I mean, after going on thirty years maybe he's been on the job a mite too long–
well, could be time we do something about it."

"He works cheap," Samuel Sprague pointed out.

"Can't much call it work," said Abner Perkins, "in any town
peaceable as this."

"Except," said Benjamin Starr, "for them high-school kids
using my car lot nights for rumpus-raising and playing them
stereo machines to all hours. I tell Ralph about it, and what's he
say? He says to me, 'Well, they're young and full of oats the way
we once was. We grew out of it and so will they.' That's our police chief talking, mind you."

"Talking about what?" said a voice from the doorway, and
the selectmen all swiveled heads to coldly regard their police
chief. Unlike the company he was joining, Ralph Biggs was ex-
ceedingly well fleshed, his double chin draped over his shirt
collar, his belly overlapping his belt. His uniform–the town's
choice of grey with brown piping–needed pressing; when he
removed his cap the white hairs fringing his shining pate indicated that he had been a long time away from any barber chair.
To add to this study in dishevelment he was clutching a large,
dingy plastic bag bulging with papers and cardboard folders.

On the bag was inscribed in red lettering *Smith's Market—Quality Meats and Groceries.* He smiled at the company. "And just what was your police chief talking about?"

More to the point," said Samuel Sprague, "you asked for this meeting, and seems like you're the one late to it."

"Few minutes at most," said Ralph Gibbs. "Had to get a man to take over my desk. Ain't easy when the department's this shorthanded."

"Shorthanded?" snorted Benjamin Starr. "With four men on days—"

"That includes me," said Ralph Gibbs, seating himself at the foot of the table with the plastic bag on what there was of his lap.

"Including you," said Benjamin Starr. "For this size town to have as much as four paid police for days and two for nights—"

Samuel Sprague rapped his knuckles on the table. "Ben, pipe down. Ralph told me this business we're here for is real important, so let's get to it. I therefore call to order this confidential meeting—"

"Meeting in executive session," corrected Jacob Sprague.

"—meeting in executive session—meaning strictly confidential—of this Board of Selectment of the township of Huxtable Falls. Go on, Ralph, speak your piece."

"Thank you kindly, Sam," said Ralph Gibbs. He spilled the contents of the shopping bag on the table and stacked them into an untidy heap.

"What's all that?" asked Abner Perkins.

"Four months of police work, Abner," said Ralph Gibbs. "Real fine big-city police work, if I do say so myself." He sat back and eased open the remaining closed button of his jacket. "Well then, gentlemen, all this starts with some disappearances in these parts."

"Disappearances?" said Fraser Smith. "Of what?"

"People, Fraser. Folks heading up the road towards Huxtable Falls here but never made it. Never made it anywhere, far as some of these records in front of me shows. First was summertime three years ago. Two high-school boys from Antico town went bicycling off to get a look at Canada. Never heard of again."

"Stale news, Ralph," remarked Benjamin Starr. "Them Antico people made a considerable fuss about it at the time."

"Fact," said Ralph Gibbs. "Then two years ago, also summertime, there was that young Greendale couple, fellow and girl, headed Canada way on their motorbike, and, far as anyone yet knows, rode right off into limbo, so to speak."

"Not married neither," said Fraser Smith. "So I heard."

"Not married neither," agreed Ralph Gibbs. "Just young, healthy, and sinful. And now among the missing. Then last summer there was that young married couple set off from Inchester, backpacking up to the north woods, and that was the last seen of them. Nobody outside of Inchester recollects getting even a look at them going by. And the girl was mighty pretty, judging from her picture. Not the kind to be overlooked that easy."

"Maybe not," said Fraser Smith. "Saw that picture on the TV news when she was first suspected missing. Real handsome leggy girl all right."

"But out of Inchester," protested Benjamin Starr. "And those others were out of Antico and Greendale. So except for those towns being in the same county as us, I don't see what this has to do with Huxtable Falls."

"Which," said Ralph Gibbs, "was my line of thought, too, up to last Fourth of July. Tourist party stopped by headquarters that day to ask directions. So I took out the old state map to point them right, and whilst at it my eye was caught by something there."

"Do tell," said Benjamin Starr drily.

"Like, for instance, all three of them towns is southward of us, oh, maybe seven, eight miles away. Now squint your eyes and picture it. Antico's right there on the main highway and Inchester and Greendale ain't that far away on each side of it on them county blacktops. Antico folks going north just use the highway right through here. Those from Inchester and Greendale, well, their blacktops join up with the highway from each side at Piney Junction a mile south of our town limits."

"Real keen police work, Ralph," said Fraser Smith. "So you know the county map, do you?"

"Fact, Fraser. But the worrisome part is that every one of them young folks that disappeared had to pass right through town here to wherever they was headed. And for not one single soul in Huxtable Falls to ever get a glimpse of them? Makes you wonder if any of them got this far at all, don't it?"

"You mean," said Samuel Sprague, "if anything did happen to them, you're pinning it down to around the Junction?"

"Closer than that, Sam. Just take notice that right inside our town limits near the Junction is the old Samson estate. Right?"

"Wrong," put in Abner Perkins. "That property hasn't rightly been the Samson estate for quite a spell now."

"Good point, Abner," said Ralph Gibbs. "Since you got them outsiders to take a five-year lease on it—and four years are already used up—maybe we should call it the Doctor Karl Jodl estate. Especially with all that work the Doctor's payng you to fix it up. Looks sure he'll pick up that option to buy next year, don't it?"

"My business," said Abner Perkins. "And the Doctor's. Not yours. And if you—"

"Hush up, Abner," said Samuel Sprague. He aimed his jaw at Ralph Gibbs. "What about Doctor Karl Jodl, Ralph? Seems to be a nice fellow, far as anyone knows. A little stand-offish maybe, but respectable, him and that whole crew he moved in with him on the estate."

"Seems to be," agreed Ralph Gibbs. "Anyhow, what it comes to is sort of a problem that's too much for me. So before I work out the bottom line I'd like the opinion of you folks here. And before you provide that opinion just listen close."

"About Doctor Jodl?" said Samuel Sprague.

"That's right, Sam. Like, to start with, the fact that him and his crew settled four years ago for a five-year lease on the Samson estate, lease money to apply to purchase price if and when there was a sale. True, Abner? You made the deal, so you'd know."

"It was a fair deal," said Abner Perkins shortly.

"Kind of a happy surprise, too, wasn't it? That big old mansion and them outbuildings rotting away, twenty acres of ground overgrown, that swamp in back oozing right up to the buildings. Didn't look like you'd ever get rid of that property. Then all of a sudden—"

"It was a fair deal all around," Abner Perkins said.

"—and all of a sudden along comes this Mr. Thomas from the Doctor—"

"Tomas," said Abner Perkins. "Toe-mass. Tomas."

"Beg pardon, Abner. Mr. Toe-mass. Along he comes, the Doctor's check in hand, to sign the papers, and next thing you look to have struck gold in that property. I mean, what with all that contract work to bring it back to shape, buildings and grounds. Swamp's all drained now except for its far end, ain't it? Place does look pretty, all right."

"Honest work, every inch," said Abner Perkins. "Buildings and grounds."

"That's your style, Abner, no denying it. Then one night before work's hardly got started, along comes this fleet of hired haulage vans, all doing buisness out of California, and quite a lineup of fancy cars with California plates, and next morning the Doctor and his people are settled in snug as can be. Maybe twenty of them by my count."

"Twenty?" said Samuel Sprague.

"Well, figuring in the Doctor and his lady–that Madam Solange–and what looks to be assistant doctors and house help and security men, somewhat around twenty." Ralph Gibbs nodded toward Fraser Smith. "Seems they do all their marketing at Fraser's place, too. His books ought to show enough to back that figure up."

"You looking to be my bookkeeper now, Ralph?" said Fraser Smith.

"Not likely, Fraser. Anyhow, gentlemen, there we have a whole new community, so to speak, hitched onto Huxtable Falls. Standoffish and highly prosperous. And not far from the Junction, where it seems young healthy folks have a way of disappearing now and then."

"And you are soured on the Doctor for living there?" asked Abner Perkins coldly.

"You're rushing me out of turn, Abner," said Ralph Gibbs. I was just getting around to asking how much anybody here ever sees of them folks close up. Aside from that Mr. Tomas who looks to be sort of manager of the works, and shows up all sunshine and smiles around town. Anybody here ever get a real close look at the Doctor and that Madam Solange?"

"Well," said Samuel Sprague. "I've seen them waiting in that limo in town square a couple of times. What's more, I give them a nod, they give me a nod. Nothing mysterious about it."

"Seen them, too," said Fraser Smith. "Nice-looking couple. High-toned. Old-fashioned mannerly. They just don't want their feet stepped on by busybodies, that's my guess."

"And mine," said Benjamin Starr. "They're in the limo now

and then when it gasses up. Never argue price for repairs or for any of them new cars they order. And those cars are always top dollar. And they pay all bills on the dot. Stand-offish? Why not? Maybe they've got more important buisness in mind than some."

"You mean like medical business, Ben?" asked Ralph Gibbs.

"That's what I mean."

"Ralph," said Samuel Sprague impatiently, "you know as well as us it's medical business. That Mr. Tomas never made any secret of it. Doctor Jodl's a heart man, top rank. Doing some big research for the government. With a fat grant from Washington, D.C. to pay for it. Can't say I truckle to public money going that direction, but there's nothing unlawful about it, is there?'

"Well, maybe just a mite, Sam. Like, for instance, Doctor Karl Jodl is not on any government grant at all. And he is not a heart man, any rank."

The selectmen gaped. Finally Samuel Sprague said, "Not doing heart research? No grant?"

"Neither," said Ralph Gibbs.

"But from what I heard—"

"Same as we all heard, Sam, from that Mr. Tomas. However"—Ralph Gibbs dug into the pile of papers on the table and came up with a well stuffed folder. He slid it across the table to Samuel Sprague—"however, what you've got there, Sam, is some letters between me and the government people in Washington. And the state people in California. Read 'em close. Take your time about it."

The selectmen kept eyes on Samuel Sprague as he took his time about it, his brow furrowing. Then he looked up at them. "No grant," he said. "No heart man. Leastways, that's what I make of it." He looked at Ralph Gibbs. "What I can't make of it is this medical stuff. This hemodynamics talk. What's it mean?"

"Blood," said Ralph Gibbs.

"Come again?"

"Blood, Sam. That red stuff that leaks out when you cut yourself shaving." Ralph Gibbs tapped the stack of papers before him. "It's all here. Seems that's where the Doctor's an expert. On the Coast he had those two outfits: the Jodl Institute for Hemodynamic Research and the Jodl Clinic for Rejuvenation, both tied tight together. And you saw those figures there

for his last ten years' profits, didn't you? Money coming in by
the barrel. All that part is from the private investigation agency
I hired out here. Private but reliable."

"Hired?" said Abner Perkins. "Out of the police budget?"

"Worth it, Abner. Especially if Sam here tells you about that
letter from the state of California itself saying why that institute
and that clinic were all of a sudden shut up."

"Well, Sam?" said Abner Perkins.

"It's down here in black and white, Abner. Just two words is
all. 'Unacceptable procedures.' "

"Meaning?"

"Meaning," said Ralph Gibbs, "that a lot of beat-up old mil-
lionaires around the world were getting themselves rejuvenated some way the state of California didn't truckel to."

"Without saying why it didn't, more than this?"

"Nary a hint, Abner. When I pushed them on it all I could
get was goodbye and good luck."

"And goodbye's the right word, Ralph," said Abner Perkins.
"All right, so the Doctor's living on his own money, not any
government handout. All the better. And that institute and
clinic could have bent some California rules, but what about it?
He didn't open them up again here, did he? You don't mind
me saying it, Ralph, but you have gone so far off the track that
you want to lay everybody missing from the county on that
man just because he's new to these parts."

"Didn't want to, Abner. Just couldn't help it, once I got to the
Europe part of it."

"Now it's Europe?" Abner Perkins rose abruptly. "Look, I
have got a hot supper waiting for me at seven, and I don't–"

"Abner," said Samuel Sprague, "hush up and sit down." He
addressed Ralph Gibbs. "And don't you play games, Ralph.
What's Europe got to do with this?"

"Ever hear of Interpol, Sam?"

"I might have. Some kind of international police, right?"

"Well, more like an information place to help police in one
country get lined up with those elsewhere. Help make
connections, so to speak."

"And how come Huxtable Falls needs any such connections?"

"Well," said Ralph Gibbs, "according to these California documents, Doctor Karl Jodl landed there from Switzerland where

he used to have another such institute and clinic. And the Switzerland government people told me they was just shut up tight one day. Want to guess why?"

"Unacceptable procedures?" said Samuel Sprague.

"You get the cigar, Sam. So then I got in touch with Interpol and had them look up Doctor Jodl. Didn't get much from them really, but did get friendly with one of their men over the phone."

"Our headquarters phone?" said Benjamin Starr. "To Europe?"

"We'll get to that later, Ben. Right now the point is that this fellow steered me to a private agency in Switzerland that would look real close into people's private business, for a price. And yes, Ben, before you come out with it, it cost money signing up that outfit. But, as duly noted before, it was worth every cent."

"Worth it?" said Fraser Smith. "Lord almighty, you must have run right through your whole department budget already."

"Pretty near, Fraser. And even gone into my own pocket. But here and now"–Ralph Gibbs detached several folders from the stack–"is what you could call the history of Doctor Karl Jodl in Europe from way back when. Copies of everything that agency sent, along with old photos from magazines and newspapers there. There's a set for each of you gents so as not to waste time." He passed the folders around the table, then sat back comfortably in his chair. "Just say the word when you're ready."

For fifteen minutes by the Naval Observatory clock there was intense concentration around the table on the contents of the folders. Samuel Sprague finally closed his folders very gently. He waited until the laggards had finished their reading and a frowning examination of the photographs. All faces around the table, excluding the police chiefs, reflected bewilderment.

"Well?" said Ralph Gibbs.

"There's something crazy here, Ralph," said Samuel Sprague.

"My thought, too, Sam, when I plowed through that mess first time around."

"It was?"

"Had to be. After all, here was all that Europe information put together. The whole works. Birth certificate from Austria, schooling, medical training, marriage, that rejuvenation clinic up in the mountains there, then Italy right across the border and another clinic, then Switzerland and still another, and those dates just didn't make sense. And those photos even less. Had to be at least three different people here, I told myself, not one Doctor Karl Jodl. Except, however you add it up, it comes out only one."

"Lord almighty, Ralph," said Fraser Smith, "it can't be. It makes that man a hundred years old. And that woman—that Madam Solange—near as much. I've seen them this close. I'd figure him to be maybe forty, if that much. And she don't go much over thirty by any reckoning."

"That's how it looks, Fraser, not how it is. The dates on these papers and pictures are all truthful. Allowing for the old-fashioned clothes and hairdos, can you tell me that those aren't photos of Doctor Karl Jodl and his wife and nobody else? Fact is, she's the clincher. Maybe the original Karl Jodl would have had a son and grandson and great-grandson who was every one in turn his spitting image and for some reason wanted to make out they themselves was all the original when they grew up. But we know each of them did not marry women who one and all just happened to be the spitting image of Mrs. Doctor Karl Jodl. No way could that happen. So that leaves just one answer that makes sense. And it's all down in those papers, like it or not."

"The clinics," said Samuel Sprague heavily. "Hemodynamics. Total transfusion."

"Total's the payoff word, Sam," said Ralph Gibbs. "Take a few quarts of fresh young blood, add a dab of some secret chemicals, pump out all the old stuff, pump in all new, and look what you've got. Why, it could be the biggest thing any doctor ever come up with—except it might be a little too total for some people's good. Specially some healthy young folks who wouldn't be offered any vote in the matter, would they?"

"Not much," said Samuel Sprague. "But I still can't get it into my head that a man like that—"

"Right," Abner Perkins cut in. "Because this whole thing is wild-eyed speculation, that's all. That man never set up any such clinic here, did he? There's no reason in the world to think what you all look like you're thinking."

"Just one, Abner," said Ralph Gibbs. "He and his wife do look mighty spry for their age. And there's something more to take into account. Kind of touching, too, in a way."

"Touching?" said Samuel Sprague. "What's that supposed to mean?"

"Means I put in a stretch a few times this summer up in that brush in Samson's Hill with the binoculars. Couldn't see inside the main house that way, but could get a good look at the grounds roundabout."

"Why?" said Samuel Sprague. "Trying to find out if any customers in Rolls-Royces were sneaking in to get rejuvenated?'

"You are sharp, Sam, that I'll give you. That's why, all right. And never did see any such customers. What I did see was the Doctor and his lady doing a slow ramble through those fancy gardens up to what's left of the old swamp. Just walking along slow and easy, talking to each other and mostly holding hands. Sometimes they'd set themselves down on one of them iron-work benches and have a kissing party. Those are high-powered binoculars all right. And one thing came clear through them. I figure that man's a little crazy more ways than one, but one way I know for sure. He is crazy in love with that woman. Easy to see why, too, with her looks and style. And that's what it's all about. Whatever it takes he is going to keep her just the way she is for as long as he can. And himself right there along with her."

"Whatever it takes," said Samuel Sprague.

"Afriad so, Sam. That's the catch."

"Only if you buy all this foolishness," said Abner Perkins.

"Abner," said Samuel Sprague, "you know that what we've got here is no foolishness, so quit trying to make it sound that way." He turned to Ralph Gibbs. "Now what? You aim to get out a warrant against the Doctor?"

"Lord almighty," said Fraser Smith.

"But there's no bodies," said Benjamin Starr. "Only some people missing."

"Just the same, Ben," said Ralph Gibbs, "there's enough here to make quite a case. And whether Doctor Karl Jodl wins it or loses it, he's a marked man afterwards. How do you think the newspapers and TV will handle this right across the country? Still and all–"

"Yes?" said Samuel Sprague.

"Still and all, Sam, I can see two directions to move. This thing's too big for me anyhow. Best to go down to Concord and lay it all out for the state people. Let them take over. After all, it covers more than Huxtable Falls, don't it? There's three other towns nearby with what you might call a vested interest in it."

Samuel Sprague considered this. "That's one direction, Ralph. What's the other?"

"Well now, Sam, one thing is pretty sure. We cut loose on Doctor Karl Jodl and company, they'll take off from these parts quick as they can. Fact. So putting myself in your place—"

"My place?'

"Yours and Jacob's, what with you two owning our good old Merchants Bank. I was thinking of you two waving goodbye to the biggest customer the bank's got. A six-figure depositor no less."

"Who told you about that?" demanded Samuel Sprague.

"Don't matter who, Sam. What matters is it's the truth. As for Abner there and his real-estate business, well, he stands to have that white elephant Samson estate dumped right back in his hands. No closing the sale for it, no fat contract afterwards to keep the place in shape. Same for Ben there and his car business. No more Doctor Jodl for luxury buys, no more high-price repairs on that whole fleet the Doctor's lined up for his kind services. And I guess I don't have to remind Fraser that the Doctor and his crowd have to be the market's number-one customers for sure. I mean, what with those loads of fancy meat and trimmings being trucked out there every few days. Am I making myself clear?'

"Some," said Samuel Sprague. "Not all. What's on your mind, Ralph?"

"Well now, what's on my mind is that all this started because some folks turned up missing from towns roundabout. But let's look at it this way. That's not my business, it it? They want the answers I got, let them go hunt them up like I did. Get the point now, Sam?"

"Except for what you left out. What makes you so sure that next summertime, let's say, a couple of our own young folks won't turn up missing from right here in Huxtable Falls?'

"Fair question, Sam. But I guarantee nobody as smart as Doctor Karl Jodl looks to make waves right here in home port.

No chance of that. That's how it's been since he settled down here; that's how it'll keep on."

"All the same, Ralph—"

"So I could just tuck all these papers here back in this shopping bag and lock it up nice and tight in my house. Which, for that matter, is where it's been kept all along. Strictly my own private business so far. Nobody else's."

"Even so, Ralph," said Abner Perkins, "if you'd just heave all that stuff in the fire—"

"No, don't see it quite that way, Abner," said Ralph Gibbs. "And there's still some items on the agenda."

"Such as?" said Samuel Sprague.

"Well, for one thing, seems there's been talk amongst you gentlemen that after me holding down my desk for nigh thirty years, it's time to put the old horse out to pasture. Fact is, I like my job. It'll do my morale a lot of good to know I'm set in it until I say otherwise."

"What else?" said Samuel Sprague.

"Matter of repayment, Sam. That Europe agency cost me cash out of my pocket. Can't see making repayment a town budget item, so best way to handle it, I figure, is for each of you gents to make out a check for one thousand Yankee dollars, payable to cash, and hand it over to Jacob here at the bank first thing tomorrow. He puts it all straight into my account, and there we are, no fuss, no big noise about it."

"Maybe not," said Jacob Sprague, "but that kind of transaction by the whole Board of Selectmen—"

"I didn't finish yet, Jacob," said Ralph Gibbs. "Didn't mention that I have already set up a meeting with the state people down to Concord three P.M. tomorrow. I figure around noon tomorrow I'll know whether to call it off or drive down there."

"Noon tomorrow," said Samuel Sprague. "And that finishes the agenda?'

"Not yet, Sam. There's them pay raises that keep getting left out of the budget every year. What I see for next year is a twenty percent raise across the board. That's for everybody in my department, including me. And two shiny new police cars with all extras, because them heaps we have now got were due for the scrap pile long ago. And that is the whole agenda." Ralph Gibbs rose and dumped the papers and folders before him into the shopping bag. He made a circuit around the table, sweeping the rest of the documents into it. He planted his cap squarely on his head. "Shouldn't rightly be here when the vote's taken, so I'll get along home now. Anyhow," he said from the door, "hate to miss the TV news any night. Never know what'll show up on it."

All eyes were on the door as it very gently closed behind him. The sound of footsteps down the corridor faded away.

"Lord almighty," whispered Fraser Smith.

The Naval Observatory clock on the wall ticked loudly, marking off a minute and then some.

"Well," said Samuel Sprague, "it looks like Ralph left us a motion here to vote on. No need to spell it out again, line for line. Anybody stand against it?" He waited a seemly time, then rapped his knuckles on the table. "The motion is adopted unanimously."

Benjamin Starr raised his hand.

"Yes, Ben?" said Samuel Sprague.

"Well, it's about the new police cars, Sam. Looks to me that Starr's Cars could get a special discount from the manufacturer that'll—"

"No way." Samuel Sprague shook his head in reproach. "That is a conflict of interest for you, Ben, and you know it. Anything else?"

"That was it," said Benjamin Starr sadly.

"Then this meeting is herewith adjourned," said Samuel Sprague.

Death of a Harvard Man
Richard M. Gordon

For reasons which he considered sufficient and which we need not consider here at all, young Dyer, Harvard '56, had decided to take arms against a sea of troubles and, by opposing, end them.

To do this as decently as he might, he had left his native Boston where any such act of self-expression is looked on askance and had journeyed to New York where the nonconformist and the dramatic fail to raise even an eyebrow. They were better able to handle this sort of thing in New York, he felt, and in any case, he would rather his shattered remains were collected by the callous hands of insensitive strangers than by the shocked and disapproving hands of his fastidious Boston friends.

He had had a busy day, but now his affairs were in order: his last will and testament lay on the dresser of his room at the Harvard Club among three touching letters of farewell and apology to his parents, his fiancee, and the Alumni Secretary of the Class of '56. He was prepared to meet the sole confidants of his fellow Bostonians, the Cabots.

He had chosen the 42nd Street Station of the Sixth Avenue Subway as his point of departure from this vale of tears. It was dark, dank, depressing, and, at 4:30 on a Sunday morning, nearly deserted. There was only a ragged bum sprawled on a bench at the rear of the platform, an empty pint bottle which had contained a cheap California Muscatel beside him. The derelict was staring vacantly into his own world of sordid misery—a world which could not possibly touch on young Dyer's world of high tragedy.

Young Dyer paced impatiently as he waited for his train. And then, as far away uptown in the darkness, there came a rumbling. The approaching train was only a local, but young Dyer was not going far. He watched fascinated as the lights materialized out of the gloom of the tunnel. Destiny and a Sixth Avenue local rushed down upon him as he poised tensely at the edge of the platform.

But young Dyer was the sort of man (boy, rather) who could not, even in his extremity, resist an ironic gesture to demonstrate his superiority to the common, non-Harvard humanity which was content to persist in a world he was rejecting.

With an exaggerated bow to the bum on the bench, he uttered the despairing cry of the gladiators of Rome: *"Morituri te salutamus!*—we who are about to die salute you!

Rather surprisingly, before he could turn to the business at hand, there was a reply. The derelict, reclining languidly like a spectator in a loge at the Colosseum, turned up his thumb and said, *"Vive!"*—the "Live!" of the Caesars.

Young Dyer was stopped in his tracks but not on them. By the time he had collected himself, the first car of the local had passed him, and the train was grinding to a halt.

"I thought I had better stop you," said the tramp, rising. His voice was well modulated, and his accent strangely familiar. "It's none of my business, of course," he continued, "but it does seem rather wasteful that a man who has his youth, his health, a Brooks Brothers suit, and a knowledge of Latin should squander all these assets under the wheels of a train. There are those who have a great deal less and still manage to carry on."

Youn Dyer was ashamed; he looked down at his hand-lasted, hand-stitched, three-eyelet oxfords, and realized they contrasted sharply with the cracked, lop-heeled, shapeless lumps of dirty leather on the feet of the older man. He had been a bit lacking in courage, he thought. After all, he was a Harvard Man. There was always a comfortable, dignified place in the world for one such as he, if not in Boston, in the wilderness elsewhere. His pioneer blood came to the fore; in spite of all the slings and arrows of outrageous fortune, he would continue living.

"Thank you," he said simply and sincerely. "You saved my life, and I'd like to help you get back on your feet again. A pair of shoes...a new suit...I've got some extra things in my room at the Harvard Club. Come with me—it's not far, just over at 44th and..."

"I know where it is," interrupted the derelict, taking young Dyer by the arm. I spent some time there myself years ago." And then, through the swelling roar of a southbound express, young Dyer heard the bum say, "I'm Hugh Haven, Class of '34—"

With a cry of horror, Dyer tore himself from the other's grasp and hurled himself under the wheels of the oncoming D train...

Of course, we could end it here—it ended here for young Dyer. But here are at least three other possible endings...

Ending One

Hugh Haven, Harvard '34, shook his head sadly as he sauntered unhurridly toward the exit. For some reason, which it is just as well not to examine, an old college song came as if of its own accord to his lips. *"With Crimson in Triumph Flashing..."* he hummed absently to himself as he started up the stairs to the street.

There would now be a delay on the downtown express, and he thought he might as well again try to get a taxi. It is difficult to get a driver to pick you up when you are returning from a masquerade after winning first prize for authenticity as a bum. However, Mr. Haven was, on the whole, well satisfied with his prize-winning costume and the impression it made even on passing strangers.

Ending Two

Hugh Haven Glass, of 34 West 3rd Street, shrugged disconsolately and ambled away from the gathering crowd.

"Now why did he do that?" he said to himself, wondering if the young man had been hard of hearing. "I only wanted to give him my name and address in case he wanted to send me a check."

In his days as a busboy at the Harvard Club bar, before he was fired for reaching above himself into the members' rooms upstairs, he had learned all about Harvard Men—what they drank, how they dressed, how they spoke. He had even learned a bit of Latin while he was there.

Ending Three
Hugh Haven, Yale '34, smiled a satisfied smile and relapsed on his bench. He hummed *Boola Boola* softly under his breath. Once again Yale had triumphed over her ancient adversary.

LIZZIE BORDEN IN THE P.M.

Robert Henson

I read about her death in the local papers–it was news even here–"Lizzie Borden Again" for the last time, so to speak.

She entered the hospital under an assumed name. They knew who she was, of course, and she knew they knew. Pure Lizzie, the whole thing!

No other details–only a rehash of the murders and trial, I read just far enough to see if the dress was mentioned.

I wrote to Miss Jubb to say I'd heard. On the way home from the post office I fell and broke my hip. That same night, in the hospital, I dreamed Lizzie pushed me. I was lying on the sidewalk. "Why, Lizzie?'

She said what she had said thirty years before in Fall River jail: "You've given me away, Emma." Then she turned her face away, as she had done then, and said again: "Remember, Emma, I will never give in one inch–never!"

Well, Lizzie, you never did, I thought, waking. But neither did I, though for twelve years you kept after me.

I finally left her–moved clear away–first to Providence, then here. Miss Jubb sometimes smuggled in a bit of news–"After all, she is your sister!"–but I never saw her again.

I heard from her once, indirectly, when she threatened legal action to keep me from selling my share in the Borden Building. I knew she could have no sound business reasons, with mills closing and property values going down in Fall River. I sent word through my lawyer that I intended to proceed.

But then newspapers got wind of the suit. I made myself unavailable–Lizzie talked: Father had wanted the building to perpetuate his name–she could not conceive why I wanted to endanger family ownership–selling would be disloyal to his memory, etc.

I knew that holding onto a poor investment would be even more disloyal to Andrew J. Borden. However, I offered to sell my share to no one but her. I was even prepared to take a loss.

She refused: the building must be ours, not hers.

Ah, Lizzie, I thought, will you never give up?

Reporters became more numerous–the past began to exercise its fascination–I capitulated. I did not have her toleration for publicity. I knew how she would interpret my retreat, but I had never been able to prevent her misconstructions–I did not hope to now.

She dropped the suit but not all the reporters went away. A young man from the *Providence Journal* persisted. I could not evade him–my address had become too well known. Yet he was very courteous. He surprised me by asking through the screen door if the *Journal's* coverage of the trial was my reason for refusing to talk to him: "I've been reading our back files–I understand how you may feel..."

"No, that was before your time–I do not blame you."

"The *Journal*, I believe, was your father's favorite paper."

"Yes. Not that that helped when the time came."

"In one thing our coverage was like everyone else's–there was nothing but respect for you. Affection might be a better word," he said.

"I was not the consideration. Most papers–yours excepted– were also well disposed toward my sister."

"There was perhaps more admiration than affection for Miss Lizzie," he said, begging me not to be offended.

"Admiration for my sister is surely not something that could give offense," I said, "except perhaps to the *Journal*."

"My erring employer!" he smiled.

I unlatched the screen. "Well, I will speak with you briefly if it will help you."

"At the time of her acquittal," he said, "it was predicted that the verdict wouldn't be acceptable to everyone–hasn't that proved true?"–"Yes, only too true."–"In all these years no one else has ever been arrested or accused or even suspected."–"Well, that is strange, but I do not blame Lizzie for that."–"It played no part in your decision to leave her?"–"I remained with her for twelve years!"–"You never had any reason your-self to find the verdict unacceptable?"–"My lips must remain sealed as to my precise reason for leaving–I remained with her," I heard myself saying, "until conditions became unbear-able."

"Unbearable?"

"And now I deserve to be left in peace."

I paid for my indiscretion. Reporters again descended. For a second time I had to call upon Miss Jubb–"It will not die!" I said. She hurried over from Fall River and helped spirit me away. She is the only person who knows my present where-abouts.

She apologized for not coming in person to tell me about Lizzie's funeral. Poor soul! she's old as I am. But I understand what she meant: if she could just tell me she could make it seem less–Lizzie. As if I expected anything else!

She wrote that Lizzie had an operation about a year ago from which she never really recovered–in fact, she felt so strongly that she was going to die that she made plans for her own funeral and left them in a sealed envelope with Helen Leighton.

Miss Leighton was her latest close friend–a young woman–from Boston, not Fall River. According to Miss Jubb, people liked her but made fun of her a little after she took up with Lizzie. She became obsessed with the idea that Fall River had mistreated Lizzie, but would maintain in the same breath that Lizzie said and did nothing to influence her.

She faithfully carried out Lizzie's last wishes: the funeral to be held at home–someone to sing "Mu Ain Countree"–a select list of people to be invited. Miss Jubb was one.

When the mourners arrived there was no Lizzie–only Miss Leighton pale as death. She had just learned that Lizzie had been buried the night before. Lizzie had left the undertaker in-structions, a funeral service to him. On the contrary, she speci-fied that after the laying out the coffin was to be closed, draped in black, and taken by night–it must be the same night–to Oak Grove cemetery. There it was to be lowered into the grave by Negroes–dressed in black. She specifically forbade any other attendants.

He had carried out her instructions to the letter, including the malicious timing.

Poor Miss Leighton! Most of the people on that select list came out of mere curiosity. She must have realized too late that Lizzie only wanted to spite them–and she would have to partly admit that they deserved it. I pictured her standing in the parlor–she cannot quite condone Lizzie's action–cannot quite condemn it. People file past her in the awkward silence. She is just beginning to understand what was required of a friend to Lizzie Borden.

Lizzie did not exchange class rings with a friend when she graduated from high school. She gave hers to Father. We had just got home from the exercises. "I want you to wear it always."

Father was not sentimental but he was always solicitous of Lizzie's feelings. Perhaps he felt tht she had been more disturbed by Mother's death than I was, though she was only two at the time; while I was twelve. And she was only four when he remarried–she found it natural to call Abby "Mother." I did not, and received permission to use her first name. A few years before the murders, we both changed to "Mrs. Borden."

Lizzie soon found that attempts to treat her as a mother only embarrassed and alarmed her. From the beginning, she could scarcely be prevailed upon to go out of the house or do anything in it except eat. She took to staying upstairs as much as possible–she would come down only for meals or between-meals foraging. Her weight, before many years passed, made even these descents laborious.

Lizzie turned back to me–she came to dislike Mrs. Borden intensely. I did not. I just could never grow fond of her–of her sloth, her physical grossness. I compared her to Mother and found her wanting. I did not, however, think of her as coming between Father and me. The older Lizzie grew, the more she behaved as if every token of affection for Mrs. Borden were stolen from her. She fought back.

Father said he would attach the ring to his watch chain "No, you must wear it on your finger!"–he said it was too small–

"Then wear it on your small finger!"–he started to put it on his right hand–"Not that hand, Father!" I remember how he hesitated–the least thing was liable to send her off into one of her peculiar spells–then, silently, he worked the ring onto the small finger of his left hand. It clashed unavoidably with his wedding band. Abby said never a word. I saw her a few minutes later groaning up the stairs with a mutton sandwich, a wedge of apple pie, and a pitcher of iced tea with half an inch of sugar boiling up from the bottom.

When Lizzie was excited her eyes seemed to grow larger and paler–color and expression would drain away–she would stare hard, but at something no one else could see. The effect was not pleasant, though reporters at the trial found it "incandescent," "hypnotizing," and so on–descriptions she cherished. No one found the mottling of her skin attractive. Even as a girl Lizzie did not blush in the usual sense–blood rising in her face would not blend with the pallor of her skin but fought an ugly battle all along her jaw and straggled out in her cheeks. Often when these signs of inner emotion were most evident her voice and manner would indicate total self-possession: "I have received Mr. Robinson's bill. Twenty-five thousand dollars. I will not pay it."

Noting the inner stress, I did not mention her new house on French Street nor any of the other extravagances that had followed her acquittal far more quickly than Mr. Robinson's fee.

"I thought he was my friend–he called me his little girl."

"He saved your life, Lizzie."

She stared. "I was innocent, was I not?'

"Mr. Robinson made the jury see it."

"You did not think it was self-evident?"

"It is not a matter of what I thought."

Well, I won't pay it! I won't be robbed, I won't be blackmailed!"

"Blackmailed!"

'Don't you see the dilemma Mr. Robinson is trying to put me in? No innocent person would be charged such a fee. If I pay, it will be said that I bought an acquittal."

"And if you don't?"

"That I wasn't willing to pay for one."

I hardly knew where to begin. "Why would he create such a

dilemma?"

"You can't guess?"

"No."

"Mr. Robinson doesn't believe me innocent," she said flatly. "This is his way of saying so. I will not pay it!"

Either then or later—for we went over and over every point—she said: "You look so downcast, Emma. If it will make you feel better, you may pay him."

"How could it make me feel better, unless you lacked the money?"

"True," she said. "And you've had enough expenses from the trial as it is."

"I? I have had no expenses."

"Yes," she said, staring hard. "it is common knowledge."

Either then or later, when I wearied of playing games, I asked bluntly: "Are you speaking of Bridget?"

"Yes—of the way she dressed at the trial—her ticket back to Ireland—the farm she bought there. She couldn't possibly have saved enough from the wages Father paid her."

"Servant-girls may believe she was bribed," I said sharply, "but no sensible person does."

"No sensible person believed that Bridget couldn't recall what dress I was wearing that morning, or whether I had changed from cotton to silk."

"If she remembered and chose not to tell, it was because she did not think the matter important. Her silense did not become an expense."

She opened her fan and looked at me over the edge. It was Mr. Robinson who persuaded her to carry a black fan during the trial. She had never used one before but so much attention was paid to it tht she was never afterward without one. To my occasional annoyance: "Put that away. Coyness does not become either of us. I will tell you now that I made arrangements to help Bridget financially during the trial. She was, after all, unemployed for almost a year. She chose to spend the money on showy dresses—that was indiscreet, but I was not bribing her and therefore had no right to object. However it may have looked, my conscience was clear. When the trial was over she wanted to go home—that is natural—and Ireland is her home."

"It is all so easily explained, yet you have never explained it before."

"It was my own affair."

"Oh Emma," she suddenly said in a tone of peculiar satisfaction, "you are not a good liar! You believe I changed from the cotton to the silk that morning! You believe Bridge lied when she said she couldn't remember!"

"Lizzie, Lizzie! if you say you wore the silk all morning, I believe you. If Bridget lied when she said she could not remember anything to the contrary, she lied upon her own motion. The money I gave her was not a bribe!"

"It was a reward."

"It was neither—it was a simple gift!"

She would not pay Mr. Robinson but I found her at work on a gift for Mr. Moody. I thought at first she was adding to her own scrapbook of clippings and memorabilia of the trial. Then I saw two police photographs mounted opposite each other— Father—half sliding off the couch—profile streaked with blood— Mrs. Borden—wedged between the bed and bureau—feet awkwardly splayed...

"Where—how—did you get these?"

"I asked for them. Oh, not for myself—" and she showed me the flyleaf: "For Mr. William Moody, as a memento of an interesting occasion."

"Lizzie, you cannot!"

"It's a duplicate of my own—except for those additions."

"Oh, Lizzie, at the very least this is not in good taste!" For some reason the remark made her laugh out loud. I persisted: "It is—inappropriate—it will seem that you are taunting him."

"Not at all," she replied, fetching string and wrapping paper. "Mr. Moody is a young man on the threshold of his career. Even though he lost this case, his connection with it cannot but help him. He will be grateful."

The assistant prosecuting attorney!

That time the house was broken into—in broad daylight— about a year before the murders—the police questioned and questioned Bridget. A little gold watch and some jewelry were missing from Mrs. Borden's dressing table. She discovered the theft when she returned from one of her rare outings, a drive with Father to Swansea. The rest of us had been home all day— none of us heard any suspicious noises. It was Lizzie who discovered how the thief got in: someone had left the cellar door unbolted–the lock had been picked with a nail–Lizzie pointed to it still hanging in the keyhole.

The police came back next day to question Bridget further. Maybe she had opened the cellar door for an accomplice...Lizzie had to be sent to her room–she could not stop talking and interfering. Father had already asked the police not to release news of the theft to the papers–now he asked them to drop the investigation altogether. "You will never catch the real thief..." The word "real" struck me as odd at the time, but I believe he was trying to let the police know that he had no suspicion at all of Bridget.

That night he locked and bolted the door between Lizzie's bedroom and the one he and Mrs. Borden used. It had never been locked before, it was never unlocked again.

I knew Lizzie would forgive Father anything–I braced myself for an attack on Mrs. Borden for that silent accusation. Instead she seemed to put the matter completely out of her mind.

But a few weeks later, while Alice Russell was paying a visit, Lizzie suddenly began a rambling account of the theft. Alice had not heard of it before–after a few questions she fell tactfully silent. Lizzie said Father had been right to call off the investigation. Robberies so bold yet limited in scope (nothing taken but what belonged to Mrs. Borden!) could seldom be solved. Even the police said so. All we could do was try to prevent a repetition–as she had done by putting a lock on her side of the door. If a thief came up the backstairs again, he would no longer be able to pass from Father's room into hers and so to the front of the house...

I heard this in startled silence. Later I checked. There indeed on Lizzie's side of the door was a shiny new lock.

Of the people who dropped away after the trial I missed Alice Russell most of all–she had been my best friend. Lizzie once made the astonishing suggestion that I exchange calls with her again.

"You know I cannot do that, Lizzie."

"Why not?–unless you have some quarrel I don't know about."

"We have not quarrelled, for we have not spoken since she testified against you."

She was toying with her fan. "She did not testify against me. She told what she saw. It could not hurt me."

I said wanly, "I wonder that you can put it out of your memory so easily."

"Well," she said negligently, "what did she have to tell except that she saw me tearing up an old dress? But you saw me, too—you knew the dress. When I told you I was going to burn it, you said, 'Yes, why don't you?'"

"In that," I said bitterly, "I had to contradict her."

"Is she angry about that? She can't be so petty!"

"I do not know how she feels."

"If she wanted her reputation for accuracy to go unchallenged, she shouldn't have waited three months before telling her story."

I could have wept. "Out of fondness for me, Lizzie! When she could bear it no longer she sent to beg my forgiveness!"

"Ah, now I understand a little better your desire not to see her again," Lizzie said on that note of satisfaction I was learning to dread. "She needn't have implicated you."

"She did not implicate me."

"Forced you to contradict her, then."

"You did that! I told about the dress-burning the way your remembered it."

She rose and walked about the room, opening and shutting her fan. "Why did you let me burn it, Emma, when you still believed I had changed?"

According to Alice I had tried—I had not said, "Why don't you?" but "I would not do that if I were you!" She was coming back from church—on Sunday after the murders on Thursday—I let her in the back door—followed her through the entry into the kitchen—Lizzie was standing between the stove and the coal closet—she had a blue dress in her hand—with brown stains on the skirt. I knew she had stained a blue dress with brown paint several months earlier—several times she had mentioned throwing it away. I also knew the police were looking for a blue dress with blood stains on it. I could have said either, "I would not do that if I were you" or "Why don't you?" Either.

"Alice may resent my contradicting her testimony," I said, "but she would never misinterpret my reasons for doing so."

"Do you think that I do?"

I would not answer.

She was never satisfied if I said I did not remember, or had not been paying attention, or had lost my way in the technicalities, contradictions, details...Yet when Mr. Moody opened for the prosecution I remember thinking, So there it all is—so *that's* their side, just as if nine months had not gone by, with an inquest and preliminary investigation. Mr. Robinson could bring tears to my eyes but I could seldom apply what he was saying to the point at hand. Mr. Moody was mercilessly clear and orderly. Watching Lizzie during his presentation, I thought, Innocence alone can account for that detached expression.

Only when he came to the very end did her eyes and complexion show a change. The case against her, he said, had always had a weapon, a motive, and an opportunity. The real puzzle had been the absence of a blood-stained dress. He promised to clear up this mystery—the prosecution would present new testimony by a witness who had seen Lizzie burning a bloody garment!

I felt my blood turn to ice—Alice was going to testify. Lizzie opened her fan—shut it. In later years, sensational journalism had her swooning virtually every day. In fact she did so only once. Just as Mr. Moody finished and started for his table she fainted dead away.

Mr. Moody's triumph was short-lived. In the days following, so many rulings from the bench favored the defense that he was rumored to have urged the District Attorney to withdraw from the case—throw the responsibility for freeing Lizzie upon the Court. There was much ugly comment upon the fact that the presiding judge was one of Mr. Robinson's appointees when Mr. Robinson was governor of the state. The District Attorney, however, did not withdraw. Apparently he did not feel as strongly as Mr. Moody that the trial was a mockery of justice.

Still, it was not to him that Lizzie sent her "memento of an interesting occasion."

Eventually she paid Mr. Robinson but announced that her door would be closed to him. Not that he had ever made any attempt to call. Neither had Mr. Jennings, her other lawyer, our family lawyer. After we moved up on the hill, he simply dropped away.

The house seemed far too large to me, but Lizzie said she

planned to entertain extensively and would need room. She was no longer content with one maid—she engaged a "staff"—a housekeeper, a second maid, a cook, a Negro coachman. What, I wondered silently, will I do with myself all day?

One afternoon I came back from shopping and found a workman carving the word "Maplecroft" on the front doorstep. I broke my silence.

"What is this?"—"The name I've given the house."—"What does it mean?"—"It doesn't mean anything, I simply like the sound of it."—"You are making a mistake."—"In what way?"—"Naming a house will be thought inappropriate, in bad taste."—"By whom?"—"Everyone, and especially those whom you would least like to think it."

"Dearest Emma," she said, "you can only mean yourself. And while I value your opinion, you're too close to me to realize that I can't be what I was before."

"No, you cannot. More is now expected."

"Well, that is my point," she said, and would discuss it no further.

But people who accuse Lizzie of "social climbing" because she bought the house on French Street do not understand that Father could have moved up on the hill at any time—he would only have been taking his place among his peers. But he was not concerned with external signs of his standing. Lizzie's hints and pleas fell on deaf ears.

It was the only thing he would not do for her—he sent her on the Grand Tour—paid dressmakers' bills without complaint—stretched her allowance with gifts of money...This generosity somewhat contradicted his basic nature but I never resented it. In such things as property and stocks he treated us equally, and he praised me where he could never have praised her—for wise management. He took both of us into his business confidence, however. I can recall only one time when he did not—and that was when he put a house in Mrs. Borden's name without telling us. We learned of it only by accident.

Lizzie was extraordinarily agitated: "She has persuaded him to go behind our backs! He would never have done this by himself!"

I agreed it was unlike him.

"What shall we do?"

I said we could do nothing except hope it would not happen again. That was not enough for Lizzie: "I shall let her know what I think of her!" She ceased to call her Mother. She went further—she would speak if they met but would not talk. Her silences were brooding—palpable—disquieting even to me. Mrs. Borden was clearly miserable, though her appetite was unaffected.

Father found a rental duplex and put it in our names. It was worth to each of us exactly what Mrs. Borden's house was worth. I was astounded by the crudeness of this attempt to atone for his secrecy and favoritism. Lizzie responded by refusing to take any more meals with him and Mrs. Borden. The house was heavy with tension.

He came to me for help. I had always had the room adjoining his and Mrs. Borden's. It was larger than Lizzie's, better furnished, and cheerier with two windows on the south. It fell to me when we first moved to Second Street only because I was the older. Now Father asked if I would exchange with Lizzie.

I said, "Yes, if you think it will raise her spirits."

But he would not directly admit his motive: "She has to go through your room to reach the hall closet. She shouldn't always be distrubing you."

True, eighteen or twenty of her dresses hung in the hall closet—her own would not hold them all. I said, "It is a considerate suggestion."

"I want you to offer it as your own," he said in his driest voice.

I thought for a moment. "She will not be deceived."

"Will you do it?"

"Well, I will say that the subject came up and that we agreed on the idea."

As I did. But he did not profit much from the exchange. Close on its heels came the daylight robbery. By then I was taking my meals with Lizzie and had ceased to call Mrs. Borden by her first name...

I had nothing to do the livelong day—I began to occupy myself at Central Congregational. Lizzie was scathing: "You've become a regular pew-warmer, Emma. You never were before. Why this sudden compulsion?"

"I am under no compulsion. I go freely."

"But you can't stay away freely, that's the point!"

I did not answer.

She leaned her cheek on her fan and gazed as me poignantly: "Perhaps Miss Jubb is your reason. If so, why not say it? I know you need someone besides me."

I ached to hold her in my arms at that moment, comfort her, as when she was a child and had no mother but Emma. I had never cultivated the people who rallied round her during her trouble–I did not feel neglected when they dropped away. She seethed as if from an injustice.

For ten months the people we now lived among but seldom saw had made her their special care. They extolled her in the press as a person of the highest character and most delicate sensibilites–charged that she was being sacrificed to inept police performance and indifferent law enforcement–called her a martyr to low-bred envy or political opportunism–the scapegoat periodically demanded by the moneyless and propertyless. Mrs. Holmes, Mrs. Brayton, Mrs. Almy, and their like kept her cell filled with fresh flowers. Only persons with influence obtained seats in the courtroom–and how many of them female! What a murmur of feminine admiration went up when she entered the first day in her dress of severest black but latest fashion–great leg-of-mutton sleeves–ruching of black lace–a black-lace hat to set off the pallor of her face. And from one hand (the other lay on Reverend Buck's arm) drooped the quickly famous long black fan.

When the words "Not guilty" were at last pronounced these same admirers wept, fainted, sank to their knees in prayers of thanks giving. Mrs. Holmes gave a splendid reception. All the people Lizzie had always admired were there to admire her. How could she escape the conclusion that she had done something for them?

We returned to Second Street next day. While we waited for the housekeeper to answer the bell, Lizzie kept glancing about. Only yesterday forty reporters or more were vying for her attention, people holding up children for her to kiss...Now the street was deserted.

We went in. I made a move toward the parlor but Lizzie walked straight ahead to the sitting room. She did not seem to notice the bare space along the wall–left by the couch where Father had been hacked to death. She was taking the pins out of her hat. "Do take another peek outside, Emma. Someone may be there."

I refused. "It is over," I said.

Gradually she saw that it was, though in more ways than the one I meant. She did not ask why—she retaliated. Formerly she had been a mainstay of Central Congregational—now she said spitefully, "Let Mariana Holmes find someone else to cook and serve dinners for newsboys!"

Reverend Buck tried without much enthusiasm to reconcile her, then turned the task over to his assistant. Reverend Jubb was more solicitous, going so far as to bring his sister with him each time. But after two visits Lizzie refused to come downstairs. I was their only catch.

"Aren't you afraid someone will think you are trying to atone for something?" Lizzie asked with a disagreeable smile.

Her other guess, about Miss Jubb, was closer. If I helped with the Christmas dinner for newsboys or kept accounts for the Fruit-and-Flower Mission, the reason was Miss Jubb's friendship. That and the fact that I had nothing to do all day long—except think.

Their clothing lay in a heap in the cellar for three days, then the police gave me permission to bury it—behind the stable—with an officer watching. Then I scrubbed the blood off the doorjamb downstairs—the baseboard upstairs—thinking, So little here, so much on their clothes...Father's had spurted forward—only one splash hit the doorjamb by his head—the murderer might have entirely escaped being spattered. But he had straddled Mrs. Borden's body, they said, after felling her with the first blow—he could scarcely have avoided stains below the knees. Yet her blood shot forward, too—onto the baseboard—so possibly he could have walked along the street without attracting attention—once he got out of the house...

It was their clothing that was soaked—pools of blood had spread out on the floor. Lizzie's shoes and stockings were spotless—so was her blue-silk dress. There had been no cries or sounds of struggle to alert her. Both died with the very first blow, medical examiners said. The senseless hacking that followed was—just that.

I had been at the seashore. Alice met me at the station, all in tears. Lizzie was waiting at home, dry-eyed. I do not know why she sent for Alice instead of one of her own friends upon discovering Father's body. It was poor Alice who went upstairs and found Mrs. Borden.

In the carriage she said: "Lizzie came to see me last night–burst in, really. I felt quite concerned–she looked, well, distraught. She said she was depressed and wanted to talk to someone–she said she couldn't shake off the feeling that something terrible was going to happen–she felt as if she should sleep with her eyes open...Shall I mention all this, Emma?"

"It will come out."

I never asked, never hinted that Alice should either speak or be silent on any matter. She stayed with us the entire week following the murders. So much of what she told me before Lizzie was arrested is mixed up in my mind with what she told afterward in court. Was it when she met me at the station, or late, that she mentioned a bundle on the floor of my closet? Detectives had been searching for a murder weapon, she said, but they had been very considerate–they had not turned things completely upside down. In my room they had not even disturbed the bundled-up blanket in the closet...I could not think what she meant–I left no such bundle–I found none when I got home.

Mrs. Borden had received twenty blows, all from behind–Father ten. He had been taking a nap–one side of his face had been sliced away–the eye sliced in half. In the coffin, that side was pressed into the pillow. Lizzie bent down and kissed the upturned cheek. Her ring was still on his little finger.

Crowds lined the route to the cemetery. The hush was eerie. When Lizzie stepped out of the carriage at the gate it was possible to hear someone whisper, "She's not wearing black!"

It was like a portent of the future. I asked her if the printer had made an error when I saw "Lisbeth Borden" on her new calling cards. She had never been called anything but Lizzie.

"It's not an error. Lisbeth is my name now, and you must call me by it."–"I cannot do that."–"You mean you will not."–"Is it a legal change?"–"You know it isn't."–"Then of what use is it?"–"Oh, *use!*"–"Very well, for what reason at all do you wish to take a different name?"

She was silent, then with a curious little smile she said, "I'll tell you–if you'll tell my why you've taken to wearing nothing but black."

"There is no mystery in that."

"Surely you're not still in mourning."

"Not mourning exactly. I have never cared much for clothes. You know that. These now seem appropriate."

"That is becoming your favorite word."

"I am a limited person."

"Then this is a permanent change in your dress?'

"I have not thought of it that way—it may be."

"Well, and I'm changing my name!"

"The two things are not the same."

"True—they aren't. You must take care that your black doesn't begin to look like penance," said Lisbeth of Maplecroft.

She purchased one of the first automobiles in Fall River. I had only Miss Jubb's description of it—"long, black, like the undertaker's limousine." The Negro who had been her coachman, or perhaps another, became her chauffeur. She could be seen every day going for a drive, looking neither left nor right but staring straight ahead. By then her ostracism was complete. All too appropriately had "Maplecroft" been carved on her doorstep by a man from the tombstone works.

I went to her coachman after the unpleasantness over the book and asked him bluntly if he had been a party to it. A certain journalist had compiled an account of the case from his daily reports, court transcripts, and so forth, and was giving it the sensational title *Fall River Tragedy*. It was supposed to clear up some "doubts" that Lizzie herself had stonily refused to clear up. Fall River was agog with anticipation—the outside world, too, it was said, though the printing was being done locally. Lizzie was several times observed entering and leaving the shop. It was assumed that she was threatening legal action. But on publication day the printer announced that Miss Borden had bought up the entire printing and had it carted away the night before.

"Did you help her?"—"She say I help her?"—"The printer said she came with some Negro assistants—he couldn't identify them."—"Miss Lisbeth know what she doin' if she get colored mens..."

I caught the note of admiration—it was Bridget all over again. "If she changed her dress you must tell Mr. Jennings," I said.

"Lizzie may be foolishly afraid that innocent stains will incriminate her," Mr. Jennings patiently explained. "But to a jury a perfectly clean dress may seem more suspicious."

"A silk dress, Bridget!–heavy silk for house wear!–on the hottest day of the year!"

"If she changed from her cotton and don't want to tell, I daresay she has her reasons," Bridget said, addressing Mr. Jennings.

"Twouldn't be foolishness–not her."

"A pool of blood had dripped from the sofa when she discovered her father," said Mr. Jennings, "yet not even her hem was stained. It might be *very* foolish to maintain that."

"I can't see how me backin' up her own statement can harm her," Bridget said stubbornly. "Besides, all I'm really sayin' is, I don't *remember* what she was wearin'."

Mr. Jennings was still not easy in his mind–he went to Lizzie and pleaded with her not to conceal anything that might damage her case later. He was explicit.

She retaliated by replacing him with Mr. Robinson–but blamed me for undermining his faith in her innocence. She was lying on a cot when the matron let me in after their interview. "You have given me away, Emma."–"I only told him what I thought he ought to know for your defense."–"Bridget's word wasn't enough?"–"Bridget did not say you hadn't changed, only that she could not remember."–"And you persuaded Mr. Jennings that that wasn't enough! upon what grounds? upon what grounds?'–"Upon grounds of common sense."

"She turned her face to the wall: "I will never give in one inch–never!"

Nor did Bridget, though subjected to great pressure on the witness stand. Lizzie was wearing a blue dress but whether it was cotton or silk she did not remember. Her steadfastness deserved our gratitude, I thought, but as for bribing her, I might as well be accused of buying the coachman's silence! "Were the books destroyed?"–"Miss Lisbeth know best about that."–"Did any escape?" were any saved back?"–"She know best about that."

After Alice testified that she saw Lizzie pulling a blue dress out of the coal closet that Sunday morning, Mr. Moody asked me if we usually kept our ragbag there. The question was excluded. I could easily have answered: no, we kept the ragbag in the pantry, for cleaning cloths and such. Lizzie probably got the dress out and tossed it into the coal closet, next to the stove, while she made a fire. Mr. Moody asked why Lizzie was burning the dress at all if we kept a ragbag. Excluded. I could have said: well, we didn't save every scrap! He asked if Lizzie usually disposed of old clothes by burning them in sweltering August heat. Excluded.

When I saw her there by the stove I didn't really think of *how* she was disposing of the dress, only of the fact that she was *doing* it, and that it might look suspicious. I might very well have said, "I wouldn't do that if I were you!" And yet I knew she had a blue-cotton dress she had been planning to throw away. She was holding the dress so that the paint-stains didn't show, but it was the same one.

For all I knew it had been in the ragbag for weeks! I could just as easily have said, "Yes, why don't you?"

Under siege, as it were, we pulled the blinds and spoke to no one but each other.

"Where are the books? Have they been destroyed?"

"You needn't worry. I paid well."

"It was the worst thing you have done!"

"Yes—to the hypocritical."

"How could the book have hurt you? It could only show your innocence."

"Oh," she said with an ugly smile, "people are no longer interested in that—if they ever were."

"Then this latest act will give them comfort."

"This *latest* act!" she mocked.

"Why do you torture yourself?"

"Why have you stopped sitting on the porch in the evening?"

I did not answer. She recited coldly:

> "Lizzie Borden took an axe,
> Gave her mother forty whacks,
> When she saw what she had done,
> She gave her father forty-one."

I shuddered. "You have heard the singing from the shrubbery," she said with her peculiar relish. "You have heard the taunts."

"Urchins—from under the hill."

"All the hill listens."

"What has this to do with the book!" I cried.

Her eyes had gone pale. "The book—why, if they want that, they must come to me."—"You saved copies then?"—"They must admit they are fascinated..."

Over and over every point! Twelve years of it! What she would not tolerate from outsiders, she required of me: "Do you think Father really planned to give Swansea to her?'

"I do not know."

"He knew how much it meant to us—all the summers we spent there, from childhood on—until she came along and spoiled it."

"I should be surprised if he made the same mistake twice. He had already seen the consequences of one such secret transaction."

"If you *had* known, though, or even suspected, you'd have told me, wouldn't you? You wouldn't let me learn by accident?"

I would not answer. About two weeks before the murders I had heard some such rumor, but I was preparing to leave for the seaside and had no desire to upset her with anything so vague.

Either then or later (for she could not be satisfied) she said: "Suppose I had discovered such a plot—overheard them discussing it, say—if I had come to you, what would yuou have done?"

"Done?"

"Or suggested."

"I would have said what I said before: we can do nothing."

"Nothing—" she echoed restlessly.

"I mean, we could not undo Father's decision."

"We could have shown our displeasure again—more strongly! We could have moved away, left them—left *her*, with her everlasting gorging and grasping!"

"I had no wish to leave Father."

"He had drived the wedge."

I did not blame him. He could not have forseen her unsuitability."

"But dwelling with such an impasse! Surely there were times when youf elt you could bear it no longer!"

"I was more content than then I am now."

Yes, I said to the young man from the *Journal*, the lack of motive is puzzling, but no one who really knew Lizzie would believe that money or property could be *her* notive if she were guilty. She was not acquisitive–that is a vulgar error.

How well I remember Mr. Moody's question after he had listened to an explanation of her break with Mrs. Borden.

"A house put in her name? Is that all? There was no more to it than that?"

Even he detected that property was insufficient as an explanation...

Perhaps it was unjust that a kind of obsession with Lizzie grew up right alongside the isolation of her. Perhaps she could not have prevented it. But from the day of her acquittal she adamantly refused to reassure her admirers. Questions they had been willing to suspend during her ordeal they must be willing to suspend forever. Of that, at least, she left them in no doubt. Not that anyone ever challenged her directly, she said irritably.

"Well, they are friends, not lawyers. They are waiting until you are ready."

"Ready? I should like to know one topic upon which you think I ought to set their minds at rest."

I had one on the tip of my tongue but suppressed it: "No, that is for you to decide."

And so the questions remained. "Where was your sister during the murders?" Thirty years later! The very question I had bitten back! The first one I asked when I returned from the seaside!

"Her whereabouts were established at the trial," I said to the reporter. I could still see Mr. Moody exhibiting his plan of the house and yard. The front door was locked–the intruder had to come in the back–pass to the front–go upstairs to kill Mrs. Borden–come down to kill Father–escape out the back again– all without being seen or heard by either Lizzie or Bridget. And between the two deaths, an hour and a half gone by...

He traced Bridget's movements with a pointer: working outside when Mrs. Borden died–taking a nap in her room in the garret when Father died. But where was Lizzie when Mrs. Borden died? Ironing in the kitchen? How did the murderer manage to slip past her? Somewhere else on the ground floor? How did he muffle the crash of a two-hundred-pound body overhead? Why did she hear no cries, no sounds of struggle?

Where did the murderer hide during that hour and a half before Father came home and lay down for a nap? And where was Lizzie when the second hacking to death took place? I could still hear Mr. Moody's relentless mockery of the defense: "Eating a pear–in the loft of the barn!–where she had gone to find a piece of screenwire!–in a heavy silk dress!–in one-hundred-degree heat!"

"There were contradictions at the trial," said the reporter. "I mean, did she ever explain to *your* satisfaction where she was?"

"My satisfaction was not the question."

The dress was immaculate when the police arrived. No blood on the hem, no dust from the loft...

She had a telephone installed at "Maplecroft." It was of little use to her and proved a trap to me. She had begun to take short trips out of town, staying for a day, sometimes overnight, in Boston or Providence...On these occasions I would sometimes ring up Miss Jubb and invite her to bring her work over. One day while we were cozily occupied in my room, crocheting doilies for a church bazaar, Lizzie returned unexpectedly from Providence. I heard her speaking to the maid. I rose without haste and went to the head of the stairs. She had already started up. I remember her fur cape and her hat with the iridescent birds-wings. Her muff, oddly enough, was stuffed into her reticule.

"Miss Jubb is here, Lizzie," I said firmly. "Won't you come say hello?' "

She brushed past me–she seemed distracted, breathless: "In a moment..."

"She is taking off her things," I told Miss Jubb, but my face betrayed me. She started to put away her work: "perhaps she does not feel well..."

At that moment Lizzie swept into the room–color high–eyes luminous–both hands extended.

"Dear Mis Jubb, how very nice to see you! I've been hoping you'd call!" For the next five minutes she chattered torrentially. Miss Jubb sent me so many gratified glances that I was forced to bend my eyes upon my crocheting. "You came back early. Did you finish all your shopping?' "

"Oh, yes–or rather, no. After Tilden's I let the rest go."

"Tilden's have such lovely things," sighed Miss Jubb, who could not afford any of them.

"Shall I show you what I bought there?' cried Lizzie. She hurried out and returned with two porcelain paintings. One was called "Love's Dream," the other "Love's Awakening." Miss Jubb went into raptures over them. Lizzie said effusively: "I meant them for my wall but now I have a different plan. One will be yours, the other Emma's, as a reminder to you of your friendship. You shall not refuse me!"

Miss Jubb burst into tears. For some time she had been hinting that I kept her away from Lizzie unnecessarily. I was unpleasantly reminded of other times when Lizzie pressed gifts on people, but, reproaching myself, I said that if Miss Jubb would accept her porcelain, I would accept mine. Blushing, she chose "Love's Dream" as more appropriate for herself. Lizzie laughed heartily: "Well, Emma, appropriate or not, that leaves 'Love's Awakening' to you!"

Not that it mattered. Miss Jubb broke hers while fastening it to the wall. Too embarassed to say anything, even to me, she made a trip to Providence to have it repaired. At Tilden's the manager was summoned. When had she purchased this painting? "It was a gift." From whom? "Why, Lizzie Borden..." Then she learned that the two porcelains had disappeared, unpaid-for, on the day of Lizzie's shopping trip.

Fall River woke to the headline "Lizze Borden Again!"

Tilden's sent a detective with a warrant. Lizzie talked agitatedly with him, then came upstairs to me and said—so great was her confusion—"We must call Mr. Jennings right away!"

"An attorney is not necessary," I said. "Tilden's will not prosecute you if you go talk the matter over with them. You have been a good customer for many years."

"They have no grounds!" she began, then broke off. In a moment she said, "Well, then, I shall go to Providence. I couldn't have taken the paintings without paying for them, but who will believe me?"

"Are you certain you have no receipt?"

"Yes. I seldom pay cash at Tilden's—I forgot all about a receipt."

"The clerk will have a record, a duplicate."

No," she said, staring, "if anything it was the clerk who perpetrated this fraud—by slipping the paintings into my reticule."

"But, Lizzie, you remember paying for them!"

"I mean, he slipped them in to make me overlook the receipt."

He slipped them inside your muff, I thought, suddenly weary of trying to believe her.

Her jaw had mottled slightly: "And Miss Jubb played right into his hands."

"Miss Jubb is not to blame," I said angrily. "Miss Jubb has been greatly mortified!"

"I'm only saying that she gave the clerk his chance to raise a hue-and-cry against me."

"He would have done that the first day," I said with a cruelty I could not control, "if all he wanted was to have his name linked with that of Lizzie Borden."

She fell silent for a moment. "You're not coming with me, then? I must settle with Tilden's alone?"

"The purchase was yours alone."

"When I come back," she said, "the paintings will still be yours and Miss Jubb's."

As soon as she left the house I found a hammer–I broke "Love's Awakening" to bits.

In the spring before that terrible August, Father went out to the stable with a hatchet. Lizzie's pigeons had been attracting mischievous boys. Tools–feed–pieces of harness had been disappearing. To discourage marauders, Father beheaded the pigeons.

I began to think of leaving her.

The nurse asked today if there was anyone I wanted to get in touch with–just for company, she said, now that the doctor has decided I must not leave the hospital–"not for a while."

I said there was no one but asked to see the doctor as soon as he was free. I knew what her question really meant.

And yet I procrastinated–for I knew that if I ever left Fall River I would not come back. Lizzie could not stay away. Her trips became more frequent, more prolonged–not only Boston and Providence but New York–Philadelphia–Washington. But after a week, or two weeks, or a month away, she would return–Lizzie Borden would be seen again in Fall River.

Playbills showed how she occupied herself when her shopping was done. She did not discuss this new interest with me–I learned about her friendship with Nance O'Neil from the newspaper—inexorably "Lizzie Borden Again" arrived.

A lawsuit against Miss O'Neil would have been news in any case, a popular actress sued by her manager to recover advances and loans. But add that Lizzie Borden appeared every day in court as her champion—that Lizzie Borden hired the Lawyer who was defending her—that Lizzie Borden had given her the little gold watch that was pinned to her bosom!

She came home during a recess in the case. I had not seen her for a month. She had been at a resort hotel near Boston. According to the newspapers, she had met Miss O'Neil there, taking refuge from the cupidity of her manager. She warned me in provocative words not to tamper with Miss O'Neil's portrait of herself as a woman wronged, misunderstood, persecuted—just the kind of woman, in effect, that she was best known for portraying on the stage. "She is a gifted and sadly maligned young woman. The manager has used her ruthlessly. I will not desert her!"

"I have not suggested that you should. I know nothing about her, the case, or your friendship—except what anyone can know."

She opened and shut her fan.

"As for the newspapers, she is not ashamed to have her name linked with Lizzie Borden's."

"To which of you is that a compliment?"

"When we first met she knew me by the name I use at hotels for the sake of privacy. I merely presented myself as an admirer, someone who had seen all her plays. Later I had to tell her that the person who wished to befriend her was not Lisabeth Andrews but Lizzie Borden. She said, 'But, my dear, I've known that all along! It makes no difference to me.'"

I said nothing. She toyed with her fan. "The remark doesn't dispose you in her favor?"

"Why should it? Such professions cost her nothing but you a great deal."

"Oh, *cost!*" she said harshly. Then her tone softened: "Poor Emma! Some things are worth paying for, others aren't. You've never learned the difference."

"I have not had good teachers," I said.

After the suit was settled, Lizzie continued to rescue her from small debts and indulge her taste for trinkets and jewelry.

Miss O'Neil repaid her by introducing her to "artistic" people and consulting her (or pretending to) on personal and professional matters. I accused myself of small-mindedness. I still had Miss Jubb, she had not deserted me—why should I begrudge Lizzie this friendship, sorely in need as she was?

So when she announced that Miss O'Neil's company had been engaged for a performance in Fall River and that she was entertaining them afterward, I said briskly, "Then I'm to meet Miss O'Neil at last!"

"There's time for you to make other plans," she said. "I know you don't approve of artists—"

"I do not know any artists," I interrupted. "If I did I would judge them on individual merits, not as a group."

"Dearest Emma," she said, "I've always been able to count on you..."

I felt a familiar dread...

Caterers, florists, musicians came and went. "Maplecroft" was finally going to serve its function. Only, from my window, there was not a soul to be seen on the street unless someone delivering ice—potted palms—a grand pinao...Not even any children hanging around the front gate in a spirit of anticipation—their mothers had swept them out of sight.

I tried to help—once I went downstairs in time to collide with a delivery of wine. "Oh, don't look so stricken, Emma! It's champagne, not gin!" I thought of all those years she'd worked for the Temperance Union—how they had help prayer meetings for her during the trial. She read my mind. "Don't worry, I'm not going to break my pledge. Only my guests aren't used to lemonade and iced tea!"

Long before the guests arrived, I had decided to keep to my room. Anything, I thought, would be better than appearing with my feelings on my sleeve. I had prepared an excuse I hoped would placate Lizzie. I awaited her knock momentarily. But only the sounds of the party increasingly assaulted my door.

Shortly before eleven I crept down the back stairs and phoned Miss Jubb. She could hear the din in the background—the music, the strident laughter, the crashing of glass: "I'll be waiting in a carriage down the block."

I hurriedly began to pack an overnight bag, but now that I

hoped to escape undetected there came a knock. I opened the door on Nance O'Neil.

She glided in, casting a glance all about as if to say, "What a charming room!"–then, turning, clasped her hands entreatingly: "It is Emma, isn't it? I've so wanted to meet you! I'm naughty to force myself on you this way, but Lisbeth told me the beautiful thing you said about artists–I knew you wouldn't turn me away!"

She was extraordinarily pretty–I could understand Lizzie's infatuation with her–that delicacy of face and figure did not run in the Borden family. But her effusiveness left me ill-at-ease. Her eyes fell on my traveling bag: "You're taking a trip? Lisbeth didn't say why you hadn't come down.

"Yes–I'm sorry I cannot spend time with you."

"But you're not leaving tonight surely!" she cried. 'Won't you come downstairs for a while? Lisbeth would be so pleased–she's very proud of you!"

"No, I cannot. I am sorry she has sent you on a futile errand."

"No, no, no! I came of my own free will! Oh, I'm too impulsive–it's my greatest fault–you do think me naughty!" Here she pouted charmingly.

"You have not been naughty," I replied, "only misused. You may tell my sister I said so."

She ceased magically to convey childlike sincerity–her bearing and expression shed an atmosphere of injured pride and reproachful forgiveness. I returned to my packing, not wanting to furnish her with further opportunities to display her art.

Five minutes later I stood at the door with my bag. I turned out the light and listened. Just as I was ready to slip out, I heard voices hurrying along the hall–then a sharp rapping–then the door was flung open. I had just time to shrink into the darkness behind it.

"She's not here," Lizzie said.

"Her suitcase was on the bed..." A shaft of light fell where it had been.

"It's gone–she's gone."

"Perhaps you can overtake her," Miss O'Neil murmured plaintively.

"You don't know her," Lizzie said in a hoarse voice. She closed the door but they did not move away. "I wonder what you said to precipitate her flight?"

"I?" Miss O'Neill fairly shrieked. "I said nothing! Her flight, if that's what it was, was already planned!"

"She would never have left at this time of night–she dreads scandal too much."

"Perhaps *you* are the one who doesn't know her," Miss O'Neil unwisely remarked.

"She is my sister!" Lizzie said harshly.

"But you've often said how different you are."

"We're two sides of the same coin."

"Don't let's stand her arguing," Miss O'Neil said placatingly. "She'll come back."

"Is that what you want?" Lizzie asked in a strange tone.

"Why, what do you mean?"

"It isn't what I want–I don't want her to come back."

"Well, then, neither do I!"

"I thought not," Lizzie said with satisfaction.

"I don't know what you're trying to prove," Miss O'Neil said in a disturbed voice. "I assure you I did nothing to cause her to leave–I came to her at your request...She said you had misused me," she ended with some heat. "I'm beginning to think she was right!"

Then Lizzie became placating: "I haven't misused you– Emma spoke out of jealousy–because I feel closer to you than I ever did to her–and because you understand me better."

"I don't like that kind of jealousy, Lizzie. You must go after her and explain. Why, what is the matter?"

"You called me *Lizzie*."

"Did I? Well, talking to your sister–hearing her–you know how I simply absorb things–"

"It is not my name. But perhaps there are those who make jokes about it in private," Lizzie said grimly.

Poor Miss O'Neil! "This is beside the point! We were talking about your sister!"

"I cannot go after Emma, I cannot bring her back. She left me long before tonight. I've lived with her door locked against me twelve years. I'll hardly know she's gone."

"Don't talk about it, Lisbeth dear!"

"No, I won't burden you," said Lizzie. "And yet–I can't help feeling that somehow you took my side when you were with her–perhaps not even knowing it."

Miss O'Neil's voice, already at a distance, faded rapidly: "Come now! quickly! No, I won't listen to any more..."

After the scandal at Tyngsboro, she apparently did not. Lizzie was sadly in error if she imagined that her connection with drunkenness and misconduct would go unnoticed simply because it did not occur in Fall River but in a house she rented for a week somewhere else. Miss Jubb learned a great deal more that I would allow her to tell me—"If you are fascinated with her," I said snappishly, "you must not use me as an excuse." There need not even have been the bitter climactic quarrel that Miss Jubb got wind of. Those butterfly wings could not in any case have supported the burden of Lizzie Borden for long.

The doctor came. I said, "I want my body taken to Fall River—we have a family plot in Oak Grove cemetery."

"I've already promised to see to that, Miss Borden, and your to her requests will be honored, too."

His choice of words roused my attention: "I have asked before?"—"Yes."—"And made other requests?"—"Yes, but when you weren't quite yourself perhaps."—"What did I say?"—"You asked to be buried the same way your sister was."—"That is correct, I do not want a ceremony."—"I mean, you asked to buried at night."—"Did I?"—"You asked for Negro pallbearers only..."

I fell to thinking. "Well, I will go halfway with you," I said. "I don't mind the Negro pallbearers but I don't want the other part."

"I'm not surprised," she said. "Do you remember the day you changed rooms with Alice Russell? It was Saturday, after the police told us not to leave the house."

"You asked if someone in the house was suspected—you demanded to know who it was!"

"That night you asked Alice to sleep in your room. You took the one she'd been using. Father's and Mrs. Borden's. You put their lock and bolt between us. We never again had rooms opening freely into each other."

"Yes, I knew what you meant, even if poor Miss O'Neil did not."

"You have given me away, Emma."

"If you changed your dress you must say so."

"I will never give in."

"I have no reason to wish to be buried at night!"

"Now that's more like it." The doctor's voice startled me. "Let's have less talk about dying and more about getting well. You have a long time to live!"

Well, that is not true. In the very course of nature I cannot live *much* longer. If I die quite soon, though—say within seven days of your death, or ten days, some such noticeable number— remember, I am seventy-seven!—it will be coincidence! I hope you will not try to make any more of it than that.

THE CHALK LINE
Ryerson Johnson

For a while the children stood quietly on the granite slope be-
hind the chalk line, watching the fast tidewater in its perpetual
nudging of the rockweed. The water streamed the weed out in a
brown fringe. As though trying to escape from the anchoring
rock, the coarse tentacles writhed and twined...

Scalped smooth by glaciers in the last ice age, the grey granite
sloped gently down to Fundy tidewater. The slope was the
only thing gentle around here. Frigid sea water in the tidal
current swept past the rock, streaming out the seaweed and
tilting a bell buoy in the channel.

The boy on the sloping rock stared hard at that deep swirl of
water. "Is he watching?"

"Yes."

"Good. Don't ever let him know we're watching *him*, Lynn."

"You don't have to tell me."

The boy answered his sister with a quick move and a deliberate push with both hands. She slipped on the smooth rock
and fell. Arms flailing, shoes scraping, she slid down the granite slope into the fast-moving water.

It was the same everywhere along this part of the Maine
coast. Near the low-tide line, dingy yellow seaweed grew in
profusion—rooted firmly into the rock. So the girl did not remain long in the icy water. Her spread fingers raked into the
seaweed and held on as the tidewater streamed her legs out.
Quickly then, she reached for a fingerhold in a crack in the
sloping granite and pulled herself out.

Laughing, back up on top of the rock, her jeans and shirt
dripping water, she made a rowdy grab for her brother.

"Cut it, Lynn! Quit! You're getting me wet."

"I'm getting *you* wet! *I* can't get any wetter–I'm going in again."

"Let's both at the same time. I'll push you and you push me."

They pushed and pulled at each other. Both fell on the sloping rock and slid with a splash into the water. Their hands grabbed the waving rockweed and held on. They grinned at each other and kicked their feet derisively at the fast water trying to pull them away.

The girl put her face close to her brother's ear. "Can you see? Is he still watching?"

The boy moved his head to give his eyes a quick sweep of the spruce underbrush crowding the shore and on to the house beyond. "I think so," he said conspiratorially.

"Ugh, it's cold! Give me a push out, then I'll pull you up."

From the direction of the house, a woman's frantic screaming sounded. Running feet crunched the beach gravel on the path that led between spruces to the shore. A woman in obvious anguish burst into close view. She stopped at the place where the rock sloped down.

Seeing them, she shouted in a panic, "Come here! This minute! Do you hear? How often must I tell you?"

"Aw, Mom–"

"You could be drowned! This is some of the most dangerous water on the whole Maine coast!"

"Gee, Mom–we know how to swim."

"No one can swim in these waters!" Her frightened eyes lifted to take in the tidal current sucking past offshore ledges. In the near distance, a herring boat made slow progress, butting through the tide. "This water's too fast and too cold. Nobody can live in it. You know that."

They did know it. Most of the children who lived here the year round never learned to swim. The water was too cold. When they grew up and went with their fathers to work the herring or the lobster boats, there was this constant occupational hazard. If they fell off a boat, that was the end of it. Their heavy clothing, the swift currents working in and out between islands and ledges, and the cold water, varying only a few degrees summer and winter, accomplished its deadly work within minutes. It happened to a few every summer.

He appeared so silently, not a smidgen of sound in the

gravel under his soft-soled shoes. The children looked up and there he was in his designer slacks and English tweed jacket. A young man—younger than their mother—with a face dark, handsome, brooding. Charming when he smiled. His black hair lay in a controlled wave across his forehead. He was standing now beside their mother, a suggestion of possessiveness in his manner. It was a posture that was never wholly absent from him, and that translated eloquently to the children.

Their mother's hand reached out for his, but her attention remained on them. "You run in and get some dry clothes on." But as they started dutifully along the path to the house, she called them back and turned, distraught, to the young man. "Mark—that piece of carpenter's chalk you had yesterday when we were hanging the pictures, do you have it?"

Mark's hand dug into a jacket pocket. He brought out a piece of chalk and handed it to her.

"Thank you, dear."

The children took note of her words and tone; she was always trying to please him. While they watched, she bent and backed along, drawing a firm chalk line across the rock where the slope began to steepen. Then she straightened and fixed her stare on the children. "Don't go beyond this chalk line ever again. Not ever! Now, go ahead and get out of those wet clothes."

On the way along the landscaped path where flowering impatiens grew in colorful profusion between the evergreens, the girl stopped and looked back, then turned and ran with her brother to the house.

Their mother locked fingers with the young man as she stood staring down at the yellow rockweed roiling in the current. With an involuntary shudder, she pressed in against him. "I'll never get used to these black waters, Mark. I lived too long in Indiana, I guess. There the water is placid and cows stand in it up to their knees. But my husband was born here—"

"I understand." In a consoling gesture, he tightened his arm around her.

"Before he died, I tried to like it here for his sake. I did try! But I worry about the children every minute. I think this is the last summer I'll open the house."

Anchored into his own thoughts, he wasn't listening. "Your

children don't like me, Connie."

She nodded, aggrieved. "I don't know what's gotten into them this summer. They seemed bedeviled."

With the insinuating gentleness of the practiced lover, his arms went around her, holding her against him closely. She resisted feebly at first, an instinctive reaction, then melted into him, giving herself fully to his embrace. His mouth lowered to hers. She returned his kisses with an intensity that left her weak, then they broke apart and, arms around each other, walked slowly to the house. On the garden path, under the shadows of the evergreens just before emerging onto the open lawn, they paused.

"Change your mind, Connie."

She looked at him searchingly. Lithe, and with clear eyes and skin, she came across an easy ten years younger than she was. She pushed at her hair, as abundant if not as blonde as when she was twenty. "I do live for my children. You're right about that."

"But you're a person, too. You have yourself to think of."

"I only know," she said miserably, "I could never marry if it made my children unhappy."

"But I *like* children, Connie. I particularly *like* your children—they're so much a part of *you*. I watch them sometimes when they don't know, trying to understand them, trying to think of ways to reach them. Next to wanting you, I want them to return my affection—"

"I know. And you'll win them over. As you did me. Be patient."

"But patience isn't in me, Connie. I love you. I want to marry you now."

Her fingers touched his lips. "A little while longer, Mark." Her voice took on a pleading tone. "Please."

"I hate to wait. I never could stand waiting. And one more day without you is a year—"

The screen door slammed. The children ran across the porch, took the steps in two jumps, and came sprinting across the lawn. As with everything else here, the lawn was poodle-clipped to perfection, although it showed brown in spots because of the dearth of rain this summer. They stopped in front of their mother, dry, clean, and cool, ignoring Mark.

"Can we go on a lobster picnic today, Mom?" the boy

wanted to know.

The girl danced around her. "Can we? Can we?"

Mark started away. "See you later, Connie." To the children he made a small flat-out wave of his hand and smiled.

"Mind your mother, Bobby–Lynn. Don't go near the water."

They watched him in his easy-flowing walk across the faded grass to the house.

Bobby said, "He wants to marry you, doesn't he, Mom?"

"Yes," Lynn said, "he does, doesn't he?"

"Are you going to, Mom? Daddy wouldn't want you to."

"And he hates us," Lynn said. "He hates us to death. He's always watching to see what he can do to hurt us."

"And he'll hurt you, too, Mom–he's just after your money."

Shocked, their mother said, "What a thing to say! I don't know what's possessing you two this summer."

"It's true," Bobby said. "I read it in a book. When a younger man marries an older woman, it's for her money. And if he can't get it by marrying her, sometimes he gets it by killing her for the insurance. Did he ask about your insurance, Mom?"

She was aware this had been building up, but she hadn't been aware of the intensity of their feelings. "Stop it," she said sharply.

"Anyone could see it except a woman blinded by love," Bobby pressed on. "And the way he's always watching us, I can tell he's thinking how to kill us because we're in the way of his marrying you for your money. But we're not afraid of him. We could kill him before he could kill us." He was speaking in a fevered way, feeding on his own excitement, building up the story and not giving his stunned mother a chance to get a word in. "Oh, yes, we could kill him easy, so he'd better watch out. Easy because he's like you–he's afraid of the ocean. But we're not. We're like Daddy. We're friends of the ocean. We could get it to kill him for us and nobody would ever know."

His mother, grasping control now, caught the children to her. "Oh, your poor dears–you babies! You don't know what you're saying."

Later in the morning the children sat on the sloping granite rock just back of the chalk line.

Bobby's bare feet rubbed the line. "He wasn't either a friend of Daddy's."

"No, he wasn't." Lynn cuddled a large cloth doll, one she'd had almost from the first.

"I never heard Daddy even mention him."

"I didn't either."

Bobby's hand reached out, closed on a loose piece of rock. He threw it in the water and, leaning close to Lynn, asked furtively, "You think he's watching us again?"

"I think I heard the bushes crackle."

Bobby threw another rock. "Mom just met him at the party that time."

"Now he lives at our house."

"He'd starve if we didn't feed him."

"He could get a job somewhere—"

"He never will as long as he's got Mom's money to spend." Bobby stood up and moved lazily to one side where there was a small clutter of dried seaweed and driftwood. He picked up a large piece of driftwood and carried it to the chalk line. Being careful to keep his toes behind the line, he heaved the piece of sun-greyed wood into the water. Lynn stood up with her doll and they both watched intently while the tidal current sucked the driftwood into its certain grasp and floated it away.

"Why don't you throw your doll in?" Bobby said.

Lynn hugged the doll possessively. "Are you crazy?"

Bobby grinned, said slyly, "It would prove you're big enough to get along without dolls."

"I don't have to prove it. I know I'm big enough."

"Maybe *you* know it. I don't."

"I don't care if you don't."

"Yes you do."

"Don't!" Frowning, she looked searchingly at the chalk line under her bare feet. "It's too far for me to throw it anyway."

"Then go a little closer."

"Cross the line, you mean?"

"I dare you."

She leaned close to whisper in his ear. "What if he *is* watching? And runs out when I'm close to the water and pushes me in?"

"I'd push him in if he did."

"Big help, after I'm already gone!"

She looked back with a nervous excitement at the evergreen thicket. Something about it seemed scary. There was no air stirring, but under the sun-glare the green spruce needles, some of them browned by the summer's heat, seemed to pulse and breathe. Suddenly, she clutched the doll compulsively and stepped across the line. Step by cautious step, she moved down the sloping rock. At the seaweed edge where the water streamed, she looked back at her brother, then turned to the sea again and threw the doll in. Scurrying back to stand by her brother, they watched the current carry the doll away.

To the surprise of them both, she burst out crying. "Oh, I didn't mean to do it! I don't know why I did it! I want my dolly back!" Her voice was a small, tearful child's; she was a girl holding in abeyance for a moment the process of growing up.

Her brother, feeling guilt pangs, tried to comfort her. "We can get it back, Lynn."

Still crying, "How can we? It's gone!"

"Remember Daddy's secret?"

"What secret?"

"About this place? Anything falling into the water when the tide's going out, like now?"

She stopped crying. "That it washes ashore in Dagget's Cove, you mean?"

"That's it. Daddy tested it with all kinds of things, remember? They float in and out between the ledges, but they always end up at Dagget's Cove, a mile from here. Nobody knows that but Daddy and us."

"All right. Let's go get my doll."

From the house there was the pleasant sound of a bell.

"Lunch time," Bobby said. "We'll do it after, Lynn. Race you to the house."

The children and their mother were already at the table when Mark came in. As he settled into his chair, Lynn swapped a meaningful glance with her brother.

"Mr. Mabrey," she said, "you've got some pine needles sticking to your coat sleeve."

He shrugged. "They won't hurt anything."

Bobby said, "You wouldn't hurt anything, either, would you, Mr. Mabrey?"

Mark stared hard at Bobby. "What do you mean by that?"

"I mean did you used to squash lightning bugs on the back of your hand, and like that?"

"Bobby!" his mother admonished.

"I mean when he was a child," Bobby poured it on.

"To make your hand shine at night, he means," Lynn said to Mark, looking innocent. "Of course, it kills the poor lightning bug."

"That's enough!" their mother said severely. "Oh, why do you talk like that?"

Bobby shrugged elaborately. "Mr. Mabrey looks like somebody we saw on TV the other night, that's all. The man on television did things like that. He—"

"Stop it!" Her face flushed with embarrassment and anger. "Leave the table," she ordered. "You, too, Lynn. This minute. Go!"

They got up and started to leave.

"You can apologize first," she said sharply.

They looked at each other for reinforcement, then said it together, almost as though reciting a sing-song nursery rhyme. "We apologize, Mr. Mabrey."

The children tromped through the house and out the front door.

"Follow me," Bobby said, tight-lipped in the manner of a conspirator in a TV crime show.

"Where to?"

"I'll show you."

"Lynn followed her brother into the house again by a side door and up the stairs and down the hall to Mr. Mabrey's room.

"I've got this idea," Bobby said. "You stand outside the door and watch while I go in and do something."

"Do what?"

"You'll see."

Inside the room, Bobby prowled actively around until he found a fishing pole, dismantled and in its case. He came out with the fishing pole and a sunhat. He looked inside the hat, under the sweatband. He showed Lynn.

"It's got a name there. Afraid somebody'll steal his hat—ha ha."

"Put it on," she whispered.

He put it on. She giggled. "It's too big for you."

"Yeah."

"Wear it anyway. I dare you."

"No. I better not."

"Why?"

"Somebody might see me with it. I don't want anybody to see me with it."

They tiptoed down the stairs.

"Where are we going?" Lynn whispered.

"Dagget's Cove," he whispered back. "But first we'll hide the hat and fishing pole somewhere, and wait for Mom and Mr. Mabrey to finish lunch and get away from the dining room and kitchen."

"Why?"

"It'll take a while for the tide to float your doll to Dagget's Cove. We might be gone all afternoon–"

"I get it. We might get hungry, so we'll raid the fridge before we go."

"Right."

Lynn had a final worry. "Do you think it's all right if we leave him at home alone with mother?"

"I guess so. She's been alone with him before..."

Dagget's Cove was a tiny indentation on a vast and rugged coastline with high rocky sides and an apron of smooth beach gravel running down to tidewater. Fir and spruce made a green smudge at the cliff tops. Except for a dilapidated and long-unused wharf, the place wasn't much changed from when the Passamaquoddy Indians lived there.

Bobby and Lynn turned off the rutted Dagget's Cove road, pushed through a tangle of shore peas and wild gooseberry bushes, and came out on the deserted beach. On their purposeful way to the ocean's edge, they walked across rocks smoothed down to about baseball size by thousands of years of tide and wave action. There was nearly every kind of rock, raked off the whole of eastern Canada and carried here by the same glacier that had smoothed the in-place granite in front of their house.

The children picked their way between random pieces of driftwood and scuffed through windrows of soggy rockweed, marks of previous high tides. Tremendous tides prevailed on this Fundy coast–as much as thirty feet when the moon and the winds were right.

The children reached the water's edge and puddled up and down the beach in the bubbly wavewash. In a pool of matted seaweed, they found what they were looking for. Lynn held her dripping doll at arm's length and picked tentacles of seaweed from it. Salt water ran down and dripped from her elbow. For a long moment she held the soggy doll out and stared at it.

"Huh," she said, "now I've got it, it doesn't seem so much any more."

She let it drop to the sea floor.

Bobby was already trudging toward the wharf. She followed him onto it. The front end of the grey-weathered structure had long since fallen in. Green water lapped at the snaggle-toothed pilings. The children made their cautious way across the rotten flooring until they reached a gap too wide to cross, then dropped down and let their feet swing over the side.

While Lynn watched, Bobby took Mark's hat out of a crumpled supermarket bag he had been carrying. He put the hat upside-down on the wharf and weighted it there with a can of bait he had brought along. He joined the fishing pole, baited the hook, and dropped the line into the green water.

Some time went by, and he caught a flounder. He put the pole carefully down, stood up, and stretched. "Should of known. Nothing but flounders here this time of tide. Mom won't clean flounders, and I sure don't want to. Do you, Lynn?'

She shook her head. "No."

He unhooked the flounder and tossed it over the side. "Let's go home."

"Yes," she said soberly. "We're finished here."

The next day the children were back at their favorite playing place. For a while they stood quietly on the granite slope behind the chalk line, watching the fast tidewater in its perpetual nudging of the rockweed. The water streamed the weed out in a brown fringe. As though trying to escape from the anchoring rock, the coarse tentacles writhed and twined.

The children listened while they watched.

"He's there now," Bobby whispered.

"Yes." Lynn nodded. "Like always."

In a loud voice, Bobby said, "I dare you."

Lynn put one foot across the line and drew it back.

"Ho ho–I can do better than that." Bobby put one foot across and let it stay there.

Lynn moved both feet across and stayed there. "Now what?"

"Go closer."

"Dare me?"

"Dare you."

She moved cautiously down the granite slope, taking tiny steps. Bobby moved along beside her. They kept on until they reached the water's edge, where they crouched down, dabbling their hands in the streaming rockweed.

They heard his feet lightly scuffing the granite in his approach before they heard his voice. He stopped disarmingly behind the chalk line. "Didn't your mother tell you not to go across this line?"

Without looking back, Bobby said, "Did you hear a funny voice, Lynn–like somebody talking?"

"Yes. It *was* a funny voice, wasn't it? Not quite human."

Mark moved across the line then, slowly, silently. Still, the children didn't look around. He moved close and crouched directly behind them. He swiveled his head in a furtive glance in all directions, then his hands moved suddenly out in a hard push against the children, one had to each child, extending himself in the effort to where he was himself almost off balance.

He accomplished his intent. Both children fell forward into the water.

The children also accomplished their intent. Although they hadn't looked around, they had been ready for him. As they fell, they reached back to take a fierce grip on his barely balanced legs–Bobby clutching one and Lynn the other. He plunged into the water with them, a hard, windmilling fall. Gripped by the icy current, he was swept away.

The children held to the rockweed and climbed back, dripping, to shore.

"He tried to kill us!" Bobby said starkly.

"Yes, he did," Lynn said.

Later, at Dagget's Cove, a man's drowned body was discovered. Two of the locals, scrounging the beach for wrinkles–a barnaclelike shellfish–discovered it. On the ancient wharf they found a fishing pole and a sunhat.

"Looks like he was fishin' off the wharf an' fell in."

The other beachcomber, examining the hat, said, "Mark Mabrey–that's what it says in the hat." He looked up. "That's that young fella visitin' out to the Thornboro place, ain't it? You know–widder woman comes here summers with the two kids?"

After the informing call, the children's mother turned in shock from the phone.

The children did their best to comfort her.

"Poor Mr. Mabrey–"

"We'll be real good, Mom, and not do anything to bother you–"

"Or worry you about anything–"

"Like playing on the rock."

"It *is* dangerous playing there, Mom."

"We won't play there any more."

A TASTY TIDBIT
Janwillem van de Wetering

"All rules need to be broken at times," Victor Verburg told the Dutch journalist who was interviewing him at the estate on the coast of Maine where Verburg lived with his wife–a calm, beautiful woman he met in South America. Verburg himself was also Dutch, "a lean, tall man... a scholarly rustic with kind brown eyes and a scraggly moustache."

As a journalist, stationed in my home country, the Netherlands, where I work for a magazine, I often have to travel to the States. My last assignment, some months ago now, was the usual assortment of very different fish–a religious society in the deep South supposedly making use of deadly snakes (whoever enjoys true enlightenment doesn't get bitten), a corrupt senator willing to grant an interview, A Dutch professor who explained biological computers in his New York laboratory, and a Dutch writer who lived high up on the East Coast.

One shouldn't expect too much from shallow articles illustrated with glossy photographs–at the very best they may distract patients in dentists' waiting rooms–so if I say the results were disappointing, I only mean the final results. What I really experience is worth the trouble. But I can never express my true feelings, which leads to continuous frustration.

Those idiots with their copperheads and rattlesnakes, for instance. What a marvelous show they put on, complete with a true black necromancer, jungle drums, nude young female meditators–how beautiful. And the slimy senator, that sympathetic parasite. And the delicious old know-it-all in New York who really thinks he is *growing* computers–the multicolored interconnected worms he showed me through his electronic microscope are still in my dreams. Each interview would supply more than enough material for a novel, but I'm only a piecemeal writer, not a true author—like the fourth contact I made on that American trip, the Netherlands-born "thriller" writer, Victor Verburg.

I found him available, via a telephone call to his estate on the Maine coast, and he was kind enough to pick me up at the airport. A lean, tall man with only a touch of bulge above the belt, a scholarly rustic with kind brown eyes and a scraggly moustache, affecting a modest attitude, although he is well known—or, rather, he was. The reading public forgets quickly. Which was the reason for looking him up—he hasn't been published for a while now.

"Why don't you write any more, Victor?" I asked in the car. (He puts us on a first-name basis right away.)

"Well—" he had a pleasant, hoarse voice "—I have other interests these days."

He explained his recent activities, while the car—a long low convertible that gave me the feeling of riding on whipped cream—slid through a freshly green landscape. He said he had asked himself, once he was well established on the international market, whether he should go on. The motivation of money is limited; after a certain amount one has all that is needed. He was spending his time now on boating and study, and in his home I found a respectable library on subjects ranging from the technical origin of life through pure abstract philosophy.

His home, a large wooden structure on a low hill with a view of the sea, was surrounded by balconies and verandas, all at the center of gardens flowing toward the sea—wavy fields carrying a crop of silver-colored plants. His wife, Victor told me, was an authority on herbs. She wasn't around—it seemed she traveled a lot, searching for rare flora.

I stayed a few days. American distances are too enormous to allow for arriving and leaving on the same day, and Verburg was a pefect host. He was a gourmet cook himself but also knew all the good eating places in the neighborhood. He poured tasty but strong drinks and would talk at length but also knew how to be quiet. We went for walks and the second day he took me out in his motorboat.

The coast there consists of bays and peninsulas. My own hobby is scuba diving and Victor owned a number of complete sets of equipment. Together we dived near some large rocks where a herd of seals was sunning itself. Victor seemed to know some of them well and several young males welcomed us and accompanied us on our journey.

It took a while to get used to the rather muddy water, but I soon began to see mysteriously waving reeds, flashing bodies of cod and mackerel, brilliant jellyfish pumping themselves forward in their bizarre manner, and the subtle sepia colors of the bay's irregular bottom. We swam further and further, exploring large caves.

Then suddenly the mood changed. I didn't understand my sudden fear. The veiled light hadn't changed. Plants and fish continued their ballet. Lobsters waved their antennae and claws. But I felt threatened and seemed to be listening to the somber music of demons playing the double bass and hitting kettle drums with wrapped sticks. I couldn't see Victor but two of the seals were with me, flapping their short forepaws nervously. We had just reached another cave, larger and deeper than the others. Rocks covered with algae were set around the entrance and I thought I saw the white glistening of an enormous smooth body inside. I started inside but the seals got in my way and pushed me back.

The oxygen in my cylinders was getting low and so I floated up. Victor was waiting for me. He smiled at me from the boat and helped me aboard.

I told him about the cave and the seals' strange behavior. He nodded. "Yes, I didn't know we had strayed this far. A shark lives in there."

"I didn't think sharks would bother us in such cold waters."

"You're right," Victor said, "sharks are okay up here, but they still lust after flesh and the great white shark is the most dangerous of the lot. He won't hurt you, but he may forget himself. And this particular fellow is an especially large example of the species."

"The two of you have met?" I asked.

He started his almost soundless engine and the small boat lifted its slender bow and began to chop at the little waves, picking up speed until we planed effortlessly on the smooth surface of the bay, hardly disturbed by a soft breeze. The freshly foaming wake stretched far behind us.

"The shark and I are well acquainted," Victor told me. "He's a true giant, some thirty feet long, with wicked teeth in his evil head. But he isn't a bad chap once you get to know him. He must be quite old. I think he has retired in the cave. I never seem him near the other shore of the bay, so he must be living on whatever happens to stray within his reach here."

I forgot the shark and that evening on Victor's veranda we awaited the arrival of a full moon while sipping cognac and smoking cigars. The temperature had dropped and Victor lit the pile of debris we had gathered that morning. The largest part of his estate is covered by a forest of pines and firs and he collects the dead wood and branches so that the carpet of reddish needles may remain undisturbed.

We watched the flames that made the cognac in our glasses sparkle and I remembered that I should be asking questions. "Don't you mind losing your following?" I said.

Verburg's was an unusual career., He lived on all the continents during the early part of his life, buying and selling irregular goods. Later on, he owned his own firm in Amsterdam but migrated to America when his books began to sell. He only wrote for some seven years, but his work was well accepted and his fame spread quickly. Some years ago he was interviewed regularly, spoke on talk shows on both sides of the Atlantic, had his own column in several newspapers, and published short stories in the better magazines. Then it all came to an end.

Victor raised his glass and laughed. The light from the bonfire made his silhouette glow. "Fame? What will that do for me? Writing was a pleasurable pastime and the profit still supports me, but I've reached the last part of my life. Isn't it time to spend my mature years on something more worthwhile? I'm studying at the local university, I observe whatever interests me. Lately I've been having a good time attempting to comprehend Einstein's ideas on relativity. The universe is fascinating, even in the dark corner that is reserved for us. Having a following distracts me from my curiosity. I don't want to waste any more time courting applause."

"Do you know a lot of people here?" I asked.

He shook his head. "And I don't want to. It's not hard to make friends here, but once you do, they gobble you up. I prefer to be a hermit."

"Am I the exception?"

He drained his glass and the silence crept back between us. His large brown eyes avoided mine. "All rules need to be broken at times, and the prospect of a visitor from my own country–I am homesick maybe." He smiled as if he wanted to excuse a weakness.

I relaxed and Verburg seemed to, too. The glasses filled themselves again, the pile burned brightly, and the moon floated majestically above bay and woods.

"Fame," Victor said, pulling his chair closer to mine, "is a nuisance, especially when it attacks you through female seduction. When a man gets older, he likes to feel he's still in it." He took a long swallow from his drink. "Some years ago there was a girl here–"

The information reaching me was unsuitable for the chatty level of my magazine's articles, but I kept quiet and listened.

"My wife was ajourneying again," Victor said. "She does have to go after her plants, and–"

I had looked through the photo album in his study and seen pictures of his wife. A most beautiful woman–slender, calm, exotic. Victor said he had met Eleia in South America. She was still on this side of middle age, a handsome woman, looking a little like Raquel Welch but somewhat darker, and with luminous eyes.

"Eleia was on a trip," Victor said, "and a girl telephoned me, a girl from the Netherlands with a dear voice. She said she had read everything that I ever wrote, was completely captured by the content and style of my work, and–well, you know that sort of approach. The most welcome type of fan mail, but alive and attainable. She was staying close by, on one of the islands here." He pointed. "I can reach it within an hour by boat. You can see the island if you stand on the roof. The girl was by herself, had to caretake somebody' house, didn't know what to do with herself, found my name in the telephone book, decided to call me, and hoped she wasn't disturbing me."

"An open invitation?" I asked.

"I didn't respond," Victor said. "I'm not that crazy. Eleia is rather jealous. To invite a young female here when she was away, wouldn't that be asking for trouble?"

"You went to fetch her."

Victor sighed, "How weak is man–how strong his desire. Not that I intended to, of course, I was just going for a little trip, as I so often do, and happened to get close to the island. And then felt like going even closer, to see if the kelp was doing well near the shore–"

"And there she was, displaying her lovely form on a rock."

"How do you know?" Victor asked.

I smiled.

"Indeed, on a rock. Such a lovely girl. Some twenty-three years old, exactly the right age. I allowed the boat to nose close to her and she never hesitated, she jumped abroad."

"She recognized you? Ah, your photograph is on your books."

"Yes, but she seemed surprised all the same. She kept saying I looked so young."

"And so you do," I said. "The life here must agree with you."

"The girl was flattering me, kept babbling about my virile good looks, saying she would never have thought of telephoning me if she'd known how much I attracted her."

I grinned.

"Yes, you can laugh. Little mistakes go a long way. My last published story appeared in an anthology gathered by a disorganized genius. Each story showed the birth year of the author and in my case he was ten years out, so the girl thought I was in my sixties."

"Poor little thing."

"Smart little thing," Victor said, "with an excellent act. I ate the apple and headed for home."

"Some sexual activity?"

"After the walk across the estate, we were at each other and never stopped. She was like an unmeasurable pit and I kept falling into her without ever reaching bottom. Whatever she gave me seemed only a beginning.

"A tasty tidbit." I grinned and held up my glass. The bottle was empty and Victor staggered into the house. We had a good go at the second bottle while he told all.

The affair was idyllic. Holding hands, artist and muse trotted through the woods. They went sailing together and raced the motorboat. She learned scuba diving and the two explored the inlet's romantic depths. He read his unpublished poetry to her and she was moved to tears. ("My rhymes make my wife sick to her stomach," Victor said, "and rightly so.") The girl got on well with the seals and helped him weed the herb gardens.

She taught him new recipes. She was always cheerful. Her youthful energy kindled his own. ("My wife doesn't believe in overspending ourselves," Victor siad.)

"Real love, eh?"

"I thought so for a little while."

"You wanted to marry her?"

"The frenzy got worse and worse. After a few days, I told her I couldn't live without her. I proposed lengthy journeys. I always wanted to go to New Guinea, to study primitive masks, and what do you know, that was exactly what she wanted to do. We seemed to be made for each other."

"Are you very rich?" I asked.

"She must have been interested in my wealth. But she never asked about money. She said she was a nurse and earning a fair salary."

"Did you promise her any presents?"

Victor nodded sadly. "She said she liked small sports cars and I immediately offered to buy her one. She also wanted to learn how to fly. I said that she could become a member of the local flying club and I would give her an airplane as soon as she had her papers."

"You never saw through the magnificent soap bubble?"

The liquor had lamed the muscles of his lips and he suddenly looked like an old clown. "My wife was due to return and the girl was still around. One morning I was brushing my teeth on the balcony and realized the stupidity of the whole thing. I knew I had struck nonsense again. She had to go, as soon as possible."

"And didn't go."

"No."

"And you were too much the gentleman to push her out."

"No. Men are rather weak, don't you think? Are you any good at breaking relationships?"

"Not at all," I said helpfully.

"Good. Neither am I. Eleia came back and I introduced the two. She saw through the situation in half a second, took me aside, and asked me what I wanted. I told her to be rid of her."

"Of who? Your wife?"

He gave me a surprised look. "Are you all right in the head? The girl, of course. I love Eleia. To grow old together, can there by anything more beautiful than that?"

"So then what?"

"Eleia knows how to take care of situations," said Victor, wiping at a cognac stain on his shirt. He wanted to break off his story but I held on.

"No, finish the tale. What happened to the girl?"

Victor gazed at the bay below. "She's still there."

"What?"

"Her body cells must have been absorbed by those of the shark."

I was on my feet. "Did you feed her to the shark?"

"Not me," Victor said.

"Who?"

He kept quiet.

"Did she visit the old shark by herself?"

Victor turned his attention to the dying fire. "Not with me, didn't I say so just now? I once gave the shark a dead seal. I found the carcass on the rocks and thought the shark would appreciate the gift. I was right. Chop chop chop. That crazy animal really has a nasty mouth. Sharks devour carrion and they go after blood. Once you're wounded you have to be careful. But when you're in one piece you can safely visit him—I've often done it. He'll come to greet me and push his flank against my leg. Why don't you join me tomorrow and see?'

"Not on your life," I said, and waited.

In time, Victor continued. "The girl stayed, and so did Eleia and I, of course. A menage a trois in a way, although the girl and I didn't sleep together any more. Her presence became irritating."

"Your wife must be very good at scuba diving, too," I said. "Am I right?"

"The county's champion," Victor said proudly. "Eleia's won first prize for five years in a row. She used to be a dancer and knows how to control her body."

"So your wife took the guest along on a swim," I said, "and happened to wound her once they were submerged—with her knife, I imagine. You gave me a knife when we were diving. I strapped it to my leg. Eleia must have scratched the girl and then took her to the shark's cave. Chop chop chop."

"It may have happened that way," Victor said.

"You're not sure?"

He made an effort to smile. "Eleia came back alone and we've never discussed the matter."

I woke up the next morning with a terrible hangover, treated by Victor with strong coffee, some aspirin, and orange juice. He dropped me off at the airport. I didn't remind him of the previous evening's conversation. Authors live in a world of fantasy. I understood that he had come up with a horror story to amuse me.

A few days ago, an acquaitance I met in a cafe mentioned holidaying in the United States. I said that the world is becoming less safe by the day—only North America can be trusted. When you leave, you know you will return on the appointed day. My acquaitance disagreed. A girl he knew had left but never come back. I asked for details.

The girl was a nurse who had been babysitting someone's house on an island off the coast of Maine. When the owner of the house eventually returned, the girl was nowhere to be found.

"What happened?" I asked. "Was she out swimming and caught by the currents?"

"Her baggage was still in the house," my friend said. "She may have slipped off the rocks or gone under while swimming, but according to the U.S. Coast Guard drowned persons are invariably found. Nobody found *her*."

What can I do—press charges? Without any proof, I'll make a fool of myself. I still see Victor Verburg, telling the tale during that drunken evening, with a wood pile burning brightly and a soft white moon sailing slowly above land and seascape. I understand now why he stopped writing. All his work is motivated by and based on fear, the fear of fantasy. That time he must have come too close to reality.

I wonder if he still visits the shark, in the greenish-black cavity fifteen feet below the cheerful little white waves of his peaceful bay.

MIFFLIN MUST GO
Shannon Ocork

Mifflin hiccuped. It was a small, involuntary hiccup and he swallowed it immediately, but he was bending over his elder mistress's left elbow at the time, offering the dinner fish. Miss Marianne Wycliffe, 71, pretended not to hear. And she kept her nose from wrinkling at the butler's moist, alcoholic breath. But her eyes blinked rapidly in maidenly alarm as she reached for the serving fork. The Crown Derbyshire platter dipped toward her as it should not have done, the sauce hollandaise pooled dangerously upon the beveled rim. With a hand that trembled, Miss Marianne served herself a portion of poached salmon.

"Thank you, Mifflin," she said with a faint voice. But firmly she replaced the serving fork. And firmly she tilted up the platter.

Mifflin lurched back, straightened almost to his full height, and, listing slightly to starboard, shuffled down the Kilim carpet the length of the satinwood table to his other employer, Miss Violet Wycliffe, 69.

The younger of the two spinster sisters warily watched him approach. For a moment she thought the better thing would be to refuse the salmon entirely. But she was keen for cook's fish. Mrs. Perez was new to the Wycliffe house. She had studied in New York under Monsieur Clare and had come highly recommended by the late Mrs. Lockholm. Fish dishes were Mrs.

Perez's speciality. Miss Violet decided she would emulate her sister's bravery.

The platter swayed at her left side now. To reassure herself, she looked up at the once-elegant figure who had been in their service for forty years. He had come into the house at nineteen as underbutler, straight off the boat from London, where he had apprenticed to Lor and Lady Arleigh of Kent.

He had been tall and solid then, and, from the first, the paradigm of the perfect butler. He was always correct in manner, always fastidious in dress and impeccable in service. Among their set Mifflin had been, and still was as far as the Wycliffe sisters knew, the envy of the Connecticut shoreline.

Now as Mifflin in his cups bowed over the salmon salver, Miss Violet saw how sadly he had fallen off the mark. He had lost his paunch in the last six months and had not had his uniform refitted. His hair, two regal silver wings, was parted in the center of his head as usual. But the part was crooked. And dandruff—yes, it *was* dandruff—littered what once had been pristine shoulders of moss-green livery. His shirt was misbuttoned, too, and there was a faint brown stain on the front just where the left lapel of the jacket crossed his heart.

She must have stared too long, for when she lowered her lavender eyes and reached for the silver fork she saw that the lake of hollandaise was overflowing the platter and the baby salmon was swimming toward her lap.

With a deftness she was later to congratulate herself upon, Miss violet deflected the catastrophe. She rose from her Eighteenth Century dining chair quicker then she thought she could with her weak ankles. She righted the platter with both hands and saved the fish. But a few drops of hollandaise yellowed the table linen.

"Mifflin," she said in her tiny lilt. "Kindly watch yourself. The sauce has splattered on the cloth."

Incredibly, Mifflin hiccuped again, a loud hiccup he was unable to defeat. He tripped backward, red-faced, red-eyed. "Madam," he said when he could, "madam, please forgive me." Recklessly, he balanced the precious platter in one unsteady hand. With the other he flicked at the droplets of sauce with his service towel. Then, inexplicably, he set the fish plate upon the soiled spot and bowed ineptly. "Please excuse me," he said in his British baritone and turned his back to his mistresses.

Drifting toward the double sliding doors, he missed the hand inset by several inches, but corrected himself and disappeared in an outbreak of hiccups and nasty chuckles. From the drawing-room side, the door slammed shut.

Miss Violet spoke down the table to her sister. "Whatever shall we do, Marianne?" Her sister, being the older, took the lead in such matters.

Miss Marianne had frozen in position with a forkful of salmon halfway to her quivering lips. Still in shock, she completed her gesture, swallowing the fish without chewing, and allowed herself a little shiver. "It's gotten too much," she said. "Much too much. We've closed our eyes too long for old time's sake. He'll have to go, that's all. You know it as well as I do."

"We could lock up the liquor cabinet again," suggested Miss Violet.

"That didn't do a speck of good last time we tried it. And it's not the sherry he's drinking, Violet, it's the brandy. I'm sure he's bringing in his own so we can't measure his intake. It's some of ours one time, some of his the next. Whatever's close to hand."

"Brandy!" breathed Miss Violet. Still on her feet, she limped to the sideboard and brought the vegetable dish to her sister. She lifted the cover and sighed.

Miss Marianne dutifully spooned herself three brussels sprouts. "I caught him at it this afternoon," she said. "He had one of the crystal goblets almost full of our apricot cordial. He drank it down like that–" she snapped her fingers "–when I asked what he was drinking, and told me it was apple juice. As if I don't know brandy when I smell it."

"He does have his good days still," said Miss Violet. She carried the vegetable dish to her own place and sat down.

"Oh, it's no good pretending, dear," said her sister. "These last weeks have been a nightmare. Mifflin's out of control and there's no getting him back. And he'll only get worse. Forget about our reputation–think of his. He may have slipped badly, very badly, but we're the only ones to know it. And the party we're giving in, what is it, ten days? I shudder at the thought, Violet. I truly shudder."

Miss Violet cut herself a little salmon and gave her plate the smallest brussels sprout. "It's true," she said. "Even on his good days he's not what he used to be." At last she tasted the fish. It was wonderfully good. She had another bite and another and then the brussels sprout.

It really was too bad, she thought. Mifflin had begun drinking in the afternoons last year after their mother died and Marianne had the hip operation and had had to give up her golf. And with the golf gone, so had the socializing and the dinner parties Mifflin loved so much. Alone in the world, the two sisters grew closer and more reclusive. Older. And as a result Mifflin's duties shrank to almost nothing. He was bored, she supposed. That was it. He hadn't, of course, asked to leave. How could he? The Wycliffe family had been his whole life. It was understood he would be with them until the end.

"When Mama died," Miss Violet said, "do you remember how he cried?'

"He was devoted to Mama," said Miss Marianne. "Well, to Daddy, too. He's been really devoted to us all."

"And we've been devoted to him in return, haven't we? I'm sure we have."

"Well, not so much these last few months, dear."

"Poor Mifflin," said Miss Violet. "We'll have to give him his stipend all at once if we dismiss him. All at once and right away."

"Let's give him the choice," said Miss Marianne. "However he wants it is the way it will be."

"What a nice thought," said Miss Violet. "But how will we tell him?"

"Together," said her sister, finishing her lemonade. "We'll sit on the sofa together very close, holding hands. We'll tell him tonight."

"After the toddies?'

"Oh, yes, decidedly after the toddies. For the courage." And Miss Marianne tried to smile away the tremor in her breast.

"For the courage," agreed Miss Violet. She arranged her knife and fork on her plate. "But what about the party, Mariannce? If he could only stay sober for that, it would be the perfect finale for him, don't you think? Going out in glory?'

Miss Marianne patted her lips with damask. "I think the party would be quite impossible without him. Anyone new in the house would be lost at such an elaborate affair so early on. And our friends expect Mifflin," she said. "it would ruin everything to have to explain his absence over and over." Her flat little bosom heaved. "If only he's able."

"Perhaps we could dangle a carrot," said Miss Violet, "and suggest that his pension depended upon it."

"Yes," said Miss Marianne, "we could give that a try."

The two spinsters, last of the Wycliffe line, rose from their great chairs in somber decision, leaving their napkins to the left of their places as they had done from childhood. They passed, one stiff and straight as though the rod in her hip extended up her spine, the other stooped with arthritis, into the library across the hall where their bedtime toddies awaited.

Cook did not live in as Mifflin did. There was no need. After dinner was prepared, Mrs. Perez left in her sensible Datsun for her little home the other side of Stormfork, on the New Haven side. She drove back mornings at eleven with the daily provisions for luncheon and dinner. She had Sundays off, as did Mifflin. On Sundays the Wycliffe sisters subsisted on crackers and milk.

It was Mifflin's duty to clear the table, Mifflin's duty to handwash the dishes and flatware, Mifflin's duty to dry each piece and put it away. It was Mifflin's duty to undress the table of its dinner cloth and candelabra and redress it for breakfast in cheerful pastel, with the flowers which three times a week the florist delivered at eight. Once the flowers had come from the Wycliffe garden, but that was long ago.

Mifflin did these final chores after making up the sister's toddies and setting the tray in the library while they were still at table. At their leisure, they poured their own water from the hot pot—the brandy and sugar and cinnamon pre-mixed in the snifters by Mifflin in the kitchen. When the sisters were ready for bed, they rang for Mifflin, discussed the next day's schedule, and dismissed him for the night. This was their long-established and invariable routine.

In the library, the sisters settled themselves before the April fire. Miss Violet made up the drinks. As it was Miss Marianne's turn, she read aloud a chapter from the spy novel they were reading. Miss Violet thrilled to the chase while she longed for the persimmon pudding they had been denied by Mifflin's excusing himself. They both so loved persimmon pudding, but to go to the kitchen for it themselves would have been an unthinkable insult to their butler.

It was going on nine o'clock when Miss Marianne rang the service bell.

Mifflin was slow in coming, but when he came he seemed much his better self. Gone were the bumbling and the shuffle, gone the red in his eye and the hiccups. His hair was beautifully parted. His jacket shoulders were spotless. He stood before the sisters with immaculate white-gloved hands.

MIss Violet, so close to her sister their dresses intermingled cream and rose, had a tear in her eye. We just can't do it, she thought. No matter what he's come to, he's *ours*. But even as she thought it, she heard her sister say, "Mifflin, dear," and knew retreat was impossible.

Mifflin bowed. "Mesdames," he rumbled.

Miss Marianne told him of their decision in the sweet, direct way that had always been her advantage. She told him of the pension they had established in his name immediately following their mother's death. She told him of their deep affection, great respect, and lifelong gratitude. Mifflin paled as she spoke—paled and paled. Miss Violet listened with chin down and averted eyes. When Miss Marianne had said her piece, she asked Mifflin to remain in service through the dinner party they were giving for their new neighbors; that is, she said, if he thought he could recapture his former standard for one last evening. "It will be a lovely swan-song for you, Mifflin dear, and a courtesy to us."

Miss Marianne ceased speaking. Miss violet squeezed her sister's hand for comfort. Mifflin was still as grave and white as wax. Finally he bowed as beautifully as he had in his prime and said, "It has only been my object to comply with your every wish. I shall, when the time comes, try to do you proud. Will that be all, then, for tonight?"

Miss Marianne nodded. Miss Violet nodded. "Thank you, Mifflin, good night, Mifflin," they said for almost the last time.

"Good night, mesdames." Mifflin picked up the cloisonne tray from the Phyfe table and backed from the room with a grace they'd thought never to see in him again.

There was only a little moon when, late that night, Mifflin rose from his bed the other side of the kitchen and crept throught the garden to the shed. Vines of rambling rose which had not been cut back for years snagged at his pajama legs and long grass dampened his velvet slippes. But he was not deterred.

He pushed open the shed door with a hand protected by a rubber working glove. By a dim yellow light he searched the shelves for the weed killer. He found it in a corner of the second shelf, a rusty tin with a rose on the face and a small skull and crossbones in the upper right-hand edge.

Mifflin consulted the ingredients, peering close at the small type. Arsenic, the list began, 42%. He read no further. With a screwdriver, he pried up the oval top. With a kitchen spoon, he scooped the grey powder into a sugar dish in the shape of a child's red wagon. It was a cracked piece, disposed of by the family and kept by him, with their permission, in his room. He liked the workmanship, the charm, the insouciance of the thing.

The sugar wagon comfortably full, Mifflin tamped back down the oval top and returned the tin to its position, setting it, as best he could, into the dust lines where it has waited, untouched, season after season.

He turned out the light, closed the shed door, and slipped back to the house, one gloved hand over the top of the wagon to keep the poison from spilling.

Back in his room, Mifflin got down on his knees. Under his bed was a cache of brandy, nine bottles in a small wine cage turned on their sides. They were all apricot cordial—an inexpensive brand, but good enough, he'd thought, for him. He drank the brandy to ease the pain of the cancer. "An operation won't help you," Doctor Dunbar had said. "There's not much to be done at this late date, old boy." The doctor has written him a prescription for Nembutal, but so far Mifflin had not used it. As long as he didn't use it, he could pretend there was nothing wrong and rampant in his stomach.

He had never, despite what the sisters thought, helped himself to their fine store unless invited to, as he had been on special occasions in happier days.

With hands that shook a little, Mifflin carefully cut away the bottle's seal with a single slice of a paring knife. Putting the seal aside, he poured half the contents of the dark-brown bottle into his teapot, then he added all the weed killer he had to the bottle, spooning it in through a funnel. Then he refilled the bottle as much as he could and screwed back the top. Tight, tight. He shook the bottle hard, back and forth, up and down, around and around. When he was satisfied that the powder was dissolved, he wrapped the seal around the top again and secured it with transparent tape. Then he tore away a corner of the bottle label as an identifying mark and put the bottle back among its brothers.

He cleaned up everything, brushed up his slippers, changed his pajamas, and went to bed. He was almost instantly asleep.

The night of the party Mifflin was magnificent, virtually his glorious self of old. The guests-of-honor were the nouveau riche Trenton-Wests, and the Wycliffe sisters' party was their grand entrance into Stormfork society. The beautiful couple had begun life in Stormfork as poor Amy Trenton and plain Arnold West. But as Aimee and Arnie Trenton-West, they had risen, through clever real-estate manipulations and public charities, to become Stormfork's richest and most civically generous couple. Yet perhaps their riches were too quickly amassed and their donations too publicized, for society was slow to open its arms to them. They began their campaign to change this upon the Wycliffe sisters, long Stormfork's social arbiters. They purchased the Hemphill estate next to the Wycliffe house as their residence and named a geriatric wing they'd donated to the hospital the Wycliffe Wing. The sisters were forced to capitulate.

But as Miss Marianne said to Miss Violet after the party was over and they sat in their library among the remnants of lavish desserts, this was the last party the sisters would give. "We're too old to do this again," she said, dipping a spoon into a melted ice-cream bombe.

"And we've retired Mifflin," said Miss Violet. "It would never be the same." She was sampling almond cheesecake.

"It's better to stop now. It was a triumph, but I'm exhausted— not exhilarated the way I used to be."

"And we eat too many sweets at our parties," said Miss Violet, biting into a strawberry glace petit four.

"Yes." Miss Marianne cut herself a tiny bit of rum butterscotch pie. "And wasn't Mifflin fine?'

"I was so proud of him!" said Miss Violet with her had on her heart. "Aimee couldn't sing his praises enough."

"Well," said Miss Marianne, "shall we forego out toddies tonight? We've had so many other sumptuous things already."

"Nevertheless, I think I'll have mine," said Miss Violet. "I want to sleep well and my ankles hurt." Mifflin was in the other rooms directing the hired crew in the cleanup but, as ever, he had set out their toddy tray.

Miss Violet poured hot water into a snifter and stirred the drink with a glass stick.

"Well, I'll join you," said Miss Marianne. "I don't want to be a stick-in-the mud in my old age."

They laughed together like young girls, drank the toddies, and picked again and again at the desserts. They sat up late, until almost one, talking about other parties in days gone by.

Just as they started to go upstairs to their beds, Miss Violet felt a sharp stomach pain. "Oh, dear," she said, gasping at the strength of it. "I hope I don't get sick."

Miss Marianne was holding onto the back of the Sheraton loveseat. "I'm not felling well, either, Violet, my dear."

"As you say," said Miss Violet, "we're too old, Marianne. That's our problem. We'll feel better in the morning."

They helped each other up the broad steps to the second floor. Miss Marianne was able to undress and slip into her nightshift, but Miss Violet lay own in her crepe de chine.

"If you need me during the night you must wake me, do you promise?" Miss Marianne said, breathing rapidly through her nose.

"If you promise the same," said Miss Violet with an effort.

They slept a while. But a second pang came to each of them and then a third, and after that the pain stayed. Doubled and tripled. Each in her turn stumbled to the bath and vomited, but still the pain stayed—and spread.

When they could no longer endure it, they rang for Mifflin. Miss Marianne couldn't remember ever ringing for Mifflin so late or ever before ringing for him from their bedroom.

He did not come at once.

Miss Marianne managed to say, "Perhaps he can't hear it or doesn't understand the bell so late at night."

Miss Violet only moaned weakly in her bed.

Miss Marianne rang for Mifflin again and again. Faintly, she could hear the bell buzzing far away in his room. She thought he must have already left them or that he must be sick himself. But at last she heard a shuffling tread on the staircase.

The light flashed on in the hall. Mifflin, in pajamas and bathrobe, swayed drunkenly in the doorway. He held himself

erect by a hand against the doorjamb. Seeing his mistresses in
distress, his eyes widened. He looked ready to faint.

"Dr. Dunbar," croaked Miss Marianne. "Tell him it's an
emer–" The pain took her voice.

Mifflin backed from the room. "Yes, madam–right away,
madam." He fled, a-tilt, down the stairs.

Miss Marianne glanced at the turquoise-and-silver clock on
her side table. The hands read 3:15. Miss Violet had lost con-
sciousness. She was curled around her stomach, breathing
slow, ragged breaths.

Dr. Dunbar arrived at the Wycliffe house at about 5:30 A.M.,
having received an emergency call from his telephone service
at 4:42. When he arrived, a sober, correct Mifflin apologized for
taking so long to summon him. He couldn't find the doctor's
home telephone number, he said, and he had had difficulty
convincing the answering service to put the call through. Then
Mifflin showed him to the sisters' room.

Both women were delirious with pain and beyond help. Dr.
Dunbar did what he could to make them comfortable, but they
died within an hour of his coming. Miss Violet went first.
Within minutes, Miss Marianne followed.

Dr. Dunbar telephoned the police and the bodies were removed for autopsy.

The police questioned Mifflin immediately. He told them
about the dinner party the evening before. "Mesdames were
usually restricted in their diets," Mifflin said. "But they im-
bibed freely of the champagne last night and of the different
desserts. They were up later than usual. I heard them mount
the stairs about one. I did not see them after the guests de-
parted, as I was cleaning up and they did not ring. Until much
later, that is." That was all Mifflin could tell them. He had, he
said, been in Wycliffe employ all his adult life, and other than
a few broken bones, some mild colds, and Miss Violet's arthritis, the two sisters had enjoyed an exemplary health.

As the day was Sunday and cook's day off, Mrs. Perez was
summoned by the police. Told of the sisters' deaths, she sat
down with a thump on a kitchen chair and fanned herself.
"Wouldn'tcha know it," she said. "I was so happy in this job.
Lovely ladies, the two of them. Real appreciators. Let me cook
for them any way I wanted, anything I wanted, and then

thanked me for it." She rapped the kitchen table with her knuckles. "It's us who're the losers, mister. We, the living. We've lost more'n them."

"What have we lost, Mrs. Perez?" inquired Lieutenant Axelrod.

The cook raised her chin and looked him in the eye. "Why, we've lost grace," she said "Why, grace and genteel ways. Sweet little voices and the most lovely manners you ever saw. Angels, that's what we've lost, mister. Angels. Don't tell me no."

Lieutenant Axelrod was silent for several seconds as Mrs. Perez nodded her head and rapped her knuckles. Then he said, "Could you tell me about the food served last night? What you cooked?"

Mrs. Perez drew herself up. "Are you insinuating anything about *my* food? I'll have you know I've worked for the best families in Stormfork. Five years with Mrs. Lockholm, may she rest in peace, and before that eight years with Mrs. Melody Combes. Not Cora. Melody. How's that for proper credentials?" She rapped her knuckles on the metal table so hard it echoed. "There has never, *never* been any question about *my* food, mister. Why, I do everything myself. Ground up. I choose my own ingredients, skin every onion. I studied under Monsieur Clare, you know. You'll find no flies on me. No, sir."

It took some time to calm her, but Lieutenant Axelrod with a gentle voice and great patience gradually induced Mrs. Perez to give him the menu for Saturday night.

There had been cocktails and appetizers, with which the cook was not concerned. The appetizers had been catered by Sarton's and delivered hot, straight to the drawing room, which adjoined the dining room where dinner was laid. The two rooms were Mifflin's territory. He had made the cocktails. He had served the hors d'oeuvres.

Dinner had been, first, a crab bisque. "Rose-beige my bisque is, and you won't find the like of it anywhere else this side of the Atlantic. I'm famous for my bisques. It's cayenne gives the lovely pink color." Then had come broiled tomato cups filled with grilled mushroom caps and minced bacon. The main course was breast of chicken Florentine. "That's flattened chicken breast rolled around sauteed spinach and garlic in my secret spiced oil." And glazed baby carrots and Caesar salad. A pear sherbet had completed the meal, and Spanish coffee.

Champagne had been the dinner wine. "Not strickly legit, okay, but champagne, mister, is never wrong, no time. And it was a party, doncha see. Festive."

Desserts had been supplied by the different guests. There had been twenty at table and everyone had eaten heartily and well. "And no one else got sick I heard of." Mrs. Perez had left the house at 10:30 with a small bottle of champagne given her by the sisters and a bonus check for her extra work. Mrs. Perez still had the champagne in her pocketbook. She took it out and waved it under Lieutenant Axelrod's nose. "And the check for fifty dollars goes into the bank on Monday," she said and banged on the kitchen table.

"I cooked it, he served it." She gestured toward Mifflin. "I went home he stayed. And there you are, that's all I know." Her nostrils flared. "Only maybe a little more." She leaned close. "He musta done it. In pique, ya see. He's just been—" she put her mouth very close to the Lieutenant's ear "—bumped. Dis*missed* for cause." She pantomimed drinking with an upraised hand, thumb moving back toward her open mouth.

Mifflin denied his dismissal and denied harming his mistresses. Their love of him was such, he said, he thought he had been mentioned in their wills.

While the police waited out the autopsy report, both cook and butler were retained in the house. Mifflin kept to his room, drinking steadily. Mrs. Perez made lunch for Lieutenant Axelrod and Officer Duff: tomato-and-cheese omelettes and watercress salad.

A copy of the sisters' joint will was found in Miss Marianne's Louis XIV escritoire. The trust established for Mifflin was there. It gave him a generous stipend for the rest of his life. The sister's checkbook was also brought forth. In it was the stub for check #4309: twenty-five-thousand dollars in cash to Mr. Bernard Milcox Mifflin for severance pay. The check stub was seven days old.

Confronted, Mifflin admitted there had been a "misunderstanding." The sisters had dismissed him and paid him off, but they had not meant it. He had been derelict in duty and they had punished him, but he had reformed, he said, and they had rescinded the discharging. He had not cashed the severance check. He showed it to Lieutenant Axelrod with fingers that shook.

Dr. Dunbar called the Wycliffe house with the autopsy results. Miss Marianne and Miss Violet had died from arsenic poisoning. A massive amount.

Mifflin was arrested, formally charged, and booked. His bail was set at $50,000.

In the early evening, Mifflin's bail was posted and he was released. He returned to the Wycliffe house. Mrs. Perez and the police were gone and the house was empty.

The telephone rang. Mifflin answered it, wondering. It was Mrs. Trenton-West. She offered him immediate employment and told him it was she and her husband who had posted his bail. They would also assume his court costs.

Mifflin wept. "This is so kind of you," he said, "to open your house to me when I might be a monstrous murderer. I am overcome."

Mrs. Trenton-West minimized her efforts on Mifflin's behalf. "Your room is ready here," she said. "I shall expect you tomorrow morning."

The next day, still weeping, Mifflin packed his things. With several belts of brandy to brace himself and with his two valises on a rolling rack, he walked the half mile to the old Hemphill estate and presented himself at the side door.

Mrs. Trenton-West opened the door to him. She was wearing an apron over a tennis dress of linen lace. She appeared to be making brunch—a bowl of batter and a portable mixer stood on the tiled island in the middle of the enormous kitchen.

"As you can see," she said, cocking her handsome head, "I haven't got a steady cook yet. But I've got you. Come in."

Mifflin left his bags outside, entered, and stood respectfully before her. He had his speech all ready. "I came," he said, "to thank you personally for all you've done for me. But I cannot work for you, dear lady. I shall never work in service again. I am not well enough. I shall stand my trial and take my punishment if convicted or retire if they let me go. I came to assure you the monies you posted in my behalf will not be lost and to kiss your hand for your lovely kindness."

Aimee Trenton-West thrilled at Mifflin's dignity of bearing. "Let's understand each other, Mifflin," she said, staring at him as at a prized antique. "I know very well you're no murderer. What do you take me for? But even if you were, that wouldn't stand in my way one bit. I didn't get to where I am without risk.

Do you understand? I'd do anything, *anything*–now do you understand?–for the perfect butler."

Mifflin bowed. He was remembering the dessert of Aimee Trenton-West. Persimmon pudding, the Wycliffe sisters' favorite. She had sent it over early in the afternoon. There had been only the two cups, pretty *muguet des bois* cache pots of Sevres porcelain rimmed in royal blue. They were signed only, "with delicious thanks."

Miss Marianne and Miss Violet had eaten the puddings in the quiet of the library before the party began. After they had finished, they asked Mifflin to fill the cups with little flowers and set them on the table at dinner.

So now Mifflin did understand. But no longer did he pale when struck by thunderbolts. Mifflin had toughened.

He straightened. "In that case," he said in his peerless British mumble, "perhaps you will allow me, this one time, to finish preparing luncheon for you and Mr. Arnold. I could serve in, let us say, an hour?'

"Delighted!" said Mrs. Trenton-West. Here was a butler she could live with. She whipped off her apron and handed it over to him and fluffed out her tawny hair. "Arnie's down at the stable. I'll run and tell him–he'll be as excited as I am. But first I'll show you to your room."

The room was large and wood-paneled. There were horse prints on the wall, Stubbs' reproductions. A wide window looked in the direction of the Wycliffe house. It was a handsome room for an Englishman, but Mifflin barely noticed. He unpacked quickly, only his uniform and toilet articles and the unopened bottle of arsenic-full brandy he had mixed last week with the intention of ending it all when he left the Wycliffe employ.

He shaved for the second time that morning. He scented. He brushed up his uniform and shined his shoes. Then he split the seal on the brandy and poured half of it into a silver pocket flask he then tucked into his jacket pocket.

He checked the dining room. The table had already been laid. He went to the kitchen. It was surrounded by windows. Looking out, he saw Mr. Trenton-West on a great chestnut hunter cantering around the lawn in riding coat and jodhpurs. The man did not ride well. He rocked in the saddle like a cowboy and drummed the horse's sides with his stirrups. Mrs. Trenton-West was watching her husband, laughing and flicking a black buggy whip whenever the chestnut swung within its reach.

Mifflin put on the apron, picked up the portable mixer, and set the batter spinning. Chutney crepes, he thought. They'll like that. And green beans almondine. He pulled out the silver flash and poured in the tainted brandy. Golden-brown lines whirled into thick yellow. The batter warmed to the color of eggshell.

In all probity, he thought, it was the least he could do for his mistresses. He knew he was no longer what he used to be. But Miss Marianne and Miss Violet had been right. Standards. One had to try to live up to them. To the end.

And, after all, he smiled to himself thinking ahead to his trial, he might as well be hung for a horse as a hare. The mixer sang under his hand.

THE DAY THE CHILDREN VANISHED

Hugh Pentecost

One bright, clear winter's afternoon, between Clayton and Lakeview, a school bus with nine children and a driver disappeared from the face of the earth–vanished into thin air on a two-mile stretch of road where disappearance was utterly impossible!

On a bright, clear winter's afternoon the nine children in the town of Clayton who traveled each day to the Regional School in Lakeview disappeared from the face of the earth, along with the bus in which they traveled and its driver, as completely as if they had been sucked up into outer space by some monstrous interplanetary vacuum cleaner.

Actually, in the time of hysteria which followed the disappearance, this theory was put forward by some distraught citizen of Clayton, and not a few people, completely stumped for an explanation, gave consideration to it.

There was, of course, nothing interplanetary or supernatural about the disappearance of nine children, one adult, and a special-bodied station wagon which was used as a school bus. It was the result of callous human villainy. But, because there was no possible explanation for it, it assumed all the aspects of black magic in the minds of tortured parents and a bewildered citizenry.

Clayton is seven miles from Lakeview. Clayton is a rapidly growing quarry town. Lakeview, considerably larger and with a long history of planning for growth, recently built a new school. It was agreed between the boards of education of the two towns that nine children living at the east end of Clayton should be sent to the Lakeview School where there was adequate space and teaching staff. It was to be just a temporary expedient.

Since there were only nine children, they did not send one of the big, forty-eight passenger school buses to get them. A nine-passenger station wagon was acquired, properly painted and marked as a school bus, and Jerry Mahoney, a mechanic in the East Clayton Garage, was hired to make the two trips each day with the children.

Jerry Mahoney was well liked and respected. He had been a mechanic in the Air Force during his tour of duty in the armed services. He was a wizard with engines. He was engaged to be married to Elizabeth Deering, who worked in the Clayton Bank and was one of Clayton's choice picks. They were both nice people, responsible people.

The disappearance of the station wagon, the nine children, and Jerry Mahoney took place on a two-mile stretch of road where disappearance was impossible. It was called the "dugway," and it wound along the side of the lake. Heavy wire guardrails protected the road from the lake for the full two miles. There was not a gap in it anywhere.

The ground on the other side of the road rose abruptly upward into thousands of acres of mountain woodlands, so thickly grown that not even a tractor could have made its way up any part of it except for a few yards of deserted road that led to an abandoned quarry. Even over this old road nothing could have passed without leaving a trail of torn brush and broken saplings.

At the Lakeview end of the dugway was a filling station owned by old Jake Nugent. On the afternoon of the disappearance the bus, with Jerry Mahoney at the wheel and his carload of kids laughing and shouting at each other, stopped at old man Nugent's. Jerry Mahoney had brought the old man a special delivery letter from the post office, thus saving the RFD driver from making a special trip. Jerry and old Jake exchanged greetings, the old man signed the receipt for his letter—which was from his son in Chicago asking for a loan of fifty dollars—and Jerry drove off into the dugway with his cargo of kids.

At the Clayton end of the dugway was Joe Gorman's Diner, and one of the children in Jerry's bus was Peter Gorman, Joe's son. The Diner was Jerry's first stop coming out of the dugway.

It was four thirty in the afternoon when Joe Gorman realized that the bus was nearly three-quarters of an hour late. Worried, he called the school in Lakeview and was told by Miss Bromfield, the principal, that the bus had left on schedule.

"He may have had a flat, or something," Miss Bromfield suggested.

This was one of seven calls Miss Bromfield was to get in the next half hour, all inquiring about the bus. Nine children; seven families.

Joe Gorman was the first to do anything about it seriously. He called Jake Nugent's filling station to ask about the bus, and old Jake told him it had gone through from his place on schedule. So something had happened to Jerry and his bus load of kids in the dugway. Joe got out his jeep and headed through the dugway toward Lakeview. He got all the way to Jake Nugent's without seeing the bus or passing anyone coming the other way.

Jake Nugent was a shrewd old gent, in complete possession of all his faculties. He didn't drink. When he said he had seen the bus–that it had stopped to deliver his letter–and that he had watched it drive off into the dugway, you had to believe it. Cold sweat broke out on Joe Gorman's face as he listened. The dugway had a tendency to be icy. He had noticed coming over that it hadn't been sanded. Joe hadn't been looking for a major tragedy. But if the bus had skidded, gone through the guard-rail...

He used Jake's phone to call the Dicklers in Clayton. The Dicklers' two children, Dorothy and Donald, were part of Jerry's load and they were the next stop after Joe's Diner. The Dicklers were already alarmed because their children hadn't come home.

Joe didn't offer any theories. He was scared, though. He called the trooper barracks in Lakeview and told them about the missing bus. They didn't take it too seriously, but said they'd send a man out.

Joe headed back for Clayton. This time his heart was a lump in his throat. He drove slowly, staring at every inch of the wire guard-rails. There was not a break anywhere, not a broken or bent post. The bus simply couldn't have skidded over the embankment into the lake without smashing throught the wire guard-rail.

Joe Gorman felt better when he came out at his diner at the

Clayton end. He felt better, but he felt dizzy. Five minutes later Trooper Teliski came whizzing through from Lakeview and stopped his car.

"What's the gag?" he asked Joe.

Joe tried to light a cigarette and his hands were shaking so badly he couldn't make it. Teliski snapped on his lighter and held it out. Joe dragged smoke deep into his lungs.

"Look," he said. "The bus started through the dugway at the regular time." He told about Jerry's stop at Nugent's. "It never came out this end."

A nerve twitched in Teliski's cheek. "The lake," he said.

Joe shook his head. "I–I thought of that, right off. I just came through ahead of you–looking. Not a break in the guard-rail anywhere. Not a scratch. Not a bent post. The bus didn't go into the lake. I'll state my life on that."

"Then what else?" Teliski asked.

"It couldn't go up the mountain."

"I know," Joe said, and the two men stared at each other.

"It's some kind of a joke," Teliski said.

"What kind of a joke? It's no joke to me–or the Dicklers. I talked to them."

"Maybe they had permission to go to a special movie or something," Teliski said.

"Without notifying the parents? Miss Bromfield would have told me, anyway. I talked to her. Listen, Teliski. The bus went into the dugway and it didn't come out. It's not in the dugway now, and it didn't go into the lake."

Teliski was silent for a moment, and then he spoke with a solid attempt at common sense. "It didn't come out this end," he said. "We'll check back on that guard-rail, but let's say you're right. It didn't skid into the lake. It couldn't go up the mountain. So where does that leave us?"

"Going nuts!" Joe said.

"It leaves us with only one answer. The station wagon never went into the dugway."

Joe Gorman nodded. 'That's logic," he said. "But why would Jake Nugent lie? Jerry's an hour and three-quarters late now. If he didn't go in the dugway, where is he? Where *could* he go? Why hasn't he telephoned if everything is okay?"

A car drove up and stopped A man got out and came running toward them. It was Karl Dickler, father of two of the missing children. "Thank God you're here, Teliski. What's happened?"

"Some kind of a gag," Teliski said. "We can't figure it out. The bus never came through the dugway."

"But it did!" Karl Dickler said.

"It never came out this end," Joe Gorman said. "I was watching for Pete, naturally."

"But it did come through!" Dickler said. "I passed them myself on the way to Lakeview. They were about half a mile this way from Jake Nugent's. I saw them! I waved at my own kids!"

The three men stared at each other.

"It never came out the end," Joe Gorman said, in a chocked voice.

Dickler swayed and reached out to the trooper to steady himself. "The lake!" he whispered.

But they were not in the lake. Joe Gorman's survey proved accurate; no broken wire, no bent post, not even a scratch...

It was nearly dark when the real search began. Troopers, the families of the children, the selectmen, the sheriff and twenty-five or thirty volunteer deputies, a hundred or more school friends of the missing children.

The lake was definitely out. Not only was the guard-rail intact, but the lake was frozen over with about an inch office. There wasn't a break in the smooth surface of the ice anywhere along the two miles of shore bordering the dugway.

Men and women and children swarmed through the woods on the other side of the road, knowing all the time it was useless. The road was called the "dugway" because it had been dug out of the side of the mountain. There was a gravel bank about seven feet high running almost unbrokenly along that side of the road. There was the one old abandoned trail leading to the quarry. It was clear, after walking the first ten yards of it, that no car had come that way. It couldn't.

A hundred phone calls were made to surrounding towns and villages. No one had seen the station wagon, the children, or Jerry Mahoney. The impossible had to be faced.

The bus had gone into the dugway and it hadn't come out. It hadn't skidded into the lake and it hadn't climbed the impenetrable brush of the mountain. It was just gone! Vanished into thin air!

Everyone was deeply concerned for and sympathetic with the Dicklers, and Joe Gorman, and the Williams, the Trents, the Ishams, the Nortons, and the Jennings, parents of the missing children. Nobody thought much about Jerry Mahoney's family, or his girl.

It wasn't reasonable, but as the evening wore on and not one speck of evidence was found or one acceptable theory advanced, people began to talk about Jerry Mahoney. He was the driver. The bus had to have been driven somewhere. It couldn't navigate without Jerry Mahoney at the wheel. Jerry was the only adult involved. However it had been worked—this disappearance—Jerry must have had a hand in it.

It didn't matter that, until an hour ago, Jerry had been respected, trusted, liked. Their children were gone and Jerry had taken them somewhere. Why? Ransom. They would all get ransom letters in the morning, they said. A mass kidnapping. Jerry had the kids somewhere. There weren't any rich kids in Clayton, so he was going to demand ransom from all seven families.

Thus Jerry Mahoney became a villain because there was no one else to suspect. Nobody stopped to think that Jerry's father and Jerry's girl might be as anxious about his absence as the others were about the missing children.

At nine thirty Sergeant Mason and Trooper Teliski of the State Police, George Peabody, the sheriff, and a dozen men of the community including Joe Gorman and Karl Dickler stormed into the living room of Jerry Mahoney's house where an old man with silvery white hair sat in an overstuffed armchair. Elizabeth Deering, Jerry's fiancee, was huddled on the floor beside him, her face buried on his knees, weeping.

The old man wore a rather sharply cut gray flannel suit, a bright scarlet vest with brass buttons, and a green necktie that must have been designed for a St. Patrick's Day parade. As he stroked the girl's blonde hair, the light from the lamp reflected glittering shafts from a square-cut diamond in a heavy gold setting he wore on his little finger. He looked up at Sergeant Mason and his small army of followers, and his blue eyes stopped twinkling as he saw the stern look on the Sergeant's face.

"All right, Pat," Sergeant Mason said. "What's Jerry done with those kids?" Pat Mahoney's pale-blue eyes met the

Sergeant's stare steadily. Then crinkles of mirth appeared at the corners of his eyes and mouth.

"I'd like to ask you something before I try to answer that," Pat Mahoney said.

"Well?"

"Have you stopped beating you wife, Sergeant?" Pat Mahoney asked. His cackle of laughter was the only sound in the room...

There are those who are old enough to remember the days when Mahoney and Faye were listed about fourth on a bill of eight star acts all around the Keith-Orpheum vaudeville circuit. Pat Mahoney was an Irish comic with dancing feet, and Nora Faye–Mrs. Mahoney to you–could match him at dancing and had the soprano voice of an angel.

Like so many people in show business, Pat was a blusterer, a boaster, a name dropper, but with it all a solid professional who would practice for hours a day to perfect a new routine, never missed an entrance in forty years, and up to the day young Jerry was born in a cheap hotel in Grand Rapids, Michigan, had given away half what he earned to dead beats and hopeless failures.

The diamond ring he wore today had been in and out of a hundred hock shops. It had been the basis of his and Nora's security for more years than he liked to remember.

If you were left alone with Pat for more than five minutes, he went back to the old days–to the people he had idolized, like Sophie Tucker, and Smith and Dale, and Williams and Wolfus, and Joe Jackson. He'd known them all, played on the same bills with them. "But," he would tell you, and a strange radiance would come into the pale-blue eyes, "the greatest of them all was Nora Faye–Mrs. Mahoney to you."

Once he was started on his Nora, there was no way of stopping Pat Mahoney. He told of her talents as a singer and dancer, but in the end it was a saga of endless patience, of kindness and understanding, of love for a fat-headed, vain little Irish comic, of tenderness as a mother, and finally of clear-eyed courage in the face of stark tragedy.

Mahoney and Faye had never played the Palace, the Broadway goal of all vaudevillians. Pat had worked on a dozen acts that would crack the ice and finally he'd made it.

"We'd come out in cowboy suits, all covered with jewels, and jeweled guns, and jeweled boots, and we'd do a little soft show routine, and then suddenly all the lights would go out and only the jewels would show—they were made special for that—and we'd go into a fast routine, pulling the guns, and twirling and juggling them, and the roof would fall in! Oh, we tried it out of town, and our agent finally got us the booking at the Palace we'd always dreamed of."

There'd be a long silence then, and Pat would take a gaudy handkerchief from his hip pocket and blow his nose with a kind of angry violence. "I can show you the costumes still. They're packed away in a trunk in the attic. Just the way we wore them—me and Nora—the last time we ever played. Atlantic City, it was. And she came off after the act with the cheers still ringing in our ears, and down she went on the floor of the dressing room, writhing in pain.

"The she told me. It had been getting worse for months. She didn't want me to know. The doctor had told her straight out. She'd only a few months she could count on. She'd never said a word to me—working toward the Palace—knowing I'd dreamed of it. And only three weeks after that—she left us. Me and Jerry—she left us. We were standing by her bed when she left—and the last words she spoke were to Jerry. 'Take care of Pat,' she says to him. 'He'll be helpless without someone to take care of him.' And then she smiled at me, and all the years were in that smile."

And then, wherever he happened to be when he told the story, Pat Mahoney would wipe the back of his hand across his eyes and say, "If you'll excuse me, I think I'll be going home."...

Nobody laughed when Pat pulled the old courtroom wheeze on Sergeant Mason about "have you stopped beating your wife." Pat looked past the Sergeant at Trooper Teliski, and Joe Gorman, and Karl Dickler, and Mr. and Mrs. Jennings, whose two daughters were in the missing bus, and George Peabody, the fat, wheezing sheriff.

"The question I asked you, Sergeant," he said, "makes just as much sense as the one you asked me. You asked me what Nora's boy has done with those kids? There's no answer to that question. Do I hear you saying, 'I know what you must be feeling, Pat Mahoney, and you, Elizabeth Deering? And is there anything we can do for you in this hour of your terrible anxiety.' I don't hear you saying that, Sergeant."

"I'm sorry, Pat," Mason said. "Those kids are missing. Jerry had to take them somewhere."

"No!" Liz Deering cried. "You all know Jerry better that that!"

They didn't, it seemed, but they could be forgiven. You can't confront people with the inexplicable without frightening them and throwing them off balance. You can't endanger their children and expect a sane reaction. They muttered angrily, and old Pat saw the tortured faces of Joe Gorman and Karl Dickler and the swollen red eyes of Mrs. Jennings.

"Has he talked in any way queerly to you, Pat?" Mason asked. "Has he acted normal of late?"

"Nora's boy is the most normal boy you ever met," Pat Mahoney said. "You know that, Sergeant. Why, you've known him since he was a child."

Mrs. Jennings screamed out, "He'd protect his son. Naturally he'd protect his son. But he's stolen our children!"

"The Pied Piper rides again," Pat Mahoney said.

"Make him talk!" Mrs. Jennings cried, and the crowd around her muttered louder.

"When did you last see Jerry, Pat?"

"Breakfast," Pat said. "He has his lunch at Joe Gorman's Diner." The corner of his mouth twitched. "He should have been home for dinner long ago."

"Did he have a need for money?" Mason asked.

"Money? He was a man respected—until now—wasn't he? He was a man with a fine girl in love with him, wasn't he? What need would he have for money?"

"Make him answer sensibly!" Mrs. Jennings pleaded in a despairing voice.

Joe Gorman stepped forward. "Pat, maybe Jerry got sick all of a sudden. It's happened to men who saw action overseas. Maybe you saw signs of something and wouldn't want to tell of it. But my Pete was on that bus, and Karl's two, and Mrs. Jennings' two. We're nowhere, Pat—so if you can tell us anything! Our kids were on that bus!"

Pat Mahoney's eyes, as he listened to Joe Gorman, filled with pain. "My kid is on that bus, too, Joe," he said.

They all stared at him, some with hatred. And then, in the

distance, they heard the wail of a siren. The troopers' car was coming from Lakeview, hell-bent.

"Maybe it's news!" someone shouted.

And they all went stumbling out of the house to meet the approaching car—all but Elizabeth Deering, who stayed behind, clinging to the old man.

"I don't understand it," she said, her voice shaken. "They think he's harmed their children, Pat! Why? Why should they think he'd do such a thing? Why?"

Old Pat's eyes had a faraway look in them. "Did I ever tell you about The Great Thurston?" he asked. "Greatest magic act I ever saw."

"Pat!" Elizabeth said, her eyes widening in horror.

"First time I ever caught his act was in Sioux City," Pat said. "He came out in a flowing cape, and a silk hat, and he..."

Dear God, he's losing his reason, Elizabeth Deering told herself. Let the news be good! Let them be found safe!

The police car with its wailing siren carried news, but it was not the sort the people of Clayton were hoping to hear.

It was reassuring to know that within a few hours of the tragedy the entire area was alerted, that the moment daylight came a fleet of army helicopters would cover the area for hundreds of miles around, that a five-state alarm was out for the missing station wagon and its passengers, and that the Attorney General had sent the best man on his staff to direct and coordinate the search.

Top officials, viewing the case coldly and untouched by the hysteria of personal involvement, had a theory. Of course there had to be a rational explanation of the disappearance of the bus, and Clyde Haviland, tall, stoop-shouldered, scholarly-looking investigator from the Attorney General's office, was ordered to produce that explanation as soon as possible upon his arrival in Clayton. But beyond that, officials had no doubt as to the reason for the disappearance: this was a mass kidnapping—something novel in the annals of crime.

Since none of the families involved had means, Haviland and his superiors were convinced the next move in this strange charade would be a demand on the whole community to pay ransom for the children. The F.B.I. was alerted to be ready to act the moment there was any indication of involvement across state lines.

While mothers wept and the menfolk grumbled angrily that Jerry Mahoney, the driver, was at the bottom of this, official-dom worked calmly and efficiently. The Air Force turned over its complete data on Technical Sergeant Jerry Mahoney to the F.B.I. Men who had known Jerry in the service were wakened from their sleep or pulled out of restaurants or theatres to be questioned. Had he ever said anything that would indicate he might move into a world of violence? Did his medical history contain any record of mental illness?

Sitting at a desk in the town hall, Clyde Haviland reported on some of this to George Peabody, the sheriff, the town's three selectmen, Sergeant Mason, and a couple of other troopers. Haviland, carefully polishing his shell-rimmed glasses, was a quiet, reassuring sort of man. He had a fine reputation in the state. He was not an unfamiliar figure to people in Clayton be-cause he had solved a particularly brutal murder in the neigh-boring town of Johnsville, and his investigation had brought him in and out of Clayton for several weeks.

"So far," he said, with a faint smile, "The report on Jerry Ma-honey is quite extraordinary."

"In what way?" Sergeant Mason asked, eager for the scent of blood.

"Model citizen," Haviland said.

"No one has a bad word for him. No bad temper. Never held grudges. Never chiseled. Saves his money. His savings account in the Clayton bank would surprise some of you. On the face of it, he's the last person in the world to suspect."

"There has to be a first time for everything," Karl Dickler said. He was a selectman as well as one of the bereaved parents.

"It's going down toward zero tonight," George Peabody, the sheriff, said glumly. "If those kids are out anywhere—"

"They're one hell of a long way from here by now, if you ask me" Sergeant Mason said.

Haviland looked at him, his eyes unblinking behind the lenses of his glasses. "Except that they never came out of the dugway."

"Nobody saw them" Mason said. "But they're not there so they did come out."

"They didn't come out," Joe Gorman said. "I was watching for them from the window of my diner."

"There were the three seconds you were getting something out of the icebox in your pantry," Mason said.

"And I suppose everyone else along Main Street had his head in a closet at just that time!" Joe Gorman said.

"Or someone reached down out of the heavens and snatched that station wagon up into space," Haviland said. He was looking at Peabody's pudgy face as he spoke, and something he saw there made him add quickly, "I'm kidding, of course."

Peabody laughed nervously. "It's the only explanation we've had so far."

Karl Dickler put his had up to his cheek. There was a nerve there that had started to twitch, regularly as the tick of a clock. "I like Jerry. I'd give the same kind of report on him you've been getting, Mr. Haviland. But you can't pass up the facts. I'd have said he'd defend those kids with his life. But did he? And the old man—his father. He won't answer questions directly. There's something queer about him. Damn it, Mr. Haviland, my kids are—out there, somewhere!" He waved toward the frost-coated window panes.

"Every highway within two hundred miles of here is being patrolled, Mr. Dickler," Haviland said. "If they'd driven straight away from here in daylight—granting Mason is right and everybody was in a closet when the station wagon went through town—they'd have been seen a hundred times after they left Clayton. There isn't one report of anyone having seen the station wagon with the school-bus markings." Haviland paused to light a cigarette. His tapering fingers were nicotine-stained.

"If you'd ever investigated a crime, Mr. Dickler, you'd know we usually are swamped with calls from people who think they've seen the wanted man. A bus—a bus load of kids. Somebody *had* to see it! But there isn't even a crackpot report. If there was some place he could have stayed under cover—and don't tell me, I know there isn't—and started moving after dark, he might get some distance. But alarms are out everywhere. He couldn't travel five miles now without being trapped."

"We've told ourselves all these things for hours!" Dickler said, pinching savagely at his twitching cheek. "What are you going to *do*, Haviland?"

"Unless we're all wrong," Haviland said, "we're going to hear from the kidnappers soon. Tonight—or maybe in the morning—

by mail, or phone, or in some unexpected way. But we'll hear. They'll demand money. What other purpose can there be? Once we hear, we'll have to start to play it by ear. That's the way these cases are."

"Meanwhile you just sit here and wait!" Dickler said, a kind of despair rising in his voice. "What am I going to say to my wife?"

"I think all the parents of the children should go home. You may be the one the kidnappers contact. It may be your child they put on the phone to convince you the kids are safe," Haviland said. "As soon as it's daylight—"

"You think the kids *are* safe?" Dickler cried out.

Haviland stared at the distraught father for a minute. Then he spoke, gently. "What kind of assurance could I give you, Mr. Dickler? Even if I tried, you wouldn't believe me. People who play this kind of game are without feelings, not rational. When you fight them, you have to walk quietly. If you scare them, God knows what to expect. That's why I urge you all to go home and wait." He dropped his cigarette on the floor and heeled it out. "And pray," he said...

Elizabeth Deering, Jerry Mahoney's girl, was sick with anxiety. Jerry was foremost in her mind; Jerry, missing with the children; Jerry, worse than that, suspected by his friends. But on top of that was old Pat Mahoney.

He hadn't made the slightest sense since the angry crowd had left his house. He had talked on endlessly about the old days in vaudeville. He seemed obsessed with the memory of the first time he had seen The Great Thurston in Sioux City. He remembered card tricks, and sawing the lady in half, and his wife Nora's childish delight in being completely bewildered. He seemed to remember everything he had seen the man do.

Elizabeth tried, but she could not bring Pat back to the present. The tragedy seemed to have tipped him right out of the world of reason. She was partly relieved when she heard firm steps on the front porch. The other part of her, when she saw Sergeant Mason and the tall stranger, was the fear that they had news—bad news about Jerry.

Mason was less aggressive than he had been on his first visit. he introduced Haviland and said they wanted to talk to Pat. Elizabeth took them back into the living room where old Pat still sat in the over-stuffed armchair.

Mason introduced Haviland. "Mr. Haviland is a special investigator from the Attorney General's office, Pat."

Pat's eyes brightened. "Say, you're the fellow that solved that murder over in Johnsville, aren't you?" he said. "Smart piece of work."

"Thanks," Haviland said. He looked at Pat, astonished at his gaudy vest and tie and the glittering diamond on his finger. He had been prepared for Pat, but not adequately.

"Sit down," Pat said. "Maybe Liz would make us some coffee if we asked her pretty."

Mason nodded to Liz, who went out into the kitchen. He followed her to tell her there was no news. Haviland sat down on the couch next to Pat, stretched out his long legs, and offered Pat a cigarette.

"Don't smoke," Pat said. "Never really liked anything but cigars. Nora hated the smell of 'em. So what was I to do? You go to vaudeville in the old days, Mr. Haviland?"

"When I was a kid," Haviland said, lighting a cigarette. "I never had the pleasure of seeing you, though, Mr. Mahoney."

"Call me Pat," Pat said. "Everyone does. I was nothing, Mr. Haviland. Just a third-rate song-and-dance man. But Nora— well, if you ever saw my Nora..."

Haviland waited for him to go on, but Pat seemed lost in his precious memories.

"You must be very worried about your son, Pat," he said.

For a fractional moment the mask of pleasant incompetence seemed to be stripped from Pat's face. "Wouldn't you be?" he asked, harshly. Then, almost instantly, the mask was fitted back into place, and old Pat gave his cackling laugh. "You got theories, Mr. Haviland? How're you going to handle this case?"

"I think," Haviland said conversationally, "that the children and your son have been kidnapped. I think we'll hear from the kidnappers soon. I think, in all probability, the whole town will be asked to get up a large ransom."

Pat nodded. "I'll chip in this diamond ring," he said. "it's got Jerry out of trouble more than once."

Haviland's eyes narrowed. "he's been in trouble before?"

"His main trouble was his Pop," Pat said. "Sometimes there wasn't enought to eat. But we could always raise eating money on this ring." He turned his bright, laughing eyes directly on Haviland. "You figured out how the bus disappeared?'

"No," Haviland said.

"Of course it doesn't really matter, does it?" Pat said.

"Well, if we knew—" Haviland said.

"It wouldn't really matter," Pat said. "It's what's going to happen now that matters."

"You mean the demand for money?"

"If that's what's going to happen," Pat said. The crackling laugh suddenly grated on Haviland's nerves. The old joker did know something!

"You have a different theory, Pat?" Haviland asked, keeping his exasperation out of his voice.

"You ever see The Great Thurston on the Keith-Orpheum circuit?" Pat asked.

"I'm afraid not," Haviland said.

"Greatest magic act I ever saw," Pat said. "Better than Houdini. Better than anyone. I first saw him in Sioux City—"

"About the case here, Pat," Haviland interrupted. "You have a theory?"

"I got no theory," Pat said. "But I know what's going to happen."

Haviland leaned forward. "What's going to happen?"

"One of two things," Pat said. "Everybody in this town is going to be looking. They're going to be looking for that station wagon in the lake, where they know it isn't, and they're going to be looking for it in the woods, where they know it isn't. That's one thing that may happen. The other thing is, they buy this theory of yours, Mr. Haviland—and it's a good theory, mind you—and they all stay home and wait to hear something. There's one same result from both things, isn't there?"

"Same result?"

"Sure. Nobody in Clayton goes to work. The quarries don't operate. The small businesses will shut down. People will be looking and people will be waiting..."

"So?"

"So what good will that do anyone?" Pat asked.

Haviland ground out his cigarette in an ashtray. "It won't do anyone any good. The quarry owners will lose some money. The small businesses will lose some."

"Not much point in it, is there?" Pat said, grinning.

Haviland rose. He'd had about enough. Mason and Elizabeth were coming back from the kitchen with coffee. "There isn't much point to anything you're saying, Mr. Mahoney."

Pat's eyes twinkled. "You said you never saw The Great Thurston, didn't you?"

"I never saw him," Haviland said.

"Well, we'll see. If they're supposed to stay home and wait, they'll stay home and wait. If they're supposed to be out searching, they'll be out searching. Ah, coffee! Smells real good. Pull up a chair, Sergeant. By the way, Mr. Haviland, I'll make you a bet," Pat said.

"I'm not a betting man," Haviland said.

"Oh, just a manner-of-speaking bet," Pat said. "I'll make you a bet that tomorrow morning they'll be out searching. I'll make you a bet that *even if you order them to stay home and wait*, they'll be out searching!"

"Look here, Pat, if you know something..."

A dreamy look came into Pat's eyes. "Nora was so taken with The Great Thurston that time in Sioux City I went around to see him afterwards. I thought maybe he'd show me how to do a few simple tricks. I pretended it was for Nora, but really I thought we might use 'em in our act. He wouldn't tell me anything—that is, not about any of his tricks. But he told me the whole principle of his business."

"Sugar?" Elizabeth asked Haviland. Poor old man, she thought.

"The principle is," Pat said, "to make your audience think only what you want them to think, and see only what you want them to see." Pat's eyes brightened. "Which reminds me, there's something I'd like to have you see, Mr. Haviland."

Haviland gulped his coffee. Somehow he felt mesmerized by the old man. Pat was at the foot of the stairs, beckoning. Haviland followed.

Elizabeth looked at Mason and there were tears in her eyes. "It's thrown him completely off base," she said, "You know what he's going to show Mr. Haviland?" Sergeant Mason shook his head.

"A cowboy suit!" Elizabeth said, and dropped down on the couch, crying softly. "He's going to show him a cowboy suit."

And she was right. Haviland found himself in the attic, his head bowed to keep from bumping into the sloping beams. Old Pat had opened a wardrobe trunk and with the gesture of a waiter taking the silver lid off a tomato surprise, revealed two

cowboy suits, one hanging neatly on each side of the trunk–
Nora's and his. Chaps, shirt, vest, boots, Stetsons, and gun belt–
all studded with stage jewelry.

"...and when the lights went out," Pat was saying, "all you
could see was these gewgaws, sparkling. And we'd take out the
guns..." And suddenly Pat had the two jeweled six-shooters in
his hands, twirling and spinning them. "In the old days I could
draw these guns and twirl 'em into position faster than Jesse
James!"

The spell was broken for Haviland. The old guy was cuckoo.
"I enjoyed seeing them, Mr. Mahoney," he said. "But now, I'm
afraid I've got to get back..."

As soon as dawn broke, Haviland had Sergeant Mason and
Sheriff George Peabody take him out to the scene of the disappearance. Everyone else was at home, waiting to hear from the
kidnappers. It had been a terrible night for the whole town, a
night filled with forebodings and dark imaginings. Haviland
covered every inch of the two-mile stretch of the dugway. And
he couldn't get away from the facts. There was no way for it to
have happened–but it had happened.

About eight thirty he was back in Clayton in Joe's Diner,
stamping his feet to warm them and waiting eagerly for eggs
and toast to go with his steaming cup of black coffee. All the
parents had been checked. There'd been no phone calls, no
notes slipped under doors, nothing in the early-morning mail.

Haviland never got his breakfast. Trooper Teliski came
charging into the diner just as Joe Gorman was taking the eggs
off the grill. Teliski, a healthy young man, was white as parch-
ment, and the words came out of him in a kind of choking sob.
"We've found 'em," he said. "Or at least we know where they
are. Helicopters spotted 'em. I just finished passing the word in
town."

Joe Gorman dropped the plate of eggs on the floor behind
the counter. Haviland spun around on his counter stool. Just
looking at Teliski made the hair rise on the back of his neck.

"The old quarry off the dugway," Teliski said, and gulped
for air. "No sign of the bus. It didn't drive up there. But the
kids." Teliski steadied himself on the counter. "Schoolbooks,"
he said. "A couple of coats–lying on the edge of the quarry.
And in the quarry–more of the same. A red beret belonging to
one of the kids–"

"Peter!" Joe Gorman cried out.

Haviland headed for the door. The main street of Clayton was frightening to see. People were running out of houses, screaming at each other, heading crazily toward the dugway. These who went for their cars scattered the people in front of them. There was no order—only blind panic.

Haviland stood on the curb outside the diner, ice in his veins. He looked down the street to where old Pat Mahoney lived, just in time to see a wildly weeping woman pick up a stone and throw it through the front window of Pat's house.

"Come on—what's the matter with you?" Teliski shouted from behind the wheel of the State Police car.

Haviland stood where he was, frozen, staring at the broken window of Pat Mahoney's house. The abandoned quarry, he knew, was sixty feet deep, full to within six feet of the top with icy water fed in by constantly bubbling springs.

A fire engine roared past. They were going to try to pump out the quarry. It would be like bailing out the Atlantic Ocean with a tea cup.

"Haviland!" Teliski called desperately.

Haviland still stared at Pat Mahoney's house. A cackling old voice rang in his ears. "I'll make you a bet, Mr. Haviland. I'll make you a bet that even if you order them to stay at home and wait, they'll be out searching."

Rage such as he had never known flooded the ice out of Haviland's veins. So Pat had known! The old codger had known *last night!*

Special Investigator Haviland had never witnessed anything like the scene at the quarry.

The old road, long since overgrown, which ran about 200 yards in from the dugway to the quarry, had been trampled down as if by a herd of buffalo.

Within three-quarters of an hour of the news reaching town, it seemed as if everyone from Clayton and half the population of Lakeview had arrived at the quarry's edge.

One of the very first army helicopters, which had taken to the air at dawn, had spotted the clothes and books at the edge of the abandoned stone pit.

The pilot had dropped down close enough to identify the strange objects and radioed immediately to State Police. The stampede had followed.

Haviland was trained to be objective in the face of tragedy, but he found himself torn to pieces by what he saw. Women crowded forward, screaming, trying to examine the articles of clothing and the books. Maybe not all the children were in this icy grave. It was only the hope of desperation. No one really believed it. It seemed, as Trooper Teliski had said, to be the work of a maniac.

Haviland collected as many facts about the quarry as he could from a shaken Sheriff Peabody.

"Marble's always been Clayton's business," Peabody said. "Half the big buildings in New York have got their marble out of Clayton quarries. This was one of the first quarries opened up by the Clayton Marble Company nearly sixty years ago. When they started up new ones, this one was abandoned."

In spite of the cold, Peabody was sweating. He wiped the sleeve of his plaid hunting shirt across his face. "Sixty feet down, and sheer walls," he said. "They took the blocks out at ten-foot levels, so there is a little ledge about every ten feet going down. A kid couldn't climb out of it if it was empty."

Haviland glanced over at the fire engine which had started to pump water from the quarry. "Not much use in that," he said.

"The springs are feeding it faster than they can pump it out," Peabody said. "There's no use telling them. They got to feel they're doing something." The fat sheriff's mouth set in a grim slit. "Why would Jerry Mahoney do a thing like this? *Why?* I guess you can only say the old man is a little crazy, and the son has gone off his rocker too."

"There are some things that don't fit," Haviland said. he noticed his own hands weren't steady as he lit a cigarette. The hysterical shrieking of one of the women near the edge of the quarry grated on his nerves. "Where is the station wagon?"

"He must have driven up here and—done what he did to the kids," Peabody said. "Then waited till after dark to make a getaway."

"But you searched this part of the woods before dark last night," Haviland said.

"We missed it somehow, that's all," Peabody said stubbornly.

"A nine-passenger station wagon is pretty hard to miss," Haviland said.

"So we missed it," Peabody said. "God knows how, but we

missed it." He shook his head. "I suppose the only thing that'll work there is grappling hooks. They're sending a crane over from one of the active quarries. Take an hour or more to get it here. Nobody'll leave here till the hooks have scraped the bottom of that place and they've brought up the kids."

Unless, Haviland thought to himself, the lynching spirit gets into them. He was thinking of an old man in a red vest and a green necktie and a diamond twinkling on his little finger. He was thinking of a broken window pane—and of the way he'd seen mobs act before in his time.

Someone gripped the sleeve of Haviland's coat and he looked down into the horror-struck face of Elizabeth Deering, Jerry Mahoney's girl.

"It's true, then," she whispered. She swayed on her feet, holding tight to Haviland for support.

"It's true they found some things belonging to the kids," he said. "That's all that's true at the moment, Miss Deering." He was a little astonished by his own words. He realized that, instinctively, he was not believing everything that he saw in front of him. "This whole area was searched last night before dark," he said. "No one found any schoolbooks or coats or berets then. No one saw the station wagon."

"What's the use of talking that way?" Peabody said. His eyes were narrowed, staring at Liz Deering. "I don't want to believe what I see either, Mr. Haviland. But I got to." The next words came out of the fat man with a bitterness that stung like a whiplash. "Maybe you're the only one in Clayton that's lucky, Liz. You found out he was a homicidal maniac in time—before you got married to him."

"Please, George!" the girl cried. "How can you believe—"

"What can anyone believe but that?" Peabody said, and turned away.

Liz Deering clung to Haviland, sobbing. The tall man stared over her head at the hundreds of people grouped around the quarry's edge. He was reminded of a mine disaster he had seen once in Pennsylvania: a whole town waiting at the head of the mine shaft for the dead to be brought to the surface.

"Let's get out of here," he said to Liz Deering, with sudden energy.

Clayton was a dead town. Stores were closed. Joe's Diner was closed. The railroad station agent was on the job, handling dozens of telegrams that were coming in from friends and relatives of the parents of the missing children. The two girls in the telephone office, across the street from the bank, were at their posts.

Old Mr. Granger, a teller in the bank, and one of the stenographers were all of the bank staff that had stayed on the job. Old Mr. Granger was preparing the payroll for the Clayton Marble Company. He didn't know whether the truck from the company's offices with the two guards would show up for the money or not.

Nothing else was working on schedule today. Even the hotel down the street had closed. One or two salesmen had driven into town, heard the news, and gone off down the dugway toward the scene of the tragedy. A few very old people tottered in and out the front doors of houses, looking anxiously down Main Street toward the dugway. Even the clinic was closed. The town's doctors and nurses had all gone to the scene of the disaster.

Down the street a piece of newspaper had been taped over the hole in Pat Mahoney's front window. Pat Mahoney sat in the big overstuffed armchair in his living room. He rocked slowly back and forth, staring at an open scrapbook spread across his knees. A big black headline from a show-business paper was pasted across the top.

MAHONEY AND FAYE
BOFFO BUFFALO

Under it were pictured of Pat and Nora in their jeweled cowboy suits, their six-shooters drawn, pointing straight at the camera. There was a description of the act, the dance in the dark with only the jewels showing and the six-shooters spouting flame. "Most original number of its kind seen in years," a Buffalo critic had written. "The ever popular Mahoney and Faye have added something to their familiar routines that should please theater audiences from coast to coast. We are not surprised to hear that they have been booked into the Palace."

Pat closed the scrapbook and put it down on the floor beside him. From the inside pocket of his jacket he took a wallet. It bulged with papers and cards. He was an honorary Elk, honorary police chief of Wichita in 1927, a Friar, a Lamb.

Carefully protected by isinglass were some snapshots. They

were faded now, but anyone could see they were pictures of Nora with little Jerry at various stages of his growth. There was Jerry at six months, Jerry at a year, Jerry at four years. And Nora, smiling gently at her son. The love seemed to shine right out of the pictures, Pat thought.

Pat replaced the pictures and put the wallet back in his pocket. He got up from his chair and moved toward the stairway. People who knew him would have been surprised. No one had ever seen Pat when his movements weren't brisk and youthful. He could still go into a tap routine at the drop of a hat, and he always gave the impression that he was on the verge of doing so. Now he moved slowly, almost painfully—a tired old man, with no need to hide it from anyone. There was no one to hide it from; Jerry was missing, Liz was gone.

He climbed to the second floor and turned to the attic door. He opened it, switched on the lights, and climbed up to the area under the eaves. There he opened the wardrobe trunk he'd shown to Haviland. From the left side he took out the cowboy outfit—the chaps, the boots, the vest and shirt and Stetson hat, and the gun belt with the two jeweled six-shooters. Slowly he carried them down to his bedroom on the second floor. There Pat Mahoney proceeded to get into costume.

He stood, at last, in front of the full-length mirror on the back of the bathroom door. The high-heeled boots made him a couple of inches taller than usual. The Stetson was set on his head at a rakish angle. The jeweled chaps and vest glittered in the sunlight from the window. Suddenly old Pat jumped into a flat-footed stance, and the guns were out of the holsters, spinning dizzily and then pointed straight at the mirror.

"Get 'em up, you lily-livered rats!" old Pat shouted. A bejeweled gunman stared back at him fiercely from the mirror.

Then, slowly, he turned away to a silver picture frame on his bureau. Nora, as a very young girl, looked out at him with her gentle smile.

"It'll be all right, honey," Pat said. "You'll see. It'll be another boffo, honey. Don't you worry about your boy. Don't you every worry about him while I'm around."

It was a terrible day for Clayton, but Gertrude Naylor, the chief operator in the telephone office, said afterward that perhaps the worst moment for her was when she spotted old Pat

Mahoney walking down the main street—right in the middle of the street—dressed in that crazy cowboy outfit. He walked slowly, looking from right to left, staying right on the white line that divided the street.

"I'd seen it a hundred times before in the movies," Gertrude Naylor said afterward. "A cowboy, walking down the street of a deserted town, waiting for his enemy to appear—waiting for the moment to draw his guns. Old Pat's hands floated just above those crazy guns in his holster, and he kept rubbing the tips of his fingers against his thumb. I showed him to Millie, and we started to laugh, and then, somehow, it seemed about the most awful thing of all. Jerry Mahoney had murdered those kids and here was his old man, gone nutty as a fruitcake."

Old Mr. Granger, in the bank, had much the same reaction when the aged, bejeweled gun toter walked up to the teller's window.

"Good morning, Mr. Granger," Pat said, cheerfully.

"Good morning, Pat."

"You're not too busy this morning, I see," Pat said.

"N-no," Mr. Granger said. The killer's father—dressed up like a kid for the circus. He's ready for a padded cell, Mr. Granger thought.

"Since you're not so busy," Pat said, "I'd like to have a look at the detailed statement of my account for the last three months." As he spoke, he turned and leaned against the counter, staring out through the plate-glass bank window at the street. His hands stayed near the guns, and he kept rubbing his fingertips against the ball of his thumb.

"You get a statement each month, Pat," Mr. Granger said.

"Just the same, I'd like to see the detailed statement for the last three months," Pat said.

"I had to humor him, I thought," Mr. Granger said later. "So I went back in the vault to get his records out of the files. Well, I was just inside the vault door when he spoke again, in the most natural way, 'If I were you, Mr. Granger,' he said, 'I'd close that vault door, and I'd stay inside, and I'd set off all the alarms I could lay my hands on. You're about to be stuck up, Mr. Granger.'

"Well, I thought it was part of his craziness," Mr. Granger said, later. "I thought he meant *he* was going to stick up the bank. I thought that was why he'd got all dressed up in that cowboy outfit. Gone back to his childhood, I thought. I was scared, because I figured he was crazy. So I *did* close the vault door. And I *did* set off the alarm, only it didn't work. I didn't know then all the electric wires into the bank had been cut."

Gertrude and Millie, the telephone operators, had a box seat for the rest of it. They saw the black sedan draw up in front of the bank and they saw the four men in dark suits and hats get out of it and start up the steps of the bank. Two of them were carrying small suitcases and two of them were carrying guns.

Then suddenly the bank doors burst open and an ancient cowboy appeared, hands poised over his guns. He did a curious little jig step that brought him out in a solid square stance. The four men were so astonished at the sight of him they seemed to freeze.

"Stick 'em up, you lily-livered rats!" old Pat shouted. The guns were out of the holsters, twirling. Suddenly they belched flame, straight at the bandits.

The four men dived for safety, like men plunging off the deck of a sinking ship. One of them made the corner of the bank building. Two of them got to the safe side of the car. The fourth, trying to scramble back into the car, was caught in the line of fire.

"I shot over your heads that first time!" Pat shouted. "Move another inch and I'll blow you all to hell!" The guns twirled again and then suddenly aimed steadily at the exposed bandit. "All right, come forward and throw your guns down," Pat ordered.

The man in the direct line of fire obeyed at once. His gun bounced on the pavement a few feet from Pat and he raised his arms slowly. Pat inched his way toward the discarded gun.

The other men didn't move. And then Gertrude and Millie saw the one who had gotten around the corner of the bank slowly raise his gun and take deliberate aim at Pat. She and Millie both screamed, and it made old Pat jerk his head around. In that instant there was a roar of gunfire.

Old Pat went down, clutching at his shoulder. But so did the bandit who'd shot him and so did one of the men behind the car. Then Gertrude and Millie saw the tall figure of Mr. Haviland come around the corner of the hotel next door, a smoking gun in his hand. He must have spoken very quietly because Gertrude and Millie couldn't hear him, but whatever he said made the other bandits give up. Then they saw Liz Deering running across the street to where old Pat lay, blood dripping through the fingers that clutched at his shoulder.

Trooper Teliski's car went racing through the dugway at breakneck spped, siren shrieking. As he came to the turn-in to the old quarry, his tires screamed and he skidded in and up the rugged path, car bounding over stones, ripping through brush. Suddenly just ahead of him on the path loomed the crane from the new quarry, inching up the road on a caterpillar tractor. Trooper Teliski sprang out of his car and ran past the crane, shouting at the tractor driver.

"To hell with that!" Teliski shouted.

Stumbling and gasping for breath, he raced out into the clearing where hundreds of people waited in grief-stricken silence for the grappling for bodies to begin.

"Everybody!" Teliski shouted. "Everybody! Listen!" He was half laughing, half strangling for breath. "Your kids aren't there! They're safe! They're all safe—the kids, Jerry Mahoney, everyone! They aren't here. They'll be home before you will! Your kids—" And then he fell forward on his face, sucking in the damp, loam-scented air.

Twenty minutes later Clayton was a madhouse. People running, people driving, people hanging onto the running boards of cars and clinging to bumpers. And in the middle of the town, right opposite the bank, was a station wagon with a yellow school-bus sign on its roof, and children were spilling out of it, waving and shouting at their parents, who laughed and wept. And a handsome young Irishman with bright blue eyes was locked in a tight embrace with Elizabeth Deering.

Haviland's fingers shook slightly as he lit a cigarette. Not yet noon and he was on his second pack.

"You can't see him yet," he said to Jerry Mahoney. "The doctor's with him. In a few minutes."

"I still don't get it," Jerry said. "People thought *I* had harmed those kids?"

"You don't know what it's been like here," Liz Deering said, clinging tightly to his arm.

Jerry Mahoney turned and saw the newspaper taped over the broken front window, and his face hardened. "Try and tell me, plain and simple, about Pop," he said.

Haviland shook his head, smiling like a man still dazed. "Your Pop is an amazing man, Mr. Mahoney," he said. "His mind works in its own peculiar ways...The disappearance of the bus affected him differently from some others. He saw it as a magic trick, and he thought of it as a magic trick–or, rather, as *part* of a magic trick. He said it to me and I wouldn't listen. He said it is a magician's job to get you to think what he wants you to think and see what he wants you to see. The disappearance of the children, the ghastly faking of their death in the quarry– it meant one thing to your Pop, Mr. Mahoney. Someone wanted all the people in Clayton to be out of town. Why?

"There was only one good reason that remarkable Pop of yours could think of. The quarry payroll. Nearly a hundred thousand dollars in cash, and not a soul in town to protect it. Everyone would be looking for the children, and all the bandits had to do was walk in the bank and take the money. No cops, no nothing to interfere with them."

"But why didn't Pop tell you his idea?" Jerry asked,

"You still don't know what it was like here, Mr. Mahoney," Haviland said. "People thought you had done something to those kids; they imagined your Pop knew something about it. If he'd told his story even to me, I think I'd have thought he was either touched in the head or covering up. So he kept still–although he did throw me a couple of hints. And suddenly, he was, to all intents and purposes, alone in the town. So he went upstairs, got dressed in those cowboy clothes, and went, calm as you please, to the bank to meet the bandits he knew must be coming. And they came."

"But why the cowboy suit?" Liz Deering asked.

"A strange and wonderful mind," Haviland said. "He thought the sight of him would be screwy enough to throw the bandits off balance. He thought if he started blasting away with his guns they might panic. They almost did."

"What I don't understand," Liz said, "is how, when he fired straight at them, he never hit anybody!"

"Those were stage guns–prop guns," Jerry said. "They only fire blanks."

Haviland nodded. "He thought he could get them to drop their own guns and then he'd have a real weapon and have the drop on them. It almost worked. But the one man who'd ducked around the corner of the building got a clean shot at him. Fortunately, I arrived at exactly the same minute, and I had them from behind."

"But how did you happen to turn up?" Jerry asked.

"I couldn't get your father out of my mind," Haviland said. "He seemed to know what was going to happen. He said they'd be searching for the kids, whether I told them to wait at home or not. Suddenly I had to know why he'd said that."

"Thank God," Jerry said. "I gather you got them to tell you where we were?'

Haviland nodded. "I'm still not clear how it worked, Jerry."

"It was as simple as pie a la mode," Jerry said. "I was about a half mile into the dugway on the home trip with the kids. We'd just passed Karl Dickler headed the other way when a big trailer truck loomed up ahead of me on the road. It was stopped, and a couple of guys were standing around the tail end of it.

"Broken down, I thought. I pulled up. All of a sudden guns were pointed at me and the kids. They didn't talk much. They just said to do as I was told. They opened the back of the big truck and rolled out a ramp. Then I was ordered to drive the station wagon right up into the body of the truck. I might have tried to made a break for it except for the kids. I drove up into the truck, they closed up the rear end, and that was that. They drove off with us—right through the main street of town here!"

"Not ten minutes later," Jerry went on, "they pulled into that big deserted barn on the Haskell place. We've been shut up there ever since. They were real decent to the kids—hot dogs, ice cream, soda."

"So we just waited there, not knowing why, but nobody hurt, and the kids not as scared as you might think," Jerry laughed. "Oh, we came out of the dugway all right—and right by everybody in town. But nobody saw us."

The doctor appeared in the dooway. "You can see him for a minute now, Jerry," he said. "I had to give him a pretty strong sedative. Dug the bullet out of his shoulder and it hurt a bit. He's sleepy—but he'll do better if he sees you, I think. Don't stay too long, though."

Jerry bounded up the stairs and into the bedroom where Pat Mahoney lay, his face very pale, his eyes half closed. Jerry knelt by the bed.

"Pop," he whispered. "You crazy old galoot!"

Pat opened his eyes. "You okay, Jerry?"

"Okay, Pop."

"And the kids?"

"Fine. Not a hair of their heads touched." Jerry reached out and covered Pat's hand with his. "Now look here, Two-Gun Mahoney..."

Pat grinned at him. "It was a boffo, Jerry. A real boffo."

"It sure was," Jerry said. He started to speak, but he saw that Pat was looking past him at the silver picture frame on the dresser.

"I told you it'd be all right, honey," Pat whispered. "I told you not to worry about your boy while I was around to take care of him." Then he grinned at Jerry, and his eyes closed and he was asleep.

Jerry tiptoed out of the room to find his own girl.

THE RHODE ISLAND LIGHTS
S. S. Rafferty

The autumn of 1736 was kind indeed to the coast of the northern colonies. Normally expected foul winds and fouler weather turned out to be a cool, clear sky and a placid sea lapping gently like a puppy against the eddyrock from Boston to New York. For the first time in 18 months, Captain Jeremy Cork and I were once again ensconced in our natural surroundings at the Oar and Eagle at Sea Bluff on the Connecticut littoral.

"Well, by jing," I said, opening the letters that had come by the post rider early that evening, "it appears that your social puzzles have produced some coin at last."

He was sitting at what he euphemistically calls his "work" table, absorbed in a newly-arrived book from England. He looked up and grunted a slight note of interest.

"You remember Squire Delaney of the Rhode Island colony?"

"Of course, Oaks. We helped him in the Narragansett Pacer affair."

"Yes, well, he has seen fit to give your spermacite candle factory in Warwick a substantial contract. It's rather astounding, though. What could he possibly do with two–pound candles? My God, it says here, 'For delivery to the Pharos at Point Judith.' Could Delaney have fallen in with some pagan ritual?"

Cork closed the book and looked up at me with that smirk-a-mouth he uses when he is about to jape me. "Perhaps we ought to refuse the contract. We wouldn't want to be party to the Dark Arts, hey?"

Now there you have it. As Cork's financial yeoman, I am patiently building him an empire of holdings that may some day make him the richest man in the Americas. However, it is part of his sport to ignore my efforts and waste his time in the solution of crimes, which he calls "social puzzles." He has other unprofitable pastimes which are not mentionable in Christian company. This present piece of sarcasm about refusing the Delaney contract was a backhanded reminder that I once proposed the importation of shrunken heads from Spanish America. I said, give the public what it wants, but he was against it.

"I didn't say 'Dark Arts,' sir, you did. I was merely curious about the use of so large a candle, and in such quantity."

"Actually, Oaks, I am guilty of bad imagery. White Arts would have been a better choice."

I looked at him querulously, and he went on, "Even in the absence of all the information, we have the thread of the tapestry. Where does the good Squire live?"

"In the Rhode Island colony."

"More specifically, at Point Judith, does he not?"

"Yes, he owns his horse ranch, as he calls it, and everything in sight."

"And does not Point Judith's recent notoriety bring anything to mind?"

"Of course, the shipwrecks! Four, over the summer, I believe. Shifting sandbars and tricky shoals, the *Gazette* reported."

"And here we have a wealthy, public-spirited man ordering immense candles—"

"A lighthouse! He's building a lighthouse."

"Or Pharos, as mariners term it. But if he is now ordering his light source, I would guess that the Pharos is already built. Now that is something I want to see."

With *The Hawkers*, the ship he owns but never sails in, away to the Indies, we were forced to make the trip overland, and arrived at the Delaney ranch three days later.

I must point out here that our party also included Tunxis, a tame Quinnipiac, who serves as Cork's shadow and as my vexation. Although he speaks passable English, the Indian always talks to Cork in Injun jabber, and a three-day trip spent with two men laughing over incomprehensible jokes is not my recommendation for pleasant travel.

I once heard a back-stair rumour that Cork was related to the Quinnipiac by blood. I would have no truck with that notion. However, when observing Cork's demeanour once he entered the woods and wild, I admit to some doubts. He and Tunxis possess uncanny hearing, and I swear their sense of smell is even better than their eyesight. Perhaps it is these underlying animal instincts that give Cork his reputation as a detector.

In any case, I spent three days ahorse with two boys on a frolic with Nature.

In a previous visit to the Delaneys, I marvelled at the luxury of their center-hall mansion. It had changed only for the better, now sprouting another wing. This annex, I assumed, was to accommodate the issue of the ever-fruitful Madame Delaney. As we were to learn later, the Delaneys, having produced seven brawny sons, were now one shy of matching that mark with females.

We arrived at dinnertime, but were not in peril of taking potluck. At the Delaney table it is always pot-wealth. There was the normal complement of cod chowder, steamed lobster and clams, and, of course, great hot bowls of succotash and pork. But, goodwife that she was, Madame Delaney also served one of the original dishes for which she is justly famous. On this evening it was a platter of succulent squabs, which were as curious as they were delicious. Under Cork's prodding, she told us that they were spit-roasted and basted with a pungent, salty liquor used in China, called sauce of soy. I know little of the Chinese, but their bellies must be content. Since Tunxis refuses to eat or sleep under a roof, he took his repast outdoors.

Later we were sitting in the drawing room with clay bowls and mugs of Delaney's usquebaugh, a potent corn liquor of dark Scotch-Irish reputation, when I brought up a point that had bothered me since we arrived.

"When we turned into your property, Squire, I could see two towers far off on the Point. Yet your order said a Pharos."

"Technical terminology, Oaks," Cork cut in. "One or several lights in one place are considered a unit, and referred to in the singular. I assume, Squire, that you have gone to the expense of two towers to give sailors a seamark that is clearly different from others along the coast."

"That and more," the Irishman said.

"Is it worth doubling the investment, just to be different?" I asked.

Cork refilled his bowl and said, "You'll have to forgive Oaks, Squire. He is a businessman, not a navigator."

"Nor am I, Captain, but mariners tell me it is worth the investment. Perhaps if you will explain it to Oaks, it will further clarify my own mind."

"Surely. Well, Oaks, you have certainly been at sea at night. It is something like waking up in a pitch-black room."

"I leave that to the helmsman," I said.

"And whom does he leave it to? Like an awakened man in a dark room, he can bump into things, not having a bearing on a fixed point. However, when our man at sea bumps into something, it is not a chair or a footstool, producing but a stubbed toe. No, my friend, his obstacle can be a reef or shoal, which can tear the bottom from his craft and send her under."

"What about stars?"

"Helpful in deep water, but when near a landfall, you require well defined objects ashore. Most charts are not well defined. The sextant is only valuable in skilled hands, and then, of course, there are starless nights. But we are digressing into science. The Squire had put up two lights to tell all at sea who might be off course that the two lights are Point Judith and nowhere else, and I compliment him on his public spirit."

"Oh, that I could accept it, Captain," said the Squire, with a moan. "But I cannot. The Pharos was built to protect my own good name, as well as the men at sea."

"Go on, man," the Captain said, squinting his eyes in interest.

"You might have read of the shipwrecks off these shores over the past year."

"Yes," I said, "the *Boston Weekly Gazette* mentioned them."

"But what they didn't mention was the ugly rumour that spread in these parts and which implied that I had somehow contrived to cause these wrecks for salvage rights."

"Did you salvage them?"

"Yes, Captain, the first one. But after the rumours I stopped.

God help me, my eldest son is at this moment apprenticed to the master of a coaster. Would I be so callous?"

"Indeed not. But tell me, why do you carry the financial load alone? Other townships have raised Pharos with lotteries. Why not here?"

"The townspeople, like those everywhere, resent the wealthy, and feel they can't afford it. Those lottery-built light-houses are near ports where a lighthouse tax is collectable. Such is not the case here. I bear the load, but alas, not out of public spirit."

"Tell me, Squire," Cork asked, "is there any suspicion that the wrecks might have been caused by foul play?"

"It's a perplexing question. The shoals off our shore are treacherous, and the sandbars seem to have shifted, so accident is highly possible. I have personally surveyed the surrounding waters at low tide, and I had a young fellow from Yale draw up some charts. When word got out that I was going to erect a lighthouse, a single one, all hell broke loose from here to Narragansett."

"But why?" I asked. "You would be protecting shipping by warning them away from underwater hazards."

"And away from Narragansett Bay, or so the dockmen up there claim. As Cork said, night navigation is tricky at best, and if my lone light was a beacon of danger, there was fear that a ship's master would steer a northerly parallel course to the light and up in Buzzard's Bay, which would enrich New Bedford."

"That's nonsense," Cork growled, "and can be proved so."

"Captain, did you ever try to explain logic and reason to a group of more than three or four men? Especially on a technical subject?"

"Touche," Cork said, with a smile.

"Well, how do two lighthouses solve the problem?" I asked.

"The Yale student suggested it. Our charts show that a deep channel cuts through the shoals. If a means could be found to guide a ship through it at night, a master could safely change from a northerly course to a westerly line, go through the channel, and then swing northeast towards Narragansett."

"Aha." Cork slapped his knee and tossed his head back. "I should have seen it at once when I noticed that the two towers are not in parallel line. The second tower is set back, is it not?"

"Twenty-five feet."

"So you have not only a distinctive seamark, but a unique navigation aid. You present the sailor with a simple light-in-one sighting."

"That's precisely the term John Knox, the student, used."

Following this discussion was becoming as difficult as listening to Cork and Tunxis talk Injun. "Forgive me, gentlemen," I said, "but this is all beyond me."

"Shall I explain, Squire?"

"Pray do. I barely understand it myself."

"Probably because the academician likes to cloak his knowledge in long words. Actually, a light-in-one sighting is simple, but it is more easily demonstrated than explained. May I conduct an experiment for Oaks here so that he might understand?"

The Squire seemed delighted with the entertainment, and Cork set to it. "First, Oaks, you will go into that closet on the far wall. When you emerge, the room will be in darkness except for these two candles, which will be burning on the table to represent the two towers on the Point.

"Now, when you emerge from the closet, you will be facing north, and the floor area in front of you will be cleared of all furniture. This will represent the safety of deep water. Now, as you walk due north, keep your eye on the candles. At a certain point, you will see the two lights start to merge into one. It is no illusion, Oaks. The lights really aren't moving, *you* are. Now the trick is to get you to change to a westerly course. That would be to your left, and bring you forward without breaking your neck on the stools I will have scattered there to represent the shoals."

"Captain," I said suspiciously, "I don't mind barked shins, but a broken neck?"

"Have faith in the system, Oaks, as must the mariner. When the lights merge into one, you will turn to your left and proceed so through the aisle I will have made between the stools, to represent the channel. Now I have a question, Squire. Are the lanterns designed to emit light on a 180-degree radius?"

"Yes, that's the reason for the immense candles."

"To be sure. So when Oaks is safely through the aisle, he will again see two lights."

"Correct."

"Then you have nothing to fear, Oaks. Now into the closet

while I scale the mathematics to fit our simplified situation in this room. Well, come, my boy, you will be just as safe as in your own bed."

On Cork's guarantee I left my dark closet and entered the room.The candles burned brightly on the table to my left, and I gingerly walked forward. I was amazed to see the candles appear to move, and when they merged into one, I turned left with some trepidation. To my surprise all went well, and when the candles were two again, I turned north again.

"Amazing," I said after the other tapers were lit and the furniture put back to rights.

"Well, you must appreciate that this was a crude example of how a light-in-one works," Cork said, taking some more usquebaugh. "This student, this Knox fellow, has obviously made precise calculations, to place the lights in their proper positions."

"He was at it for weeks, spending nights out in a skiff while my son Secundus and I lit fires from rude poles placed ashore at different angles and heights. Once we had the proper mathematics, we started construction. In the last three weeks of operation we personally have traversed the channel at least fifty times. Three ships' masters have also taken their crafts through successfully.

"Copies of the charts were sent to all the major ports to the south and the harbourmasters have written back that they have made the information known to north-bound ships."

"And what of fog or heavy rain?" I asked.

"I am sorry to say that the lights are useless in foul weather, but we have tried to overcome that weakness by firing a star rocket every hour on the hour. At least it will be some warning, and will keep the taint of malicious rumour from my good name. Being accused of placing false lights to lure ships upon the rocks is a heinous charge."

"And punishable by death under Admiralty Law," Cork added with a note of grimness. "But it seems your troubles are over. Is John Knox still with you? I should like to meet him."

"To be sure. He is manning Tower One, while Secundus is in Tower Two. We have decided to hire keepers, but not for a while."

I smiled to myself at the Squire's penchant for naming things by number. A less precise man would have called the first tower the forward tower, and the second the aft, or rear, tower. But what could you expect from a man who named his seven sons Primus, Secundus, Tertius, and so on? He once told me that he originally planned to use the names of the Apostles, but was forewarned by his wife that he was overreaching himself. The female Delaneys were being named for the nine Muses. The Squire is clearly a man of stern determination.

"So, my lads," he said, raising his mug, "I give you the Point Judith Pharos, long may it shine." As he said it, Delaney walked to a large bow window and threw back the drapes. "There are my beauties," he said and raised his glass anew.

Out in the distance, through a starless night, were the dark landsides of the towers, eerie halos of light radiating above their silhouettes as their fiery faces shone out to sea. As we watched the halos glistening, Cork explained that the halo was called a corona, and the rears of the lanterns were much like a view from the dark side of the moon. Then suddenly a toll of bells and the wail of handhorns sounded off in the distance.

"Why, it's like New Year's Eve," I said, jokingly. Cork touched my arm and cocked his head into the sounds. He turned and looked at the Squire, who was white with fear.

"Oh, God," Delaney said, lips trembling, "a shipwreck!"

The ensuing hours of that horror-filled night will never be erased from my memory. Out in the darkness lay a sinking ship, its timbers grinding chillingly like the broken spine of a wounded and thrashing beast. Small boats with survivors bobbled in the surf as citizens from the surrounding countryside rushed to aid them. It was near dawn when the last of the longboats dispatched from shore returned from a sweep of the wreck area.

As the longboat was hauled onto the beach, the last survivors tumbled out. One was a young sailor of no more than 20. His hand was bleeding, and one of the countrymen came forward to help him. As he lifted the lad to carry him, he cried out in anger, "It's Primus Delaney, it is. The old devil Squire is at it again!"

By noon the Squire and Primus had been placed under arrest and locked in the brig of a Royal Frigate in Narragansett harbour. The charges were barratry, collusion to shipwreck, and murder, since three hands were lost in the tragedy. The towers were closed by Royal Navy order, and the Delaney household was in chaos.

Before the two Delaneys were clapped in irons, however, Cork was able to piece together the gist of what had happened at sea.

The doomed ship was the *Queen of Tortuga*, out of New York, bound for Narragansett. Her master, who was injured but alive, was Captain Amos Whittleby. At the time of the wreck he had been below deck, having left Primus as the watch officer, and helmsman Fergus Kirk at the wheel.

According to Primus, he had been given charts of his father's new enterprise and was anxious to use the navigation aid. On sighting the two beacons, he sounded the ship's bell and ordered Kirk into the channel-crossing manoeuver.

"The lights were joining beautifully," he told us earlier that morning, while being fed hot broth by his mother. All the survivors had been taken to the Delaney home for care, but it was obvious that most of the crew were suspicious and angry. "I kept the lights in sight until they were one, and then told the helmsman to bring her into the west. All went well, and when the lights started to part again, I thought we were through the channel. In fact, I could see the fore and aft lights of a smaller craft still further west. I was about to order us back north, when the crunch of the bottom came, and—well, after that it was hell."

"And now, in broad daylight," Cork said at the time, "we can see that the wreck lies hundreds of feet from the entrance of the channel. So you were on a dead heading for the shoal all the time."

"Yet I couldn't have mistaken the lights' merge, Captain Cork. Fergus Kirk can tell you the same thing."

But it seemed the helmsman couldn't.

"Aye, the boy may be telling truth," the Scotsman told us later. "I kept my eyes peeled to the compass, and could nae say what the lights done. This I do ken, sirs. No wee laddie should have say on the course of a bark under sail."

Cork interrogated the rest of the crew, but at the time of the wreck all were at meal or asleep in the fo'c'sle. A second hand on the night watch admitted to being asleep on the forward hatch. The others on the watch were lost in the disaster.

Captain Whittleby refused to answer any questions, and replaced cooperation with threats and castigation

"You have one of two choices, Captain Cork," he snarled as his battered head was being bandaged by a crewman. "Either the light scheme is faulty, or the boy was derelict in his duty. In either case, one of the Delaneys will swing for it, and I want to be there to see the execution."

"We are assured the lights were operating properly, and the system has been tested time and again, Captain Whittleby," Cork had said with some annoyance. "But while we are speaking of dereliction, may I ask you why the youngest mate in your crew was given command of the ship in a difficult passage? Surely you shoud have been on deck, or at the least your first mate."

"The setting of watches is my own business, Captain Cork, and I resent the accusation of dereliction. Why wouldn't I trust young Delaney? He was in home waters and following his father's charts. And I'm sure, if you are a mariner, you well know the youngest eyes and ears in the crew are called on when needed in rough crossing."

"Then you admit to a rough crossing."

"He admits to nothing, sir." The speaker was the local man who had helped young Primus from the boat. His name was Myles Swaith, and he was truly no friend of the Delaneys. "I have heard of your reputation, Captain Cork—how you are able to twist and contort things to fit your own ends. But not this time. Delaney has lorded it over this vicinity for years, but now he's for it, and there's no help for him."

"There really isn't, you know," I said to Cork when we left the room. "We ourselves are witness to the lighthouses working, and if Knox's calculations are correct, then it's error on Primus' part. But if the calculations are wrong, it's the Squire's neck."

"Yes," Cork said, stroking his barba in thought, "but when you have spent some time at sea, Oaks, you learn not to trust the surface of the waves. It's what's below that counts. Let's talk to Knox and Secundus."

The lighthouse keepers were in a bedroom on the second floor. John Knox was in his mid-twenties, with flaxen blond hair and an aquiline nose. Secundus Delaney needed no description once you had seen the Squire or any of his offspring. The same red hair and round pixie face. It was as if they had all come from the same mould, which, when you thought about it, was precisely the case.

Knox sat in a chair with his head in his hands. Secundus, a lad of 18, lay despondently on the bed.

"I can't believe it, Captain," Knox said after we had introduced ourselves. "I am positive of my calculations. We tested them over and over again. If anyone should be blamed, it should be me."

"That's not true," Secundus said, getting up and patting his friend's shoulder. "My father and I have also used the system, and we know it works. And several ships' masters have done the same."

"All it proves is that your brother made an error," Knox said. "So what does that solve?"

"Mr. Knox," Cork broke in, "self-pity is a poor companion in dire straits. The Squire tells me that copies of the charts were sent to harbourmasters of all major ports to the south. Did you draw those charts?"

"Why, yes, I did. Oh, I see what you mean. I must have made an error on one of them, and somehow it got to New York and on to the *Queen of Tortuga*. Then I *am* to blame!"

"Possibly. But there is another aspect. The New York chart could have been changed. How were they sent?"

"By coaster, sir," Secundus explained, "out of 'Gansett. It was the quickest way."

"And Primus' copy of the chart went down with the *Queen of Tortuga*. How fortunate." Cork smiled.

"Fortunate?" Knox looked perplexed.

"Fortunate for Primus' neck. I believe there will be a trial, and I plan to defend him. I have that right, as a ship's master and owner. Now we have a point of doubt in our favour. If the Court will accept the argument that the chart could have been changed–ever so slightly, for a jot on a chart is hundreds of yards at sea–then we introduce the possibility of collusion from a third party."

Knox's face took on brightness for the first time. "Why, I never thought of that. But wait, Captain, the harbourmaster at New York–wouldn't he know?"

"I doubt that he would remember. Most seamen do not memorize charts they will never use."

Secundus smacked his hands together and let out a howl of glee. "Captain, sir, you're a marvel," he cried.

There was a commotion downstairs, and we all went down to find Primus and his father chained together and guarded by six towering Royal Marines. An English Captain named Cricker read formal charges and led the men away over the shrieks and wails of the Delaney women.

The rest of the day was spent within the legal machinery in preparation for a naval inquiry. Once in the town of Narragansett, we called on a local lawyer of some reputation. Giles Pomfret was an old eagle, trained in the Inns of Court, and regarded as a sound scholar. His offices were on the second floor of the Blue Whale, and after an explanation of the situation he sat back slowly touching the fingers of one hand to the other.

"I bow to you, Captain, in marine law, but this doubt-casting element about a chart being mysteriously changed—well, it is a thin line, sir. A very thin line, indeed, since the chart itself is fathoms down."

"That is only my first line, Mr. Pomfret, and I think you will agree that a good defense is the sum of many ramparts."

The old man nodded and then smiled. "To show you how ill equipped I am for the case, when you first said 'barratry,' my mind immediately went to the civil-law interpretation—the habitual maintenance of lawsuits or quarrels. Now in marine law, it means to sink a ship, does it not?"

"Technically, it is the use of fraud or gross or criminal negligence on the part of the master or mariners of a ship to the owner's prejudice."

"Yes. Yes, of course. And the Delaney boy being on the deck watch is the mariner in this case. But what of the charge of wrecking and murder?"

"The changed-chart theory, if proved, will obliterate all charges."

"Well, Captain"—Pomfret shook his head—"I wish you good fortune, but I'll also pray for the Delaneys at the same time. I will, however, prepare the necessary papers to allow you to represent them at the inquiry. If, however, this goes to a full Court, I suggest that you hire the finest marine lawyer money can buy."

We bid him goodbye on that sour note, and, when we were on the street, Cork walked in silence.

Finally, he stopped for a moment and said, more to himself than to me, "Strange, a lawyer in a busy port, and he knows nothing of marine law."

"It could be his age. He seems in his dotage."

"That may be," he said, and then stopped a young boy. "Hey, my lad, who is the harbourmaster in these waters?"

"That be old Peg and Patch, sir," the boy replied with a shudder.

"Old Peg and Patch, hey? And I suppose you address him so when you bid him good day?"

The lad lowered his head and then shot it up again. "When I sees him I brings myself about, sir. Beware churned waters, my old may says," he told us through a toothless grin.

"A fearsome fellow, then?"

"Like the devil himself, sir. Some says he was a pirate and lived with wild natives on a far-off isle where he was a canny-ball."

"And where would his headquarters be, lad?"

"At the foot of Tillford's dock, sir, but you won't find 'im there. Best look in Sadie's, by the Front Street." Then he said, wide-eyed, "If ye have the heart, for you 'pear to be of quality."

"Mere clothes, my lad," Cork said, tossing a coin to him.

One of the outstanding aspects of New England life is the righteous piety of the population. Yet, in its port towns, there is usually one low place where evil flourishes and slakes the appetites of men home from long voyages. Sadie's was buried deep in the cellar of an old warehouse. Through the thick and acrid smoke I could see a stairway that led to the upper part of the building, and dared not think of the evil doings that must occur up there. A crone with tousled hair paid court to our obvious means, and directed us to the harbourmaster at a table in a far corner.

From the boy's description I expected to see a demonic sot, racked with depravity. However, Captain Robert Tinker (for that was his true name) was a well kept man of 60. The appellation of Peg and Patch sprang from the spotless patch over his left eye and the ivory stump that served as his left leg from the knee down. To my further surprise he was a reasonably well-spoken Englishman of some education.

After we had taken seats, he must have noticed my own amazement, or sensed it.

"From the look on your face, Mr. Oaks, I take it you have been talking to the townspeople. I am no ogre, sirs. The eye and the limb were lost to gunfire in the service of King and Country. I guess I am resented because I was granted my post by Royal Appointment. Let me assure you, it is no sinecure."

An unbelievably buxom wench came to the table, and Captain Tinker ordered a bottle of madeira. *His* madeira.

"I take it you are here on the Delaney business, gentlemen. What service can I do for you?"

"I am told," Cork began, "that copies of the Point Judith charts were put aboard coasters and taken to southern ports."

"Aye. Four in all. Put them aboard myself, explaining in each case the Pharos to the ship's master."

"Do you recall the ships?"

"Ah, let me see, the *Tarrymae* was one."

"Excuse me, Captain," Cork interrupted, "to simplify it, which ship was New York bound?"

"The *Ice Cloud*, under Master Swaith."

"John Swaith?"

"Nay, his brother, Ishmael."

"Interesting. There were four wrecks in this area over the summer months, I gather."

"Aye. The Judith shoals were becoming a graveyard, until the Squire came along with this Pharos idea."

"Now I'm told that Delaney took salvage rights on the first bottom, but who took rights in the other wrecks?"

"The 'Gansett Corporation. After the rumours started when the *Bristol Girl* went down, Delaney wouldn't put an oar in the water. So John Swaith and a few local businessmen formed a group and took the jobs. Damned shame about young Delaney, though. Shouldn't put the deck under a youngster, I always say."

"Then you believe it to have been an accident?"

"What else, sir? I myself put the Pharos plan to the test and went through the channel like it was the Thames. Say now, don't go taking on this bilge that the Squire was a wrecker. He's as true as magnetic north."

"To be sure. You will be called as a witness if there is a trial, and I trust you will hold that position."

"You have my bond, sir."

When Cork offered to pay for the madeira, which was excellent, Tinker refused. "First one's free, Captain," he said. "It's good for business. You see, I own this place."

That evening, on our return to the Delaney ranch, we took a meagre supper in our rooms. The hearty familial spirit that had been drawn from the home had left only bleakness in its aftertide.

"It appears that the name Swaith abounds in this affair," I said, over the cold turkey and corn bread.

"Yes, the brother could have changed the charts, but we are on slanderous grounds. I want something with more meat to it."

"Your second rampart?"

"And a third, if we can find one."

With this, there was a tap; at the window, which at first I thought was rain. Getting up, Cork opened the casement to admit Tunxis. Despite the fact that we were on the second floor, the Indian's sudden appearance was not in the least jarring to me. To come to the second floor like a normal person he would have to enter under a roof, so it was natural that he would scale the trellis to converse with Cork. The climb up must have winded him slightly, or set his mind a-bubble, for he spoke in English. Thrusting a sack through the window, he said, "Here, like you say, lower beach."

"Good fellow, Chawcua, and who was with you?"

"White man named Clint."

"Good. Wait below."

When Cork had closed the window again, he returned to the table with the sack and sat down.

"What's in that thing?" I asked, sniffing the air. "A skunk?"

"No. My second line of defense, Oaks."

I reached across, opened the sack, and quickly closed it. "Animal droppings. Dung is your second rampart?"

"Evidence is often as repulsive as the crime, Oaks. Now I'm off for the third."

"Not without me," I said, getting to my feet.

"You're a stout fellow, my lad, but not this time."

"And why not? Am I some slip of a girl, some piece of frippery? I may not have the woodsy wiles of that redskin, but I'm man enough to a given task."

There were few times in my long relationship with him that I experienced true camaraderie. He reached out, clapped my shoulder, looked at me with those cold blue eyes, and smiled. "I never doubted that, my friend. Come, we have some climbing of our own to do."

My moment of gallantry stuck in my throat as we approached the base of the forward tower on the point. With the ground-level hatches of both structures sealed tight with Royal lead, Cork proposed to scale the side of the thirty-foot edifice fronting the sea.

"Not only is it dangerous, but pointless," I said, as Tunxis uncurled roping lines.

"Wrong on both counts, Oaks. The facing is of fine hammered sandstone with a wide bond, so, despite the mist, the footing is sure. As for examining the light room, it is crucial to the case. I will go first, Tunxis to follow. Once up, we will haul you up by rope."

"If you climb, I climb."

He looked at the Indian, and Tunxis nodded. A savage was giving his accord to my own valour. Perhaps, at last, I was accepted by him.

I will not embarrass myself by describing the toil and fear of the ascent. From one slippery stone to the next, never looking down into the blackness, I inched my way up into more blackness. Above me I heard the shatter of glass, as Cork broke one of the panes in the tower windows, and a sharp tug on the guy line around my waist alerted me that the end of the climb was near.

"Take care of the broken pane, Oaks," Cork whispered. "Reach above your head and you will find a rod running around the ceiling on the inside."

I swung into the window frame and got to my feet. Cork was examining the apparatus with a shielded candle. The now dark light was a wondrous machine. Twelve large candles were imbedded in a holding plate before a concave plate of polished brass. The candles, when lit, must have reflected a most powerful light out to sea.

"What are you doing, Captain?" I asked, as he tugged at the base of the holding plate.

"Solid as Gibraltar," he said. "Let's take the ladder below."

One by one we descended into a round room directly below the light chamber. It had been fitted out as living quarters for a permanent keeper, when he was eventually hired. A chair and a writing table were at one side of the room. Tunxis lit the lamp with his candle while Cork rummaged around. He found nothing in the table drawer, and obviously nothing of interest in the few books on the shelf.

"Looks like a wild goose," I said, sitting on the chair, still winded from the climb and the excitement.

"Perhaps," Cork muttered as he pulled back a curtain hanging on ring hoops to expose a bed.

"Are lighthouse keepers allowed to sleep?"

"We all must, eventually, Oaks. With the coal-fired beacons along the English coast, there is little chance of the light going out, so the keepers sleep. I'm sure that when Delaney hires a regular keeper, he will keep a night watch."

"Keepers, you mean," I corrected him. An opportunity I rarely have.

He looked at me from the shadows cast by the lamp and gave me that smirk-a-mouth again. "You! A man of ledgers and coin! My word, Oaks, that is astounding. One man can handle both towers. Stationed in this forward tower, he could see if the rear tower was lit at all times. What's below there, Tunxis?"

The Indian's head poked up the ladderway hatch from the deck below.

"Supplies, candles."

"Well," I said, "what next? I hope we are not going to climb the other tower."

"No need. Come, lads, there is nothing more here." Cork snuffed the lamp.

When we arrived back at the house, Tunxis went wherever he goes, and we entered to find a note from Lawyer Pomfret. Cork did not read it in front of Madame Delaney, but waited till we were in our rooms. He then tore open the sealed envelope and read quickly.

"They move with great haste in this matter." He tossed the paper to me and I read it with a sinking heart. Disregarding all the niceties and legal terms, its essence was that a Naval Court of Inquiry would convene two days hence to take advantage of the fact that Admiral Fenley-Blore, of his Majesty's fleet, was in the area, and had agreed to preside over the panel.

"My, my, a flag officer, no less. Is that good or bad, Captain?"

He shrugged. "All bad pennies have an obverse. If we lose, there is little chance for appeal in London. A Fleet Admiral's stamp will settle it forever."

"And if we win, that also ends it forever. "But two days is so short a time to prepare."

"For us, yes. I feel other forces have been planning for weeks.
But no use wailing over it. We must set some things to our advantage. Fetch me Secundus, will you, while I pen a note."

A note indeed. It was a missive of polite flattery and obei-
sance to Admiral Fenley-Blore. Cork expressed concern over
the meagre accommodations available in Narragansett to a
naval hero of the Admiral's stature. He went on to describe the
luxury of the Delaney home and extended its hospitality to
further add to the Admiral's comfort, and suggested that the
Court be convened in the main hall of the Delaney mansion in
order that the Admiral's august presence have the proper dignified surroundings. The most amusing part was his signing it,
"Your obedient servant." Cork has bowed to no man, and I am
sure he has never been obedient.

Secundus was dressed for the night ride, and took the letter.
"Mind, lad, for the Admiral's hands, and no other's. By the bye,
before you go. Was anyone aware that your brother's ship was
making for these waters?"

"Surely. It was posted in the harbourmaster's office. Not the
exact day, but on or about, you know."

"Estimated date of return, yes. Well, off you go."

The Admiral arrived the next afternoon with two aides.
Fenley-Blore was an English sailor of the old line. In the days
of Queen Bess he would surely have been one of the Sea Dogs.
A shortish man, he tended toward portliness in his twilight
years. But the weight of girth and age had not slowed his step
or his agile mind. Cork, the sly fox, fawned over him like a lass
to a fiddler.

It wasn't until the next morning that I saw through the reason for Cork's uncommon actions. We were at breakfast, and
Fenley-Blore was saying, "Wild turkey, you say? Now that
should be good sport, hunting from horseback. But I'm afraid
we will have to get on with this inquiry business. I enjoy these
sojourns ashore, but I must get back to sea."

"I understand, Admiral," Cork soothed him, "but why not
have the best of all possible worlds? We can hunt today and
hold the inquiry tonight. You have the power to convene at
any hour, so why not at your leisure?"

"Well put. Tonight it is. Feel a bit sheepish at trying a man in in his own home, though."

"Command is not always easy, Admiral."

He had hooked him. The inquest was to be held that night.

Before I describe that evening of surprises, dejections, and finally, of uncanny solution, I must explain that I have simplified the text to avoid all the technical terms that fog understanding for the layman. I myself kept copious notes, and it took Cork three days to explain them to me. The air in the main hall that night was thick with such phrases as "points to the larboard," "keel lines," "true and magnetic course," and "lines of divination," as well as an hour's worth of talks and arguments about sails and winds and cross-winds.

The main point is that a ship was wrecked due either to negligence or to a faulty system—or so the Court claimed.

Cork went immediately to work on the changed-chart theory. He carefully laid the groundwork by describing how the copies of the chart sent to New York *could* have been changed. He was about to strengthen his question of doubt when one of the Admiral's aides leaned over and whispered into his superior's ear.

"Excuse me, Captain Cork," Fenley-Blore said, "but this line that the chart used aboard the *Queen of Tortuga* by young Delaney being missing is not correct."

I looked up at Cork, who was standing at our table facing the Court. His face showed surprise, and a chart was handed down the line of nine officers on the panel to the Admiral.

"Captain Cork," the Admiral continued, picking up the chart, "this was found with the flotsam of the *Tortuga*. It bears the inscription: *Delaney, Point Judith Pharos*. Would you kindly verify that it is the same as the original chart?"

Cork called John Knox, who was sworn in. The student looked at the cart carefully and said, "I'm afraid it's accurate, Captain," causing a murmur from the small group of townsmen who sat at the back of the long room. It appeared that Cork's first line of defense was breached, and I could see no rampart to fall back upon.

The Captain now went into skirmish manoeuvers. He called the Delaneys, and Primus and his father both took an oath to their stories. He also put on the stand a Captain Jeggs, one of the mariners who had tested the system, and he too swore to Heaven that it was a genuine chart.

Next came Fergus Kirk, who would swear to nothing except that he was Fergus Kirk. He stuck to his story that he had been watching the compass. As Kirk stepped down, a voice from the back of the room said, "If it pleases the Admiral and the panel, sir, may I be recognized?"

I turned to see Lawyer Pomfret, counsellor-at-law, representing the Virron Shipping concern of Maiden Lane, New York, owners of the *Queen of Tortuga*."

He shifted on his feet like a nervous bird, and faced the panel.

"We, of course, have an interest in this matter and its outcome, and it seems to me that the good Captain here has everyone in sight taking an oath. We can't believe both Delaneys and still have a logical explanation of the matter. Now I'm a local man and would like to see fairness tendered, but my clients demand justice."

"And, from justice, restitution?" Cork asked.

"Captain, you're a fine fellow and a superior host," the Admiral smiled, "but we will have to get more answers than we have so far."

Cork was about to resume, when Captain Jeggs motioned to him, and both men talked in low whispers for a few moments. "Admiral, I have no further need of Captain Jeggs. We have his testimony, and he has a tide to catch."

"Excused, and good weather, Captain," the Admiral said, tossing him a half salute.

"Now, gentlemen." Cork walked forward as a chair was brought up for Pomfret, who sat and crossed his spindly legs. "The crux of the matter is the Pharos system itself, and to fully understand it, the panel should see it in operation."

"No need, Admiral. We can exhibit it right here, with your permission. It's very simple. All we will need is two candles and total darkness. I would use my friend Oaks to demonstrate, but that could be viewed as prejudice, so I will call on a man who has asked for justice, Lawyer Pomfret."

The lawyer gladly accepted, and the room was set up much as we had it when I played the part of the ship. One major exception was that Cork had the panel table moved forward. That put us all facing the wall along which Pomfret would walk in darkness.

"Now, to truly imitate the conditions of the night in question," Cork said, before the tapers were extinguished, "I have fashioned a shield for the back of the candle holders. In that way, only Mr. Pomfret will be able to tell us what he sees. Now remember, Pomfret, when the lights are one, make your turn, not before or after, for those chairs could give you a nasty knock."

The lawyer left the room, and we waited, adjusting our eyes to the darkness. Cork lit the candles, for we could all see the halos above the shields. "Come ahead," he shouted, and a door opened and I could hear Pomfret slowly shuffling across the room ahead. Four, five seconds, and then he said, "I'm turning now," and then the crash of old bones and heavy mahogany chairs followed instantly.

It would have been a comic sight to see the old man lying on the floor rubbing his painful leg, had it not sunk the Squire once and for all. But then it occurred to me that Pomfret had deliberately turned too soon, in order to create a negative impression. I went forward in the low-lighted room and informed Cork in a low tone.

"Excuse me, gentlemen," Cork said to the Court, while he helped the snarling man to his feet. "It has been suggested to me that our legal friend here may have resorted to deceit to prejudice the case."

"That's a lie," Pomfret shouted, dusting himself off.

"You are correct, sir. I believe you did turn when the lights became one. Just as young Delaney did."

"Then you have proved the case against the Squire," the Admiral said.

"I have proved a case, sir. Let us see who fits the mould."

He walked over to the window and drew back the drapes to the oh's and ah's of everyone. The Admiral came to his feet and hurried to the window. "What are those lights doing on?" he roared. The two towers had glowing halos above their tops. "They were ordered sealed, and by the gods, I'll hang any man who has broken them open."

"There are ways around seals, just as there are ways around systems, Admiral. Say, isn't that a ship out there? See the fore-and-aft running lights riding the waves?"

"You're right, Cork." The Admiral spoke with sudden anxiety.

An aide who had come to the Admiral's side muttered,

"He'll have her on the beach in a moment."

The Admiral was now purple with rage. "Cork, I hold you responsible for the safety of the ship. It was lured into the cove by those blasted lights."

"I take the responsibility, sir. May I produce the master of that 'ship'?"

"How? By magic?"

"No, by voice." Cork opened the window and called, "Ahoy!"

It *seemed* like magic, for the ship turned its prow into the beach and headed straight for the window. Then, as it got closer, we could see the trick.

"It's a donkey!" the Admiral cried. "A beast with lanterns hung over its head and tail."

"And the movement of a donkey walking on the beach would give an observer at sea the illusion that he was looking at a distant ship riding the waves."

"That's an old wrecker's trick, a damnable one," Fenley-Blore swore. "But what has this demonstration to do with the Pharos being faulty?"

"If we will all take our seats again, I will explain," Cork addressed us. He now knew he was in safe water, and he played like a dolphin.

"Actually, I am presenting the evidence for acquittal in reverse. You will recall that Primus felt he was on a safe course when the beacons were joined, because the over-all plot was so well conceived, so wondrously scientific, that I couldn't believe such a shoddy element would be allowed to mar it. It was just too much sugar in the bun.

"The man out there with the animal is named Clint. On the morning after the wreck he and my Indian friend searched the beach area and found what my yeoman calls 'filthy evidence' that a beast of burden had traversed the ground. Now, Admiral, you are correct that this has nothing to do with the performance of the Pharos. I say it worked perfectly that night, and will continue to work perfectly."

"My shin seems to give that a sound argument," Pomfret put in.

"I am sorry about that, Mr. Pomfret. It was not done in malice, but perhaps with a touch—only a touch, mind you— of indignation at your performance in your office two days ago. I

am sure you are skilled in marine law, and I do not like to be
lied to. But leave it, sir. This conspiracy required a genius and a
fool, and you are neither.

"Cork, get to the point," the Admiral admonished, irritably.

"I beg pardon. Would you be kind enough to walk the same
course which was so painful to Mr. Pomfret? Oh, no, I will not
have the lights out this time. Please, sir."

The Admiral got to his feet with a look of simmering anger
and took a place at the far wall. Cork re-lit the candles and
nodded for the old sailor to start. Fenley-Blore was a quarter of
the way across when he stopped.

"What the devil are you doing, Cork? You're passing a
screen over the forward candle."

"Yes, exactly as I did when Pomfret was our ship. Only in
the lit room you can see the trick. Just as Primus Delaney could
not see the trick out over the blackness of the sea. Seize him,
Oaks."

John Knox was a slippery fellow, but I held him fast.

"You can't prove a thing, Cork," Knox said, "How could I
hold a screen in front of the candles up there? It's too big for
one man to do."

"When I said this conspiracy needed a genius and a fool, I
should have added a dupe, but I didn't want to forewarn you,
Mr. Knox. You have told us that you went to Yale College. Did
you graduate?"

"No, I went only two years."

"That's strange. Yale is a fine school, but more regarded for
its humanities and theology than for its science."

"My father was a master builder, and taught me his trade."

"Builder, yes. The construction of the towers is sound. But
what of seamanship, navigation?"

"I've read books."

"Good sailors learn their trade before the mast, as soldiers
learn their craft in battle." This last drew smiles from the entire
panel.

"I suggest you are a dupe, Mr. Knox. To devise this plan
would require years at sea, years of experience with difficult
passages. And, I might add, an accurate mathematical ability.

"As for holding a screen in front of the lamp, I agree that it
would be impossible for one man to do it alone, and if you
blew out the candles, there would be no corona, or halo, to be

seen from the back of the tower to gull us all into thinking that the light was in proper working order.

"Also, if you were simply to hold up a screen in front of the light, no purpose would be served. A ship running on a parallel line would see it one second and not the next. The abruptness of the change would make a mere cabin boy suspicious. No, Knox, the screen would have to move slowly between the lights from left to right to give the illusion that the lights were joining, long before that would really happen."

"That would be some trick," Knox said contemptuously. "What would I use? I took nothing from the tower that night, and it has been sealed since."

"You had no need to take anything away. The tools are still there in all their innocence. One thing I noted about your tower when I broke in the other night is that it is efficient. Yet the only purpose of a rod that runs around the ceiling of the front wall seems to be to give the intruders a handhold. Another inefficiency is a bed that gives the sleeper privacy, when a lone sleeper needs no privacy. Thus we have your screen or curtain, which could be attached to the rod in the light chamber and used to slowly eclipse the light source from the front, while still providing a halo at the back."

"That's fanciful conjecture, Cork."

"No, I think the two gentlemen entering the room will back it up. Did it work, Captain Jeggs?"

Jeggs and a naval officer came forward and told of sailing out off the Point while Tunxis worked the curtain in Tower One.

"You are the dupe, Knox, and you have the privilege of going to the hanging string alone if you choose. Shall I produce the fool and the genius, or would you care to throw yourself on the Admiral's mercy?"

Knox looked at Fenley-Blore and back at Cork. He was frightened now, like an animal in a trap.

"Swaith! Miles Swaith is the culprit!" he screamed. "When I came here to build only one tower, he offered me money to advise the Squire against it, because he had been wrecking the ships with that donkey trick and spreading rumours about the Delaneys. When the Squire insisted on going ahead, Miles Swaith brought me the Pharos scheme, plans, charts, and all. Believe me, Squire, I didn't know Primus was aboard that ship. When I saw the running lights through the spyglass, I didn't know it was the *Queen of Tortuga.*"

Miles Swaith was on his feet frothing at the mouth. "He can't bring me into this, he can't! I deny everything he says, and it's his word against mine."

"And your donkey against whose, Swaith? When I sent Tunxis to scour the neighborhood with Mr. Clint, he learned that you are the only one in the immediate vicinity who keeps such a beast. Oxen are used hereabouts, which, as any wrecker knows, are too slow and too even-footed to give the illusion of a cruising ship. Admiral, I give you Miles Swaith, the fool in the plot. If he had followed his master's plan, and trusted the light system alone, without using the donkey trick, we would have never uncovered the plot."

"By the Duke's guns!" The Admiral thumped the table. "When I first laid eyes on you I said, 'There is a remarkable fellow.' Now I double it, sir. You are a genius."

"I thank you, sir, but there is only one genius abounding, and we must pin him before we have the lot."

"If you can do that, my boy, I'll give you a man-of-war for a toy. I don't know when I've enjoyed myself more. Well, go on, go on." The Admiral was as gleeful as a small lad on Christmas morning.

"I have given profound thought to his identity. Swaith is discounted, for he is merely a rude and greedy bumpkin. Our student is too limited in skill. So who have we? Let me see. We need a master mariner, to be sure, and a scientist of some prowess. Forgive me, Admiral, if this description seems to fit you."

For a moment the old boy looked concerned, and then he broke into laughter. "Very remarkable fellow," he said to the aide at his side.

"But, combined with these laudable attributes, we need also a man with a smidgen of evil, with an attraction to the low life. The criminal mind operates that way. A cutpurse or a highwayman will risk his life for a bag of gold, and then squander it on wine and whores. Another forgiveness, Admiral, but when I asked your naval lieutenant to accompany Captain Jeggs on to-night's cruise, I also requested that he have your Captain of Marines arrest a suspect–the only one who qualifies as a master mariner and a scientist with a touch of evil. May I produce him?"

The commotion at the back of the room turned all our heads. There, between two Marines, was Captain Robert Tinker, the harbourmaster, old Peg and Patch, as the street urchin had so aptly named him...

Well, nothing is more jubilant than an Irishman who has just escaped the noose, and since both Delaneys were free, it was merriment in double time at the ranch. Fiddlers were called, punchbowls filled, and great sides of meat were put to the spits. The celebration lasted until dawn, when the Admiral and his party took their leave.

"Technically, he owes you a ship of the line," I said as we repaired to our rooms. "He made you that promise before witnesses."

What could we do with it, Oaks? Start a navy? You know, this idea of closing off the Pharos light with a screen is intriguing when properly done. If a clock mechanism could be devised to shield the beacon for a specific amount of time—say, seconds or minutes—ships could recognise the seamark by the frequency of the light flashes."

"Excellent idea, and possibly profitable. Put it to paper tomorrow."

"It *is* to-morrow, and I'm for sleep."

So, I fear, it is to be with all his to-morrows. Sleep. Drink. Carouse. And, of course, solve. I shall persevere in spite of him.

THE PROBLEM OF
SANTA'S LIGHTHOUSE
Edward D. Hoch

"You say you'd like a Christmas story this time?" old Dr. Sam Hawthorne said as he poured the drinks into fine crystal wineglasses. "Well, the holidays are approaching, and as it happens I've got an adventure from December of 1931 that fills the bill nicely. It didn't happen in Northmont, but along the coast, over toward Cape Cod..."

I'd decided to take a few days off (Dr. Sam continued), and took a drive by myself along the coast. It was something of a treat for me, since vacations are rare for a country doctor. But now that the Pilgrim Memorial Hospital had opened in Northmont, some of the pressure was off. If people couldn't reach me in an emergency, the hospital was there to minister to their ills.

So off I went in my Stutz Torpedo, promising my nurse April I'd telephone her in a few days to make certain everything was under control. It was the first week in December, but winter hadn't yet set in along the New England coast. There was no snow, and temperatures were in the forties. Along with every other part of the country, the area had been hard hit by the Depression, but once I'd passed through the old mill towns and headed north along the coast I saw less poverty.

Not far from Plymouth, a sign nailed to a tree caught my attention. *Visit Santa's Lighthouse!* it read, and although such commercial ventures to attract children are commonplace today, they were still a bit unusual in 1931. I couldn't imagine a lighthouse whose sole function was to entertain tots in the weeks before Christmas. But then I noticed that the word *Santa's* had been tacked on over the original name. It was enough to make me curious, so I turned down the road to the shore.

And there it was, sure enough: a gleaming white structure that rose from the rocky shoreline and proclaimed across its base, in foot-high wooden letters, that it was indeed Santa's Lighthouse. I parked my car next to two others and walked up the path to where a bright-faced girl of college age was selling admissions for twenty-five cents. She was wearing bright Christmasy red.

"How many?" she asked, peering down the path as if expecting me to be followed by a wife and children.

"Just one." I took a quarter from my pocket.

"We have a special family rate of fifty cents."

"No, I'm alone." I pointed up at the sign. "What's the name of this place the rest of the year?"

"You noticed we changed the sign," she said with a grin. "It's really Satan's Lighthouse, but there's nothing very Christmas-sounding about that. So we took the 'n' off the end of Satan and moved it to the middle."

I had to chuckle at the idea. "Has it helped business?"

"A little. But with this Depression and gasoline twenty-five cents a gallon, we don't get many families willing to drive here from Boston or Providence."

A bulging, padded Santa Claus appeared at the door just then, mumbling through his beard, "Lisa, you have to do something about those kids. They're pulling the beard and kicking me!"

She sighed and turned her attention to the Santa. "Harry, you've got to show a little patience—you can't expect me to go running in to rescue you every time they give you any trouble."

I said, "He's not so good at this Santa Claus business."

"He's much better as the pirate ghost," she agreed.

"The pirate ghost is a feature of Satan's Lighthouse?"

She gave a quick nod and offered her hand. "I'm Lisa Quay.

That's my brother, Harry. There's a legend that goes with this place—I guess it's why our father bought it."

"Buried treasure."

"How'd you guess? Pirates are supposed to have put up a false light here to lure ships onto the rocks and loot them, just as they once did off the coast of Cornwall. That's why it was called Satan's Lighthouse. When a real lighthouse was built years later, the local people called it by the same name. But of course there aren't pirates any more—except when my brother puts on his costume."

I introduced myself and she told me more about the region. She was an open, unassuming young woman who seemed more than capable of taking care of herself—and her brother, from what I'd seen. "Is your father here, too?" I asked.

She shook her head. "Daddy's in prison."

"Oh?"

"He was convicted of some sort of fraud last year. I never fully understood it, and I don't believe he was guilty, but he refused to defend himself. He has another year to serve before he's eligible for parole."

"So you and your brother are keeping this place going in his absence."

"That's about it. Now you know my life story, Dr. Hawthorne."

"Call me Sam. I'm not that much older than you."

Four unruly children came out of the lighthouse, shepherded by a frustrated Santa Claus. I watched while they piled into a waiting car and drove off with their parents. "Anyone else inside now?" Lisa asked her brother.

"No, it's empty."

"You're not making any money by my standing here," I decided, plunking down the quarter I was still holding. "I'll have a ticket."

"Come on," Harry Quay said. "I'll show you through."

The lighthouse was a slender whitewashed structure with rectangular sides that tapered toward the top, where a railing and walkway surrounded the light itself. I followed Quay up the iron staircase that spiraled through the center of the structure. The padded Santa suit didn't slow him down and he made the first landing well ahead of me. I was short of breath and welcomed the pause when he led me to a room that had been converted into a Santa's workshop.

"We bring the kids up here and give them inexpensive little toys," he explained. "Then we go the rest of the way up to the light."

"What's the room used for the rest of the year?"

"Originally it was the sleeping quarters for the lighthouse crew—generally a keeper and his wife. Of course, Lisa and I don't live here ourselves. We use the room for the pirate's den when it's not Christmas."

I glanced at the spiral staircase, anxious to get the rest of the climbing behind me. "Let's see the top."

We went up another dozen feet to the next level, where a rolltop desk and wooden filing cabinet had been outfitted with signs indicating it was Santa's office. The nautical charts of Cape Cod Bay on the walls were festooned with streamers proclaiming a landing area for Santa's reindeer-powered sleigh. There were powerful binoculars and a telescope for observing passing ships, and a two-way radio for receiving weather reports or S.O.S. messages.

"I have to watch the kids every minute up here," Harry Quay said. "Some of this equipment is valuable."

"I'm surprised it's still here if the lighthouse is no longer in use."

"My father kept them for some reason. He used to sit up here at night sometimes. It was a hobby of his, I suppose. That's why he bought the place."

I gestured toward the ceiling of the little office. "Does the light up above still operate?"

"I doubt it. I haven't tried it myself."

We climbed the rest of the way to the circular outside walkway that went around the light itself. A metal railing allowed me a handhold, but one could easily slip beneath it and fall to the ground. "You don't bring the kids up here, do you?"

"One at a time, with me holding their hand. I'm very careful."

I had to admit it was a magnificent view. On the bay side the land fell away rapidly to the water's edge, and as far as I could see the chill waters were casting up rippling whitecaps before the stiff ocean breeze. The curve of Cape Cod itself was clearly visible from this high up, and I could even make out the opposite shoreline some twenty miles across the bay.

But at this time of the year night came early and the sun was already low in the western sky. "I'd better get going if I want to reach Boston tonight," I said.

"Why go that far?" There are plenty of places to stay around Plymouth."

We went back downstairs and met Lisa at the workshop level. "Did you enjoy the view?" Isn't it spectacular?"

"It certainly is," I agreed. "You should double your prices."

"No one comes as it is," she replied with a touch of sadness.

"If the light still works, turn it on! Bring in some customers in the early evening."

"Oh, the coast guard would never allow that." She bustled about the workroom, picking up a few candy wrappers dropped by the children, retrieving a reel of fishing line and a set of jacks from one corner. "You find the darnedest things at the end of the day."

"Your brother says there are some places I could stay in the Plymouth area."

"Sure. The Plymouth Rock is a nice old place, and the rooms are clean." She turned to her brother. "Let's close up for the night."

"I'd better make sure everything's shut upstairs," Harry said.

"I'll go with you."

I started down the spiral staircase to the ground floor. I waited a few minutes, thinking they'd be following soon, but I became restless. The lighthouse had been a pleasant diversion, but I was anxious to move on.

"Wait a minute!" Lisa Quay called out as I started down the path to my car. She was at one of the middle windows, and I paused while she came down to meet me.

"I didn't mean to leave without saying goodbye," I told her, "but it's getting dark and I should be on my way."

"At least wait for Harry. He's taking off his Santa Claus suit. He'll be down in a minute."

I strolled back with her while she closed up the foldaway ticket booth and stowed it inside the lighthouse doorway. "If this weather holds out, you should get some crowds before Christmas."

"I hope so," she said. "Those four kids you saw were the only customers we had all afternoon."

"Maybe you could offer a special group-rate for–"

"What's that?" she asked suddenly, hurrying back outside. "Harry?" she called out, looking up. "Is that you?"

There was some sort of noise from above us and then Lisa Quay screamed. I looked up in time to see a figure falling from the circular walkway at the top of the lighthouse. I sprang aside, pulling her with me, as Harry Quay's body hit the ground where we'd been standing.

Lisa turned away screaming, her hands covering her face. I hurried over to her brother, my mind racing through the possibilities of getting fast help if he was still alive.

Then I saw the handle of the dagger protruding from between his ribs and I knew that help was useless.

"I don't believe in ghosts," she said quite rationally as we waited for the police to arrive. I'd used the lighthouse radio to call the coast guard, who promised to contact the state police for us. While I was inside, I'd looked in both rooms and even inside a little storeroom, but the lighthouse was empty. There was nothing on the walkway to indicate anyone else had been there, nothing on the spiral staircase to point to an unseen visitor.

"We don't have to believe in ghosts," I told her. "There's a logical explanation. There has to be. Have you ever seen that dagger before?"

"Yes. It's part of his pirate costume. The storeroom—"

"I checked the storeroom. I saw the costume hanging there. No one was hiding."

"Well, I don't believe in ghosts," she said again.

"The police will be here soon."

She fastened her hand on my arm. "You won't leave, will you? You won't leave before they come?"

"Of course not." I'd moved her away from her brother's body, so she'd be spared the sight while we waited for the police. I could see she was close to hysteria and might need my professional services at any moment.

"Without your testimony they might try to say I killed him," she said. "Even though I had no reason to."

"I'm sure they wouldn't say that," I tried to assure her.

"But no one else is here! Don't you see how it looks?"

"You were down on the ground with me when he was stabbed. I'll testify to that."

"Suppose I rigged up some sort of device to throw the knife

at him when he stepped out onto the walkway."

I shook my head. "I was up there with him shortly before he was killed. And I went up there again a few moments ago. There was nothing at all on that walkway."

"Then what killed him? Who killed him?"

Before I could respond, we saw the headlights of two police cars and an ambulance cutting through the early darkness. I had plenty of time to tell my story then, and Lisa told hers. They walked around with their flashlights, examining the body, asking questions, going through the motions. But it was clear that they didn't want to deal with a pirate ghost, much less any sort of impossible crime. I fondly wished for old Sheriff Lens back in Northmont. At least he could keep an open mind about such things.

"Did your brother have any enemies?" one officer asked Lisa.

"No, none at all. I can't imagine anyone wishing him harm."

"Can you tell me why he's wearing a false beard?"

"He'd been playing Santa Claus for the children. He was changing out of his costume when it happened."

The officer, a burly man named Springer, turned to me next. "Dr. Hawthorne?"

"That's correct."

"You say you were just passing through, not bound for any particular place?"

"Just a little vacation, I explained. "I practice in Northmont, near the Connecticut state line. The sign attracted me, and I stopped for an hour or so."

"Ever know the deceased or his sister before?"

"No."

He sighed and glanced at his pocket watch. Perhaps he hadn't had supper yet. "Well, if both of you are telling the truth, it looks like an accident to me. Somehow he slipped and fell on the knife up there, and then toppled off the walkway. Or else he killed himself."

"That couldn't–" Lisa started to say, but I nudged her into silence. The officer seemed not to notice.

As the body was being taken away, she said, "I'll have to notify Father."

"How do you go about that? Where's his prison?"

"Near Boston. I'll phone a message tonight and go there tomorrow to see him."

I made a decsion. "I'd like to go with you."

"What for?"

"I've had a little experience in solving crimes like this. I may be able to help you."

"But there are no suspects! Where would you begin?"

"With your father," I said.

I slept surprisingly well in my room at Plymouth Rock, and awoke refreshed. After a quick breakfast, I picked up Lisa at the small house in town she'd shared with her brother. "The police called this morning," she said. "They want us both to come in and make statements about what happened."

"We'll do it this afternoon," I decided. "Let's see your father first."

"What do you hope to learn from him?"

"The reason why he's in prison, among other things. You seem reluctant to talk about it."

"I'm not reluctant at all!" she bristled. "Until now I didn't really feel it was any of your business. Daddy brought us up after Mother died. What happened to him was a terrible thing. He's in prison for a crime he didn't commit."

"You said something about a fraud."

"I'll let him tell you about it."

Because of his son's death, we were both allowed to see Ronald Quay together. He was a thin man, who looked as if he might have aged overnight. His pale complexion had already taken on the look of endless incarceration, even though Lisa said he'd been locked up for only a year. She cried when he was led into the room, and the guard stood by awkwardly as they embraced.

"This is Dr. Sam Hawthorne," she told her father. "He was at the lighthouse with us when it happened."

He wanted details and I told him everything I knew. He sat across the table, merely shaking his head.

"I've done a little amateur detective work back in Northmont," I told him. "I thought I might be able to help out here."

"How?"

"By asking the right questions." I paused, sizing up the man almost as I would diagnose a patient's illness, and then I said,

"You're in prison for committing a crime, and now the crime of murder has apparently been committed against your son. I wonder if there could be a relationship between those two crimes."

"I don't–" He shook his head.

"I know it seems impossible that anyone could have killed Harry, but if someone did they had to have a motive."

"He didn't have an enemy in the world," Lisa insisted.

"Perhaps he was killed not for what he was like but for what he was doing," I suggested.

"You mean playing Santa Claus?"

"You said he played a pirate, too. And he was struck down with a pirate's dagger."

"Who could possibly–"

I interrupted her with another question for her father. "Were you engaged in any sort of illegal activity at the lighthouse?"

"Certainly not," he answered without hesitation. "I've maintained my innocence of these charges from the beginning."

"Then the fraud charges somehow involved the lighthouse?"

"Only in the most general way," Lisa replied. "At one point we tried to set up a corporation and sell shares of stock. A Boston man went to the police and accused my father of fraud because Daddy claimed he had a million dollars to build an amusement park."

"Did you ever claim that?" I asked him.

"No! Harry suggested once that we put in one of those miniature golf courses that are all the rage, but I was against even that. Certainly no one ever mentioned a million dollars."

"They must have had evidence of fraud."

He looked at his hands. "A stock prospectus we had printed, just for test purposes. It wasn't supposed to get out. Lisa can tell you we don't even own much land around the lighthouse– We couldn't have built an amusement park there even if we'd wanted to."

Lisa sighed. "That's exactly the argument the prosecutor used to convict you, Daddy."

I was aware that he'd neatly avoided the main thrust of my question by bringing up the fraud conviction. "Forget the fraud charges for the moment, Mr. Quay. What about other activities at the lighthouse?"

"I don't know what you mean," he said, but his eyes shifted away.

"The two-way radio. The powerful binoculars. The telescope. They were used to locate and contact ships offshore, weren't they?"

"Why would I-?" he began, then changed his mind. "All right. You seem to know a great deal."

"What were they landing at the lighthouse? Illegal whiskey from Canada, I imagine."

Lisa's eyes widened. "Daddy!"

"I needed money from somewhere, Lisa. Using that lighthouse for pirates and Santa Clauses was a losing proposition from the beginning."

"You told Dr. Hawthorne there'd been no illegal activity there."

"Prohibition is an unjust and unpopular law. I don't consider that I acted illegally in helping to circumvent it."

"What happened after you went to prison?" I asked. "Did Harry continue the bootlegging activities?"

"He knew nothing about it," Quay insisted.

"And yet the radio and telescope are still in place, a year later."

"He was sentimental about moving them," Lisa explained. "He wanted everything just as it was for when Daddy came back."

"You must have dealt with someone on this bootlegging operation, Mr. Quay. Couldn't that man have contacted Harry and struck a deal with him after your imprisonment?"

Ronald Quay was silent for a moment, considering the possibility. "I suppose so," he admitted at last. "That would be like him. And it would be like Harry to accept the deal without telling anyone."

"I need the name, Mr. Quay."

"I-"

"The name of the man you dealt with. The name of the person who might have contacted your son to continue with the setup. Because that might be the name of his murderer."

"Paul Lane," he said at last. "That's the name you want." The words had been an effort for him to speak.

"Who is he? Where can we find him?"

"He owns some seafood restaurants along the coast. I can

give you an address in Boston."

As we parked my Stutz Torpedo along the Boston docks a few hours later, Lisa said, "Sam, how come you're not married?"

"I've never met the right woman at the right time, I guess."

"I want to ask you something—a very great favor."

"What is it?"

"Could you stay here with me until after Harry's funeral? I don't think I could get through it alone."

"When—?"

"Day after tomorrow. You could leave by noon if you wanted to. They'll let Daddy come down from prison with a guard, and there'll be some aunts and uncles. That's all. We're not a big family."

"Let me think about it. Maybe I can."

Lane's Lobsters was a seafood restaurant that also sold live lobsters for boiling at home. A grey-haired man behind the lobster tank told us Paul Lane's office was upstairs. We climbed the rickety steps to the second floor and found him sitting behind a cluttered desk. He puffed on a fat cigar that gave him the look of a minor politician.

"What can I do for you?" he asked, removing the cigar from his mouth.

"We're interested in some lobsters," I said.

"The retail business is downstairs. I just handle wholesale up here." He gestured toward an open ice-chest full of dead lobsters.

"That's what we want—wholesale."

He squinted at Lisa. "Don't I know you?"

"You may know my brother. Harry Quay."

Paul Lane was no good at hiding his reaction. After the first shock of surprise he tried to cover it with a denial, but I pressed on. "You run a bootlegging operation, Lane, and you involved her father and brother in it."

"Go to hell! Get outa here!"

"We want to talk. Somebody killed her brother last evening."

"I read the papers. They say it was an accident."

"I was there. I call it murder."

Paul Lane's lip twisted in a sneer. "Is that so? If you two were alone with him, then you must have killed him."

I leaned on the desk between us. "We didn't come here to

play games, Mr. Lane. I think you approached Harry after his father went to prison on that fraud rap. You wanted to continue bringing your Canadian whiskey ashore at Satan's Lighthouse, and you needed Harry's cooperation. Isn't that right?"

He got up from his desk and deliberately closed the lid on the ice-chest. "I don't know what you're talking about, mister."

As a lobsterman or a bootlegger, he might have been pretty good, but just then he was being a bit too obvious. When he sat down again I lifted the lid and picked up one of the cold lobsters.

"What the hell are you doing?" he bellowed, coming out of his chair.

I turned the lobster over. Its insides had been hollowed out to make room for a slim bottle of whiskey. "Neat," I said. "I'll bet that's a popular take-out item at your restaurants."

Before I realized what was happening, his fist caught me on the side of the head. I stumbled back against the ice-chest as Lisa screamed. Two tough-looking seamen barged in, attracted by the noise. "Get them!" Lane ordered. "Both of them!"

I was still clutching the dead lobster and I shoved it into the nearest man's face. "Run!" I shouted to Lisa. Lane was out from behind his desk, trying to stop her, when I shoved him aside and followed her out the door. Then all three of them were after us and I felt one beefy hand grab at my shoulder. We made it halfway down the stairs before they caught us, and I tripped and stumbled the rest of the way to the ground floor, landing hard on my chest.

I looked up and saw one of the men take out a knife. Then I saw someone from the restaurant grab his wrist.

I recognized Springer, the state police officer who had questioned us. "Having a little trouble here, Dr. Hawthorne?" he asked.

I'd cracked a rib falling down the stairs, and while it was being taped up Springer explained that he'd gone to prison to question Ronald Quay, arriving just as we were leaving. "You seemed in such a hurry I decided to follow along. You led me here."

The Boston police and agents of the Prohibition Bureau had taken over Paul Lane's operation, seizing hundreds of barrels of good Canadian whiskey. My last glimpse of Lane was when a cop led him away in handcuffs. "Did he kill my brother? Lisa asked.

"Not personally, but he probably ordered it done. I can't name the actual killer, but I can give you a description of him and tell you how I think the murder was committed."

"I hope you're not going to say somebody threw the knife from the rocks all the way to the top of that lighthouse," Springer said.

"No," I agreed. "It's much too tall for that. And that pirate dagger is too unbalanced to have been fired from a crossbow or anything similar. The killer was right there with Harry when he died."

"But that's impossible!" Lisa insisted.

"No, it isn't. "There was one place in that lighthouse we never searched, one place where the killer could have been hidden–the rolltop desk in the office on the top floor."

"But that's absurd!" Lisa said. "It's hardly big enough for a child!"

""Exactly–a child. Or someone dressed as a child. Remember that carload of children that arrived just before me?" Didn't you think it odd the parents remained in the car–especially since the lighthouse offered a family rate? Four children came out, but I'm willing to bet that five children went in."

Lisa's eyes widened. "My lord, I think you're right!"

"One stayed behind, hidden in that rolltop desk. And when Harry came back upstairs to close up, he did his job. He was a hit man hired by Paul Lane, who'd had a falling-out with your brother over the bootlegging business. I think we'll find enough evidence in Lane's records to verify that."

Springer was frowning. "You're telling us a child was the hit man?"

"Or someone dressed as a child," I said. "Someone small– maybe a midget."

"A midget!"

"What better hit man to kill a Santa Claus than a midget dressed as a small child? Five children entered the lighthouse but only four came out. No one thought of the missing child. The supposed parents drove away, leaving a hidden killer awaiting his opportunity."

"All right," Springer said with a nod. "If Lane has a midget on his payroll it should be easy enough to discover." He started out and then paused at the door with a slight smile. "I checked up on you. Sheriff Lens back in Northmont says you're a pretty fair detective."

When he had gone, Lisa Quay said simply, "Thank you. It won't bring him back, but at least I know what happened."

Two days later I was at Lisa Quay's side as her brother was buried beneath the barren December trees of the Plymouth cemetery. As we were walking to the car, Springer intercepted us. "I thought you'd like to know that we have a line on a very short man who worked as a waiter last year in Paul Lane's New Bedford lobster house. We're trying to locate him now."

"Good luck," I said. "I'm heading home today."

My car was back at the funeral parlor and I said goodbye to Lisa Quay there. "Thanks again," she said. "For everything, Sam."

I'd been driving about an hour when I saw the boy fishing off a bridge over a narrow creek. My first thought was that December wasn't likely to be a good fishing month.

My second thought was that I'd made a terrible mistake.

I pulled the car off the road and sat for a long time staring at nothing at all. Finally I started the motor and made a U-turn, heading back the way I had come.

It was late afternoon when Santa's Lighthouse came into view, much as it had been that first day I saw the place. Lisa's car was parked nearby, but no others. The lighthouse was still closed to visitors. I pulled in next to her car and got out, walking up the path to the doorway. She must have heard the car and seen me from the window, because she opened the door with a smile.

"You've come back, Sam."

"Just for a little bit," I told her. "Can we talk?"

"About what?" She was flirting, seductive.

"About Harry's murder."

Her face changed. "Have they found the midget?"

I shook my head. "They'll never find the midget because there never was one. I made a mistake."

"What are you talking about?"

"We kept saying there were no suspects, but of course there always was one suspect. Not the least likely person but the most likely one. You killed your brother, Lisa."

"You're insane!" she flared, trying to close the door on me. I easily blocked it with my foot, and after a moment she relaxed and I stepped inside.

"The more I thought about it, the more impossible the midget hit man became. Those kids were raising a fuss, pulling on Santa's beard and otherwise calling attention to themselves. That's hardly the sort of thing our killer would have allowed. The success of his scheme as I imagined it depended upon their group being unnoticed and uncounted." Lisa stood with her arms folded, pretending to humor me.

"Then, too, there was the matter of the murder weapon. A hit man would certainly bring his own weapon, not rely on finding a pirate dagger in a storeroom.

"Third point: how did the killer lure Harry out onto that walkway, especially when he was still removing his costume and had the beard on?"

"He might have been stabbed in the office below," Lisa said, her voice a mere whisper.

I shook my head. "No midget could have carried Harry's body up that ladder. He went up there by himself, with his murderer, and with the fake beard still on, because it was someone he trusted."

"You're forgetting I was with you when he was killed."

"Correction—you were with me when his body fell from the walkway. An hour ago on the road I passed a boy fishing off a bridge. And I remembered you picking up a reel of fishing line in the workroom. It hadn't been left by a child at all. You simply needed it for your scheme. You went back upstairs, called your brother up to the walkway on some pretext, stabbed him, and left his body right at the edge where it could easily be slid beneath the railing. You tied one end of the fishing line to his body and dropped the other end over the side of the lighthouse to the ground. It was nearly dark at the time, and I didn't see it when I went out. You called me back because you needed me for your alibi. I suppose you'd been waiting for days for the right person to happen along just at dusk. You pulled on the line and Harry's body rolled off the catwalk, nearly hitting us as it fell to the ground."

"If that's true, what happened to the fishing line?"

"I missed it in the dim light when I examined the body. Then when I went upstairs to radio for help, you simply untied it from the body and hid it away."

"Why would I kill my own brother?"

"Because you discovered he was responsible for sending your father to prison. It was Harry who printed that phony stock prospectus and tried to defraud investors with dreams of an amusement park. Your father was covering up for him. When you learned about that, and learned that Harry was involved in the bootlegging scheme with Paul Lane, it was more than you could bear."

The fight had gone out of her. "At first I couldn't believe the things he'd done—letting Daddy go to prison for his crime! And then this thing with Lane! I—"

"How did it happen?" I asked her quietly.

Her voice was somber. "I waited a week for someone like you to come by—someone alone. Then I called up there and gave him one last chance. I told him he had to confess to the police and get Daddy out of prison or I'd kill him. He laughed and made a grab for the dagger and I stabbed him. I used the fishing line just like you said. It was strong but thin, and almost invisible in the fading light." She looked away. "I thought I was lucky you came along, but I guess luck doesn't run in the family."

"You have to tell Springer," I said. "He's looking for that waiter. If you let an innocent man go to prison, you'd be as wrong as your brother was."

"All that planning," she said. "For nothing."

"That was how it ended," Dr. Sam concluded. "I wasn't particularly proud of my part in the affair, and I never told the folks back in Northmont about it. When my nurse April asked about the tape on my ribs I told her I'd fallen down. But by the time Christmas came we had snow, and it was a merry holiday for all of us. Then early the following year came that business at the cemetery—which *didn't* involve a ghost. But that's for next time.

THE STONE WALL
Steve Sherman

Albert Koski began building the stone wall when his wife died. Debra was younger than he, some people saying at least by fifteen years, and probably she was. It was difficult to tell, because she wore her years like clean dresses and bright scarves, never out of fashion, always inviting and welcome—so different from her husband. Nobody could figure them together, but then couples were made like them in the back country, where men and women lived with fewer choices.

He started building the wall straight from her gravesite behind the sycamore she favored. At first people said that was good, he needed the release, he needed something demanding to take his mind off her. It was hard, honest labor, the Vermont kind. He worked at it in plain sight there by the road, and acquaintances (he wasn't the "friend" type) stopped by and said he was doing all right, making progress. It was good to have someone making stone walls again. It was a lost art, everybody putting up easy fences that rotted before the children grew up.

Albert said little in return. He kept digging and lifting and shifting the rocks and boulders into place. "One on two," he said. That was his method, the old-time method. One rock on two and the wall would hold—it wouldn't slip, the ice wouldn't topple it.—One rock on two didn't rock the wall. This was his witticism, but it usually got only silent nodding from those who heard it, and never a signal from Albert himself that he meant it to be memorable.

Those infrequent watchers stood by as he bent his hulking frame, his sweaty summer muscles still rippling and tight. No one offered help because Albert was that kind. This was his wall and it would be until it was finished. So they just watched and made a few comments now and then to show their presence.

The wall grew by great yards at a time. He worked on it day after day, week after week. Ten yards, twenty, fifty, a hundred, straight across the wavy field. Vermont had plenty of stones and Albert just kept hefting them in place. Soon the wall was a giant—a yard wide, a yard high, big stones on the inside for anchorage, small stones on the sides and top for show. In two months the wall was approaching Wesley Scott's land, and that was when the trouble started.

Albert was a worker, Wesley an inheritor. Albert worked his land, but Wesley moved in from Connecticut when his parents were killed in a plane crash at the Madrid airport. He hired help (he had plenty of money) to trim his apple orchard, paint the barn, cut the rye, keep the white house and black shutters in shape. His two roans idled through the afternoon grass, their lazy tails fluffed by the Green Mountains wind and typifying what Wesley was all about.

Those horses were irresistible to Debra, being so open-air herself. Eventually, she got to ride them, which was all right with Albert. He liked to watch her trotting far across the straw field, her black hair streaming behind like the roan's, her rhythm of exuberant symmetry gentle on the rugged backdrop of woods and rocky balds.

When people saw Debra and Wesley riding together, they didn't say much. Neither did Albert. But when she died he didn't cry, either. Instead, he buried her with perfunctory concern, lost himself in the house for a week, and then started building the wall.

Now that the wall was nearing Wesley's property line, people took particular notice. One or two would ask, "Albert, where's the wall going?"

"Up the hill," Albert would say, toss his head back in the direction, and keep right on lifting and shoving, adding up the stones.

Then the day arrived when Albert continued the wall straight across Wesley's line, straight into his field. It was a peculiar sight because Wesley's line was a stone wall, too. Albert simply breached that wall with his at a forty-five-degree angle and on up the hill he went, working at a steady, deliberate pace, undeterred—unaware, it seemed. The good honest labor now looked like a passion. All that focused him was the wall, as if the blunt straining and building was a consumption, sort of demonlike. Nothing mattered, just the bending and hefting, the sweat and the groans, and that damn wall.

Wesley, of course, was watching, too, and when Albert crossed into his property he waited a day to see what would happen. Then two more days. Finally, on the fourth morning he saw Albert continue where he had left off, straight up the hill, slicing the field in two like a slow, gouging wedge.

It was time to talk with Albert. A man's grief had to stop sometime. Enough was enough.

Wesley stood to one side of the wall and said, "Albert, you're making this wall on my land. You know that, don't you?"

Albert said nothing. He worked as if Wesley were not there.

"I can't let this go on, Albert. You're going to have to stop."

Still the burly man lifted the stones and angled them in place, edging the wall up the hill piece by piece.

"Now I know you're upset about Debra. We all are. But, Albert, I can't let this go on."

Nothing.

"You hear me, Albert? You're on my property. I want you to stop. Now!"

Albert never faltered, never once acknowledged Wesley's presence. The wall inched forward almost inevitably, as if Albert were merely its instrument, as if the wall were building itself.

Wesley grew so humiliated at being ignored that a rage flamed in him. He was a man who could not be ignored like this, a man of means and position. He hired people like this obsessed neighbor of his, and fired them, too. The rage simmered and boiled until Wesley swiveled around and stomped away, back to the house.

That night he pushed and shoved the end of the wall where Albert left off, heaving the stones to the ground, demolishing the work Albert had done that day. He couldn't destroy all of it, because for him this was as strenuous as building it, and he was no match for Albert.

The next day Albert set to work as if nothing had happened. He stooped to pick up the stones that Wesley had shoved aside and rebuilt that section steadily, inevitably. By afternoon, he reached the point of making progress again and added another two yards up the hill.

Wesley watched enraged from his second-story window. And that night he again shoved and pushed the stones asunder, destroying what the madman had built, had rebuilt. This time he used a long prying pipe to help him.

Again, the next day, Albert walked to the end of the wall and without the slightest hint of acknowledgment of the scattered stones set about to rebuild it. This time it took the full day to recast all that Wesley had ruined.

Wesley was not one to forfeit advantage. After all, he had the night and his land, his position and means, a network of influential people and lawyers, and he would not be trespassed. He would not let this field man challenge him with such peasant superiority. So again that night he pushed and shoved the stones to the ground, slipping and cursing away the thought that Albert never slipped, never cursed dead stones. This was his land. Albert had no right, and stubborness was not his exclusion. Wesley would never quit, never.

Albert rebuilt the wall the next day, and the next and the next. Soon people got wind of this incredible battle and they gave wide berth to both Albert and Wesley. They shook their heads and told each other, "Somebody has to give way. Something has to give."

For ten days and ten nights, the battle waged between the two men. It was as if Albert had turned into a living Sisyphus who struggled a monstrous round stone up a hill only to grow exhausted inches before reaching the crest and have it roll back, the corrosive frustration and suffering plunging him into eternal repetition. The difference was that Albert didn't recognize the frustration and suffering, nor even the exhaustion. And Wesley's anger had rooted too deep to consider any metaphor for his actions—he simply would not lose this ridiculous conflict to someone like Albert Koski. His stride through the village would not allow it.

As these forces of strength and pride continued day and night, the people in town grew increasingly apprehensive. Yet none dared approach either man for fear of accidentally releasing the trip-wire to some danger upon their own future. So they waited and watched.

In the end, they could only surmise. When they found Albert's body folded over the wall, his head smashed and bloodied by a stone, they knew that the sin had won. The stone lay beside Albert's head, splotched with blood. It was big enough to require two deliberate hands to lift above the head and to crash it in frenzy upon Albert's skull. His body draped over the wall in a startling scene of affection, almost an embrace, curved like love.

Wesley was found hard-eyed and sullen in his house. His hands were dirtied with grass and soil, his shirt and pants blood-streaked. At the trial his lawyer tried valiantly to paint an apocalypse of madmen locked in unforgiving, hateful insanity, but the verdict was inevitable. When Wesley was pronounced guilty of cold-blooded murder over a thoroughly minor and negotiable problem, the people in town said, "He should have known better."

Only a few in town really understood, and they remained silent. These were the ones who knew the unknowable Albert Koski. Never mind about Wesley—he was a child, Albert was a man. Albert was a builder, a protector, and he saw that those roan horses of Wesley's had eroded the house of his Debra and him. Who knows how much Wesley touched Debra in the private white house with the black shutters, except Albert. When Debra died, so then must Albert. And he did. And he punished Wesley. These people who knew Albert saw that within this meat of a man was more than a stone-wall builder. They knew, too, that they would never speak of how they thought Debra died.

A QUICK LEARNER
Bredan DuBois

Karen had always hated the rain, and when the gas-station attendant started giving Roy a hard time it didn't help things. The attendant was bent over, his yellow slicker oily-looking from the grease stains, and water was dripping off his cap. His beard was matted with water and he was heavy-looking, at least forty pounds heavier than Roy, but of course that didn't stop Roy.

"Listen, buddy," the attendant said, his voice a snarl, "I don't care how many fingers you think you put up, I saw five and I put five in the tank. You owe me three more bucks."

Roy turned to grin at Karen, but she looked away, her large brown purse in her lap, and stared out the window. The rain made everything look grey. They were someplace in New York State. It seemed like it was all made of highways, fast roads, and shopping malls. The few trees she had seen were thin and scraggly-looking, as if they were on the verge of dying. She suddenly missed Maine and the clean beaches where the pines grew right down to the rocks at the shore. What were his sister Tracy and those kids of hers doing now? She remembered their house, old and creaky for sure, but at least it was warm and dry. And if this was Thursday, there'd be a big baked lasagna.

Hush, she thought. You're here now with your man, going south. No time to think of Maine. Think of Roy, think of Roy now.

She rearranged her purse and looked over at her boy friend.

"I've got some buddies," Roy said, "but none of them look like you, guy. Look, ask my girl friend here—she saw me. I put up two fingers, for two bucks' worth. If I wanted five, I would have put up five. If I wanted ten, I would have put up both hands. But I only asked for two." He was tapping his fingers on the steering wheel and Karen felt her stomach chill. And his grin got wider. Another bad sign. Back off, she thought, Mr. Gasoline Man, back off. You don't know about that big handgun Roy's got under the front seat.

The attendant moved his face closer. "Look yourself. I ain't explaining to my boss when the register don't balance out tonight. Either you give me the money or—"

Karen quickly opened her purse, went through the envelopes in it, found the one marked "F", and drew out three greasy singles.

"Here," she said, crumpling them up and passing them past Roy before he could react. "Take it, okay? We don't want no trouble."

The attendant grunted and put the bills into his pants. Roy looked at her, stunned.

"Start the car, Roy. Let's get going."

He muttered something and turned the key. It took three tries before the engine caught and he raced out of the parking lot, not bothering to look either way. Karen caught her breath and sat back in her seat, her arms around the purse. Roy turned and glared at her, his blue eyes like chips of rock.

"Thanks. Thanks a whole hell of a lot, babe. I was doing what you always bug me about—I was trying to save money, trying to con the guy out of three bucks, and you blew it."

"I didn't want a fight."

"I don't care what you want. Where did you take the money from?"

"From the food budget."

"Food—is that right? You expect me to go hungry tonight 'cause of you? Was that what you were thinking?"

She looked out the window, her fist against her chin. I won't cry. I don't want him to see me cry. I won't do it. She repeated this over and over, as tears trickled down her cheeks. Outside it was still raining.

"No, you won't go hungry," she said. "Just get me some french fries from McDonald's tonight, I'm not that hungry."

Roy snorted. "I had that guy, Karen, I know I did. When are you going to learn to trust me?"

"She winced at his words. Ever since they had left Maine, it had been the same thing. When are you going to learn, Karen? When are you going to learn to drive better? When are you going to grow up? When are you going to learn not to cry? Learn, learn, learn–after two years since high school, she thought she wouldn't listen to that any more. She pressed her fist against her chin again.

Roy leaned over and turned on the radio. Nothing came out of the speaker until he slammed the dashboard with his fist, then the radio sputtered into life. He was four years older than she was, and when they had met at a party at her cousin's in North Berwick she knew he was the one. He had short blond hair and a good build, and she liked the solid way he walked into a room, like he had control of everything the minute he stepped inside the door. She also liked his smile, the way his teeth glistened and his eyes practically danced.

Karen looked over. He wasn't smiling, which was fine with her. She no longer thought the smile was so cute, especially after that time back in New Hampshire. She pushed the thought from her mind. No, I won't think about that. I won't think of what happened, what Roy did after he started smiling.

Roy was wearing a heavy flannel shirt and jeans, and his leather jacket was strewn across the back seat, along with her suitcase and his green duffel bag. She was wearing her best jeans and a wrinkled Western-style shirt under a jean jacket. It was her favorite shirt and she hated the wrinkles, but she had no iron.

"Here we are," Roy said, making a wide turn. "Look at that shopping center."

The shopping center was still under construction. Toward the right were some piles of dirt and yellow construction equipment. There was a clothing store, a restaurant, a couple of shops, and a bank at the far end. Roy stopped the car. The engine coughed and rumbled and he kept racing the gas to keep it going. He leaned over into the back seat and pulled a pack of cigarettes from his leather coat. He lit one up and she was glad of the tobacco smell. It masked some of the sour odors coming from their clothing in the back seat.

"See? See tha bank right there?" That's where I'll be tomor-row." Roy took a deep drag from his cigarette. His face was stubbled with whiskers. "It's right at the end of the center, which is good, gives me room. You just make a quick turn out of the parking lot and in a couple of minutes you're at a high-way. Another ten or fifteen and we're into Vermont."

"But our trip—" she began.

"What trip?"

"Florida. We're supposed to be going to Florida."

Roy stubbed out the cigarette in the overflowing ashtray. "We are, just as soon as we get some money."

"But Vermont is going back north."

"Don't tell me which is north and south, Karen, I know. But if we go south, we're running into big towns and cities, where the cops will be looking for us. We go into Vermont a couple of days, maybe a week, and let things cool off."

Florida. Oh, Florida. She had never been south of New Hampshire in all her life. It was getting on toward October and the rain was cold and the days were short, and she had read that the ocean in Florida was light-blue and warm, like bathwater. Living close to the Atlantic, she had been to those beaches lots of times, but even in the hottest day in August the waters would be dark-grey and cold.

Florida. Roy had said one night that he was going to Florida, and she had said yes, I want to come along. That had been al-most a month ago and now they were only in New York. Did Roy really want to go, or was he enjoying himself too much?

She bit her lip. "That sounds fine, I guess."

"Good." He leaned over and kissed her. She tried hard not to draw back. His breath reeked of cigarette smoke. At any other time, especially back in Maine, it wouldn't have bothered her. It bothered her now.

With the last of the money from the "R" envelope, for rooms, they rented a motel room almost at the outskirts of the city. Roy didn't like the envelope system she had devised, but she guessed he gave into it because it was the only thing that seemed to work. Roy didn't have a good head for money, he just let it slip through his fingers, but Karen knew how hard it was to get money. Growing up without a mom and dad will give you that.

The room was small, with only a single bed, a dresser, and a black-and-white TV stuck in a corner. There wasn't any phone in the room, but there was a bathroom off to one end. Karen sat on the edge of the bed. The mattress was soft and mushy, and the tassled blue bedspread was dotted with cigarette burns. Roy piled her suitcase and his duffel bag in one corner, and after using the bathroom he came out and said, "I'm going to get supper. You wanna take a shower or something?"

Karen gave him the few dollars left in the "F" envelope and he walked out, not bothering to give her a kiss.

She picked up her suitcase, dragging it into the bathroom. The linoleum was cracked, but at least there was soap in the shower. Which first, the clothes or herself? They didn't have enough money for a laundromat, hadn't had since they left Maine, so she had been washing her clothes in showers and bathtubs in the motels they stopped in, hanging up the clothes on the curtain rod and drying them with her hair dryer.

She looked into the mirror. Her face was pinched and her eyebrows were heavy, but it was her hair that repulsed her the most. She picked up a few greasy-brown strands in her hand and rubbed them together. The grittiness decided her. She was going first. The clothes could wait.

She could have spent hours in the shower, washing and re-washing her hair, making sure the last trace of dirt was gone. She turned the water up as hot as she could stand it and luxu-riated under the hot streams of water, feeling it pulsate against her shoulders. She didn't care if she went through the whole bar of soap, she lathered herself from her head down to her feet, rinsing herself off, then soaping and rinsing herself again. She loved showers, loved the clean feeling and the steam rising up around her. Her only regret was that she didn't have a ra-zor. Her legs were getting stubbly.

She rubbed the soap across her shoulders, massaging in the heat, remembering that it had been a warm day when she had first met Roy at that party. They had gone out for a while, Roy taking her to the movies or to some fine restaurants in York. He had dressed well, always smelling of cologne, and when she had asked what he did for a living he had always changed the subject. She imagined that he was some kind of secret agent or drug dealer, and in a way she hadn't been far off.

Then one day he had said he was going, heading south to Florida. By now she was convinced she was in love with him.– Going south. It sounded wonderful–more wonderful than working at the mall again in the winter, and Maine winters were *cold*. Her sister Tracy had frowned and put up something of a fight when she told her she was leaving with Roy. "I know what it's like when you got someone," Tracy had said. "But– well, remember this. You can always come back here when you're done."

Karen rinsed herself again. She remembered the first day– driving out, a six-pack of beer between them in the front seat. Her asking, "Roy, tell me what you really do?" And Roy grinning back, his blue eyes bright. "Among other things, I'm a thief." At the time, she was half drunk, so she giggled and talked about something else, but it was true. Roy was a thief. By the time they had left Maine, he had robbed a gas station, a restaurant, and a store.

At first Karen had been scared, but Roy was so smart, so cocky, and it was a thrill to see him run out of a place, gun in one hand, a bundle of cash in another. Such a thrill. Until New Hampshire.

The soap fell from her hands. She leaned against the ceramic tile and lifted her face, letting the hot water pound against her, remembering it all. A corner grocery store in some small town, Roy pulling up near it, laughing, getting out of the car with the gun in his hand. The grocer was a small, overweight man. She could see him through the plate-glass window. After Roy went in, she saw the grocer get angry. He was waving his pudgy hands around. Roy's face was angry, too, at first–and then he smiled. This made her smile, too, until he brought up the handgun. Boom. Another boom. The plate-glass window was sprayed with blood, and shattered. The grocer crumpled out of sight, Roy leaned over the counter firing until the gun was empty, that happy smile on his face, and then he ran out to her. She was too scared to scream or cry or move, and he drove the car away, grinning. "Guy tried to tell me the money was in the safe and he didn't have the combination."

Later, she was sure she must have screamed later.

She got out of the shower, drying herself off and wrapping a towel around her. Time for clothes–and Roy's if she had the time, though he didn't seem to care if his clothes were clean or not.

Hunched over the tub, letting the water run into the clothes, she recalled Tracy saying she could always come back. Yeah, Tracy, but with what? If I start hitching, Roy's going to be mad that I left him—and then he's going to chase me, big sister. He'll chase me until he finds me, and by then he'll be real mad and, no, I don't want to see Roy mad.

For supper Roy had three cheeseburgers, a large fry, and a large Coke. He had gotten a small Coke and a small fry for Karen. "You said you weren't hungry," he reminded her, and he idly watched a game show on the flickering black-and-white set as he ate.

Karen sat on the other end of the bed. The Coke was warm, the french fries were cold. She watched Roy as he ate, the way he mechanically put the food away. Don't you even taste it? she thought. Don't you feel anything? She wanted one of those cheeseburgers, damn it, and her stomach growled as she finished her fries. She was still hungry and her boy friend was wolfing down three cheeseburgers like they were nothing. So why don't your complain? she asked herself. Chicken?

God, yes, she thought.

Roy crumpled up the waste paper, belched, and then strode over to the duffel bag. He unzipped it and brought out two handguns. She recognized the one he always used. The other one was smaller, but looked just as deadly. Roy sat back on the bed, a gun in each hand.

"School time," he said, putting the unfamiliar gun down and working with the smaller one. "I want you to learn to use this, Karen."

She felt like moving off the bed. "I don't like guns, Roy."

He did something to the gun and the bullets fell out, clicking together like marbles. "Tomorrow," he said, "I'm going after a bank, Karen—I'm going after something big. At nine A.M. I'm going to be one of their first customers. Friday's payday, those cash drawers are going to be stuffed, and I'm gonna do some unstuffing. And I'm gonna need you as a backup in case something goes wrong. It's about time you pulled some weight. Here. Listen and learn."

She kept quiet and watched as he moved his hands across

the revolver, as he talked about rounds, chambers, and the hammer. She picked it up when he told her to, and without any bullets in it she practiced pulling the trigger.

When Roy was done, he leaned back and stretched, letting his muscles pop. She smiled a little and he smiled back, a good smile that reawakened something inside her.

"Roy?"

"Hmm?" he said.

"Roy, when we're in Florida, will you stop this? Stop robbing stores and banks?"

He turned and looked at her, still smiling, but the warmth was gone. "Give up what I do? Is that what you want?"

Frightened, she could only nod. His smile was now mocking. "Why, Karen, what a wonderful idea. Give up what I do best. That sounds fine. Just great. Maybe I can get a job at a Burger King or Pizza Hut—free uniforms and all the food I can sneak home. Does that sound good to you?"

She drew her legs up to her chin, wrapped her arms around herself. "Roy—"

"No, fine, I'll do that, Karen. Anything you say. I'm sure there are hundreds of jobs out there for a guy like me who dropped out when he was fifteen. I see those ads all the time, don't you? High school dropout wanted, preferably with a record. Will pay a quarter over minimum wage. And then we can get married and have a bunch of squawling kids. And maybe when I'm thirty I'll be *junior assistant fry manager or some freaking thing!*"

Karen buried her face in her legs. Can't cry. Can't let him see me cry. She looked up.

Roy bounced off the bed and grabbed his leather jacket. "I'm going out." He went to the dresser, grabbed her purse, and started pawing through it. Her wallet fell out, then her lipstick and brush. Her purse, her things.

He went through the envelopes, emptying them of all the money meant for gas, food, motel rooms, emergencies. "And I'm going to get drunk," he announced before he slammed the door.

She was half asleep when the car roared in and its lights lit up the room. She sat up in bed, wearing one of Roy's T-shirts. The room went dark when the lights went off and she held her breath. Then the door flew open and Roy stumbled in, mumbling to himself. She smelled a strong odor of beer and he cursed, his voice deep and sharp, as he knocked over a lamp. The crash made her jump and then hold herself stiffly as he sat down on the edge of the bed.

Then he slowly slid off, and coughed once, twice, and started to retch.

Oh, God, she thought, the sour smell striking her senses. She reached out and turned on the side lamp, blinking from the sudden light. Roy was crumpled on his side. The smell was awful and she thought, I've got to clean it up, I can't leave it there, and then she switched off the lamp and burrowed into the bed, pulling the blankets over her head, trying to block out the noise of his breathing and the smell.

In the morning, Karen got out of bed as quietly as she could, not wanting to wake Roy. He was rolled up in the covers next to her, a bare foot hanging off the bed. He snorted and grumbled, and his breath smelled like dead fish. She took her time walking across the room, knowing there was probably broken glass there. During the night, Roy must have gotten up off the floor and come to bed.

There was no money left in her purse, just a few pennies and a quarter. Not even enough for a cup of coffee. Maine and Florida were too far away. But the quarter in her hand was shiny. Money enough for a phone call. Maybe to Tracy. Maybe Tracy would come get her.

Karen looked at the coin in her hand. Tracy and her husband were just scraping by, they didn't have the money to come rescue her. And if she left him, Roy would always follow, she was sure of that.

Roy coughed and rolled over. Her boy friend. Ready to rob a bank in a couple of hours. And for me, she thought, just cleaning up one damn mess after another.

He didn't apologize, didn't say anything about last night, which made it worse in a way. He just whistled and checked the two handguns, and after loading up the car he stuck one gun in his waistband and handed the other to Karen. She put it in her purse. It was heavy and threw her off-stride, and she checked her watch as she got into the car. Eight-thirty.

In the car Roy said, "Remember what I said. Drop me off in the parking lot and wait until nine-oh-five, and then drive up to the bank. I'll be ready, then. Use the gun if you have to, but don't leave anything behind for evidence. "Okay," she murmured.

"Fine." Roy was grinning. "How does breakfast in Vermont sound?"

She only nodded.

When they reached the parking lot, Roy gave her a kiss, but she moved her head, offering only her cheek. It didn't seem to faze him—he strode across the lot, his hands in his pockets, walking in that same manner of control she had liked so much when she had met him.

When he was out of sight, she moved the car around in the parking lot and found a single space, far on the other side, near one of the piles of dirt where the construction work was going on. She switched off the engine and stepped out. It had stopped raining and the fresh air felt wonderful. She could see the bank from where she was standing.

So strange. To come from Maine and end up in a parking lot in New York. She was going to ask herself how did I get here, but she remembered last night and everything else and she knew what was ahead of her.

She checked her watch. Nine in the morning. She looked up. Roy was walking into the bank. She opened the car door and went back inside, but she came out again, her purse over her shoulder, her suitcase in her hand, and locked the door.

The morning sun was bright. She took a deep breath and placed the suitcase down, reaching in with one hand to her purse. She looked across the lot and saw some cars moving in around the bank and then Roy ran out, a bag in one hand, the gun in the other, and men were leaping out of parked cars, shotguns and handguns at the ready, all of the cops yelling at Roy, all of them there because of her phonecall. He was looking around wildly, and she knew what he was looking for.

She drew out the handgun and aimed it at the dirt pile and fired once, the gun kicking in her hands.

At that sound, the police at the other side of the parking lot opened fire, the sounds echoing and booming across the lot. Karen started walking away, suitcase in her hand, not wanting to look back. The gun was warm and she was about to drop it

on the ground but, no, that was evidence, and she put it back
into her purse. She had learned at least that.

NICE, WELL MEANING FOLK
N. Scott Warner

Lower down gives way to what has drifted up. The new Chevy police cruiser was driven by Sheriff Gagne because he was older, supposedly experienced, and, anyway, it was his county, right? Ezra Katz, the tall Maine Deputy with sandy hair cropped close, was next in line and so drove a yellow rustbucket of a Bronco. The vehicle parked in the dusty driveway and its weary engine spluttered to a halt. Katz got out and walked to where the body lay in the grass.

The dead man was Roy Finney, a carpenter who took odd jobs. His tarpapered home wasn't far away. The chalky face turned upward, the mouth slightly open and shriveled like a dead rose. Finney seemed to float in the bright grass, half swallowed by waves of hawkweed and mountain fern. His right temple was a dark mess, as if it had been sampled with a scoop. Beside him a cherry-red, new-looking Honda three-wheeler, a vehicle somewhere between a motorcycle and an oversized toy, was leaning crazily on its isde. Oil, spilled from the crankcase, smeared the grass and rocks. The ignition key pointed to "on," but the engine was silent.

To the west, the field rose and melted into a gritty yard surrounding a farmhouse of unpainted granite fieldstone. Its metal roof, a protection against the harsh Maine winter, glittered in the sunlight like a battered medieval helmet. A peeling barn flanked and dwarfed the building, a mountain of grassy manure looming up behind it. This was Hatch property, next to the Finney land. It didn't go far, for Mildred Hatch had been selling bits and pieces, holding onto a few acres that were no longer farmed. It was Mildred who had phoned in, claiming a body lay outside.

In the tan driveway dirt, there were faint marks that the deputy tentatively identified as boot prints. A recent, sudden shower had smudged them.

Katz knocked softly, then hard, but there was no movement around the green window shades. He stepped aside and put his face close to a pane. His knuckles rapped, and a startled face appeared on the other side. Katz stepped back and turned toward the door again. The lady of the house, a short, oldish woman in a purple sack of a dress, beckoned him inside.

"Come in Ezra," she rasped. Her tough amber face, like a dried apple, split into a grin.

A hot wind flew out from the large, undivided downstairs room. The Clarion wood stove roared, although it was at least 65 degrees outside. A dented tin kettle steamed on its hot black surface. Katz loosened his color a little and shut the door behind him. Mildred slopped hot water on instant coffee in a mug without a handle.

"Have some?"

"Sure."

He took the mug gingerly, anxious not to burn his fingertips, and sat back in a chrome-trimmed chair heavily patched with silver tape. He noticed a large wooden baseball bat leaning against the table.

Katz sipped the bitter brew. "Out of sugar and milk again," Mildred said. "Food stamps ain't what they used to be. Don't go far nowadays."

"Yep," Katz said. It hadn't been long ago that his mother had gone off stamps. That had taken some doing. "Good coffee," he said brightly.

"Nice and polite, aren't you?" Mildred said, dragging a step stool roughly across speckled linoleum. She sat down briskly, pushing heavy eyeglasses up her short nose.

"Want to tell me what you saw?" Katz asked after a carefully measured sip.

Deep furrows lined Mildred's forehead. "Not much to tell. There was that damned noise again, and a bang—must have hit that rock. Drinking, no doubt. Always drinking, he was."

"Bashed his head, Mildred."

"Ayep," Mildred agreed. "Reckon he did."

"You go look?"

"Just a bit," Mildred said. "Dead man doesn't need no ambulance, I figure, so I called the sheriff. Couldn't think of nothing
else."

"Subject drove into your yard," Deputy Katz summed up,
"made a short turn, hit that rock, fell over, and hit his head on
another rock."

Mildred wasn't listening. Her beady eyes followed a cricket
hopping on the well worn floorboards along the edge of the
linoleum. Her hand crept to the bat, there was a quick movement and a noisy grind, and the fat insect became a whorl in
the cracked linoleum. Katz noticed a good many others.

"Lots of them about now," he said. "It's the wet weather
brings them out."

Mildred cackled. "Get every single one of them. Unwhole-
some little buggers. They slip in the food."

Katz studied the bat. It was large and splintered slightly.
There were no dirty fingerprints on it as on every other object
he saw around. Mildred didn't waste time on cleanliness.

"You always get them with the bat?"

"Stamp on them, too," Mildred said. "Got to get them good."

Katz finished his coffee with one courageous gulp. "Finney
hadn't had the machine too long?"

Mildred poked carefully at a remaining tooth. "Only last
week. Didn't know how to handle it yet. Drinking didn't help."

"He come often to visit?"

"Nah." Mildred leered. "Don't encourage no bums around
here. Keep to myself."

Katz remembered seeing a car in the barn. He had seen her
in town, too. She was getting around and had some welfare,
maybe savings from selling land.

"You ever worry about getting robbed?"

"Of what?" Mildred asked.

"But Finney came to visit."

"Once in a while," Mildred said. "Not too often. Not today.
Just showing off and racing his dumb machine, making a
racket."

"What time, Mildred?"

"Got no time here." She pointed at what was left of a clock. "Sun'd been up a while."

"You phoned in at ten."

"Maybe ten," she said. "It's Saturday, ain't it?"

"Yes, Mildred," Katz said gently.

"Fridays he got drunker."

"Than what?"

"Than other days."

"Wonder where he got the money to buy that Honda." Katz said.

"Same here." Mildred waddled to the stove. "More coffee?"

"No thanks," Katz said quickly. "Bought it on time, cut the beer to make the down payment maybe. Had he been working lately?"

"With that other bum, Levesque," Mildred said. "He lives on the other side of them alders. I've seen them go off in Levesque's car."

"Last night, too?"

Mildred nodded. "Plowing up my dooryard again, them bastards."

Katz got up. "I better get going. See you, Mildred. Take it easy."

"Always do." She opened the door for him.

Finney's shack showed some effort at design, with a pretty gable sloping smoothly to a side where a shed had been started and never finished. But Katz noted other details, too. Exposed timbers on the unfinished shed were weathered to a silver grey. A stack of shingle rotted in the tall grass and shreds of tarpaper, blotched with water stains, blew about in the breeze. The roof was covered in odd-sized sheets of corrugated iron, some rusted, and there were yellow drip stains on the siding.

Katz investigated several junk cars. The closest, a Ford Galaxy, might have worked until recently—the registration was still valid, but bottles were heaped against its fenders. Blackberry shrubs grew over the other phantoms. Bags of garbage ripped and worried by animals spread their contents across the yard and path, the labels and torn packages mostly faded into a tired white by the sun and rain.

Katz fanned blackflies and mosquitos aside as he pushed the poorly hung door and stepped inside. Light streaked weakly through greasy windows. Dust settled in clouds onto the contents of the single room. A couch wrapped in dark, brittle burlap sagged under a collection of damp newspapers and discarded clothes. A low cot with a blackened, dimpled mattress stood under a staircase that seemed ready to slide away. A tower of magazines, some bound with yellowed twine, leaned into a thin shaft of light, obliterating a window. Fastfood packing littered the table and floor. An old console television set, its screen oily and dark, might still be in working order.

Katz left the shack and crossed Mildred's property, heading for alders thickly veiled in the gauze of tentworm colonies. It was raining again. Levesque's location was a lookalike of Finney's, but there was only one car, a badly rusted compact that probably started up all right. Katz noted it was overdue for an inspection. The Toyota made a brave effort to shine as it got washed by the rain.

Katz found his way between heaps of debris and approached the shack. A plastic flamingo, its eyes missing, had been stuck next to a cracked concrete slab that served as a step. "Anybody home?"

Levesque, a large, red-faced man with wooly sideburns, showed up at the door. He hadn't shaved for a while and his beergut ballooned over oily jeans, stretching the limits of a ribbed tee-shirt. A dirty hand, hanging limply, carried a beer bottle by its neck.

"The law," Levesque grunted, opening the door.

Katz followed Levesque inside.

"Someone notice my inspection is out of state?" Levesque asked. He put on a funny squeak. "Will see to it right away, officer—first thing Monday morning. Sorry about that, *sir.*"

The living room had a low ceiling the texture of cottage cheese and the carpet could have been made out of matted red hair. Levesque pointed at a chair and stumbled onto a vinyl recliner. He sat down clumsily. "Why did you put yourself out?" I have a phone, and I'm in the book. Could have saved yourself the trip." He tipped back a plastic baseball cap with the mouth of the bottle, revealing a red crease that bordered a bald patch in wet, thin hair.

Katz ignored the chair that was one leg short and sat down gingerly on a sofa that looked like it had slept in the green army blankets that partially covered its ungainly bulk. The cushions were hard as brick.

"Something else," Katz said. "Never mind the inspection for now."

"Like what?" Levesque asked brightly, slurring comfortably now.

"You went drinking with Finney last night?"

Levesque tried to sit up. "As a matter of fact, I did," he said pleasantly. "Yes, sir, we had a few—but never again, and that's right, too. Silly no-good bum."

"Finney's dead," Katz said.

"No," Levesque said, draining his bottle. "What's that?"

"Dead," Katz said softly. "Lying in Mildred's yard with his head bashed in."

Levesque thought. He closed one eye. "Good for him."

"You two didn't go home together?"

"Must have walked," Levesque said. "Kept punching me in the bar. I wasn't paying much attention so he got thrown out alone."

"You didn't mind?" Katz asked. "He wasn't your buddy?"

Levesque's forefinger wagged. "Bad influence, officer. Never drank this much until I started working with old Finney. So he's dead now, eh? Well, what do you know."

Katz looked around. There was a baseball bat near the door. The handle was sooty with dirt. He pointed it out. "Go in for a bit of sport?"

"Guns are expensive," Levesque said, studying his bottle with a fascinated, intense stare; shaking it as if hoping it might fill itself again. "Had all sorts once. Twelve-gauge shotgun, a good twenty-two, a couple of handguns. Sold them all. Now I've got to bash them."

"Bash who?"

"Them that bother me."

A cricket crawled by Katz's right foot. He stamped his boot, avoiding the insect.

"Got some bugs here," he observed.

Levesque looked. "What—them little fellows? Come to keep me company. They have pretty legs, too. Sure can hop.

"Don't they get into your food?"

"What?" Levesque tried to focus. "No, not that I notice." He burped heavily. "Out of beer again. Bah. So what do you reckon happened to old Finney?"

"Drunk?" Katz asked. "Fell off his bike?"

"Nah."

"You don't think so?"

"Stupid bastard didn't get drunk in the morning, and besides–"

"Besides what?"

"He rode pretty good."

"You didn't see him this morning?"

"No, sir," Levesque said. "Wish I had, though. Might have bashed him myself."

"Would you do that?"

"Me?" Levesque asked. "I'm a good guy. I've been to Viet Nam. I got a medal."

"Come and have a look at Finney," Katz suggested.

"Not right now," Levesque said. "I'll read about it in the paper come Monday..."

Nice people, Katz thought as he drove back in the heavy rain. Then: They aren't really bad. They all got lost somehow. This is a good place to get lost in. Water pelted the roadside hard, mottling the runny mud. Budding trees and evergreens with rust-colored needles beneath their umbrellas swayed with the wind. A grey sky sat on a seamless horizon as if determined to keep the sun out forever. The Bronco's tires slammed into potholes and ruts.

But, Katz thought on, I wish all these nice, well meaning folk got lost somewhere else.

He parked the car in the new hospital's parking lot and pulled the emergency brake, noting smooth, recently laid pavement through a hole by the shift lever. The brake lever felt loose. He looked over his shoulder and saw a small tree. If the brake didn't hold, then perhaps the tree would for a bit.

He marched into the lobby, khaki uniform spotted in dark brown. He smiled at the switchboard operator, a middle-aged woman with protruding brown eyes and a pouty mouth. She folded her puffed arms on the counter and showed him her gums.

"Could you direct me to the morgue?" Katz asked. He shook the water from his hair.

"The morgue? You must be Deputy Katz."

He frowned. Should he be associated with corpses?

"The doctor is working on your client," the heavy woman

said. "We got your call and the ambulance picked him up. The doctor won't know anything yet. Why don't you come back in an hour?"

The hospital had a coffee shop. Katz ordered some tea to wash his mouth with and there was some banana pie. The pie wasn't bad. He leafed through magazines.

The operator waddled in. "The doctor is ready for you know. Would you care to follow me?"

Katz shuddered as he got up. The elevator took him down to a corridor still smelling of fresh paint. The morgue was a tiny room that the doctor seemed to consider palatial. "Deputy Katz," the pathologist, still a young man but with a shock of white hair, said precisely, as if he were memorizing the title and name for future use. "Look what we have here. Everything in tip-top order. Much better than what we're used to in the city. Am I glad I got this job—unspoiled country, lots of space, a cottage instead of an apartment that gets burglarized twice a week, a garden. My wife just planted it. Broccoli! Leeks!"

"Glad to have you with us," Katz said obediently.

There were steel plates covering the concrete block of the far wall. In an alcove was a cabinet of blue-grey metal and glass containing surgical gowns and basins. To the left stood a deep porcelain sink with a long hose and spray nozzle curled around the wide drain. The center of the morgue contained a cutting table, a long metal altar with a beveled surface and a gutter on the side. Finney's belly had been split open, the incision spreading at the breastbone to create a flap of skin that stretched back over Finney's face. A scale hung by Finney's feet. Organs in labeled plastic bags were neatly corralled between the knees.

"Bit of a boozer," the doctor said. "Or, rather, a confirmed and terminal alcoholic, as we can see by the liver. This in here is the liver." He indicated a zip-locked bag filled with clear liquid in which swam a large purple object, yellow and brittle-looking at the edges.

"But was he drunk when he died?" Katz asked.

"No," the doctor said. "Yes, I can say that with some degree of certainty. No, Deputy Katz, this man was not drunk during the last few hours of his miserable life. I would say he had one hell of a hangover, but that's something else."

"And the wound, doctor?"

"A bad wound." The doctor rubbed his chin. "He got hit with something. Instantaneous death."

"Maybe he hit something?" Katz tried. "I mean he hit *it* rather than *it* hit him?"

"Yes," the doctor said. "That's police talk. You men think differently. Yes, I see. Well, perhaps, yes—why not? Hit a tree?"

"Why a tree?" Katz asked. "Why not a rock?"

The doctor brought a pair of tweezers. "This here is no rock, Deputy Katz. This is definitely a splinter."

"Pine," Katz said.

"Pine, do you think? I don't know about trees yet. They're all green to me. In summer, that is—maybe not in winter. I'll find out in due time. I'm looking forward to some hiking."

"Any trace of rock in the wound, doctor?"

"No. Dust, yes, bit of dirt. I'll have it analyzed. I can mail it out today."

"Ah," Deputy Katz said. "Thank you, doctor."

Lichen-smothered rocks shouldering spruce trees marked the entrance to the property, and this time Katz turned the wheel softly so as not to spin the tires in the soft dirt road. He cut power and the engine quieted with a sigh. He let the Bronco coast down the incline and winced when it rattled heavily over a deep rut. Once within sight of the small stone farmhouse, he turned the wheel and softly applied the brakes by a tight cluster of firs. Katz got out and walked soundlessly to the sand by the fountain of the house. There was a line of laundry suitable for cover. He got behind it and worked his way along the wall.

Now.

He yelled and kicked the door, then jumped back into a crouch. He waited only a little over a second. Mildred was out, swinging her bat.

"Mildred?" Katz asked.

She whirled around and the bat came down. Katz deflected the weapon with his raised arm but the blow still stung. He grabbed the handle and wrenched it free. Mildred staggered back and whimpered. "Let's go in," Katz said.

Mildred backed to the rear wall.

"You always do that when you're bothered?" Katz asked. "Let them have it, huh?"

Mildred cried.

"It's all right," Katz said.

"It's not all right!" Mildred screamed. He bugged me, like them damn crickets. I've thrown him out before. But he kept coming on that damn machine, making noise, wanting beer and what not. I got nothing to give away."

"Could have called us," Katz said. "That's what we're for, Mildred, to protect you. So you hit Finney. Then what happened?"

"Nothing," Midred said. "He wasn't dead. He rode away."

"And bashed his head on a rock when his three-wheeler tipped over?"

"Right," Mildred said. "Right."

"Not right," Katz said. "Maybe you better come with me."

"Chains?" Mildred asked. "I don't want no chains."

"No chains," Katz said.

"Can't have no-good bums tearing around my place," Mildred said in the Bronco. "I'll tell the judge. He don't want no bums around his place, either."

"You tell the judge, Mildred," Katz said, "and I'll tell him, too. Don't worry now, you'll be all right in jail."

Sheriff Gagne rested behind his desk, dapper in his starched uniform, studying his trimmed fingernails. He could see himself in the glass of the bookcase. He touched his hair that had started greying at the temples. He thought that looked nice. Katz stood on the other side of the mahogany desk.

"So Mildred bashed the fellow," the sheriff said. "Amazing, I would think it was Levesque. A pretty rowdy lot, Finney and Levesque, bound to start bashing each other."

"Levesque is kind of kindly," Katz said. "Wouldn't kill a fly." He coughed. "Well, a cricket, anyway. Seems to like the little varmits. He says they keep him company. Mildred squashes bugs."

"So I heard." The sheriff blinked at Katz. The deputy was framed in the background of the office—thin rosewood paneling, certificates, pictures of goats from county fairs, and drapes. "Well, we've got some good charges against our suspect."

"Lonely," Katz said, "for one. And crazy. Lonely folk are often out of it a bit."

"Extenuating circumstances?" the sheriff asked. He got up

and marched around his desk, stopped in front of a picture of a framed billy goat, and turned around. "Nah. First she bashes him dead, then picks him up, then she slams him on his machine, then she starts the damned thing, gets it into gear, and aims it at the rocks. First-degree murder, Katz. We won't go easy on her."

"I'll go easy on her," Katz said, "and I made the arrest."

"Yes," the sheriff said curtly. "Back to work for now. The day isn't over yet."

Katz marched out of the office and Gagne snapped the report folder with his fingers to the rhythm of the step. He studied the billy-goat photograph, his scowl weakening into a grin. Crickets, he mused to the goat. No crickets here. Just a smart deputy who likes odd people. Why not? Someone should.

A TICKET OUT

Brendan DuBois

Then there are the nights when I can't sleep, when the blankets seem wrapped around me too tight, when the room is so stuffy that I imagine the air is full of dust and age, and when my wife Carol's sighs and breathing are enough to make me tremble with tension. On these nights I slip out of bed and put on my heavy flannel bathrobe, and in bare feet I pad down the hall-way—past the twins' bedroom—and go downstairs to the kitchen. I'm smart enough to know that drinking at night will eventually cause problems, but I ignore what my doctor tells me and I mix a ginger and Jameson's in a tall glass and go to the living room and look out the large bay window at the stars and the woods and the hills. Remembering what we had planned, what we had stolen, the blood that had been spilled, the tears and the anguish, I sip at my drink and think, well, it wasn't what we wanted to do. We weren't stealing for drugs or clothes or to impress the chunky, giggly girls Brad and I went to high school with. We were stealing for a ticket, for a way out. In the end, only one of us got out. That thought doesn't help me sleep at all.

It began on an August day in 1976, about a month before Brad Leary and I were going in as seniors to our high school. That summer we worked at one of the shoe mills in Boston Falls, keeping a tradition going in each of our families. Brad's

father worked in one of the stitching rooms at Devon Shoe
while my dad and two older brothers worked on the other side
of the Squamscott River at Parker Shoe. My dad was an assistant bookkeeper, which meant he wore a shirt and tie and
earned fifty cents more an hour than the "blue-collar boys" that
worked among the grinding and dirty machinery.

Brad and I worked in the packing room, piling up cardboard boxes of shoes and dodging the kicks and punches from
the older men who thought we were moving too slow or too
sloppily. We usually got off at three, and after buying a couple
of cans of 7-Up or Coke and a bag of Humpty Dumpty potato
chips we biked away from the mills up Mast Road to the top of
Cavalry Hill, which looked over the valley where Boston Falls
was nestled. Well, maybe nestled's too nice a word. It was more
tumbled in than nestled in.

On that day, we both wore the standard uniform of the
summer, dark-green T-shirts, bluejeans, and sneakers. We were
on an exposed part of the hill, past the town cemetery, looking
down at the dirty red-brick mill buildings with the tiny windows that rose straight up from both sides of the Squamscott
River. Steam and smoke fumes boiled away from tall brick
stacks and neither of us really had gotten used to the pungent,
oily smell that seemed to stay right in the back of the throat.
The old timers never mind the smell. They sniff and say,
"Aah," and say, "Boys, that's the smell of money." We weren't so
dumb that we didn't know if Devon Shoe and Parker Shoe and
the lumberyard shut down, Boston Falls would crumple away
like a fall leaf in November.

But Brad never liked the smell.

"God," he said, popping open his can of soda. "It seems
worse today."

"Wind's out of the south," I replied. "Can't be helped."

Our bikes were on their sides in the tall grass. There was a
low buzz of insects and Brad took a long swallow from his
soda, water beading up on the side of the can. It was a hot day.
Brad's long hair was combed over to one side in a long swoop
and I was jealous of him because my dad made me keep my
hair about two inches long, with no sideburns. But then again,
Brad wore thick glasses and my vision was perfect.

"Brad," I said, "we're in trouble."

He tossed his empty soda can over his shoulder. "How are

you doing?"

"With the sixty from last week, I got four hundred and twelve."

"Idiot. You should have four hundred and fifteen like me. Where's the other three?"

"I had to buy a dress shirt for Aunt Sara's funeral last week. I tore my last good one in June and Mom's been bugging me."

"Mothers." Brad hunched forward and rested his chin on his knee.

"State says we need at least a thousand for the first year."

"Yeah."

"And we can't get part-time jobs this winter, there won't be any around."

"Yeah."

"So what do we do?"

"I'm thinking. Shut up, will you?"

I let it slide, knowing what he was thinking. We were both six hundred dollars' short for the first-year tuition at the state college. My dad had made some brave noises about helping out when the time came, but six months ago my oldest brother Tom had wrapped his '68 Chevy around a telephone pole and now he was wired up to a bed in a hospital in Hanover and my parents' bank account was shrinking every month. But at least my father had offered to help. Brad's father usually came home drunk from the mill every night, sour-mad and spoiling for a fight. I'd slept over Brad's house only once, when we were both fourteen and had just become friends. It was a Friday night and by midnight Brad's father and mother were screaming and swinging at each other with kitchen knives. Brad and I snuck out to the backyard with our blankets and pillows and we never talked about it again. But one day Brad came to school with his face lumpy and swollen from bruises, and I knew he must have told his father he wanted to go to college.

"Monroe," he said, finally speaking up.

"Go ahead."

"We're special people, aren't we?"

"Hunh?"

"I mean, compared to the rest of the kids at school, we're special, right? Who's at the top of the class? You and me, right?"

"Right."

"So we're special, we're better than they are."

"Oh, c'mon–"

"Face it, Monroe. Just sit there and face it, will you? That's all I ask right now. Just face it."

Well, he was somewhat right, but then you have to understand our regional high shool, Squamscott High. Kids from Boston Falls, Machias, and Albion go there, and those other towns are no better off than ours. And in our state there's little aid for schools, so the towns have to pay the salaries and supplies. Which means a school building with crumbling plaster ceilings. Which means history books that talk about the promise of the Kennedy administration and science books that predict man will go into space one day. Which means teachers like Mr. Hensely, who stumbles into his afternoon history classes, his breath reeking of mouthwash, and Miss Tierney, the English teacher, not long out of college, who also works Saturday and Sunday mornings as a waitress at Mona's Diner on Front Street.

"All right, Brad," I said. "I guess we're special. We study hard and get good marks. We like books and we want to go places."

"But we're trapped here, Monroe," he said. "All we got here is Boston Falls, the Mohawk Cinema, Main Street–and the Wentworth Shopping Plaza ten miles away. And a lot of brick and smoke and trees and hills. Here, straight As and straight Fs will get you the same thing."

"I know. The lumberyard or Parker or Devon Shoe."

"Or maybe a store or a gas station. We're too smart for that, damn it."

"And we're too broke for college."

"That we are," he said, resting his head on his knees. "That we are."

He remained silent for a while, a trait of Brad's. We'd been friends since freshman year, when we were the only two students who were interested in joining the debate team–which lasted a week because no one else wanted to join. We shared a love of books and a desire to go to college, but no matter how many hours we spent together there was always a dark bit of Brad I could never reach or understand. It wasn't something dramatic or apparent, just small things. Like his bedroom. Mine had the usual posters of cars and rocketships and warplanes, but his had only one picture–a framed photograph of

Joseph Stalin. I was pretty sure no one else in Brad's family recognized the picture–I got the feeling he told his father the man had been a famous scientist. When I asked Brad why Stalin of all people, he said, "The man had drive, Monroe. He grew up in a peasant society and grabbed his ticket. Look where it took him."

Brad wanted to become a lawyer and I wanted to write history books.

"Feel it," he said, his voice low, rocking back and forth. "Feel how it's strangling us?"

I felt it. If we didn't go to State, then next summer we'd be on that slippery slope where we couln't get off, a life at the mill, a life of praying and hoping for a nickel-an-hour wage increase, of waiting for the five o'clock whistle. A life where we would find our friends and amusement at the Legion Hall, Drake's Pub, or Pete's Saloon, where we would sit comfortable on the bar stools, swapping stories about who scored what winning touchdown at what state tournament, sipping our beers and feeling ourselves and our tongues getting thick with age and fear. Just getting along, getting older and slower, the old report cards with the perfect marks hidden away in some desk drawer, buried under old bills, a marriage certificate, and insurance policies.

"We gotta get out," I said.

"We do. And I know how." Brad had gotten to his feet, brushing potato-chip crumbs from his pants. "Monroe, we're going to become thieves."

The next day we were at Outland Rock, tossing pebbles into the river. We were upstream from the mills and the waters flowed fast and clean. About another mile south, after the river passed through town, the waters were slow and slate-grey, clogged with chemical foam and wood chips and scraps of leather. Outland Rock was a large boulder that hung over the river, watching the wide arcs of the ripples rise up and fade away.

"What are we going to steal?" I asked. "Gold? Diamonds? The bank president's Cadillac?"

Brad was on his stomach, his feet heading up to the bank, his head over the water. "Don't screw with me, Monroe. I'm serious."

I shook my head, tossing another rock in. "Okay, so you're serious. Answer the question."

"Cash." He had a stick in his hand, a broken piece of pine, and he stirred it in the water like he was casting for something. "Anything else can be traced. We steal cash and we're set."

The day was warm and maybe it was the lazy August mood I was in—the comfortable, hazy feeling that the day would last forever and school and September would never come—but I decided to go along with him.

"Okay, cash. But you gotta realize what we're working with."

He looked up at me, his eyes unblinking behind the thick glasses. "Go ahead, Monroe."

"Our parents still won't let us drive by ourselves, so we're stuck with our bikes. Unless you want to steal a car to get out of town—which doubles the danger. So whatever we go after has to be in Boston Falls."

"I hadn't thought of that."

"There's another thing," I said. "We can't go into the National Bank or Trussen's Jewelers in broad daylight and rob 'em. In an hour they'd be looking for two kids our age and they wouldn't have a hard time tracking us down." I lay back on the rock, the surface warm against my back, and closed my eyes, listening to some birds on the other side of the river swish-swish as Brad moved the stick back and forth in the water.

"Burglary," he said. I sat up, shading my face with one hand. "Burglary?"

"Yeah." We find someone who's got a lot of cash and break into their house. Do it when no one's home and they'll blame it on some drifters or something."

Somewhere a dog barked. "Do you realize we're actually talking about stealing, Brad? Not only is it a crime, but it's wrong. Are you thinking about that?"

He turned to me and his face changed—I had the strange feeling I knew what he'd look like in ten years.

"Don't get soft on me, Monroe. In another three weeks we'll be back at school. If we don't get more money this summer we're done for. 'Wrong.' Isn't it wrong that you and me have to grow up in a place like this? Isn't it wrong that we have to live alongside people who haven't read a book in years? Don't you think it's wrong that for lack of a few measly bucks we have to rot here?"

He bent over the rock and pointed. "Look." In the shallow water I saw a nesting of mussels, their shells wide open. "There you have," he continued, "the population of Boston Falls, New Hampshire. Sitting still, dumb and happy and open, letting everything go by them, ready to snap at anything that comes within reach." He pushed his stick into one of the mussels and it snapped shut against the wood. He pulled the stick out, the mussel hanging onto the stick, dripping water. ""See how they grab the first thing that comes their way?"

He slammed the end of the stick onto the rock and the mussel exploded into black shards.

"We're not going to grab the first thing that comes our way, Monroe. We're going to plan and get the hell out of here. That will take cash, and if that means stealing from the fat, dumb mussels in this town, that's what we'll do."

On the ride home, Brad slowed and stopped and I pulled my rusty five-speed up next to him. A thick bank of rolling grey clouds over the hills promised a thunderstorm soon. Our T-shirts were off and tied around our waists. I was tanned from working in our garden all summer but Brad was thin and white, and his chest was a bit sunken, like he'd been punched hard there and never recovered.

"Look there," he said. I did and my stomach tightened up.

A dead woodchuck was in the middle of the road, its legs stiff. Two large black grackles hopped around the swollen brown body, their sharp beaks at work.

"So it's a burglary," I said. "Whose house?"

He shrugged his bony shoulders. "I'll find the right one. I'll go roaming."

Roaming. It was one of Brad's favorite things to do. At night, after everyone at his house was asleep, he would sneak out and roam around the dark streets and empty back yards of Boston Falls. The one time I'd gone with him, I thought he was just being a Peeping Tom or something, but it wasn't that simple. He just liked watching what people did, I think, and he moved silently from one lighted window to another. I didn't like it at all. I wasn't comfortable out on the streets at night and I couldn't shake off the feeling that I was trespassing.

Brad rolled his bike closer to the dead woodchuck. "Are you in, Monroe? We're running out of time."

Thunder boomed from the hills and I glanced up and saw a

flash of lightning. "We better get going if we're going to beat the storm."

"I said, are you with me?"

The wind shifted, blowing the leaves on the trees in great gusts. "Brad, we gotta get moving."

"You get moving," he said, his lips tense. "You get moving wherever you're going. I'm staying here for a bit."

I pedaled away as fast as I could, pumping my legs up and down, thinking, I'll save a bit here and there, maybe deliver some papers, maybe just work an extra summer—there's got to be another way to get the money.

A week later. Suppertime at my house. My brothers Jim and Henry had eaten early and gone out, leaving me alone with my parents. My brother Tom was still in the hospital in Hanover. My parents visited him every Saturday and Sunday, bringing me along when I wasn't smart enough to leave the house early. I guess you could say I loved my brother, but the curled over, thin figure with wires and tubes in the noisy hospital ward didn't seem to be him any more.

We sat in the kitchen, a plastic tablecloth on the table, my mother, looking worn and tired, still wearing her apron. My dad wore his shirt and tie. His crewcut looked sweaty and he smelled of the mill. On his right shirt pocket was a plastic pen holder that said Parker Does It Right with four pens. Supper was fried baloney, leftover mashed potatoes, and yellow string beans. I tried to talk about what went on at the mill that day—a pile of boxes stuffed full of leather hiking boots had fallen and almost hit me—but my parents nodded and said nothing and I finally concentrated on quietly cleaning my plate. The fried baloney left a puddle of grease that flowed into the lumpy white potatoes.

My father looked over at Mom and she hung her head, and he seemed to shrug his shoulders before he said, "Monroe?"

"Yes?"

He put his knife and fork down and folded his hands, as if we were suddenly in church.

"At work today they announced a cutback." He looked at me and then looked away, as if someone had walked past the kitchen window. "Some people are being laid off and the rest of us are having a pay cut."

"Oh." The baloney and potatoes were now very cold.

"Tom is still very sick, and until he–gets better, we still have to pay the bills. With the cutback–well, Monroe, we need the money you've saved."

I looked at my mother, but she didn't look up. "Oh," I said, feeling dumb, feeling blank.

"I know you've got your heart set on college, but this is a family emergency–that has to come first, a family has to stick together. Jim and Henry have agreed to help–"

"With what?" I said, clenching my knife and fork tight. "They don't save anything at all."

"No, but they're giving up part of their paychecks. All we ask is that you do your part."

Then Mom spoke up. "There's always next year," she said. "Not all of your friends are going to college, are they? You'll be with them next summer."

Dad gave me a weak smile. "Besides, I never went to college, and I'm doing all right. Monroe, it's just temporary, until things improve with Tom."

Until he gets better or until he dies, I thought. I didn't know what to say next, so I finished eating and went down the hall-way to my bedroom and got the dark brown passbook from First Merchants of Boston Falls and brought it back and gave it to my father.

Back in my bedroom, I lay on the bed, staring up at the models of airplanes and rocketships hanging from thin black threads attached to the ceiling. I looked at my textbooks and other books on the bookshelves I made myself. I curled up and didn't think of much at all and after a while I fell asleep.

There was a tapping at my window and I threw the top sheet off and went over, lifting up the window screen. I stood there in my shorts, looking at Brad on the back lawn. My glow-in-the-dark clock said it was two in the morning.

"What is it?" I whispered.

"I found it," he whispered back, leaning forward so his head was almost through the open window. "I found the place."

"Whose house is it?"

"Mike Willard's."

"Mike? The ex-marine?"

"That's right," Brad said. "I've watched him two nights in a row. He goes into his bedroom and underneath his bed he's got this little strongbox–before shutting off the light and going to bed he opens it up and goes through it. Monroe, he's got tons of money in there. Wads as big as your fist."

"You saw it?"

"Of course I did. I was in a tree in his yard. He must've been saving up all his life. You never saw so much money."

The night air was warm but goosebumps traveled up and down my arms. "How do we do it?"

"Easy. He lives out on Tanner Avenue. We can get to it by cutting through the woods. His house has hedges all around. It'll be a cinch."

I chewed on my lip. "When?" I asked.

Brad grinned at me. I could almost smell the sense of excitement. "Tomorrow. It's Saturday–your parents will be in Hanover and Mike goes to the Legion Hall every afternoon. We'll do it while he's there."

I didn't argue. "Fine," I said.

The next afternoon we were in a stand of trees facing a well mowed back yard. Tall green hedges flanked both sides of the yard and the two-story white house with the tall gables was quiet. Beside me, Brad was hunched over, peering around a tree trunk. We heard a door slam and saw Mike Willard walk down his drive and down the street. His posture was straight as a pine, his white hair cut in a crewcut.

"Let's give him a few minutes," Brad said. "Make sure he didn't forget anything."

I nodded. My heart was punding so hard I wondered if Brad could hear it. I knew what we were doing was wrong, I knew it wouldn't be right to steal Mike Willard's money, but money was all I could think of. Wads as big as my fist, Brad had said.

"Go time," Brad said, and he set off across the yard. I followed. There were no toys or picnic tables or barbecue sets in Mike Willard's back yard, just a fine lawn, as if he mowed it every other day. Up on the back porch I had a strange feeling we should knock or something. I was scared Mike would come back and yell, "Boys, what the hell do you want?" or that a mailman would walk up the drive and ask if Mike was home. I almost hoped a mailman would come, but Brad picked up a rock and went to the door and it was too late. He smashed a pane of glass–the sound was so loud it seemed like every police cruiser within miles would be sent around—then he reached in and unlocked the door, motioning me to follow him inside. A small voice told me to stay outside and let him go in alone, but I followed him into the kitchen, my sneakers crunching on the glass.

The kitchen smelled clean and everything was shiny and still. There weren't even any dishes in the sink.

"God, look how clean it is," I said.

"Tell me about it. Mom should keep our house so clean."

The kitchen table was small and square, with only two chairs. There was one placemat out, a blue woven thing with stars and anchors, and I thought of Mike Willard coming home every night to this empty house, opening a can of spaghetti maybe and eating alone at his table. I looked at Brad and wanted to say, 'Come on, let's not do it,' because I got a bad feeling at the thought of Mike coming home and finding he'd been robbed, that someone had been in his house, but Brad looked at me hard and I followed him down the hallway.

The bedroom was small and cramped, with neatly labeled cardboard boxes piled on one side of the room and a long bureau on the other, on the other side of the bed. The labels on the boxes read CHINA 34, IWO 45, OCC., and things like that. Brad pointed at the walls, where pictures and other items were hanging. "Look, there's Mike there, I think. I wonder where it was taken. Guadalcanal, maybe?"

The faded black-and-white picture showed a group of young men standing in a jungle clearing, tired-looking, in uniforms and beards, holding rifles and automatic weapons. There was no name on the picture but I recognized a younger Mike Willard, hair short and ears sticking out, standing off to one side.

I heard a creak. "Shh!" I said. "Did you hear that?"

"Yeah. This is an old house, Monroe."

"Well, let's get going," I said, rubbing my palms against my jeans. They were very sweaty.

"What's the rush?" Brad said, his eyes laughing at me from behind his glasses. "Old Mike's down at the Legion, telling the boys how he won the big one back in 'forty-five. Look here."

Below an American flag and a furled Japanese flag was a sheathed curved sword resting on two wooden pegs. Brad took it down and slid it out of its scabbard. He ran a thumb across the blade and took a few swings through the air. "I wonder if Mike bought it or got it off some dead Jap."

By now I was glancing out the window, wondering if anyone could see us. Brad put the sword down and climbed onto the bed. "Hold on a sec," he said.

The bed was a brown four-poster. Brad reached under the pillows and pulled out a handgun, large and oily-looking. "A forty-five. Can you believe it? Old Mike sleeps with a forty-five under his pillow."

"Brad, stop fooling around," I said. "Let's get the box and go." But I could tell he was enjoying himself too much.

"Hold it, I just want to see if it works." He moved his hand across the top of the gun and part of it slid back and forth with a loud click-clack. "There," he said. "Just call me John Wayne. This sucker's ready to fire. I might take it with me when we leave."

He took the gun and stuck it in his waistband, then reached over and pulled a dull-grey strongbox with a simple clasp lock from under the bed. My mouth felt dry and suddenly I was no longer nervous. I was thinking of all the money.

Brad rubbed his hands across the box. "Look, partner. In here's our ticket out."

Then Mike Willard was at the bedroom door, his face red, and I could smell the beer from where I was standing, almost five feet away. "You!" he roared. "What the hell are you doing in here? I'm gonna beat the crap out of you, boys!"

I backstepped quickly, tripping over the cardboard boxes and falling flat on my butt, wondering what to do next, wondering what I could say. Brad scampered across the other side of the bed, pulling out the gun and saying in a squeaky voice, "Hold it." Mike Willard swore and took two large steps, grabbing the sword and swinging it at Brad. I closed my eyes and there was a loud boom that jarred my teeth. There was a crash and an awful grunt, and another crash, then a sharp scent of smoke that seemed to cut right through me.

When I opened my eyes, Brad was sitting across from me, the gun in his lap, both of his hands pressed against his neck. He was very pale and his glasses had been knocked off–without them he looked five years younger.

"It hurts," he said. And then I saw the bright redness seep through his fingers and trickle down his bare arms.

"God," I breathed.

"I can't see," he said. "Where's Mike?"

I got up, weaving slightly, and saw Mike's feet sticking out from the other side of the bed. I crawled across the bed and peered over. Mike was on his back, his arms splayed out, his mouth open like he was still trying to yell, but his eyes were closed and there was a blossom of red spreading across his green workshirt. I stared at him for what seemed hours but his chest didn't move. When I looked up, Brad was resting his back against the bed. Both of his arms were soaked red and I gazed at him, almost fascinated by the flow of blood down his thin wrists. His face was now the color of chalk.

"Wait, I'll get a towel," I said.

"No, you idiot. If I take my hands away, I'm dead. An artery's gone. Listen. Take the box and call an ambulance."

"I think Mike's dead, Brad."

"Shut up," he said, his teeth clenched. "Just grab the box, hide it, and get help! We're juveniles—nothing's going to happen to us! Get going!" I grabbed the box and was out of the house, running through the woods, the strongbox tight against my chest. The air was fresh and smelled wonderful, and I ran all the way home.

Three days later Mike Willard was buried with full military honors and a Marine Corps honor guard at Cavalry Hill Cemetery. I learned from his front-page obituary that his wife died five years earlier and he had a daughter who lived in Jamaica Plain, Massachusetts. I also learned that Mike had been in the Marines since he was seventeen, stationed in China in the 1930s and in the Pacific in the 1940s, island-hopping, fighting the Japanese. Then after occupation duty and a year in Korea, he pulled embassy duty until he retired. His nickname had been Golden Mike, for in all his years on active duty he'd never been wounded, never been shot or scratched by shrapnel. The newspaper said he'd come home early that day to dig out a magazine clipping to show some friends at the Legion Hall. To settle a bet.

I kept the strongbox hidden in the attic. Despite the temptation and the worries and the urging, I didn't open it until that day in May after my college acceptance letter came, followed

by a bill for the first year's tuition. Then I went up with a chisel
and hammer and broke open the lock. The wads of money
were in there, just as Brad had said, thick as my fist. They were
buried under piles of fragile, yellowed letters, some newspaper
and magazine clippings, and a few medals. The money was
banded together by string, and in the dim light of the attic I
wasn't sure of what I had. I bicycled over to Machias, to a coin
shop, and the owner peered over his half-glasses and looked
up at me, the money spread over his display case.

"Interesting samples," he said. He wore a dark-green sweater
and his hair was white. "Where did you get them?"

"From my uncle," I lied. "Can you tell me what they're
worth?"

"Hmm," he said, lifting the bills up to the light. "Nineteen
thirties, it looks like. What you have here is Chinese money
from that time, what old soldiers and sailors called 'LC,' or local
currency. It varied from province to province, and I'd say this
is some of it."

He put the bills back on the counter. "Practically worthless,"
he said. I thanked him and rode back to Boston Falls. That afternoon I burned some of the paper money along with my acceptance letter and tuition bill. I didn't go to college that fall
and ended up never going at all.

My ginger and Jameson is gone and I continue looking out
at the stars, watching the moon rise over the hill, Cavalry Hill.
And even though it's miles away, I imagine I can see the white
stone markers up there, marking so many graves.

In the end I stayed in Boston Falls and took a job at a bank. I
worked a little and now I'm an assistant branch manager. Some
years ago I married Carol, a teller I helped train, and now we're
out of Boston Falls, in Machias. It's just over the line, but I get
some satisfaction from getting that far.

Upstairs I still have the old strongbox with some of the
money, and though I don't look at it all that often I feel like I
have to have something, something I can tell myself I got from
that day we broke into Mike Willard's house. I have to have
something to justify what we did, and what I did. Especially
what I did.

After running all that distance home, I stashed the strongbox
in the attic, and as I came downstairs my parents came home.

Dad patted me on the back and Mom started supper and I thought of the strongbox upstairs and the blood and the acrid smoke and Mike Willard on his back and Brad holding his neck like that. I knew no one had seen me. Mom offered me some lemonade and I took it and went to the living room and watched television with my dad, cheering on the Red Sox as they beat the Yankees—all the while waiting and waiting, until finally the sirens went by.

Brad was buried about a hundred feet from Mike Willard a day later. On the day of his funeral, I said I was sick and stayed home, curled up in a ball on my bed, not thinking, not doing anything, just knowing that I had the box and the money.

I put down my empty glass and open the back door, hoping the fresh air will clear my head so I can go back upstairs and try to sleep. Outside there's a slight breeze blowing in from Boston Falls, and like so many other nights I go down the porch steps and stand with my bare feet cool on the grass, the breeze on my face bringing with it the stench of the mills from Boston Falls. The smell always seems to stick in the back of my throat, and no matter how hard I try I can never get the taste of it out.